THE POSTMAN FROM SPACE

by Guillaume Perreault

Translated by Françoise Bui

HOLIDAY HOUSE NEW

Our story begins with a spacial postman.
No, not a "special" postman, a spacial postman.
A postman from space.
It's simpler to say it that way.

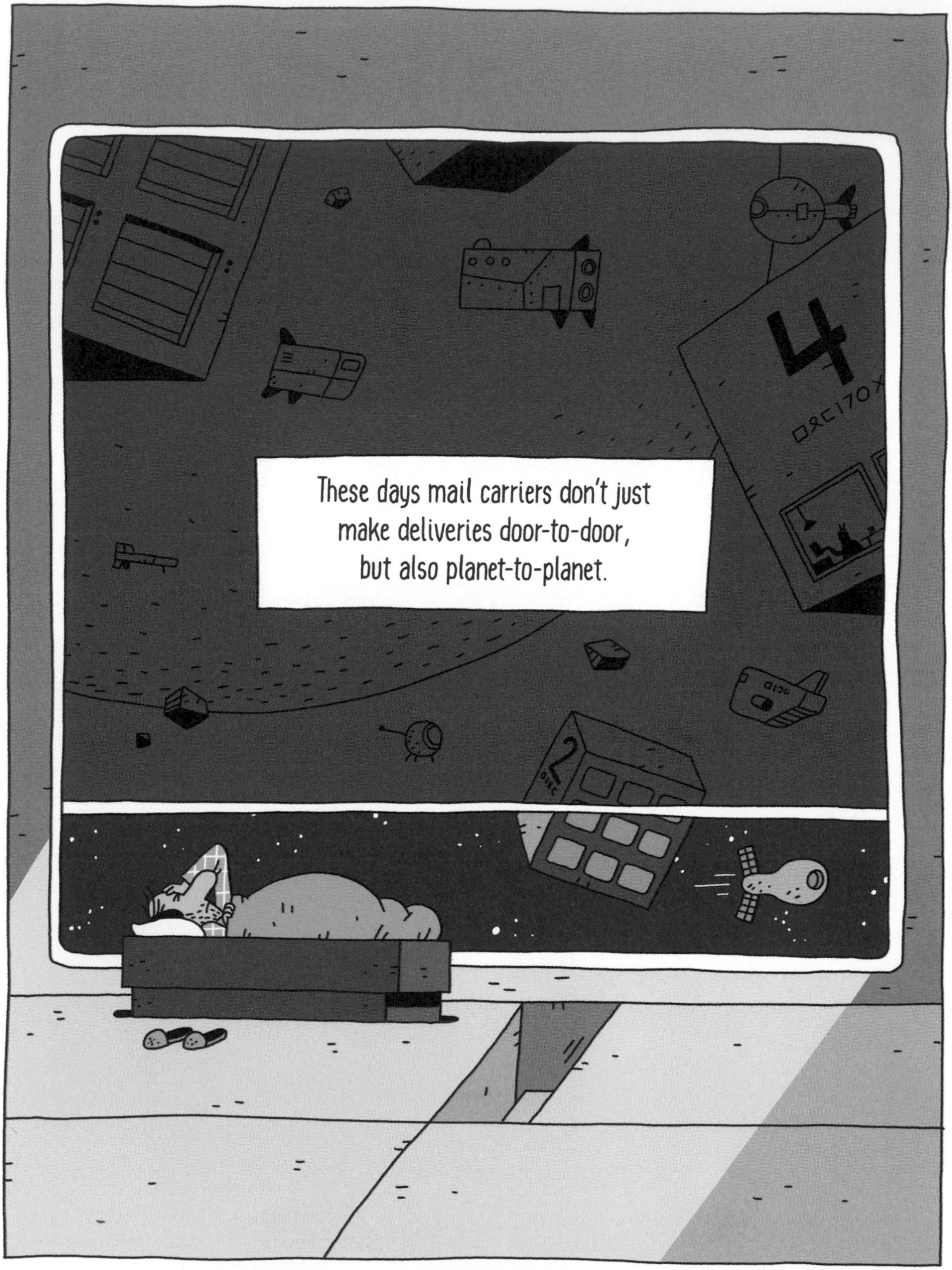
These days mail carriers don't just make deliveries door-to-door, but also planet-to-planet.

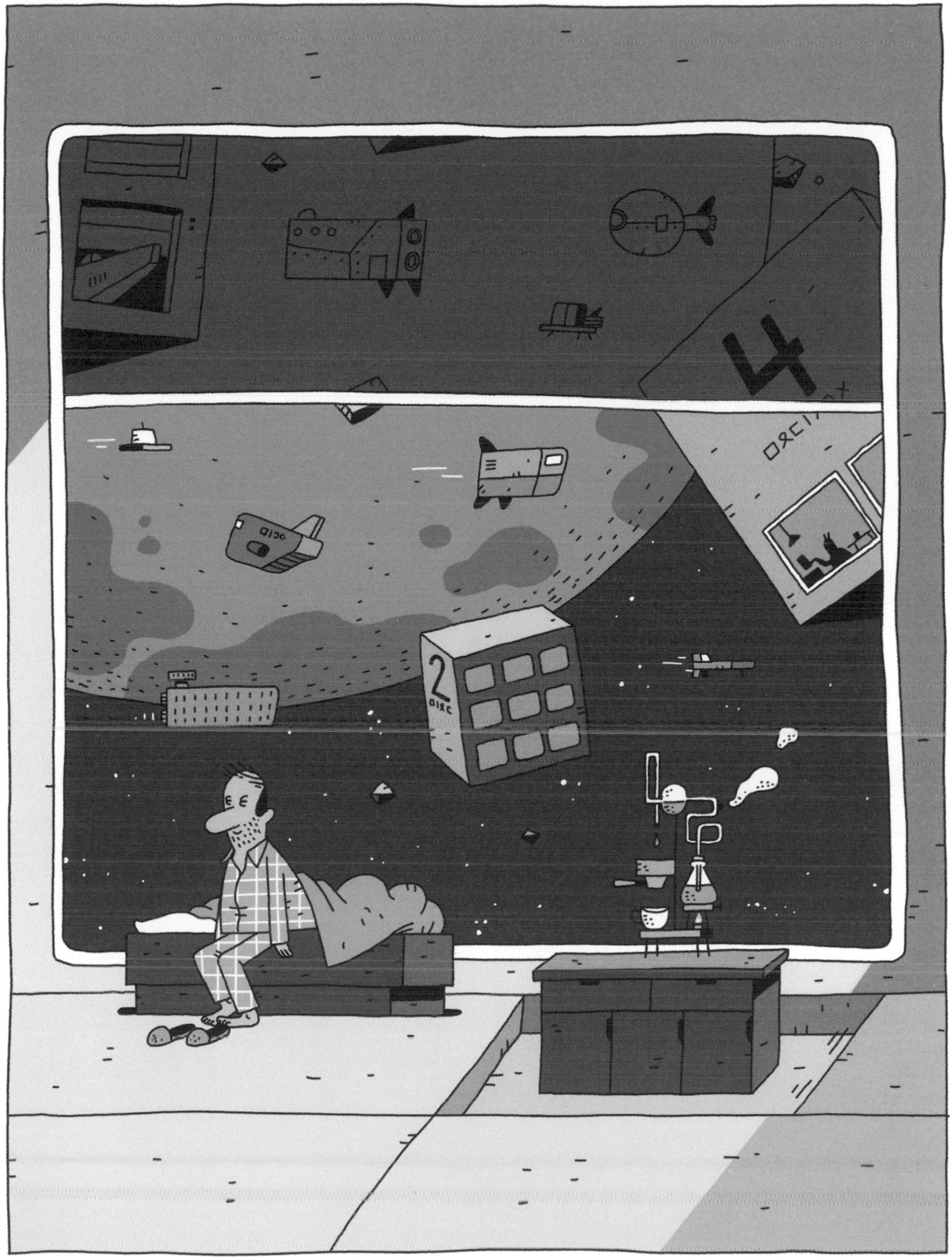

This may seem unusual to you, but for Bob
(yes, our postman's name is Bob)
it's all pretty ordinary.

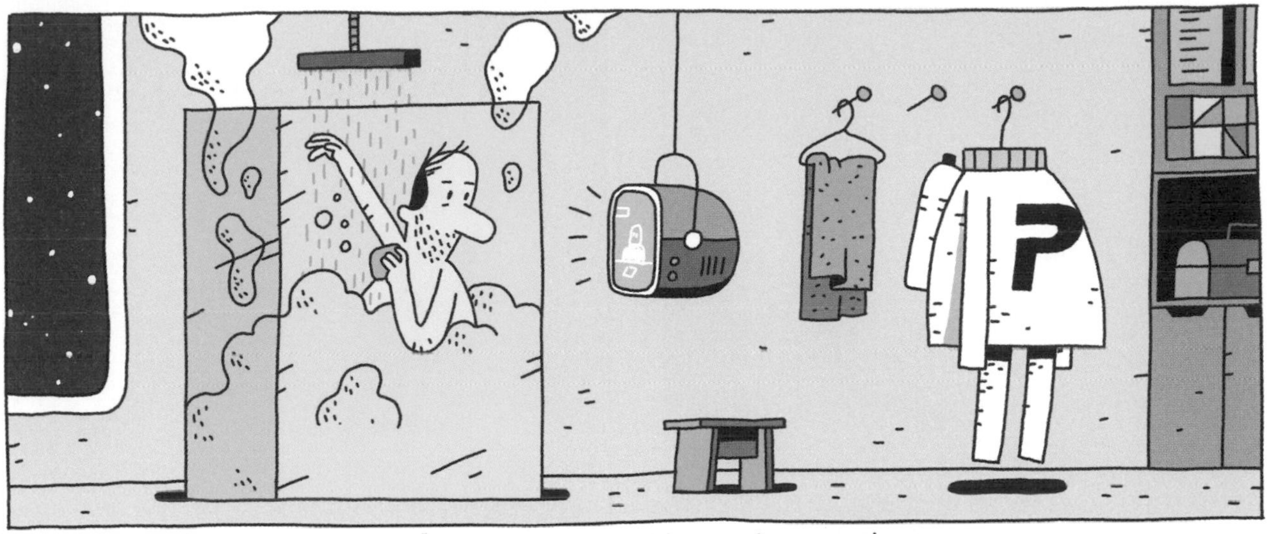

Every morning, Bob wakes up and begins his day the same way.

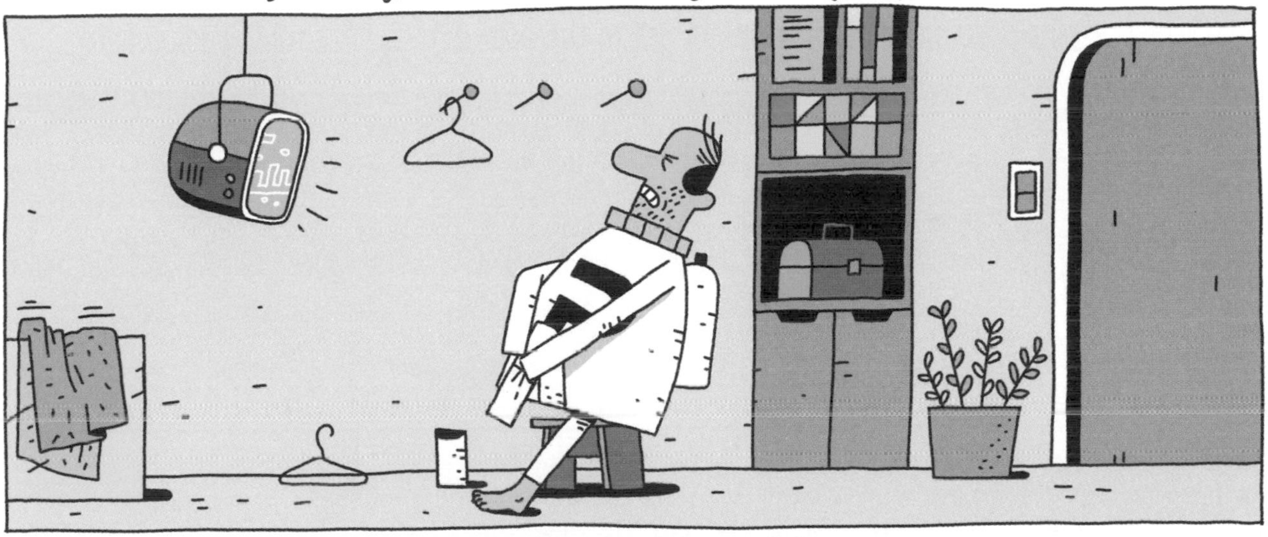

He slips into the same uniform.

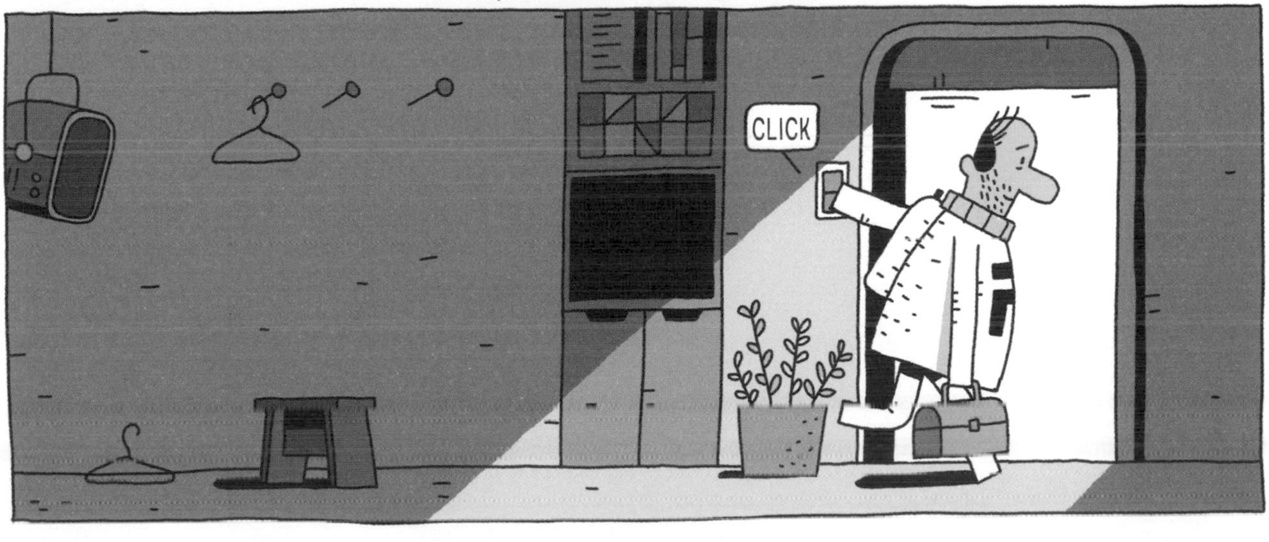
CLICK

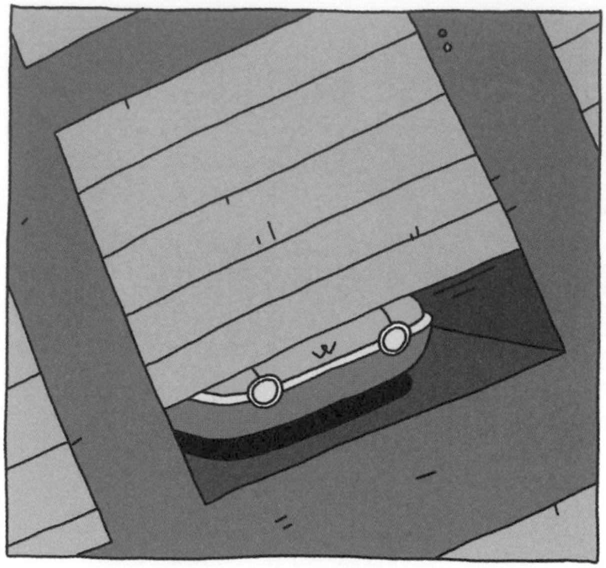

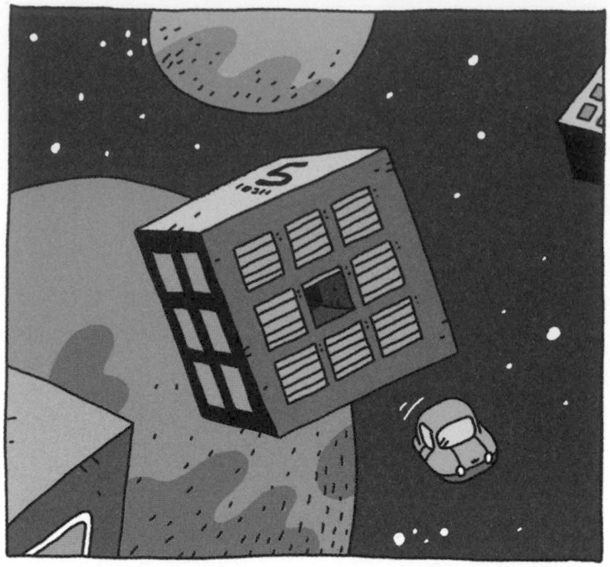

Then off he goes on the same route to get to the post office. It's simple and orderly.

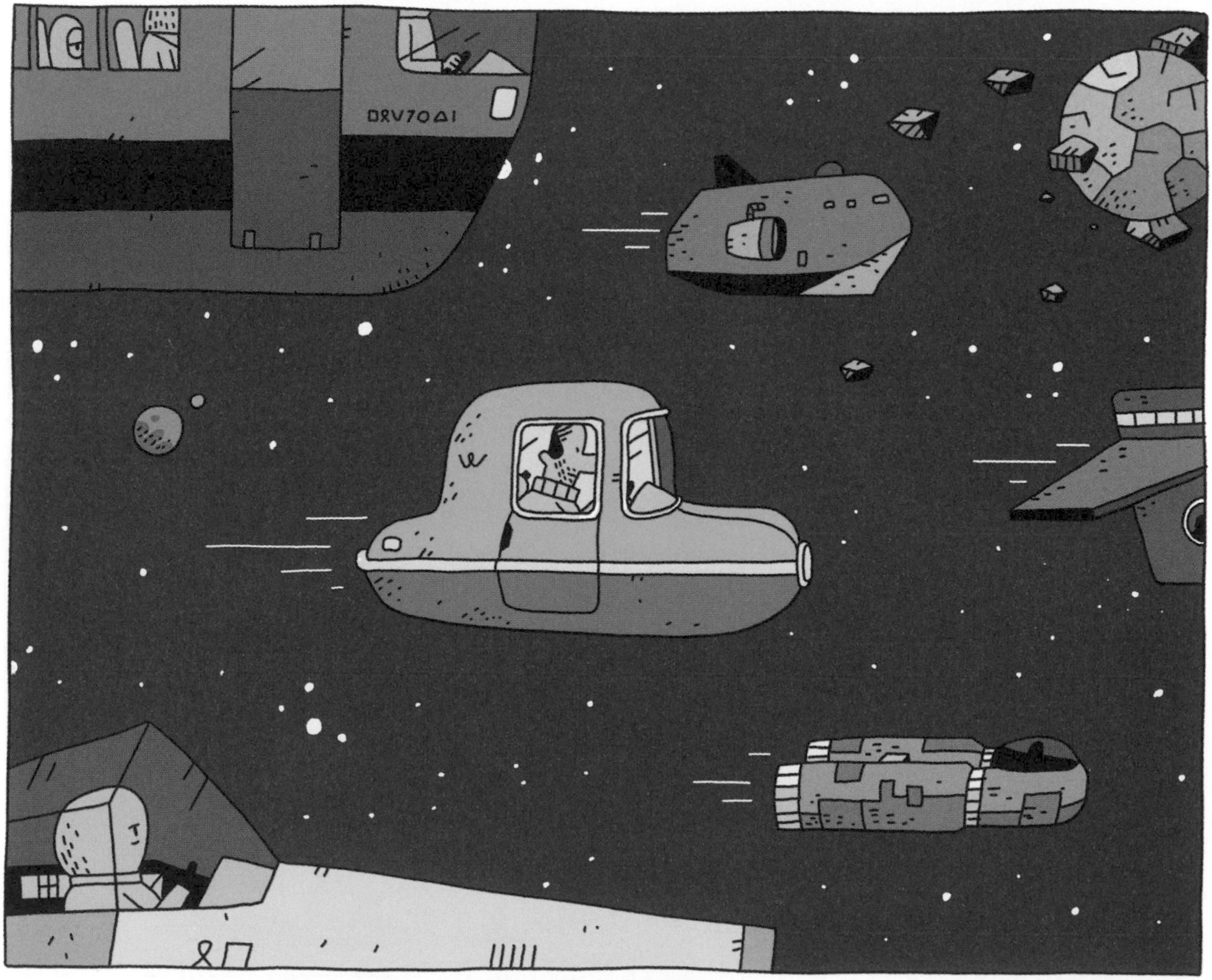

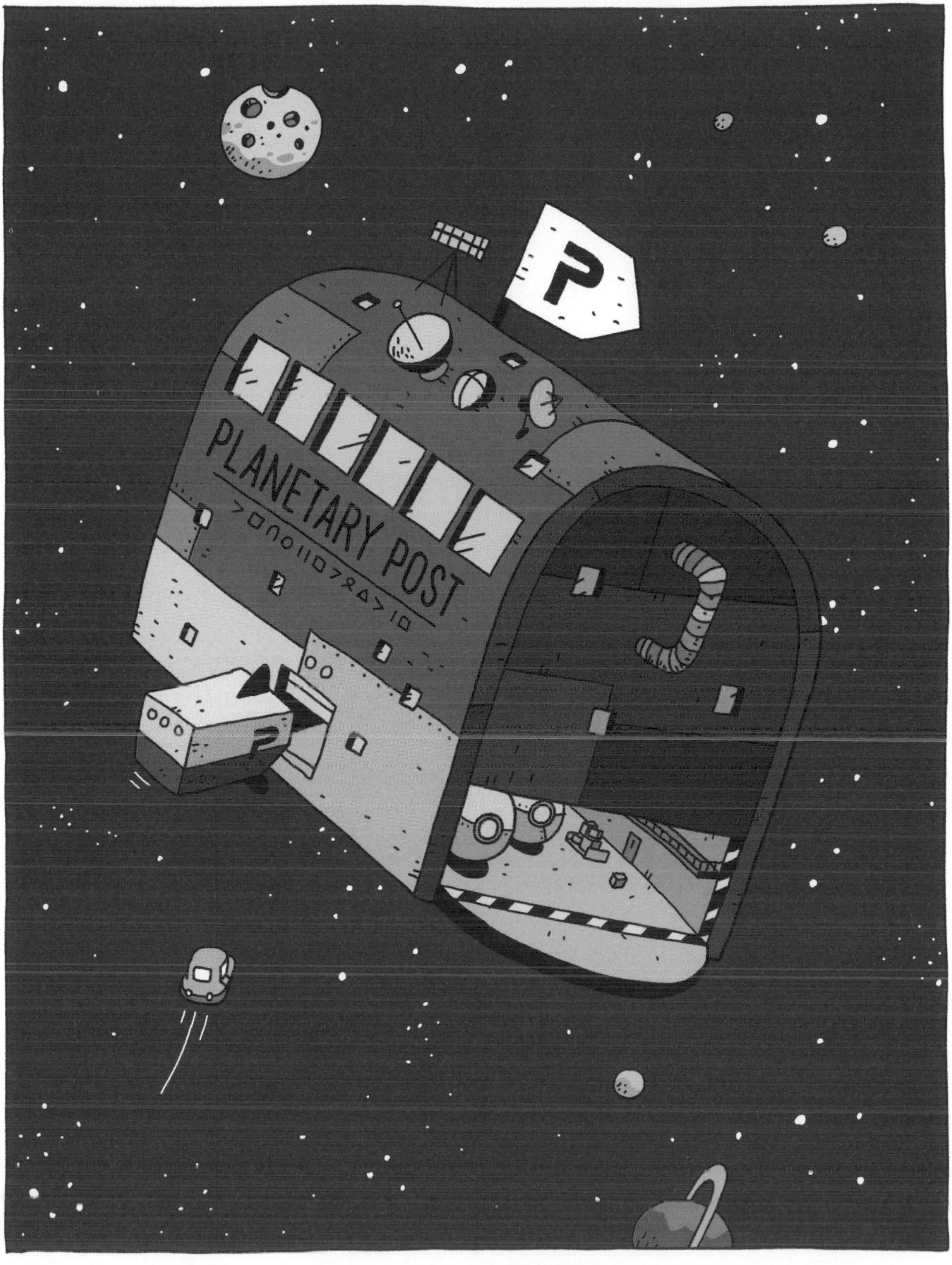
PLANETARY POST
P

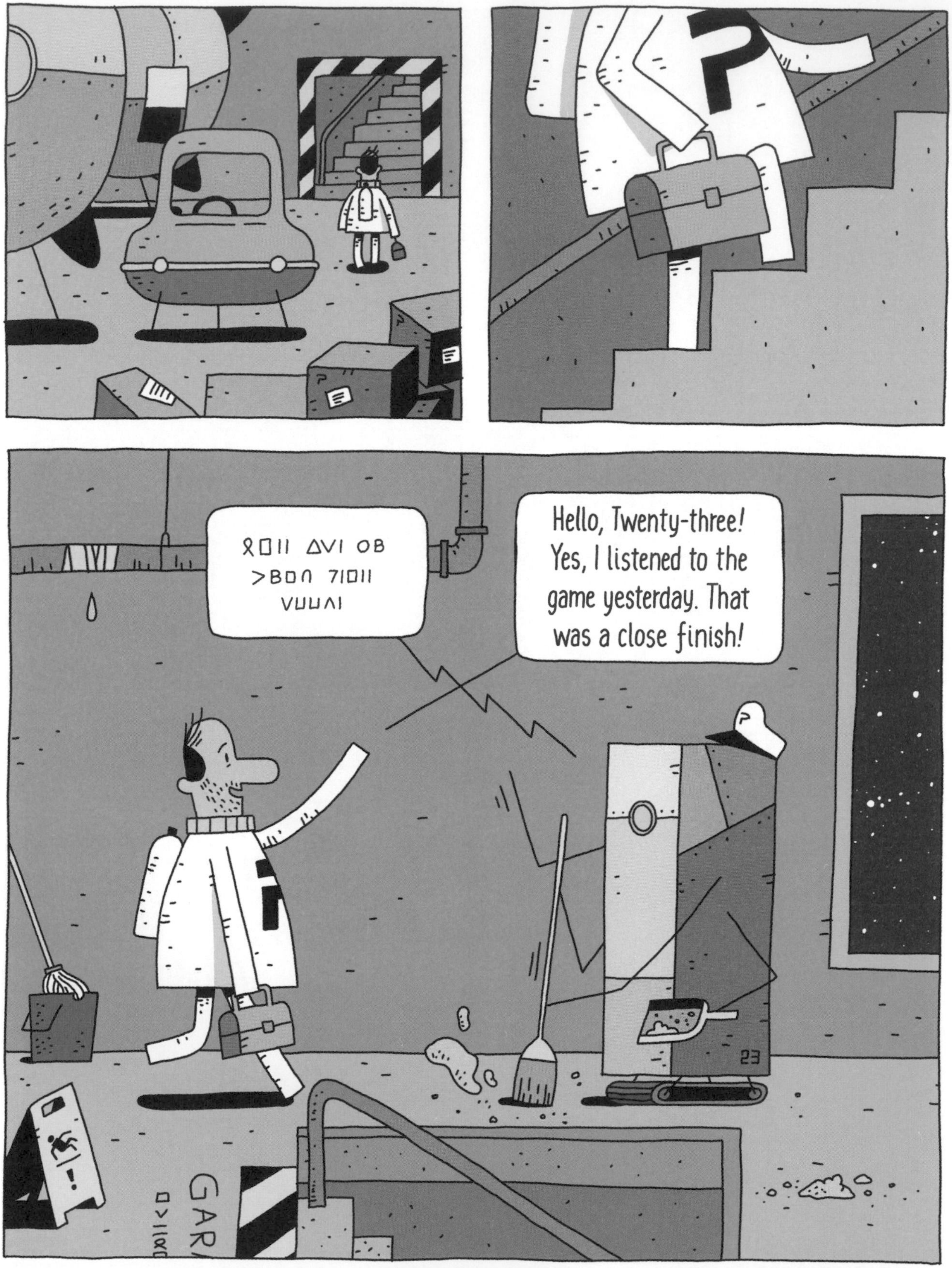
Hello, Twenty-three! Yes, I listened to the game yesterday. That was a close finish!

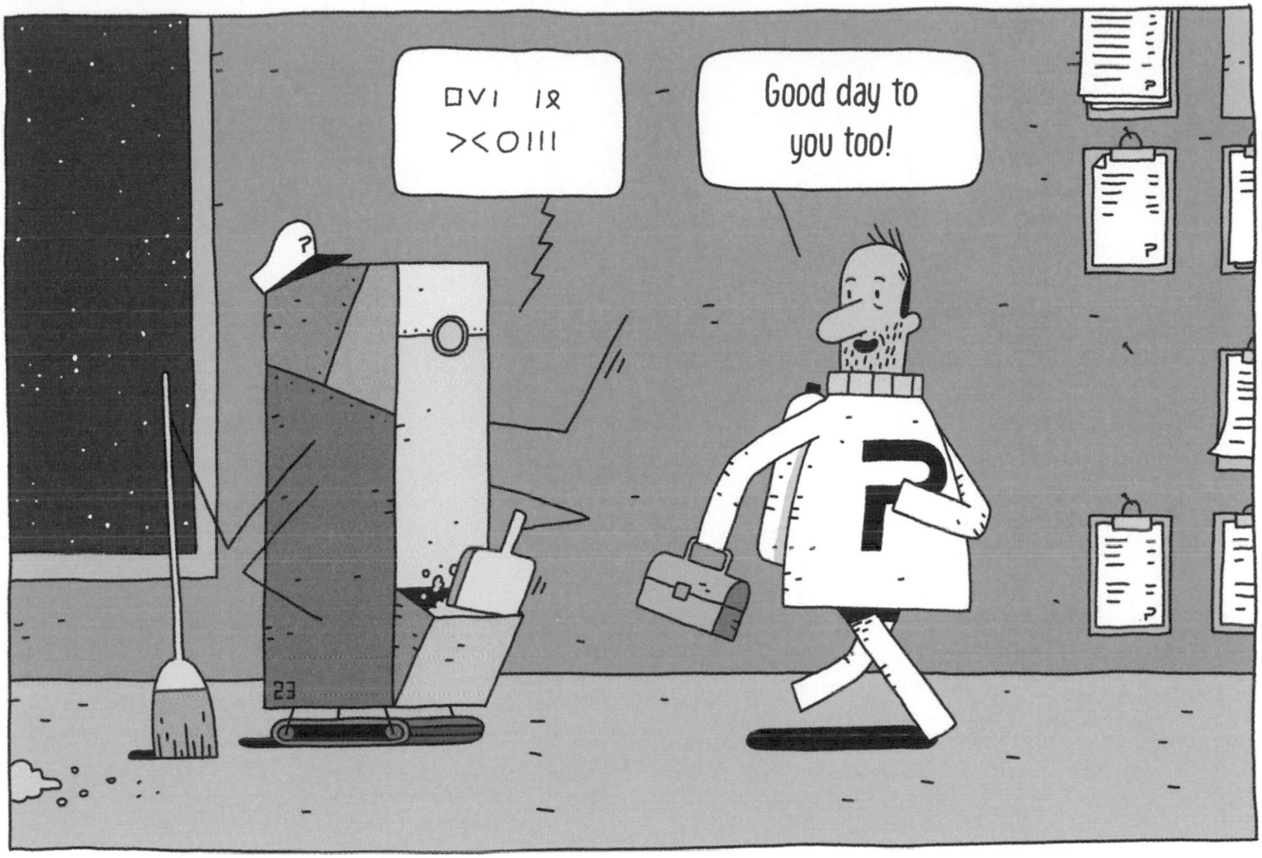
Good day to you too!

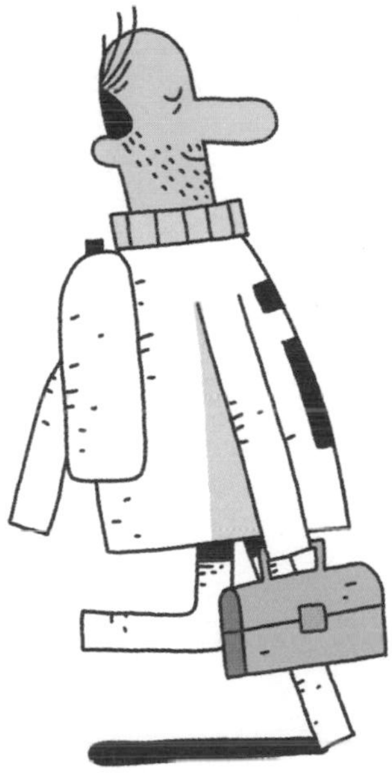

Yes, our friend the postman definitely enjoys his little routine.

Nice and easy is how he likes it.

But this morning there's a glitch. . . .

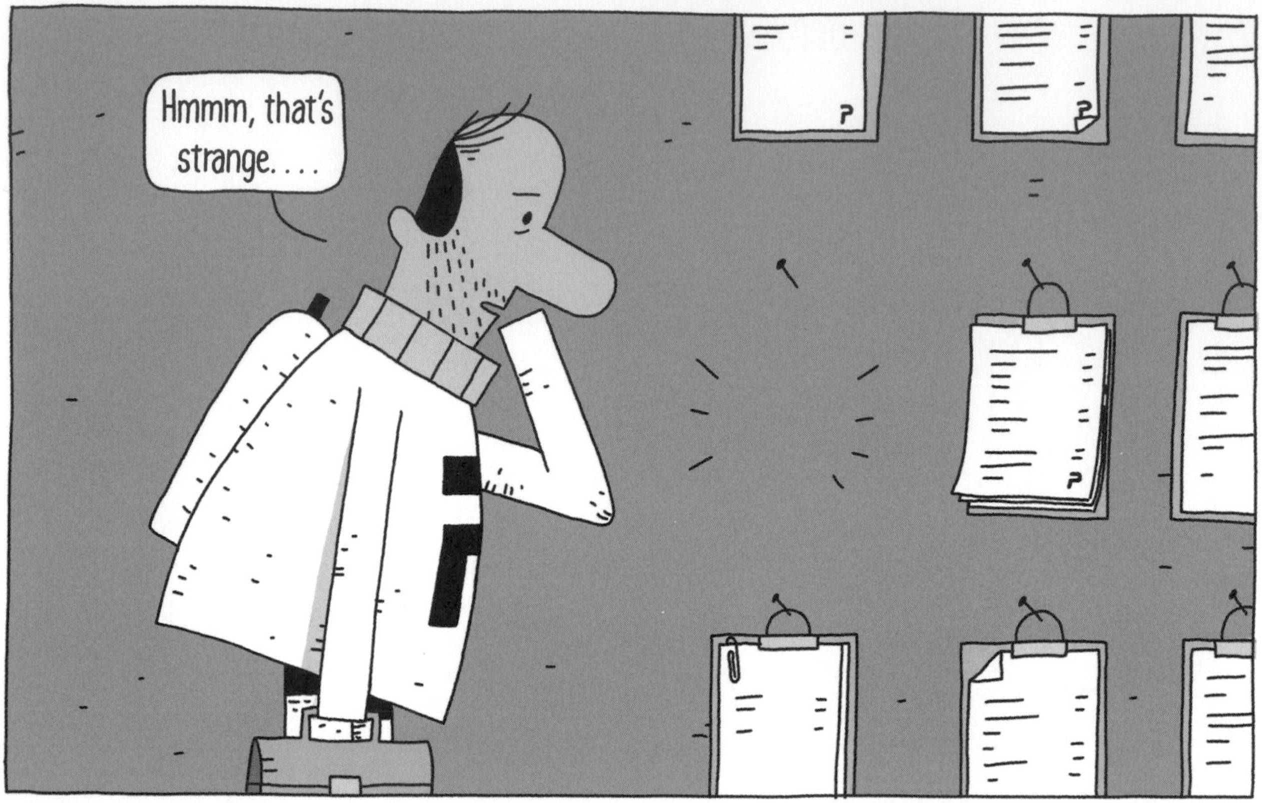
Hmmm, that's strange.....

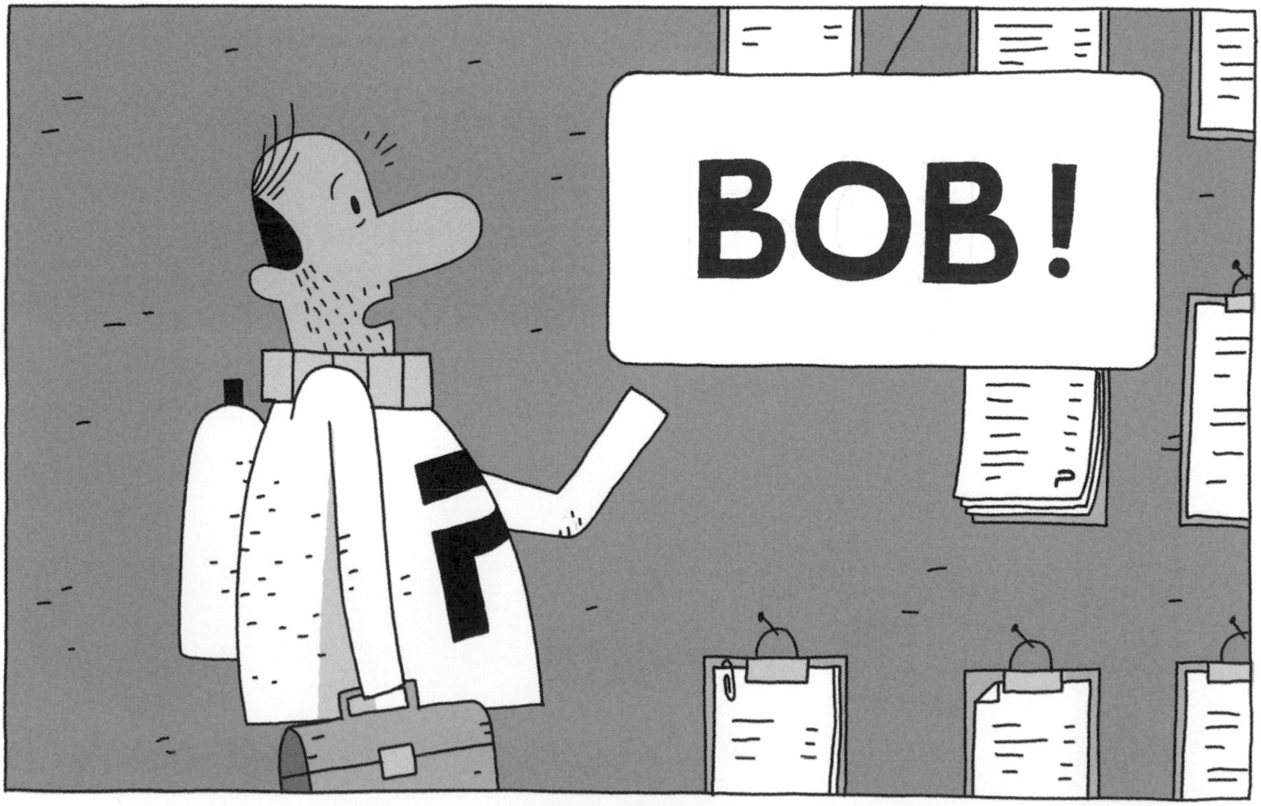
BOB!

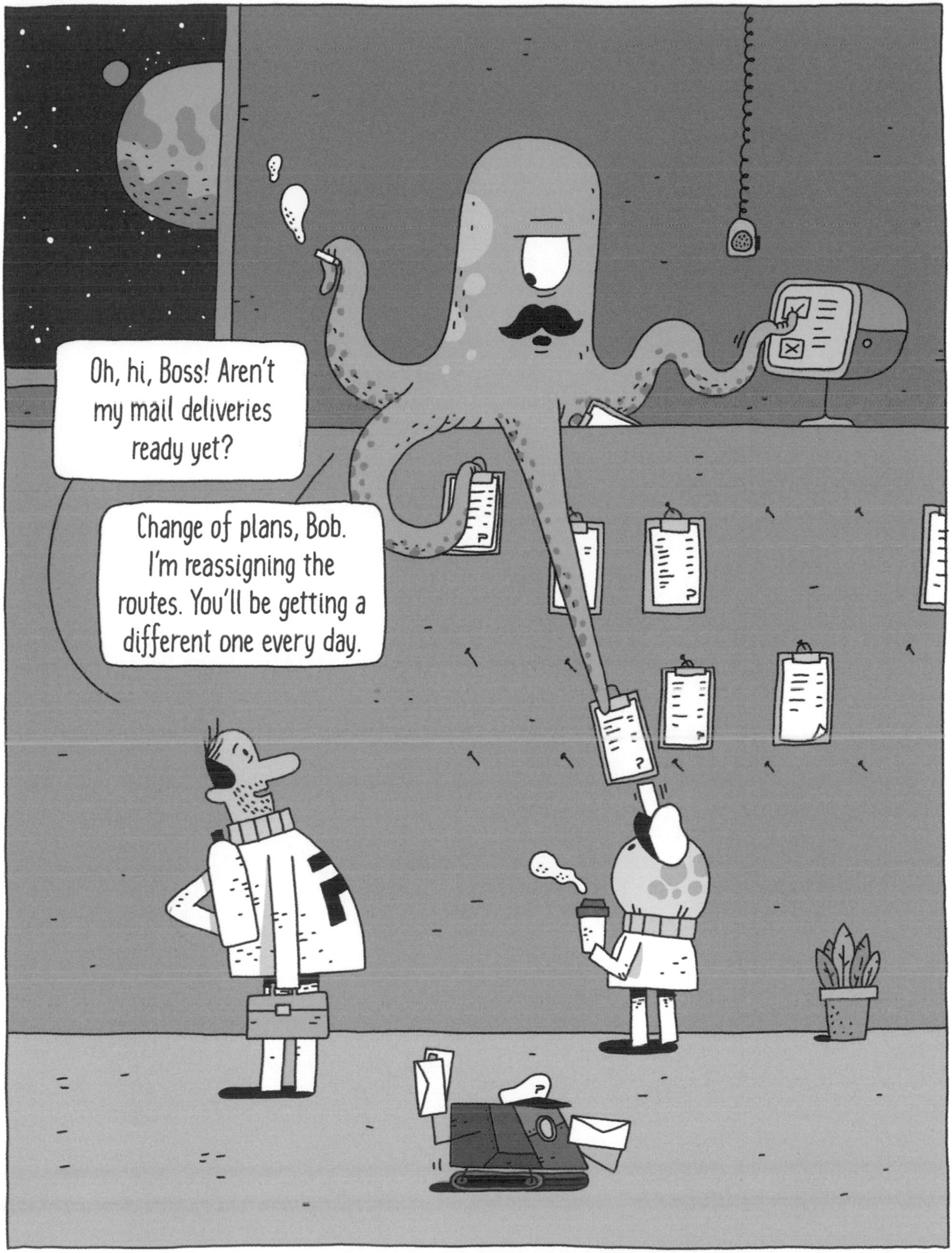
Oh, hi, Boss! Aren't my mail deliveries ready yet?
Change of plans, Bob. I'm reassigning the routes. You'll be getting a different one every day.

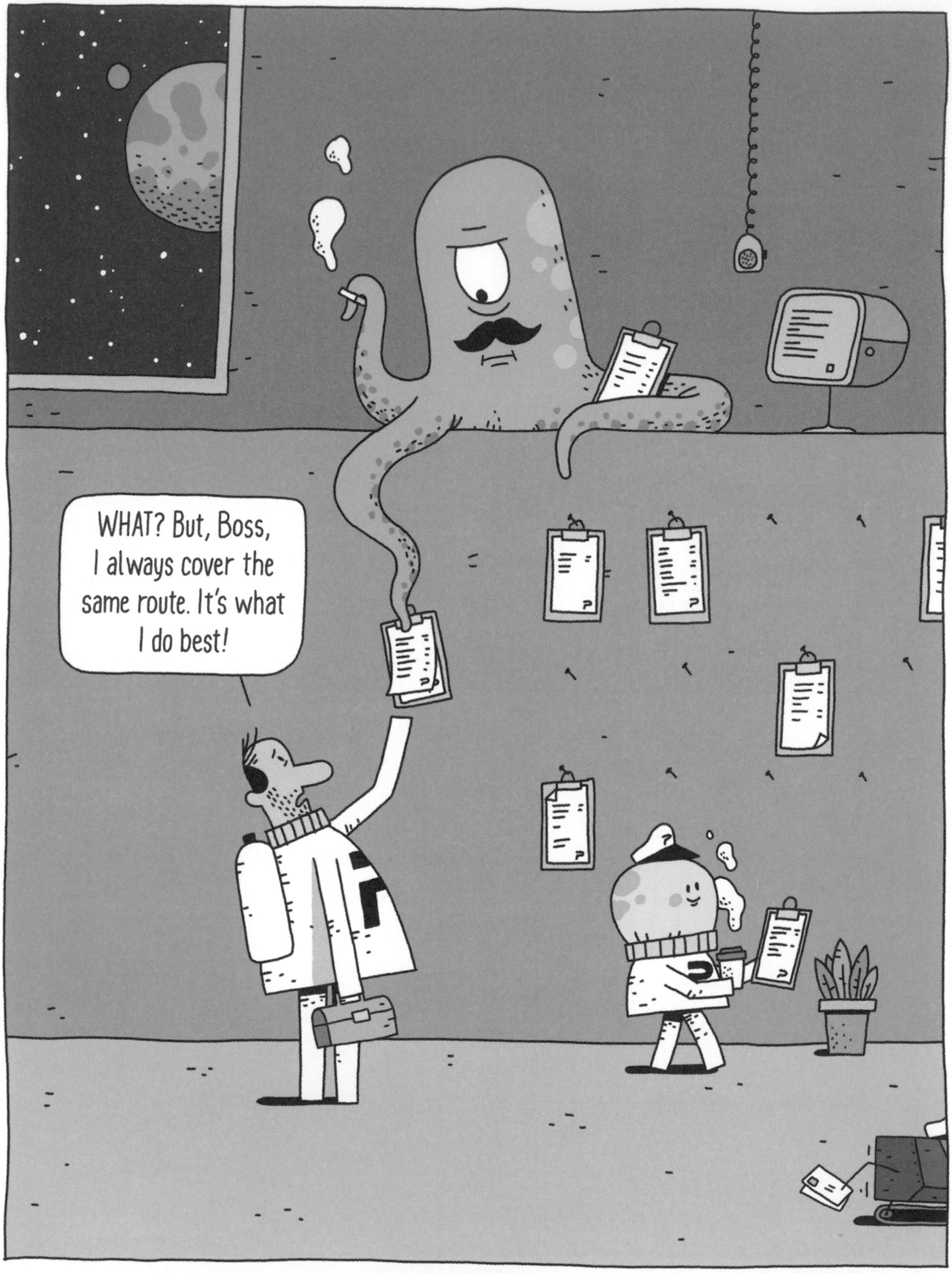
WHAT? But, Boss, I always cover the same route. It's what I do best!

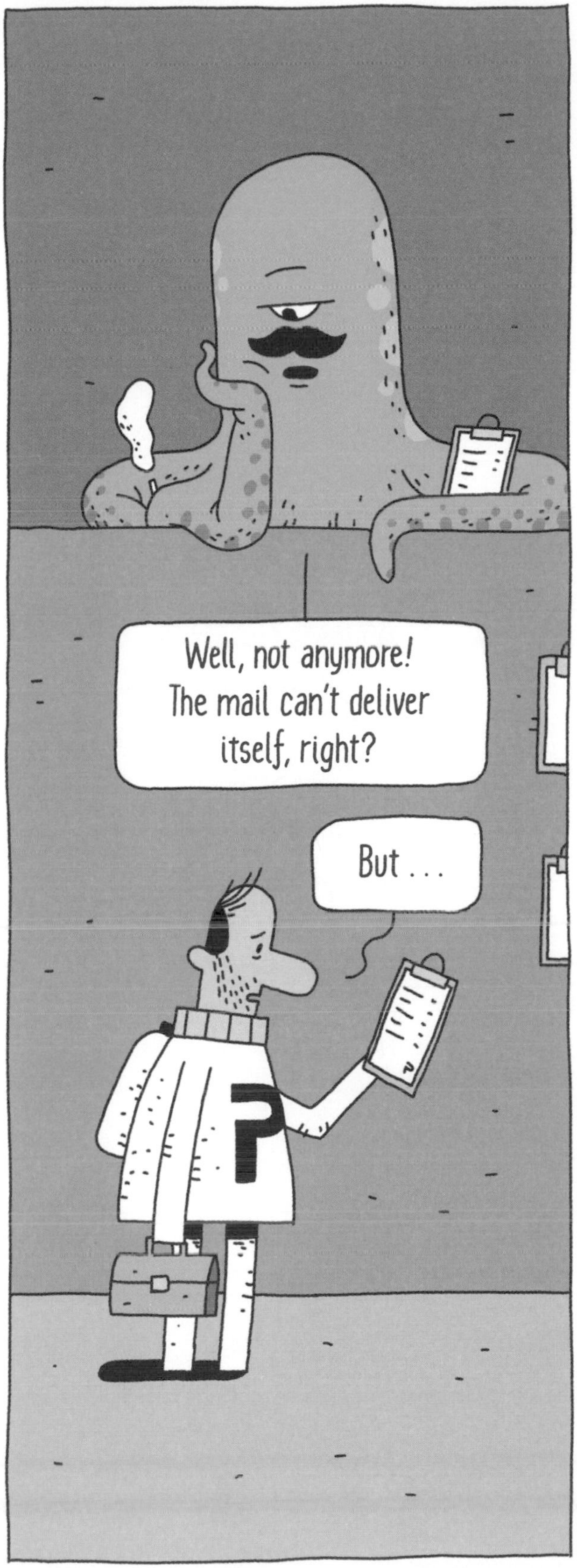
Well, not anymore! The mail can't deliver itself, right?
But . . .
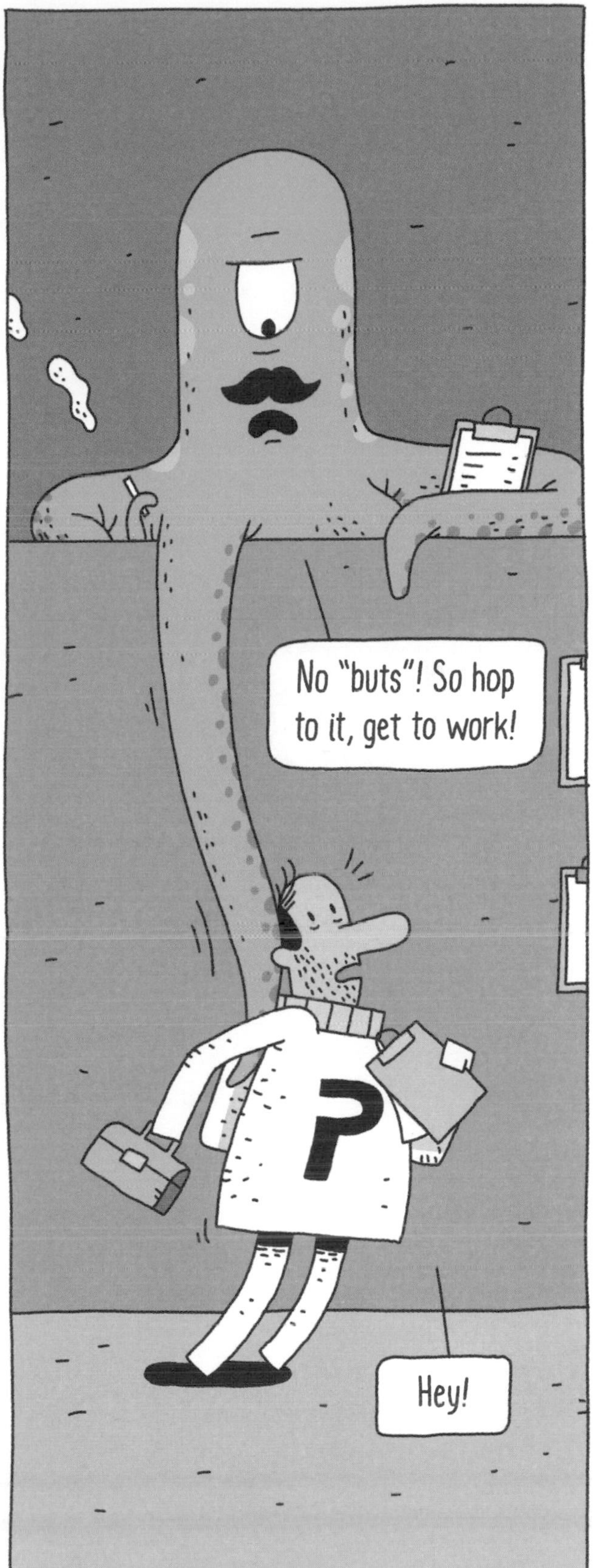
No "buts"! So hop to it, get to work!
Hey!

Bob doesn't know the new route at all.

Suddenly he feels really hot in his uniform, and
he starts to get a stomachache.

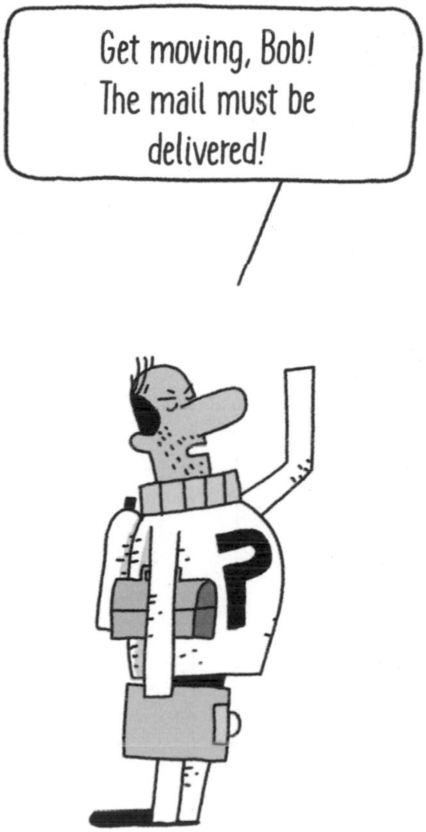
Get moving, Bob! The mail must be delivered!

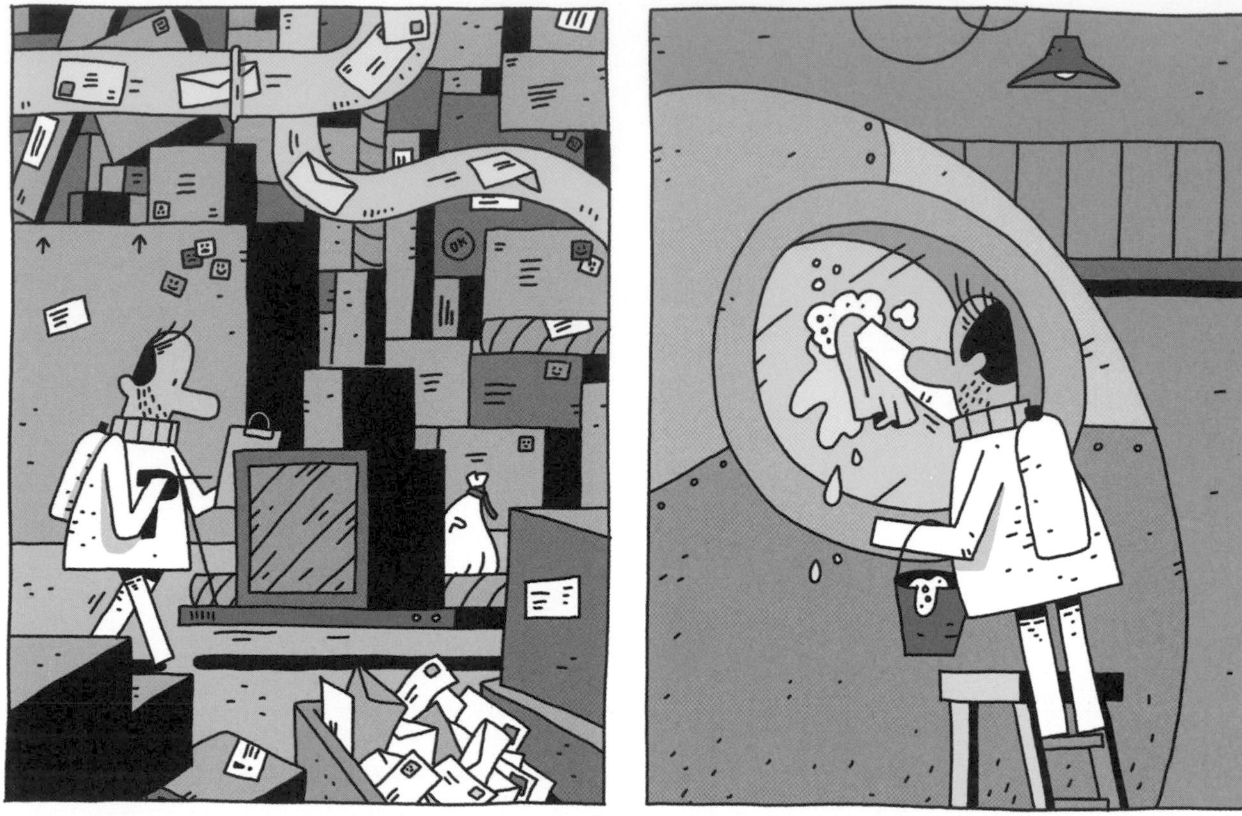

So Bob starts his day like any other. Load up, clean up, fuel up, and he's ready to go.

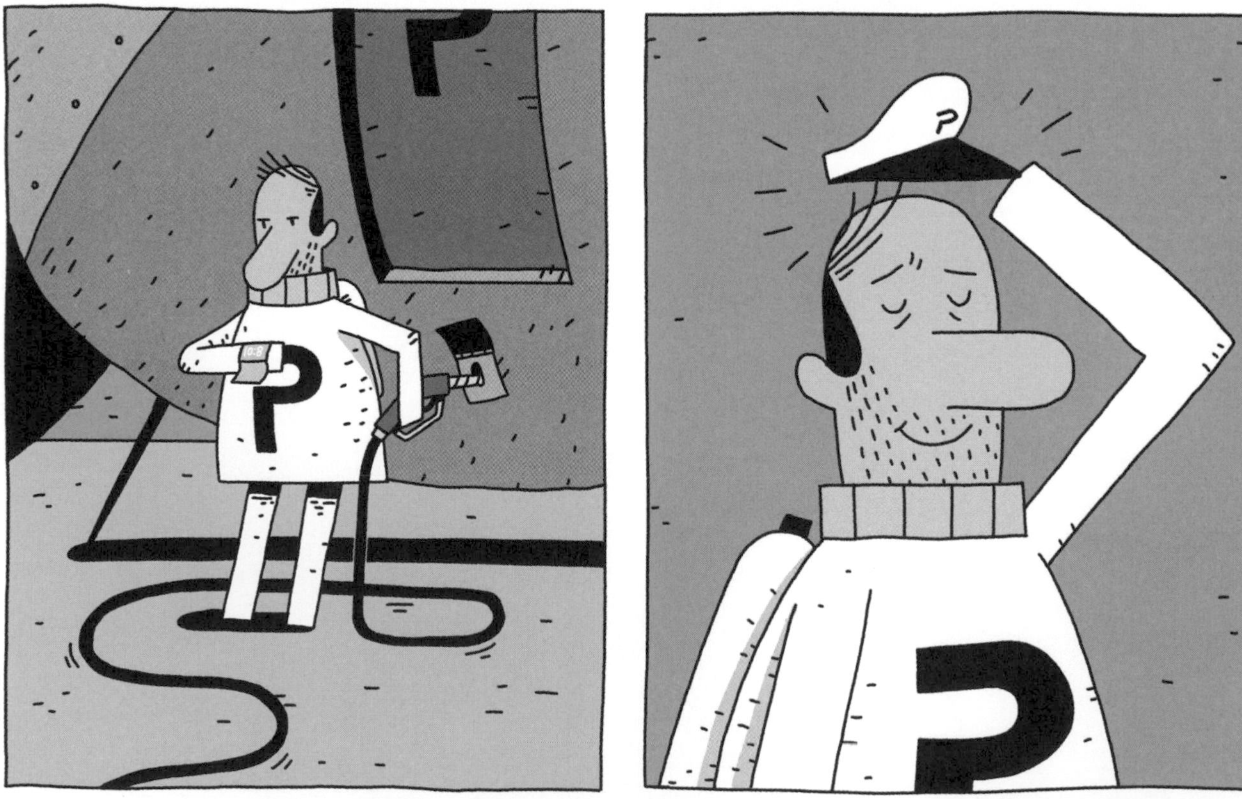

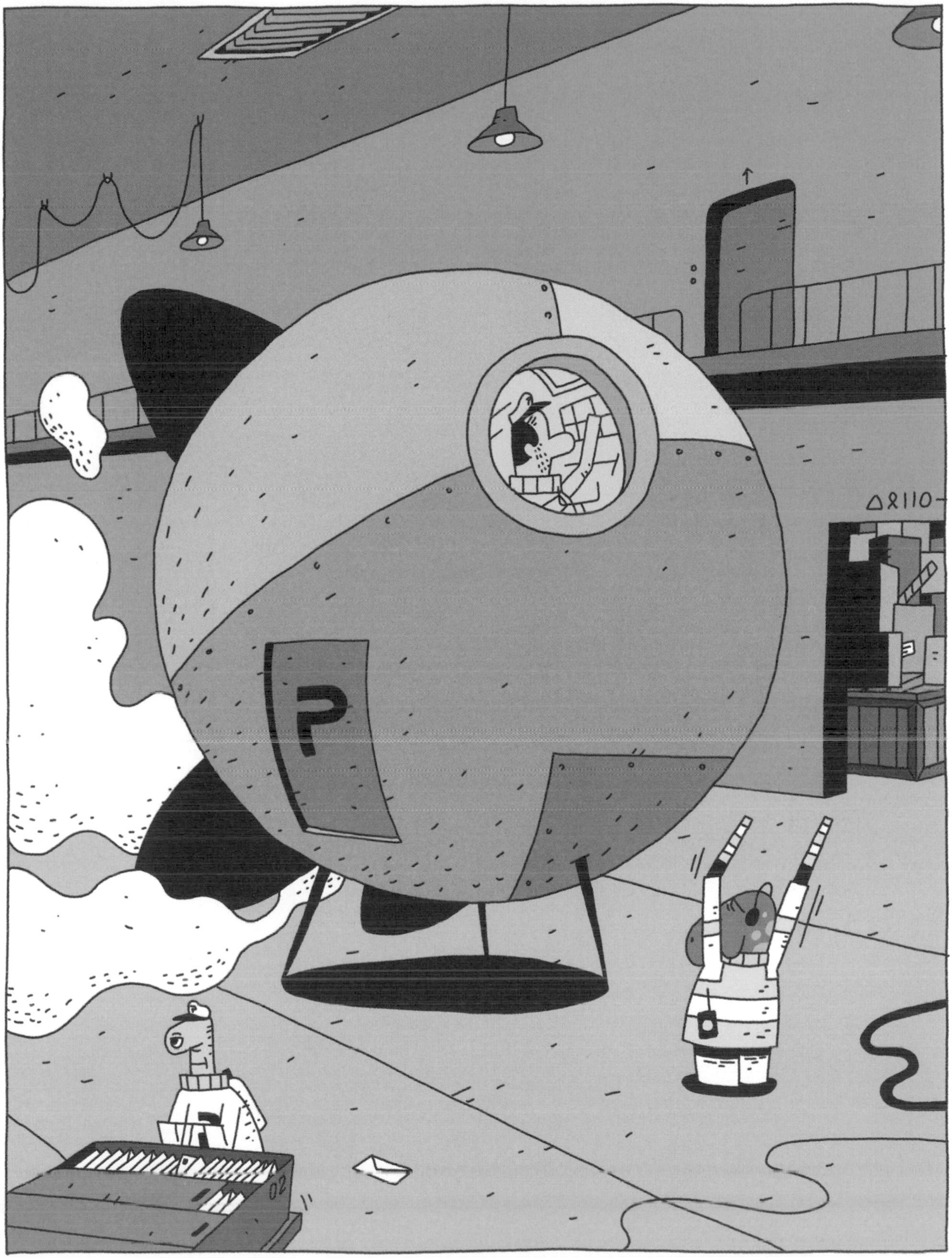
P
02

But our friend has no clue that today is a day he'll never forget.

DELIVERY
#1

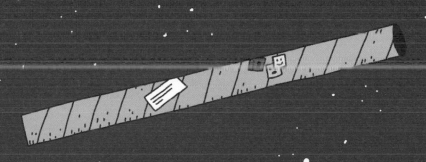

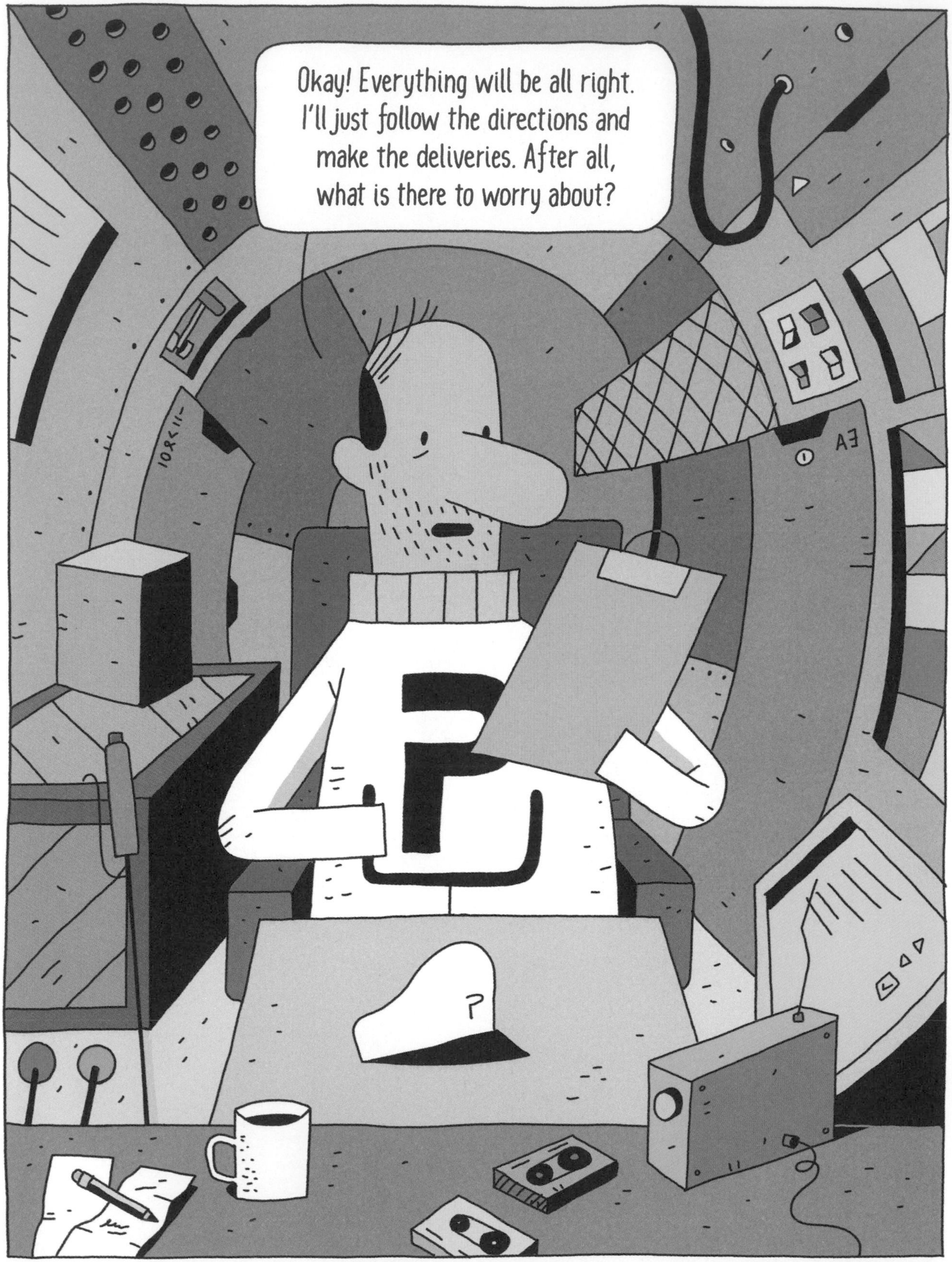
Okay! Everything will be all right. I'll just follow the directions and make the deliveries. After all, what is there to worry about?

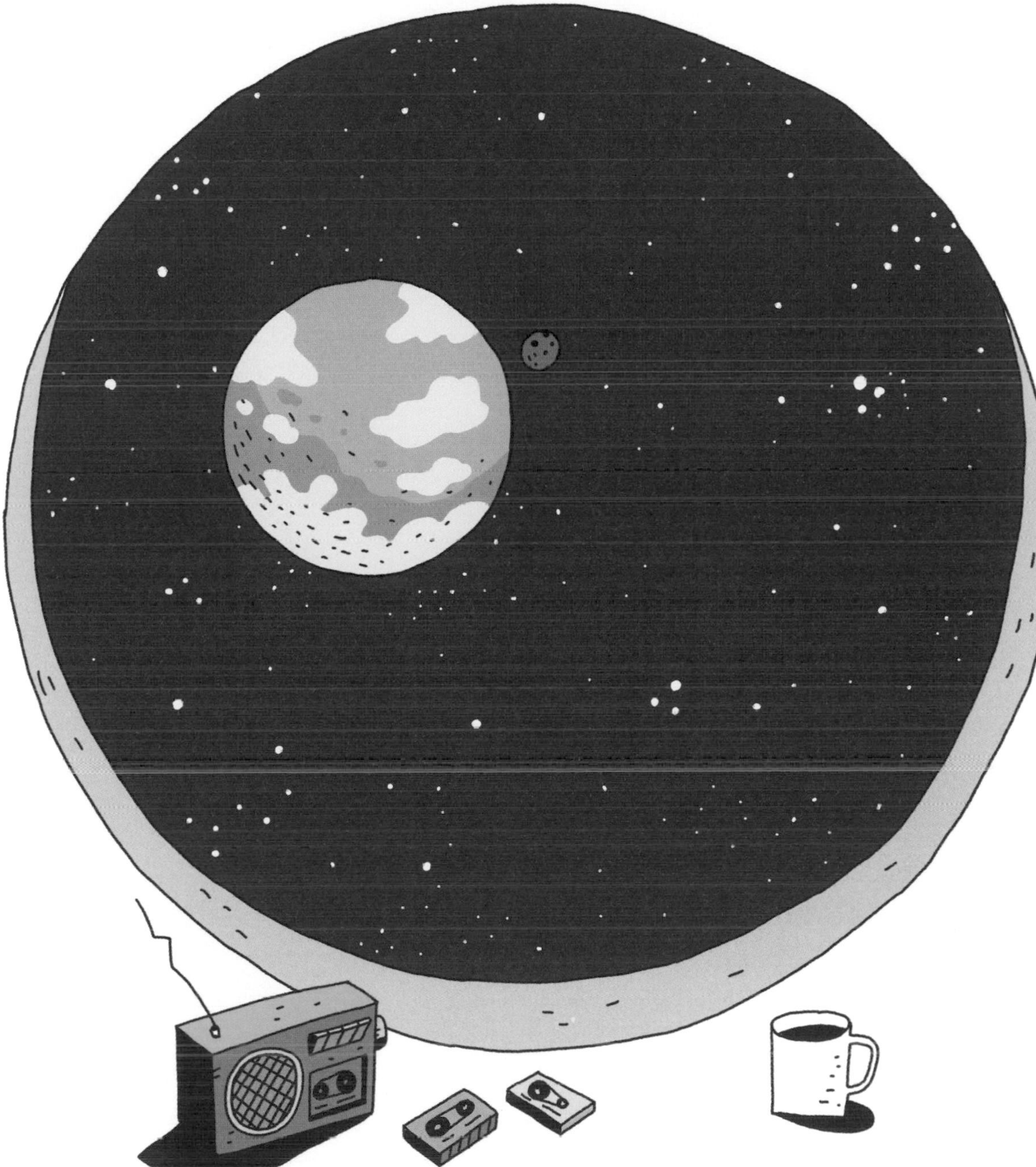

The first stop is coming up.

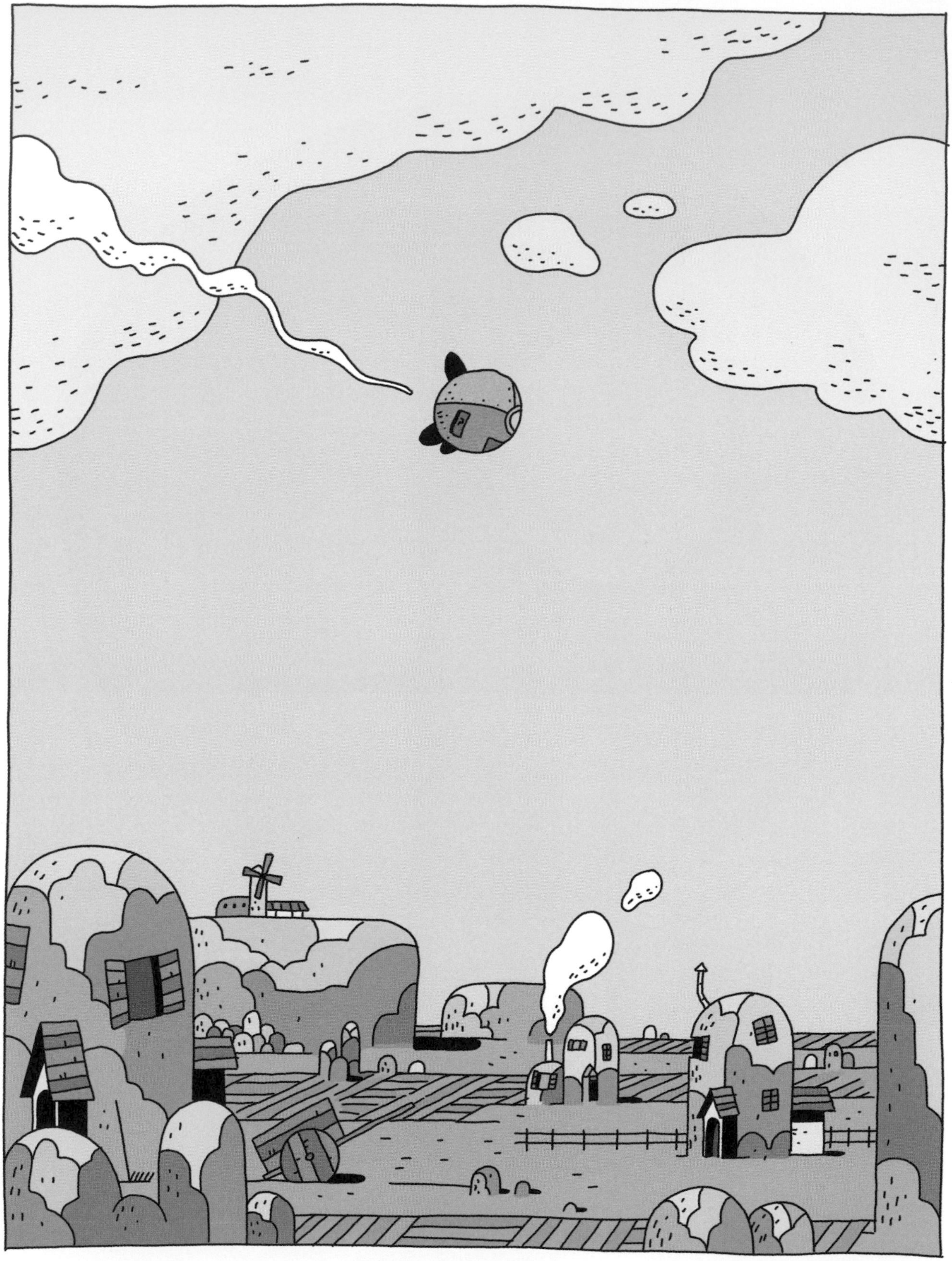

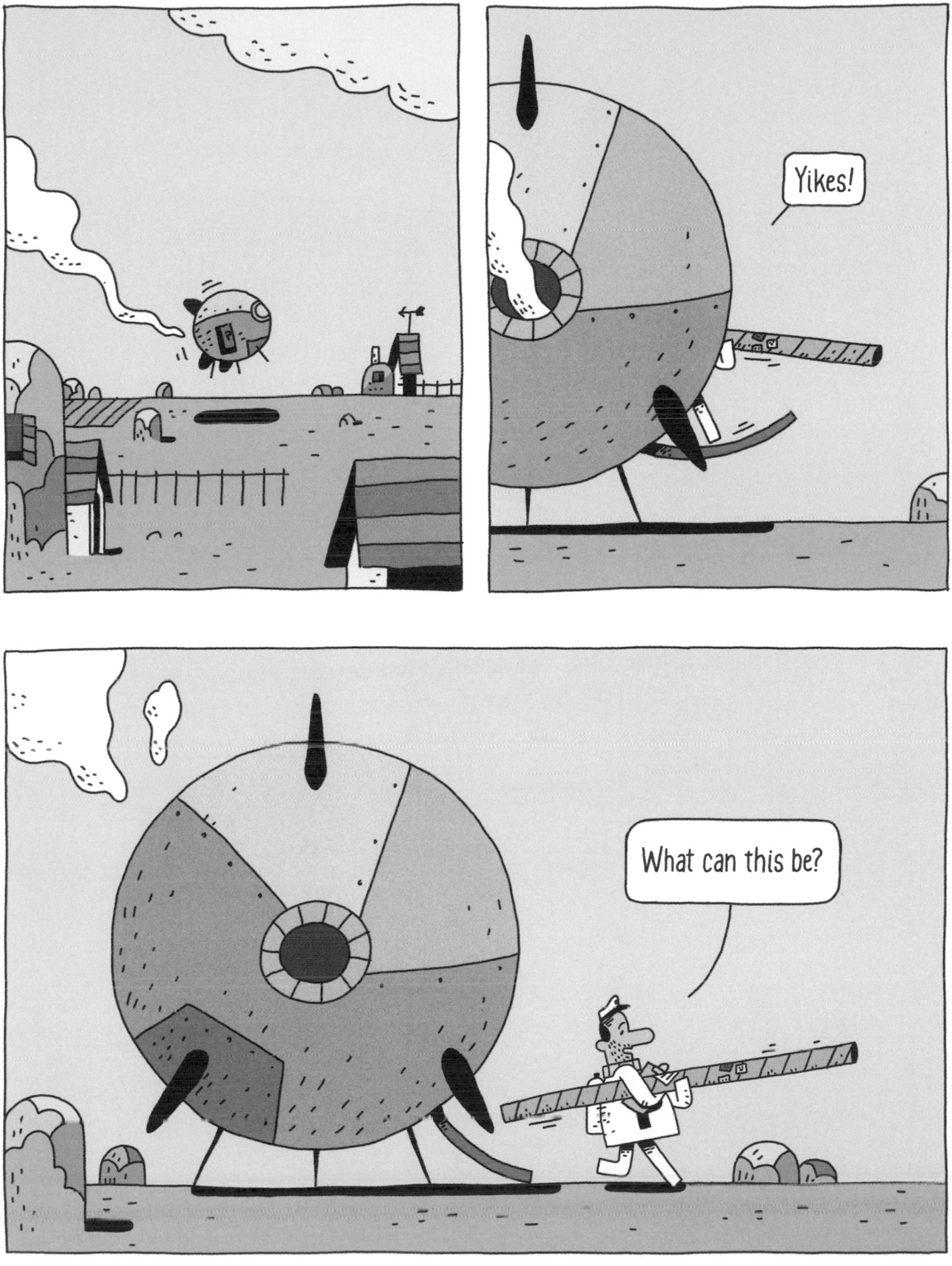
Yikes!
What can this be?

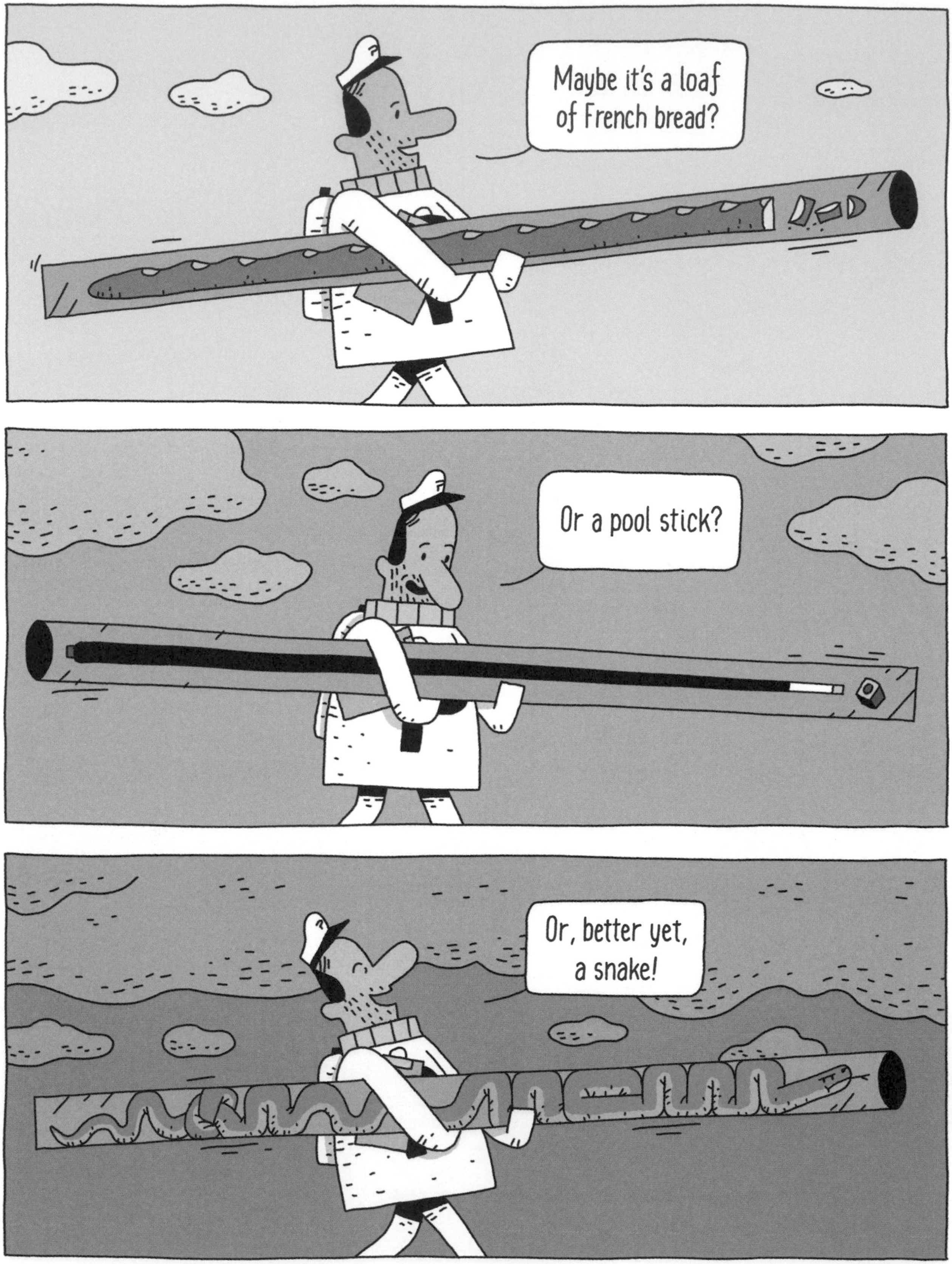
Maybe it's a loaf of French bread?
Or a pool stick?
Or, better yet, a snake!

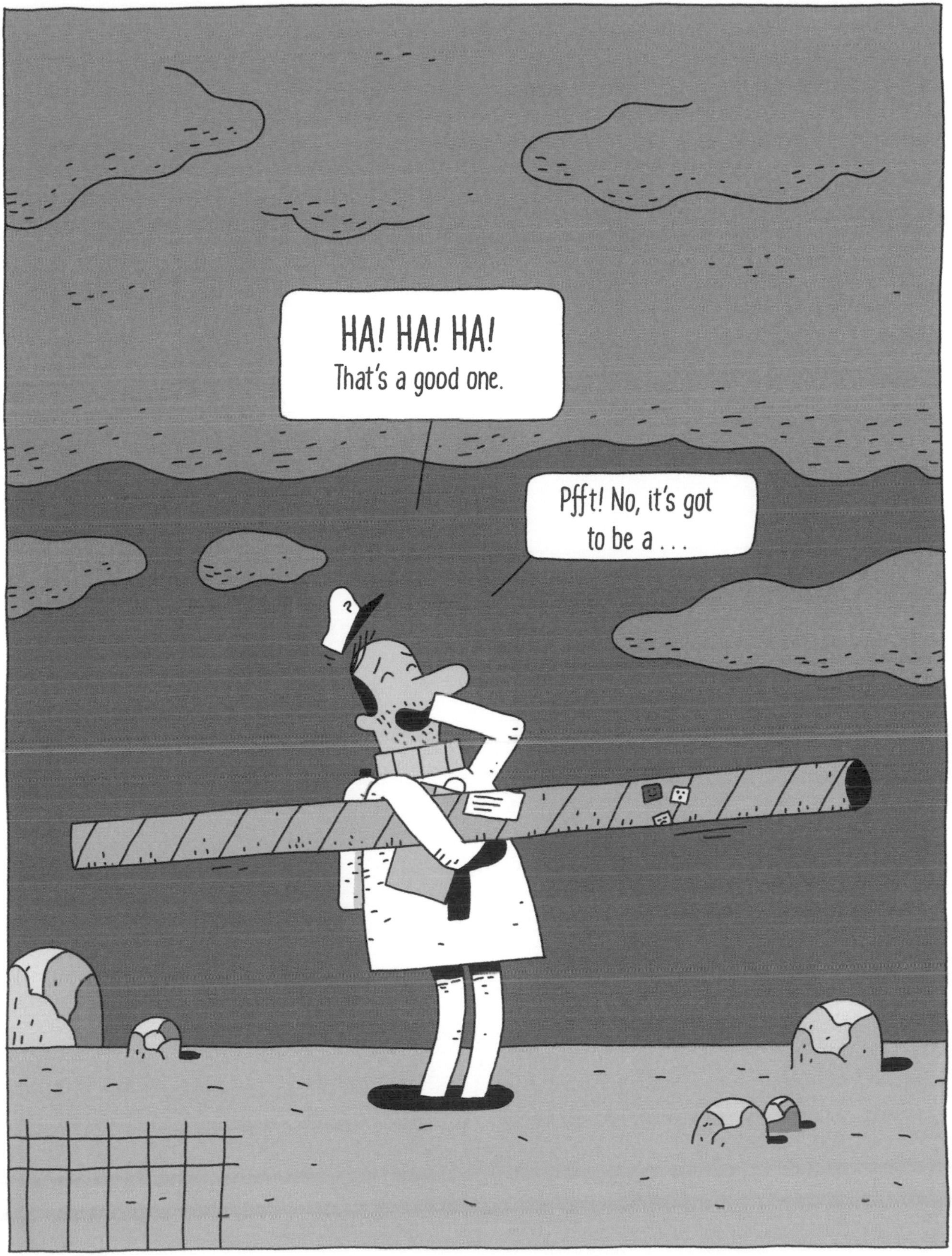
HA! HA! HA!
That's a good one.
Pfft! No, it's got to be a . . .

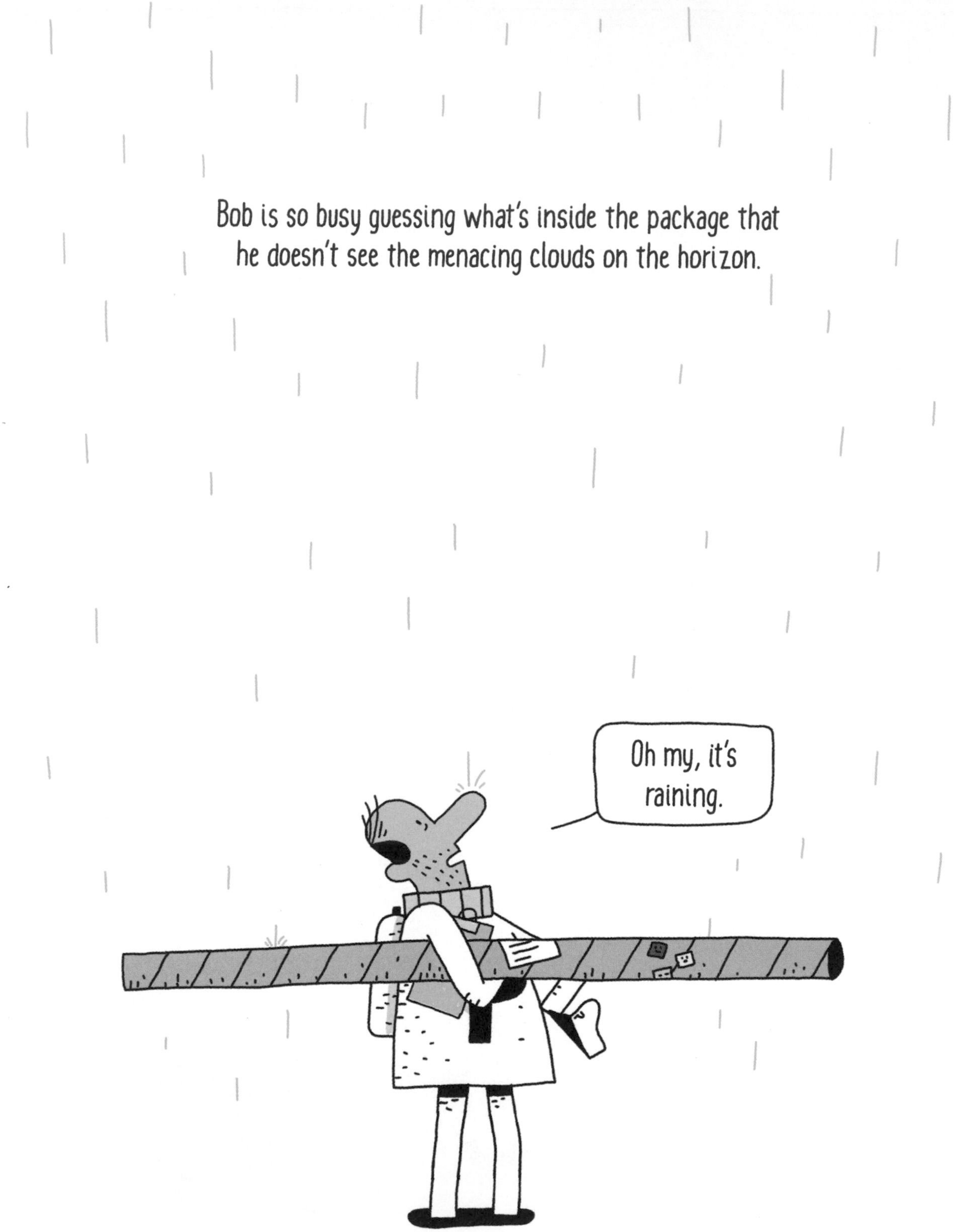
Bob is so busy guessing what's inside the package that he doesn't see the menacing clouds on the horizon.
Oh my, it's raining.

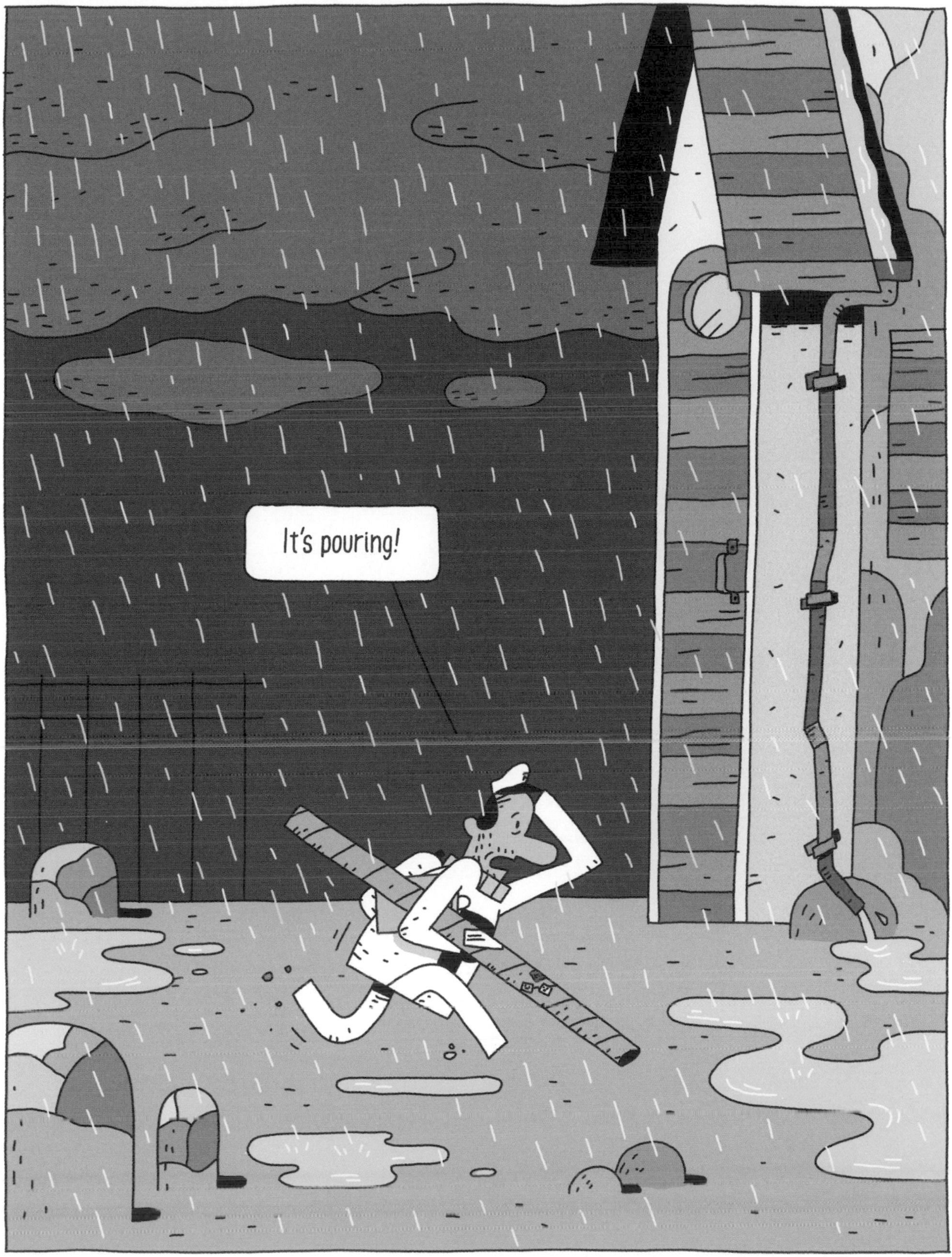
It's pouring!

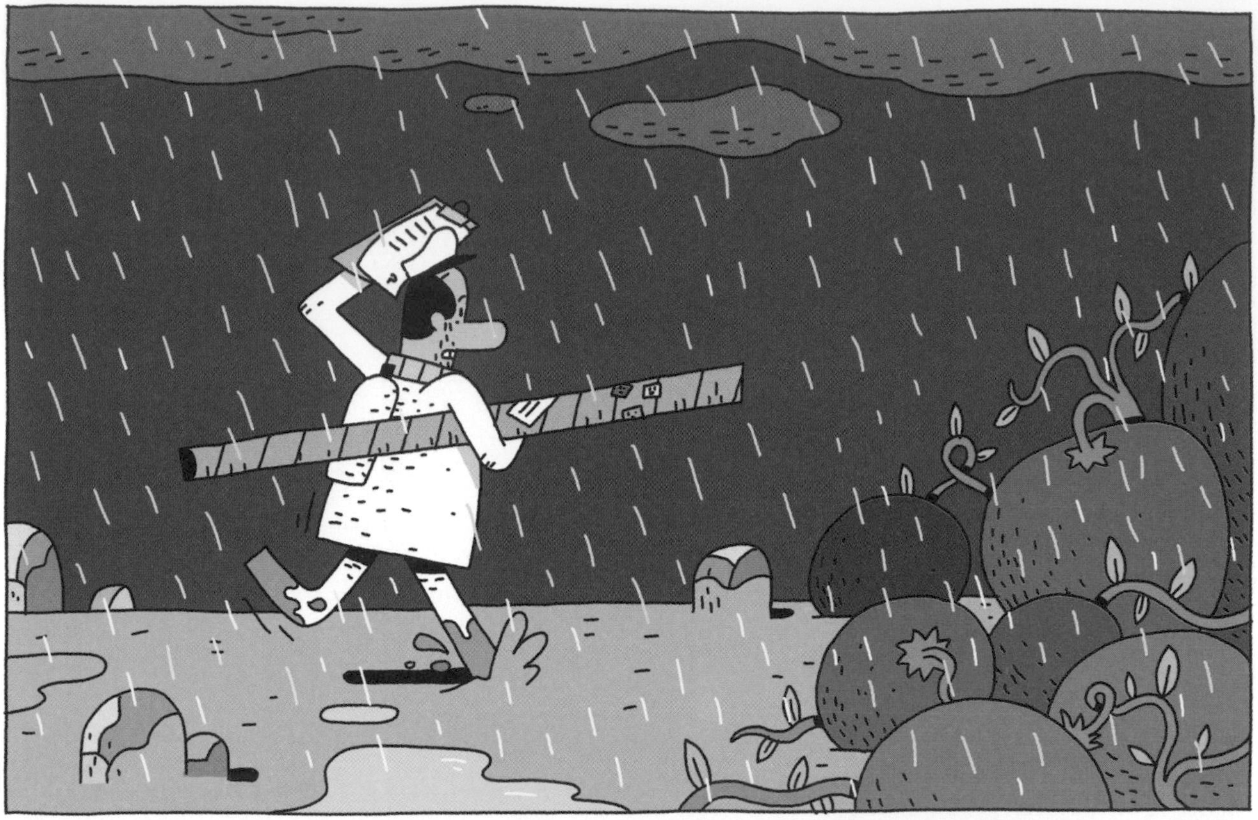

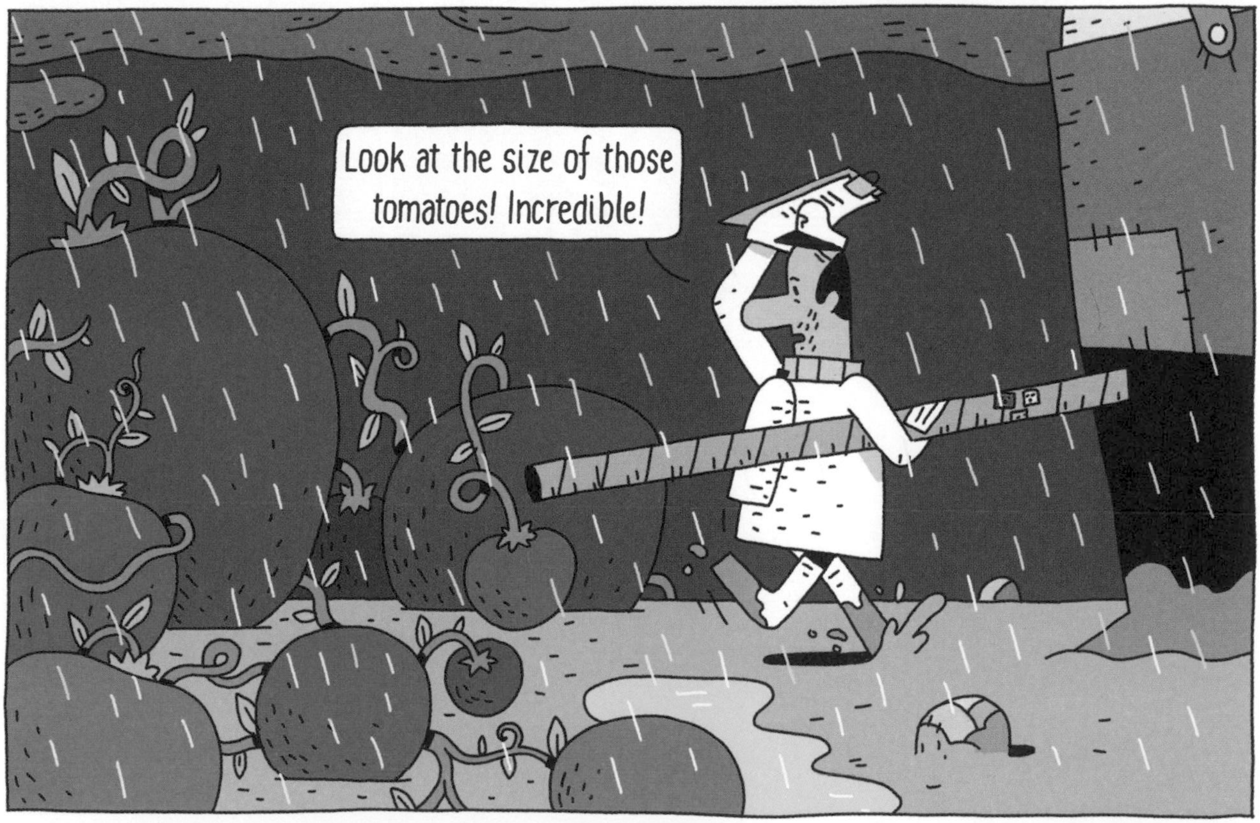
Look at the size of those tomatoes! Incredible!

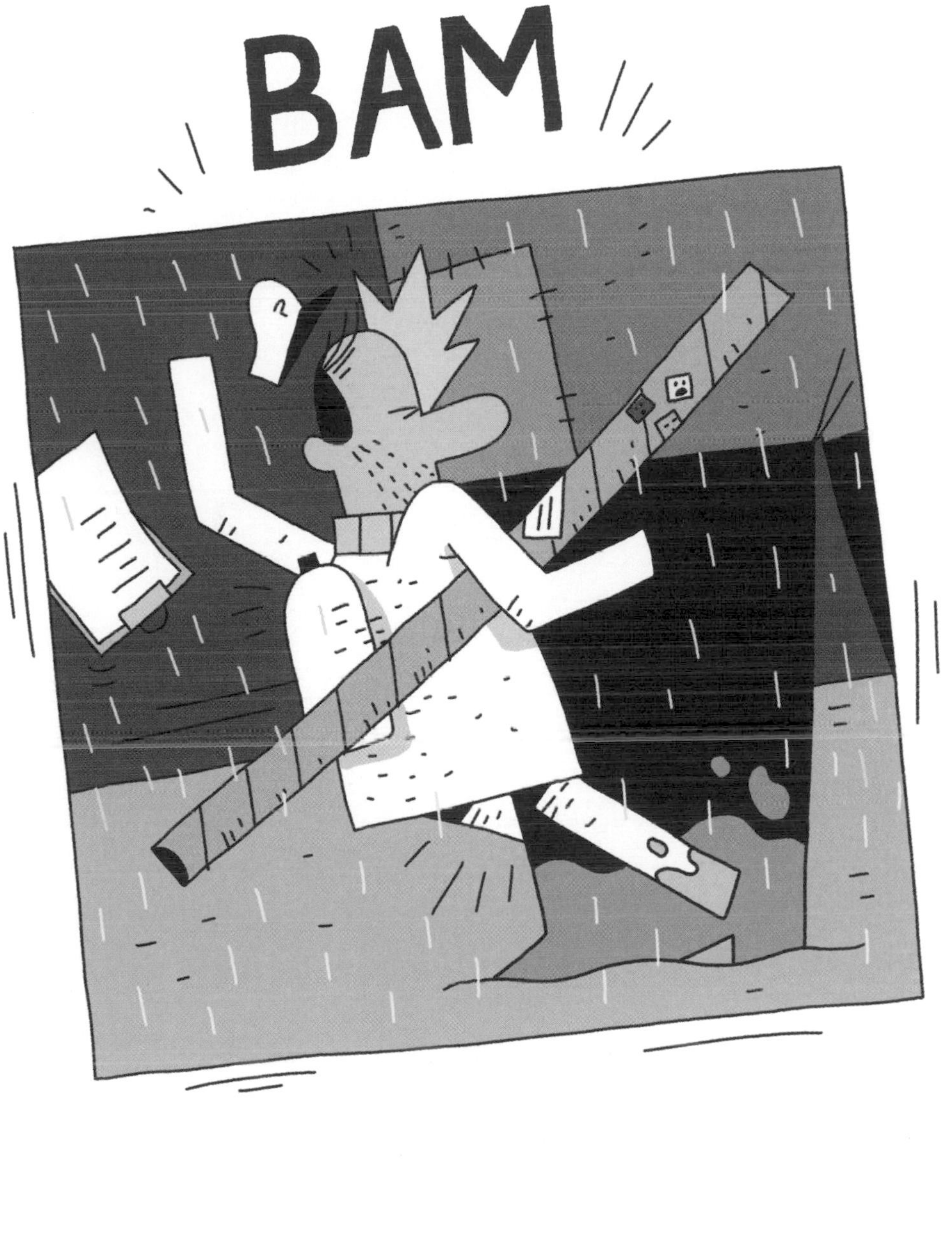
BAM

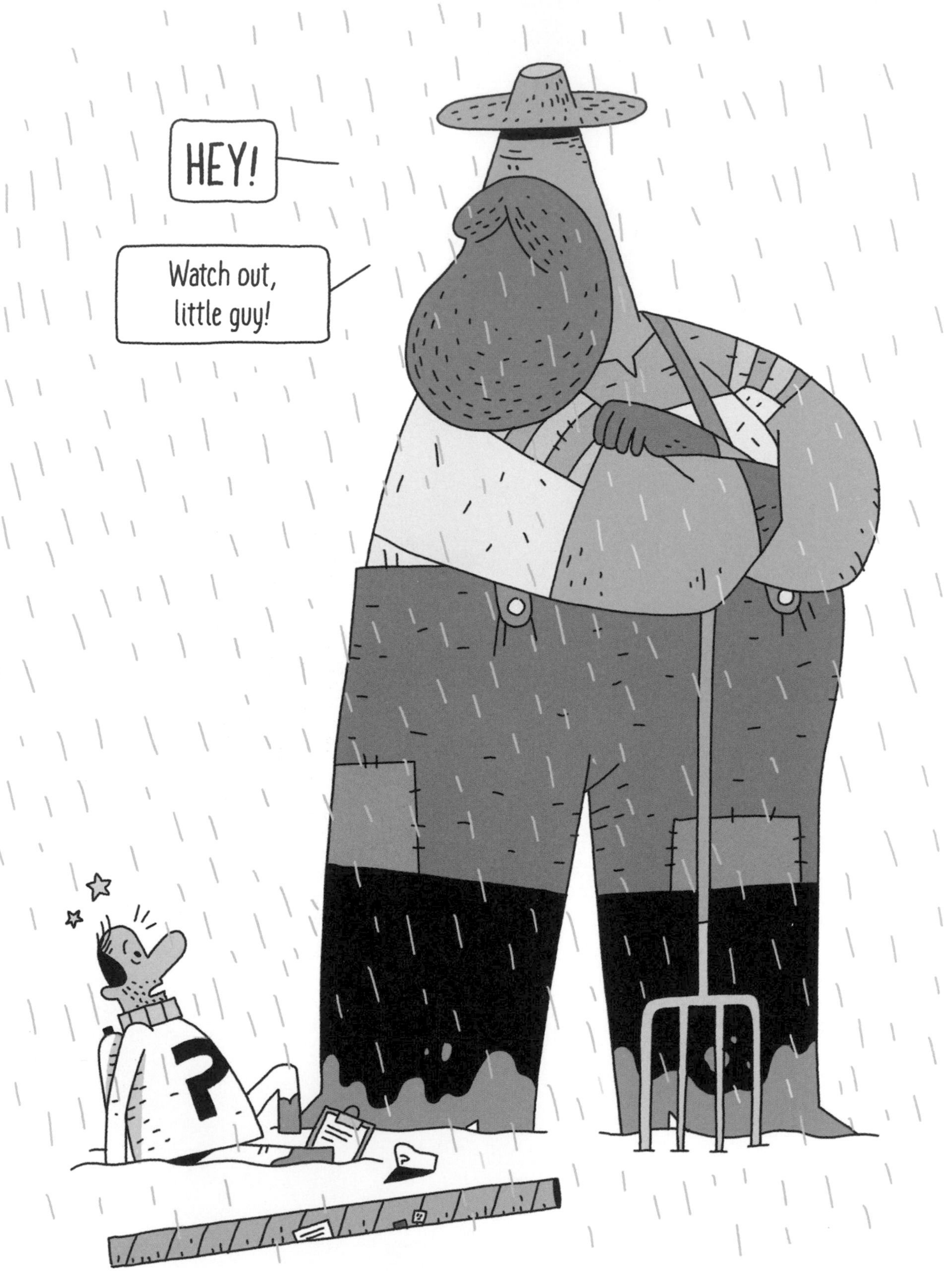
HEY!
Watch out, little guy!

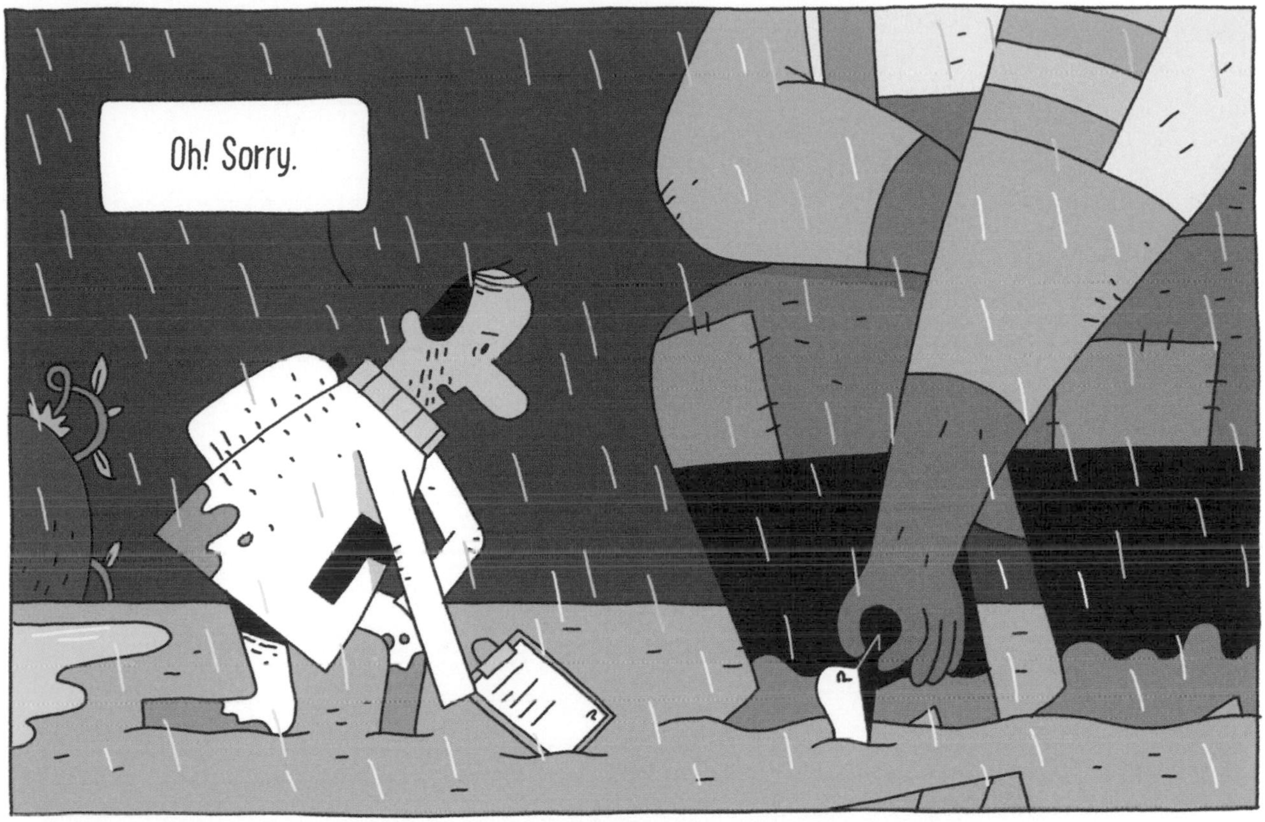
Oh! Sorry.

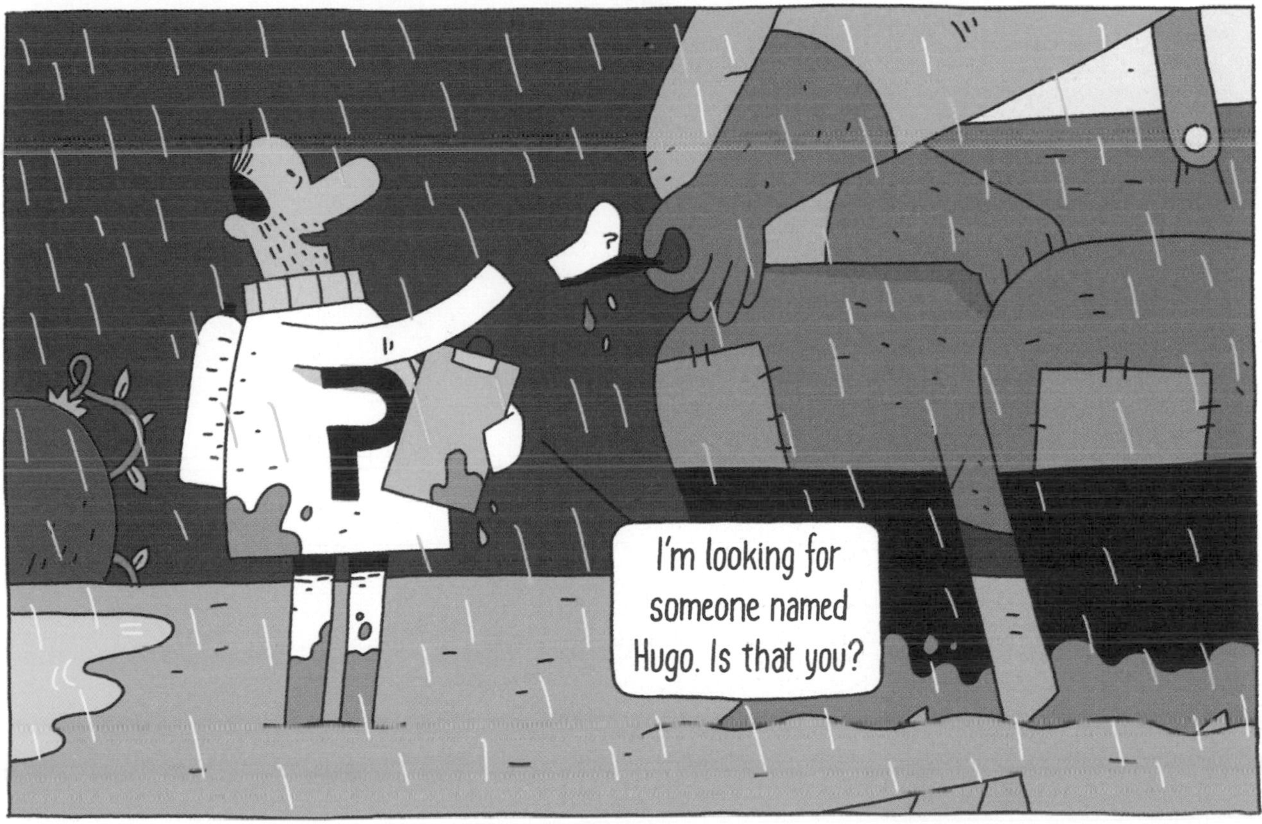
I'm looking for someone named Hugo. Is that you?

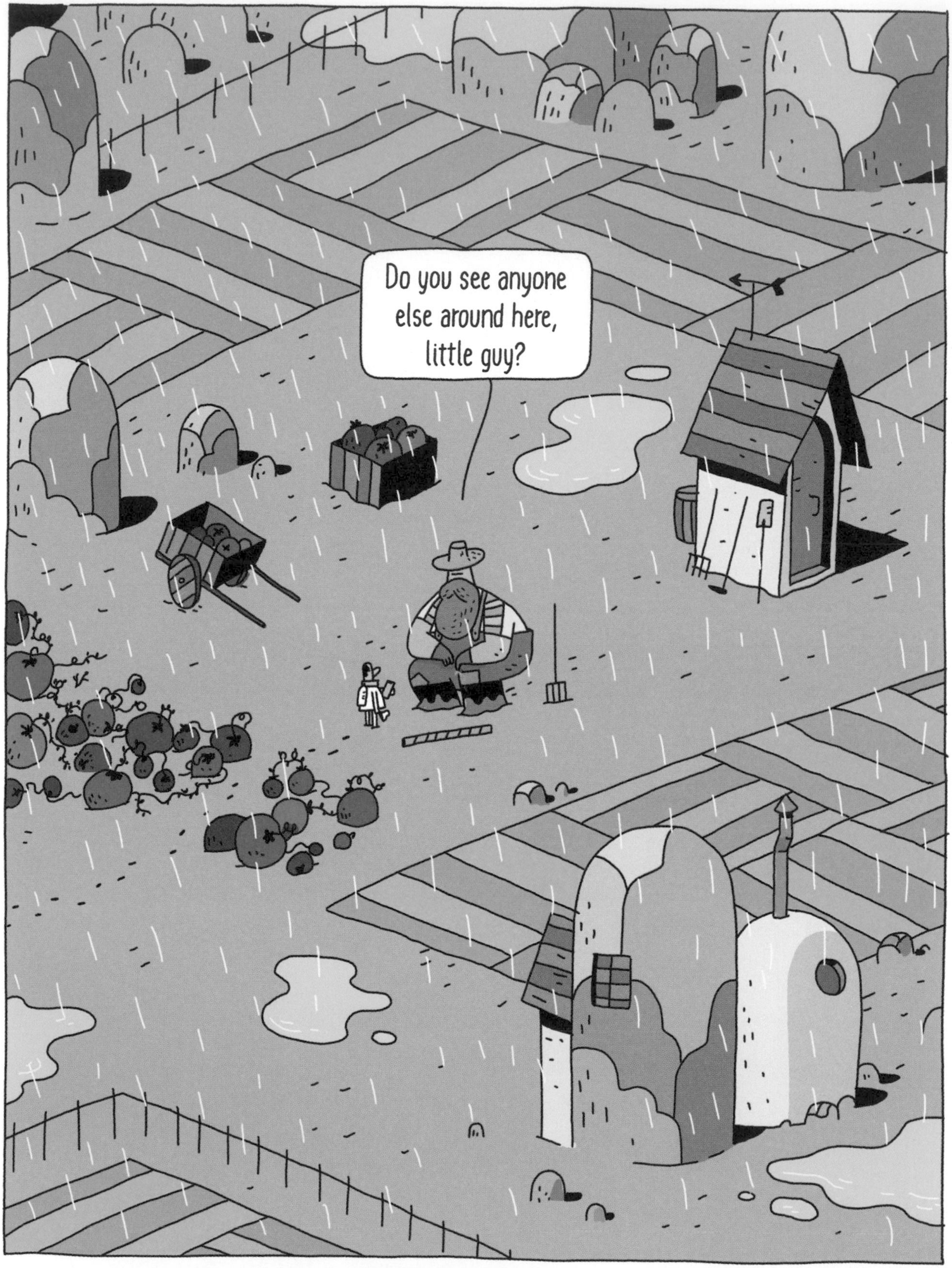
Do you see anyone else around here, little guy?

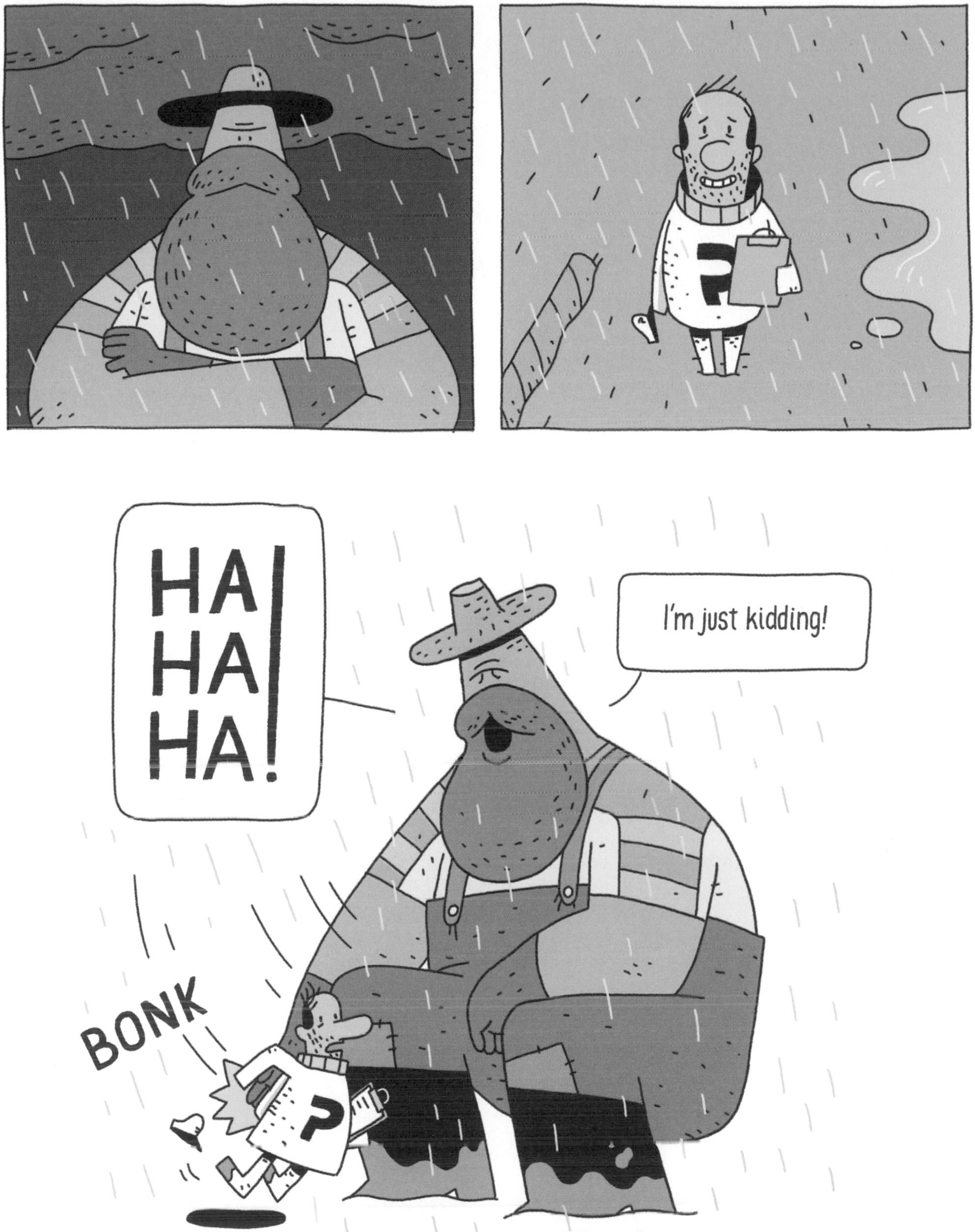
HA HA HA!
I'm just kidding!
BONK

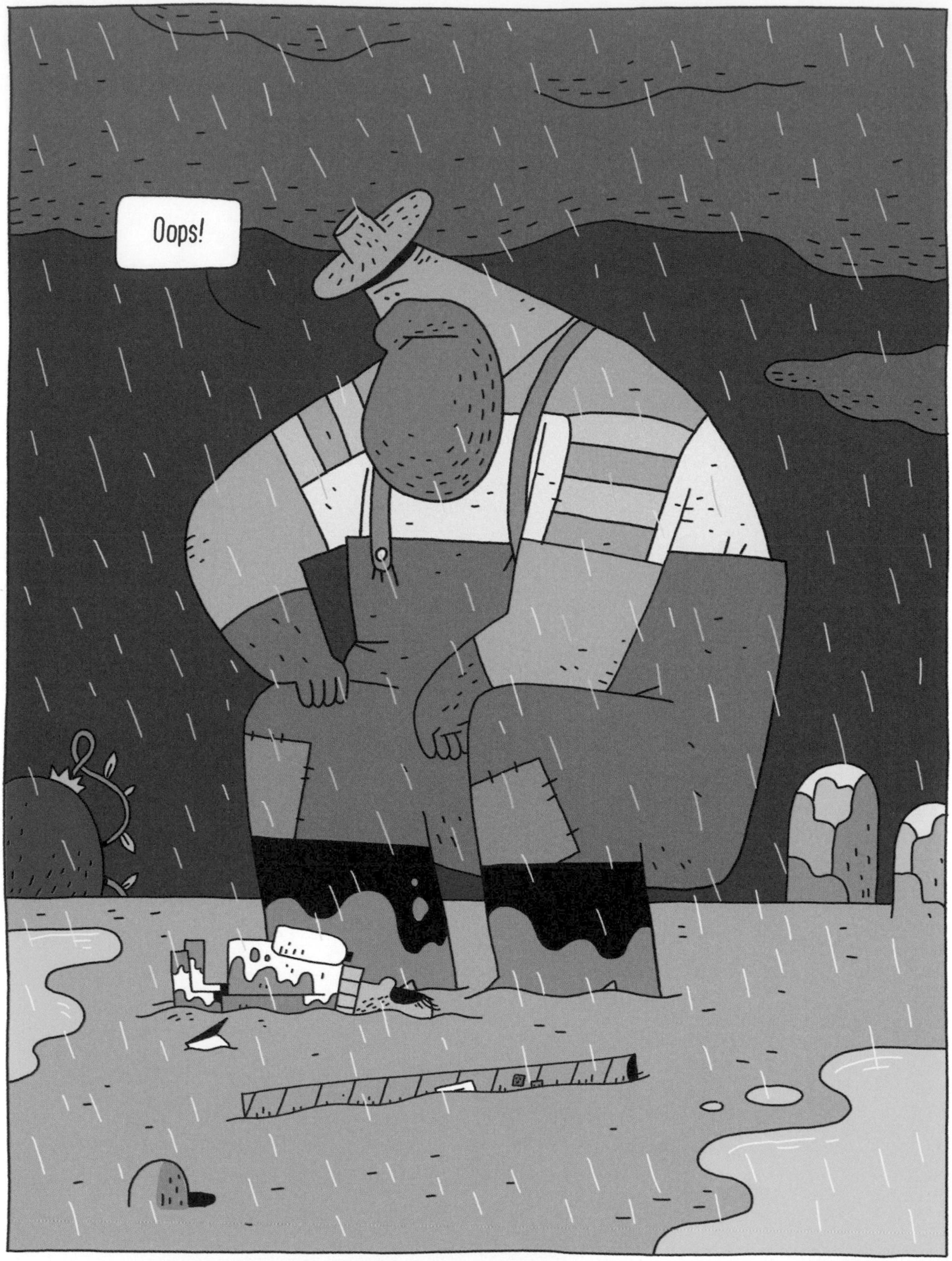
Oops!

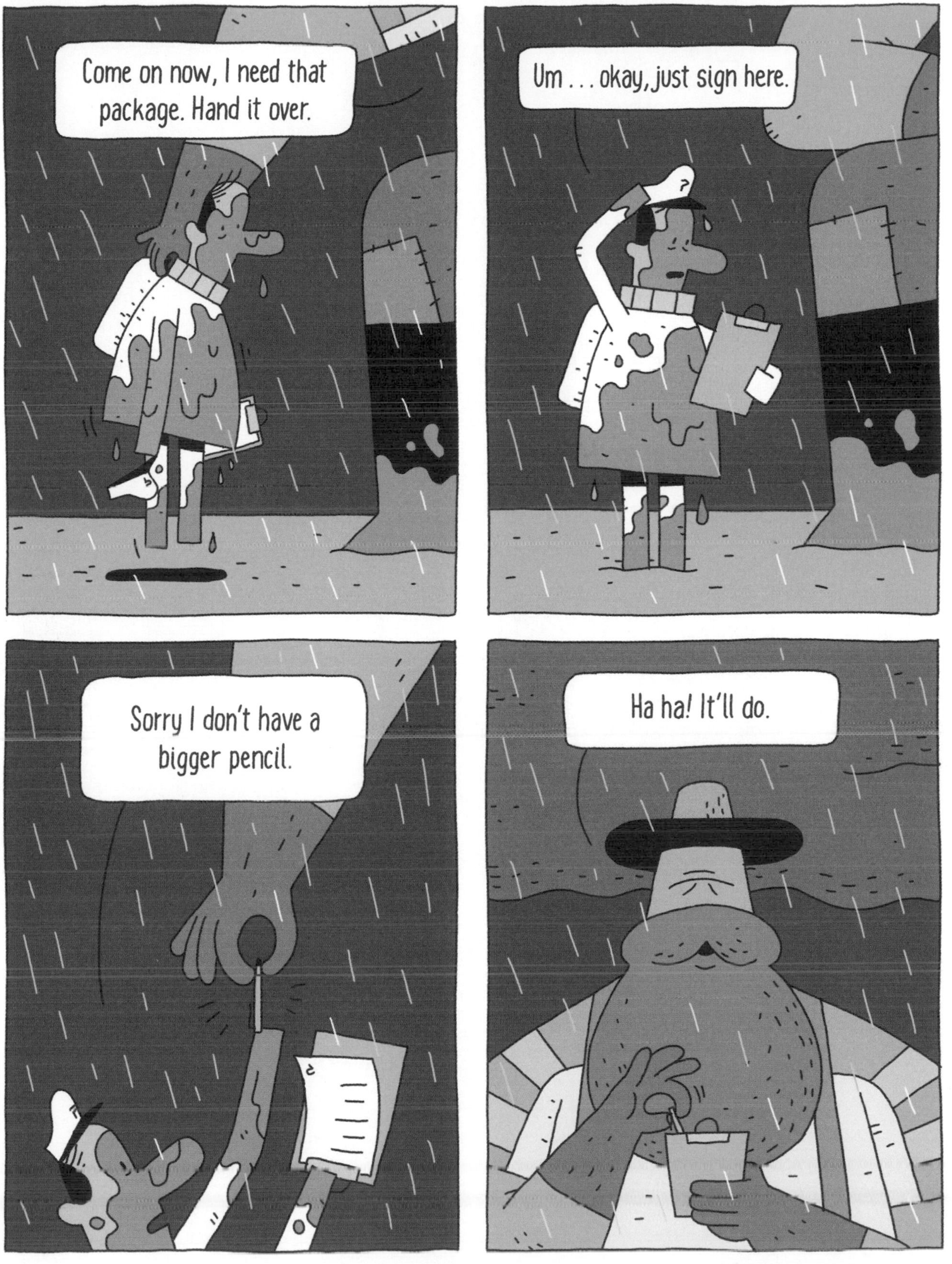
Come on now, I need that package. Hand it over.
Um . . . okay, just sign here.
Sorry I don't have a bigger pencil.
Ha ha! It'll do.

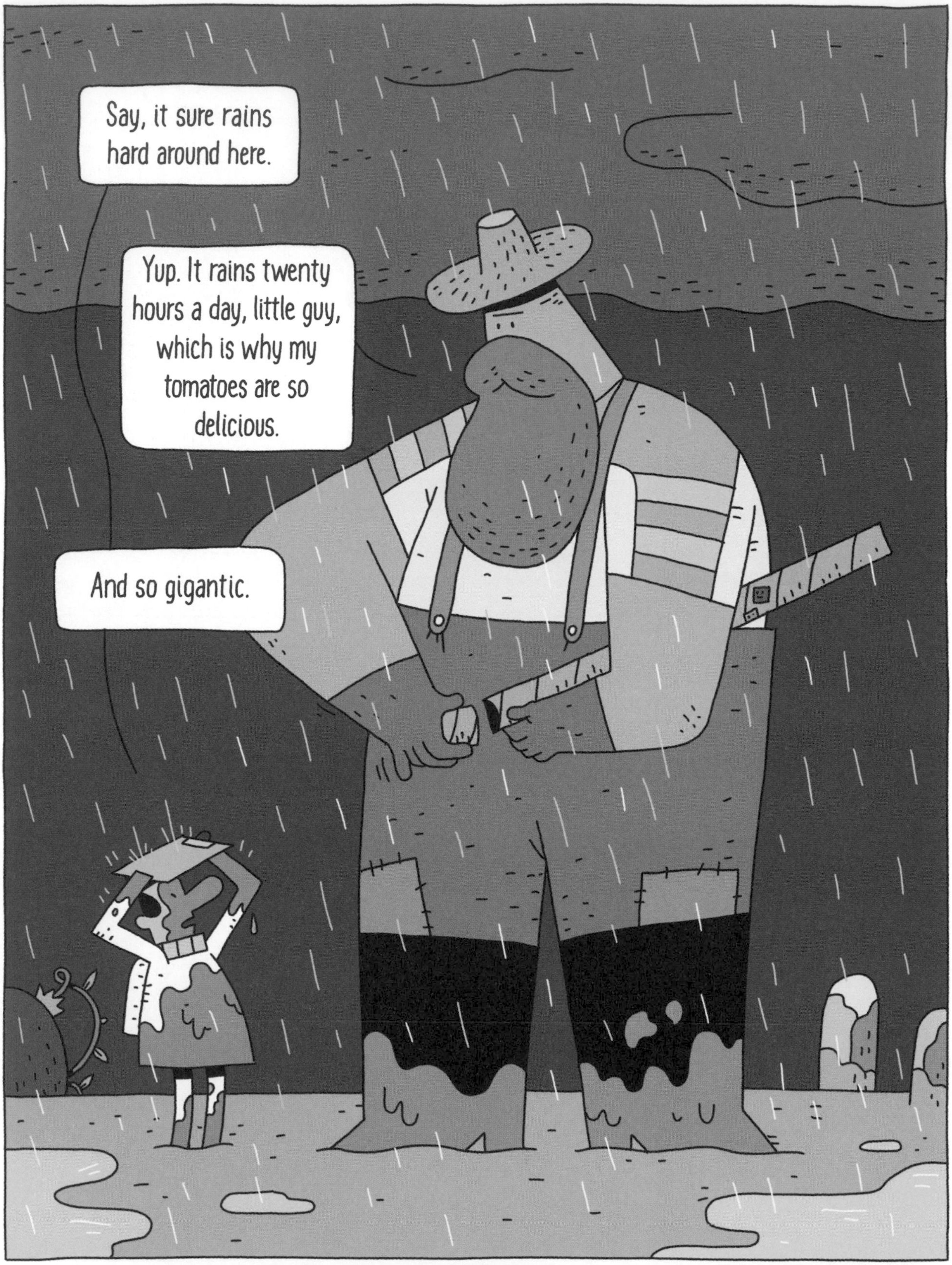
Say, it sure rains hard around here.
Yup. It rains twenty hours a day, little guy, which is why my tomatoes are so delicious.
And so gigantic.

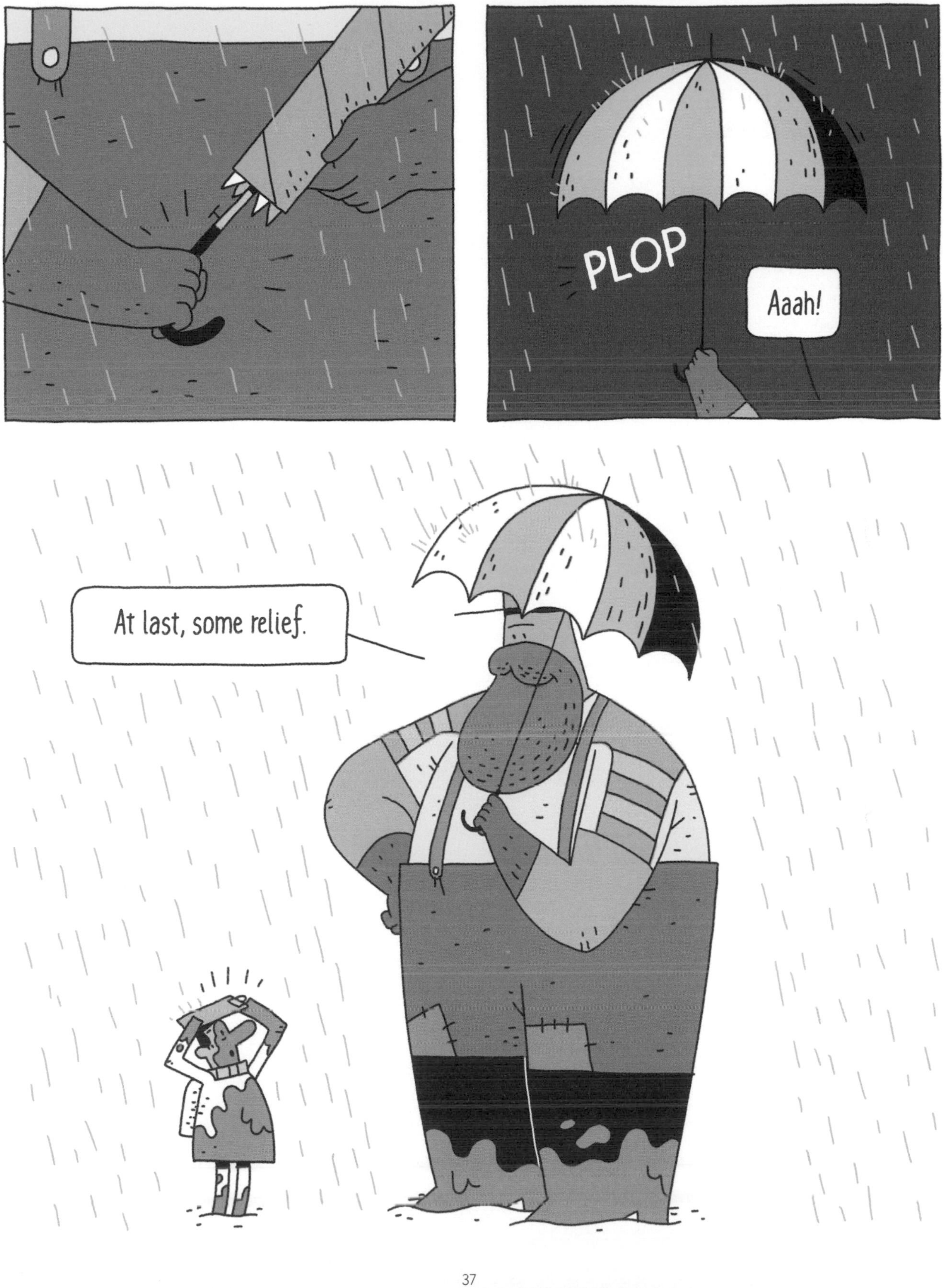
PLOP
Aaah!
At last, some relief.

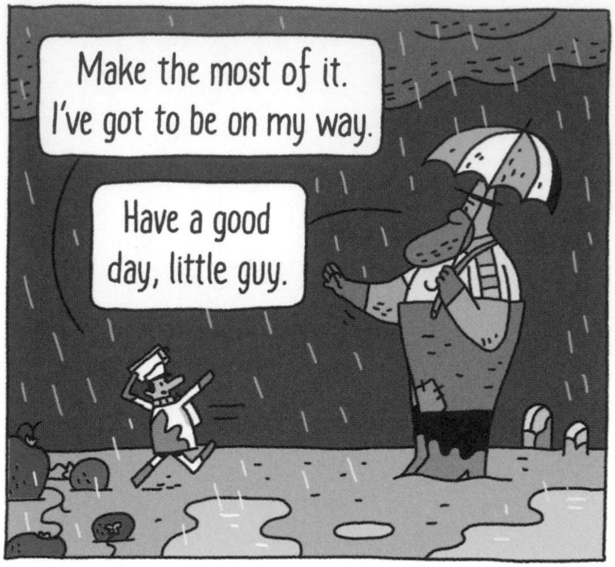
Make the most of it. I've got to be on my way.
Have a good day, little guy.

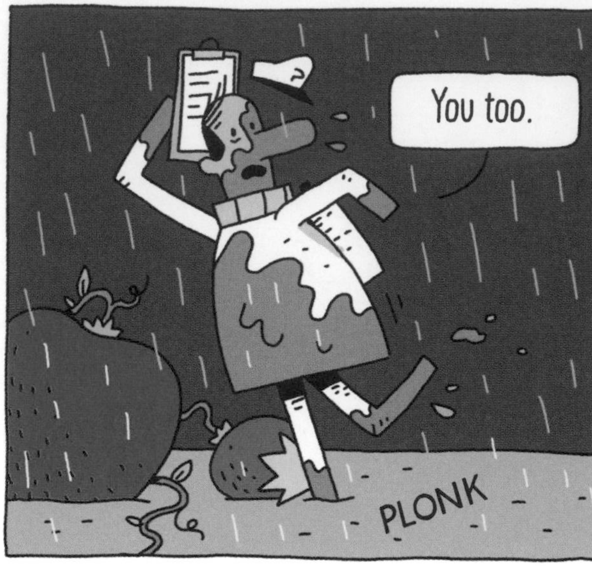
You too.
PLONK

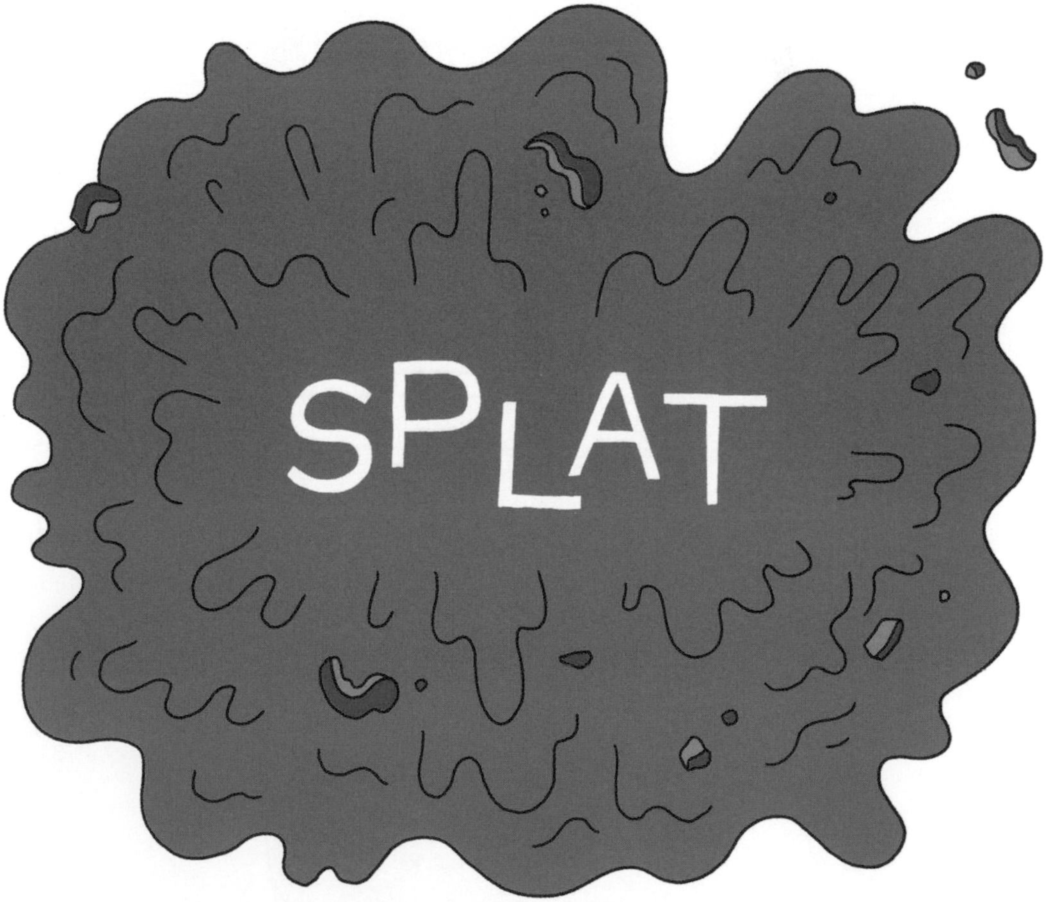
SPLAT

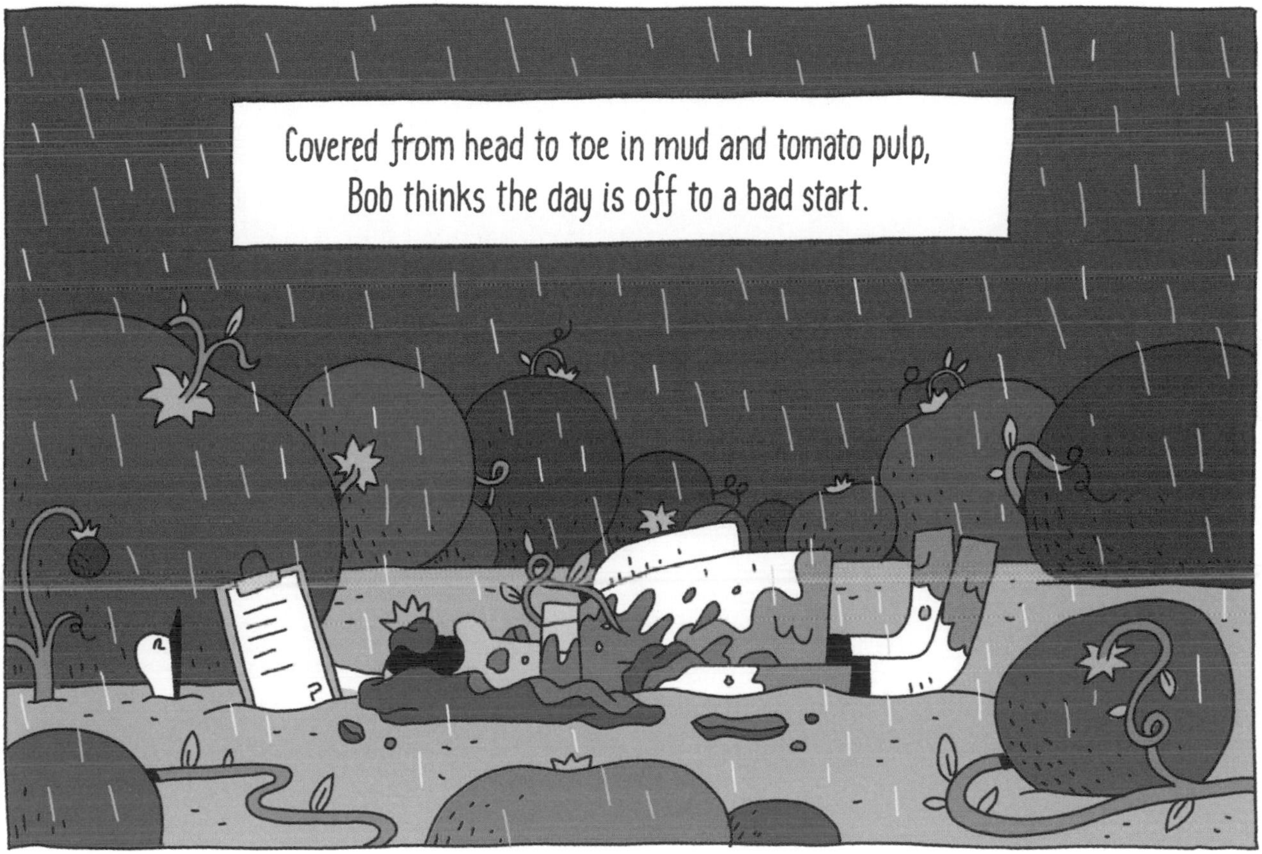
Covered from head to toe in mud and tomato pulp,
Bob thinks the day is off to a bad start.

DELIVERY
#2

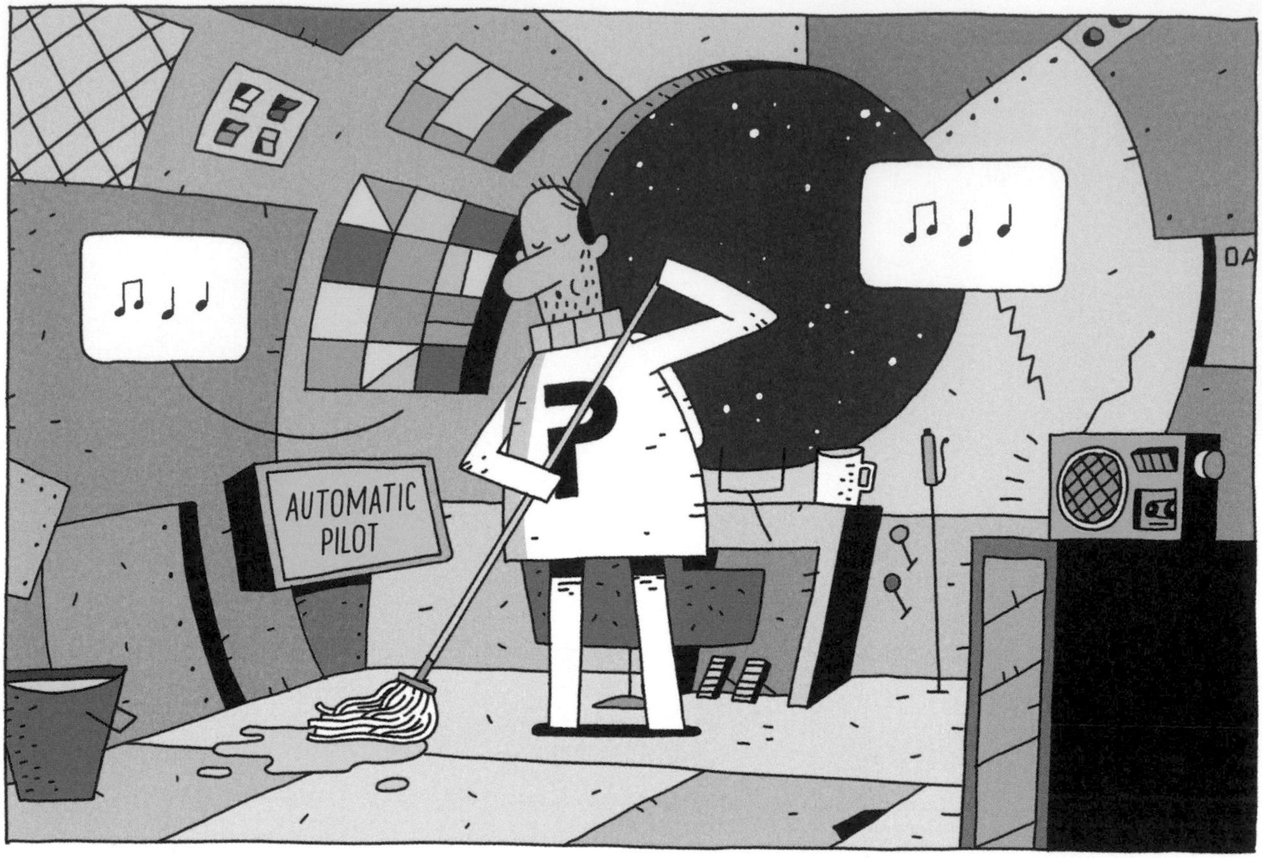
♫ ♩ ♩
♫ ♩ ♩
AUTOMATIC PILOT

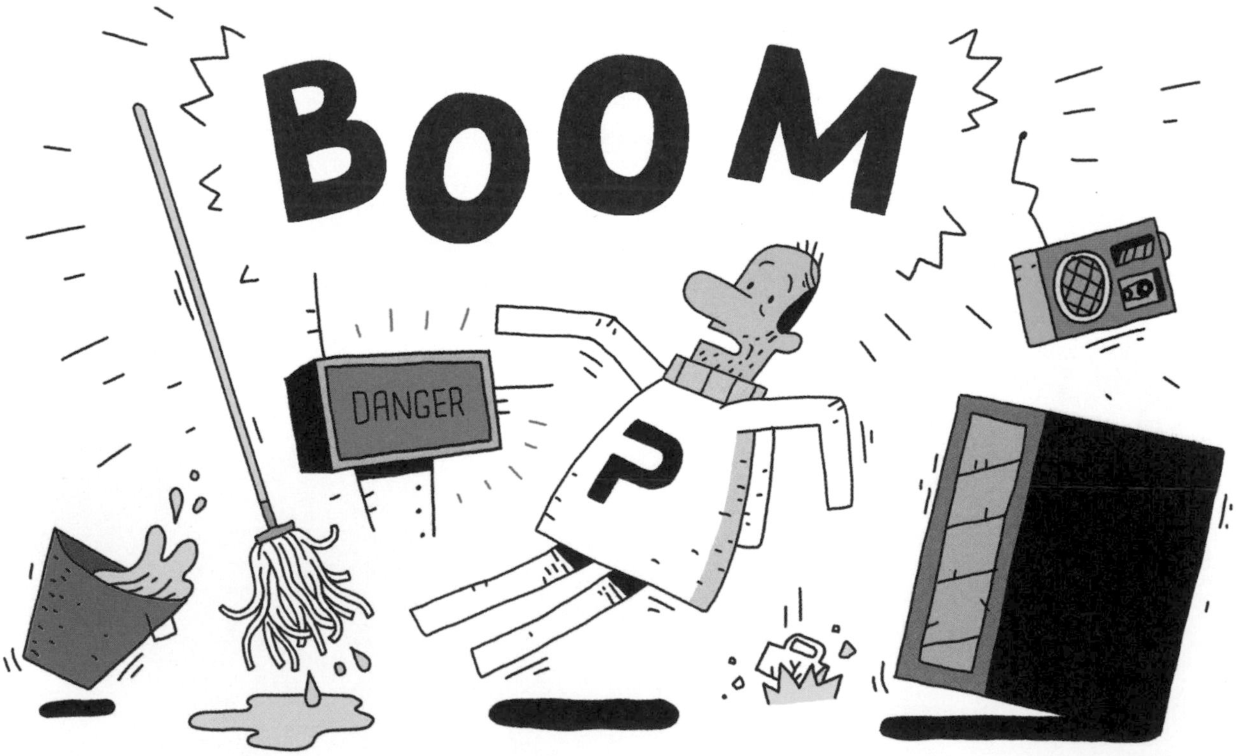
BOOM
DANGER

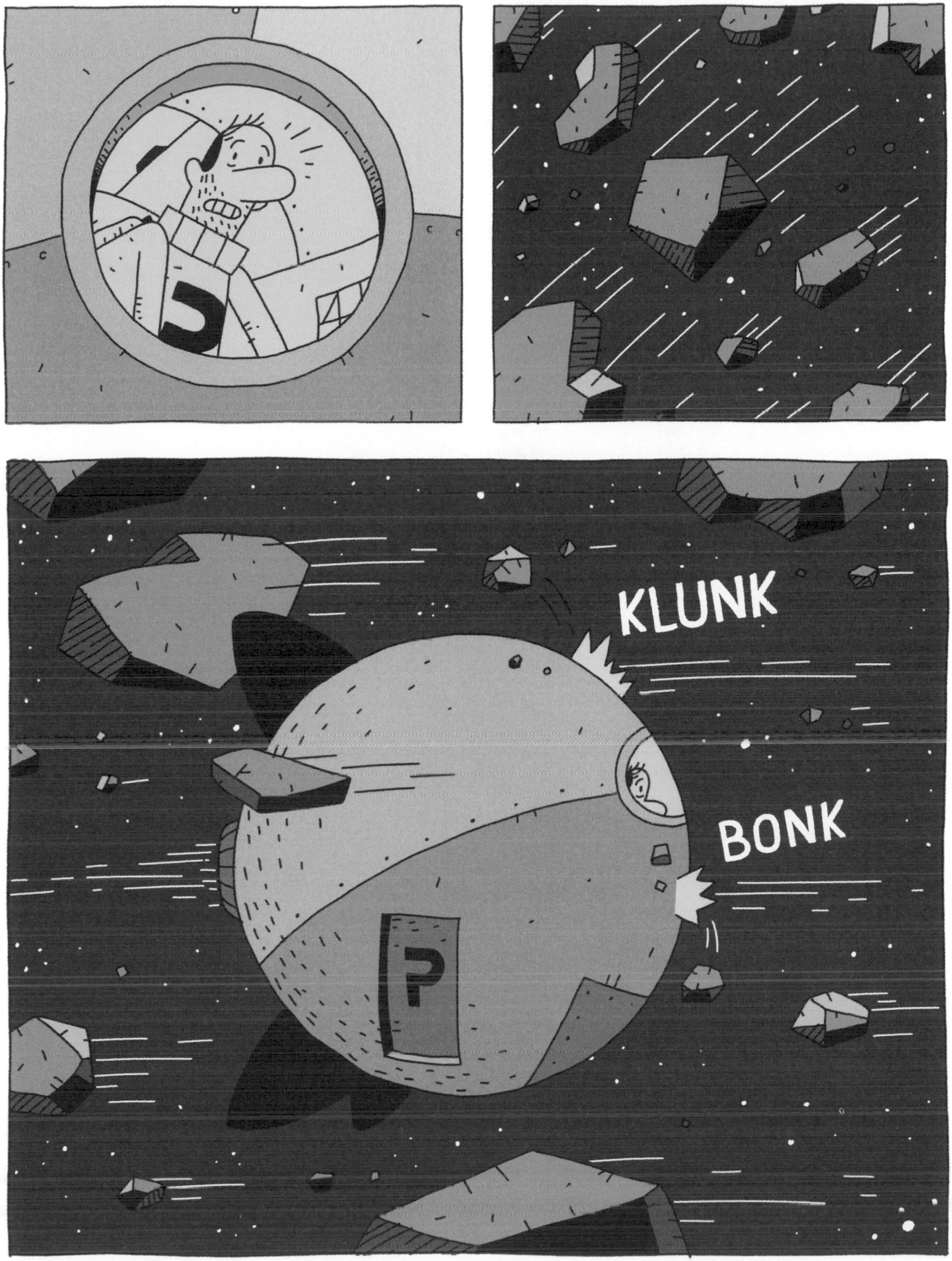
KLUNK
BONK

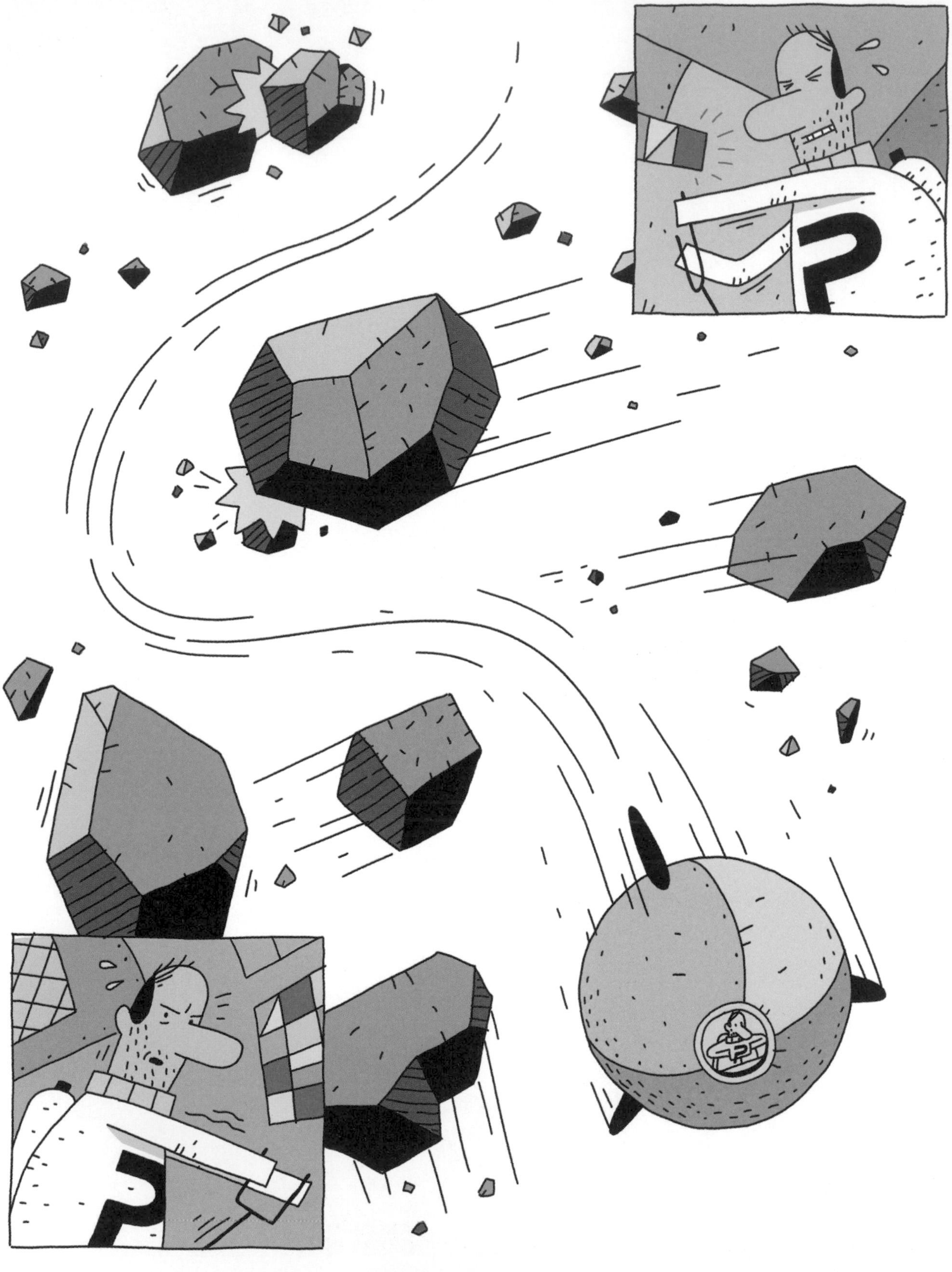

Our friend may not be a great adventurer, but thanks
to his skills as a pilot, he's able to avoid a near
collision before bringing the spacecraft to a stop.

It was a close call!

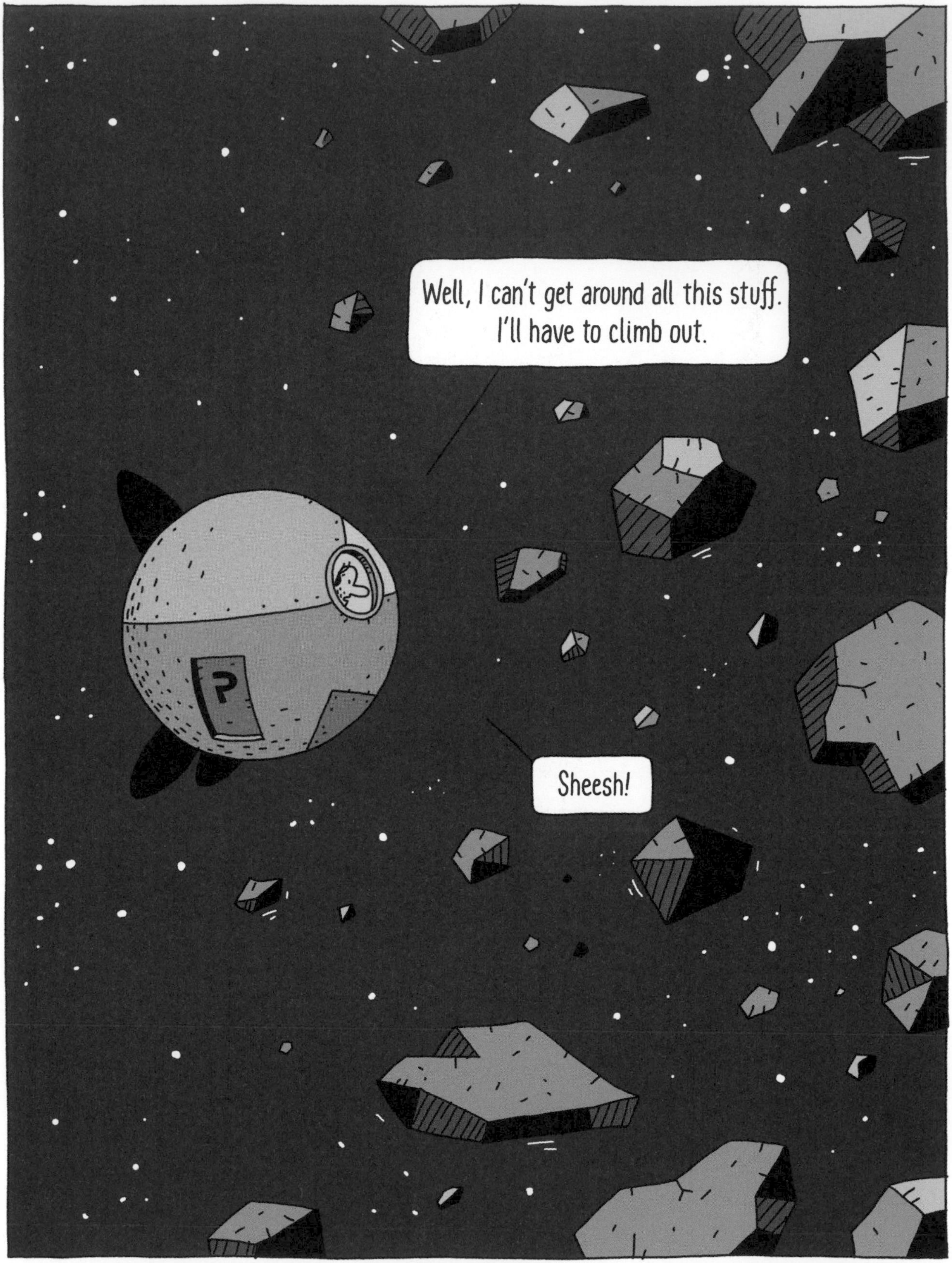
Well, I can't get around all this stuff. I'll have to climb out.
Sheesh!

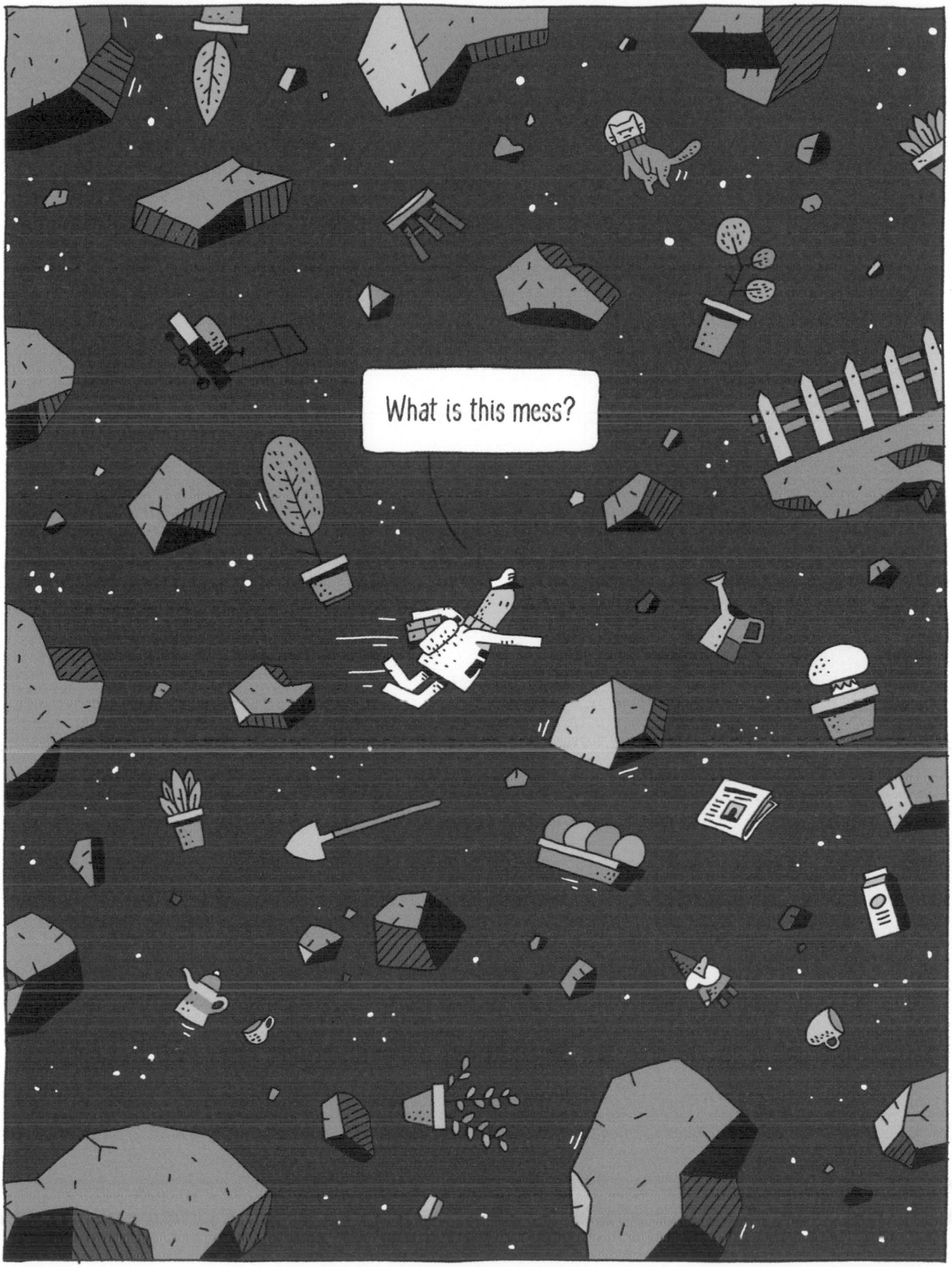
What is this mess?

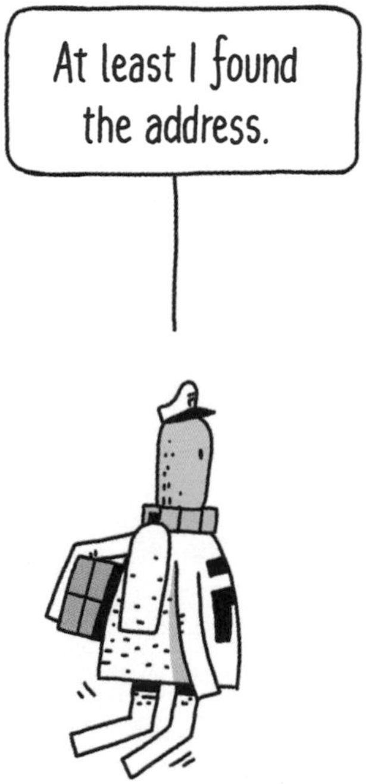
At least I found the address.

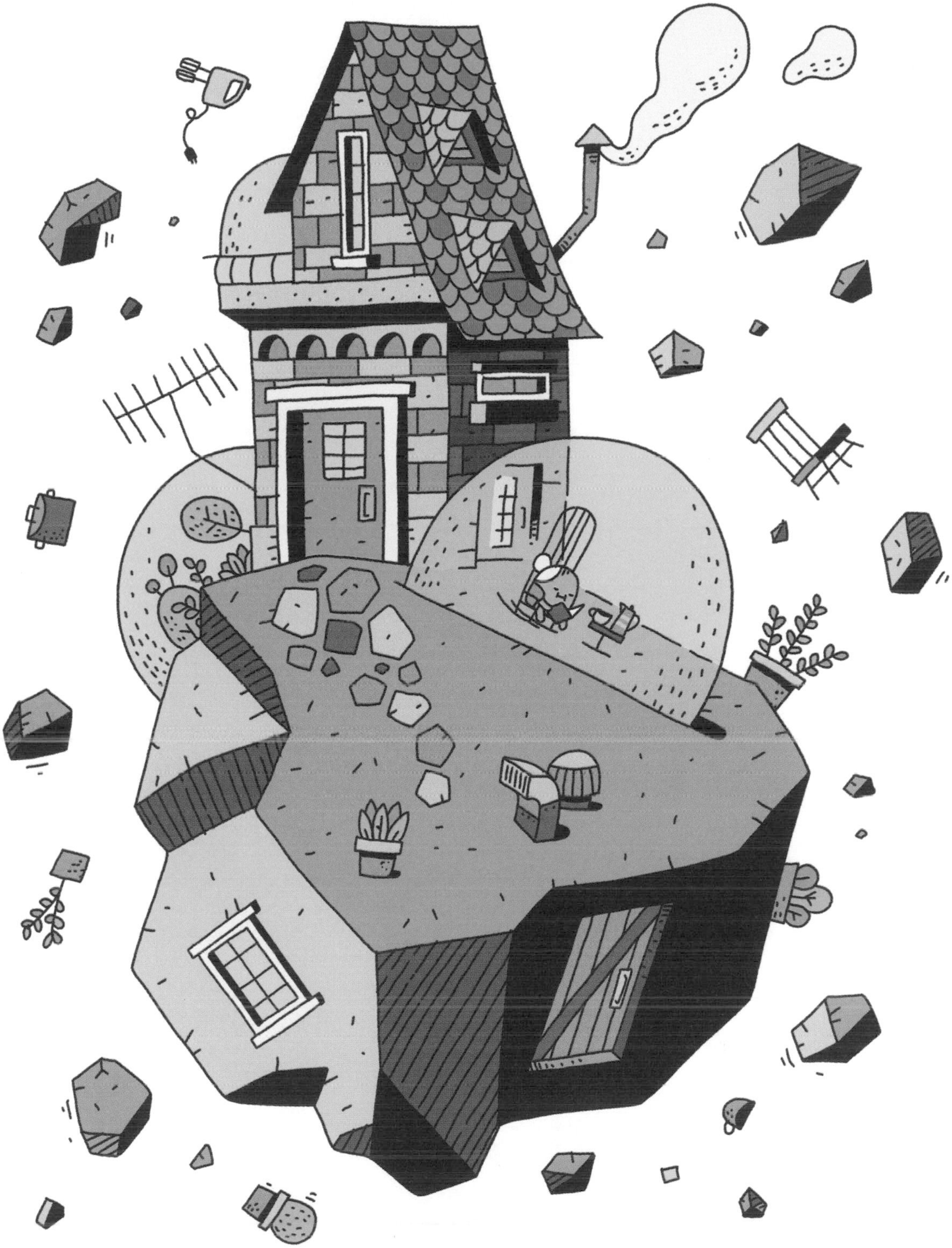

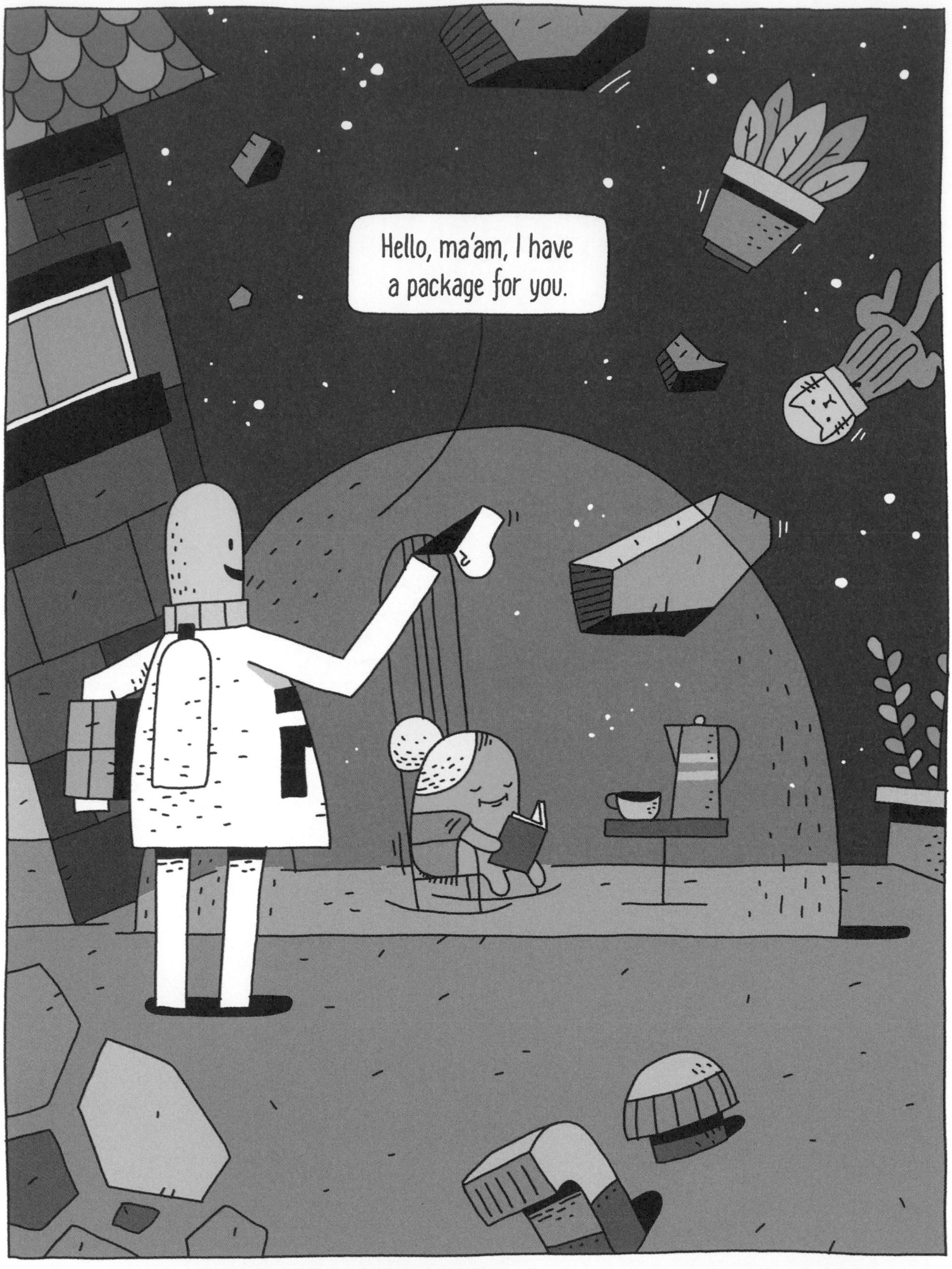
Hello, ma'am, I have a package for you.

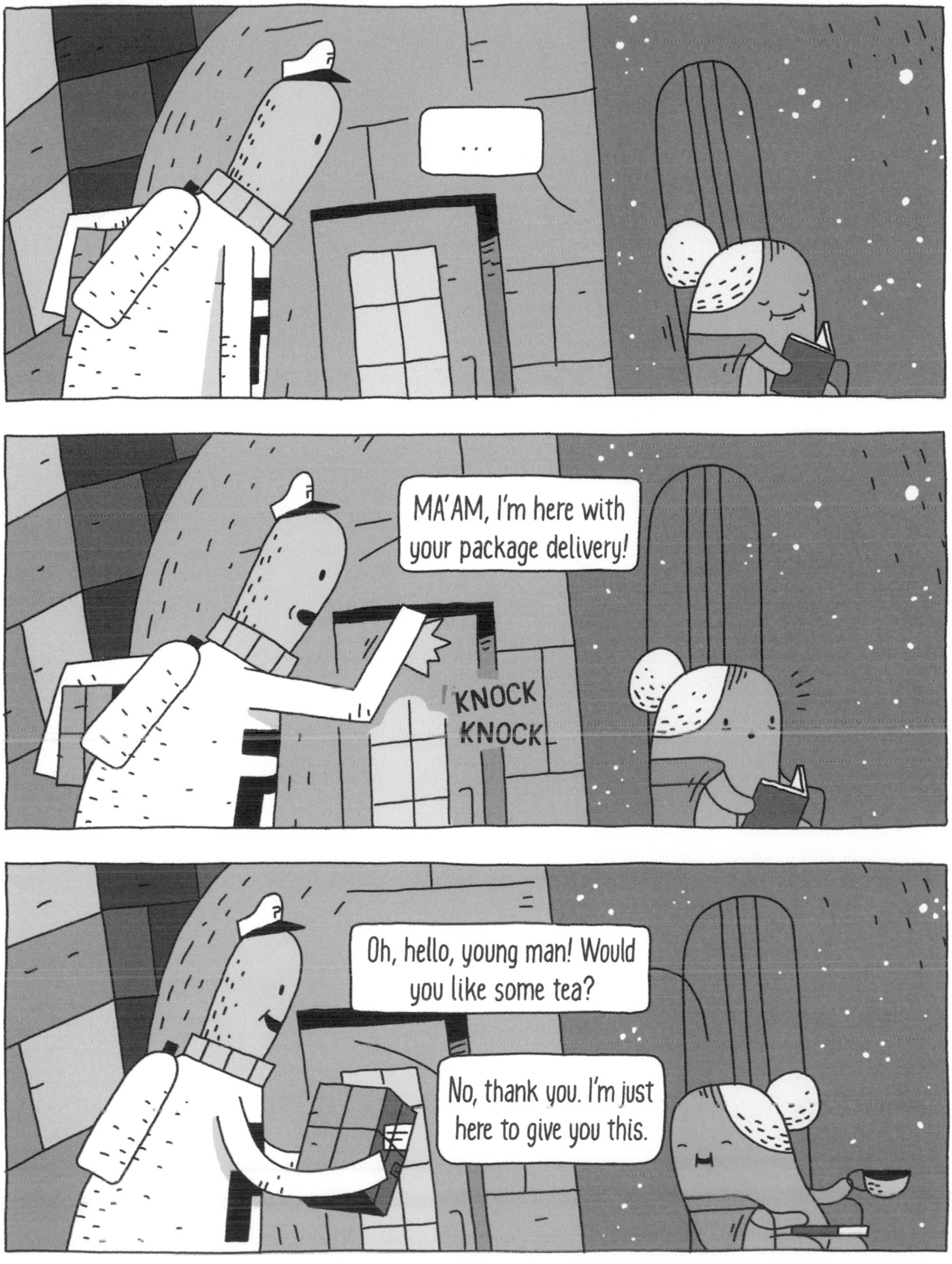
...
MA'AM, I'm here with your package delivery!
KNOCK KNOCK
Oh, hello, young man! Would you like some tea?
No, thank you. I'm just here to give you this.

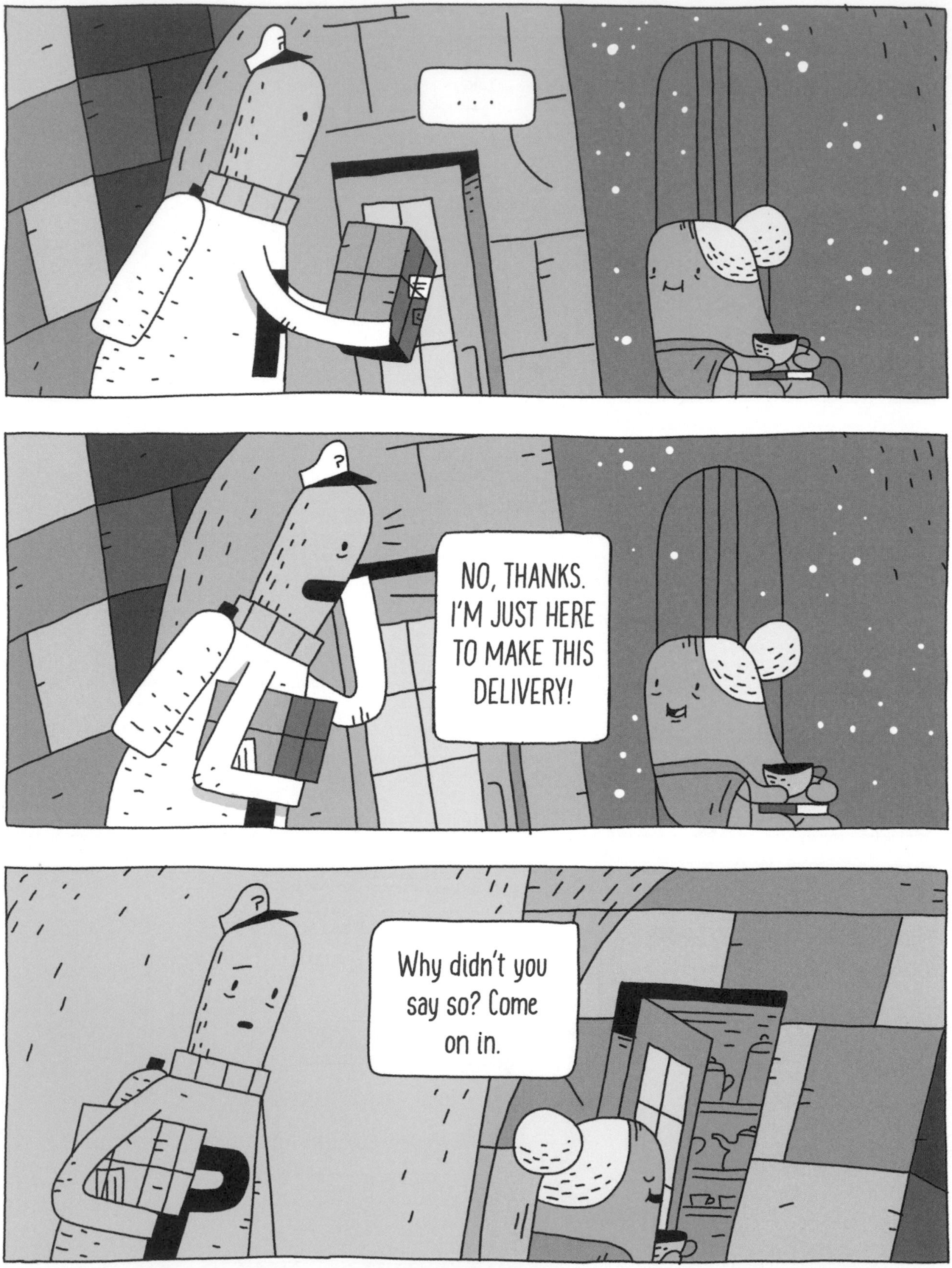
...
NO, THANKS. I'M JUST HERE TO MAKE THIS DELIVERY!
Why didn't you say so? Come on in.

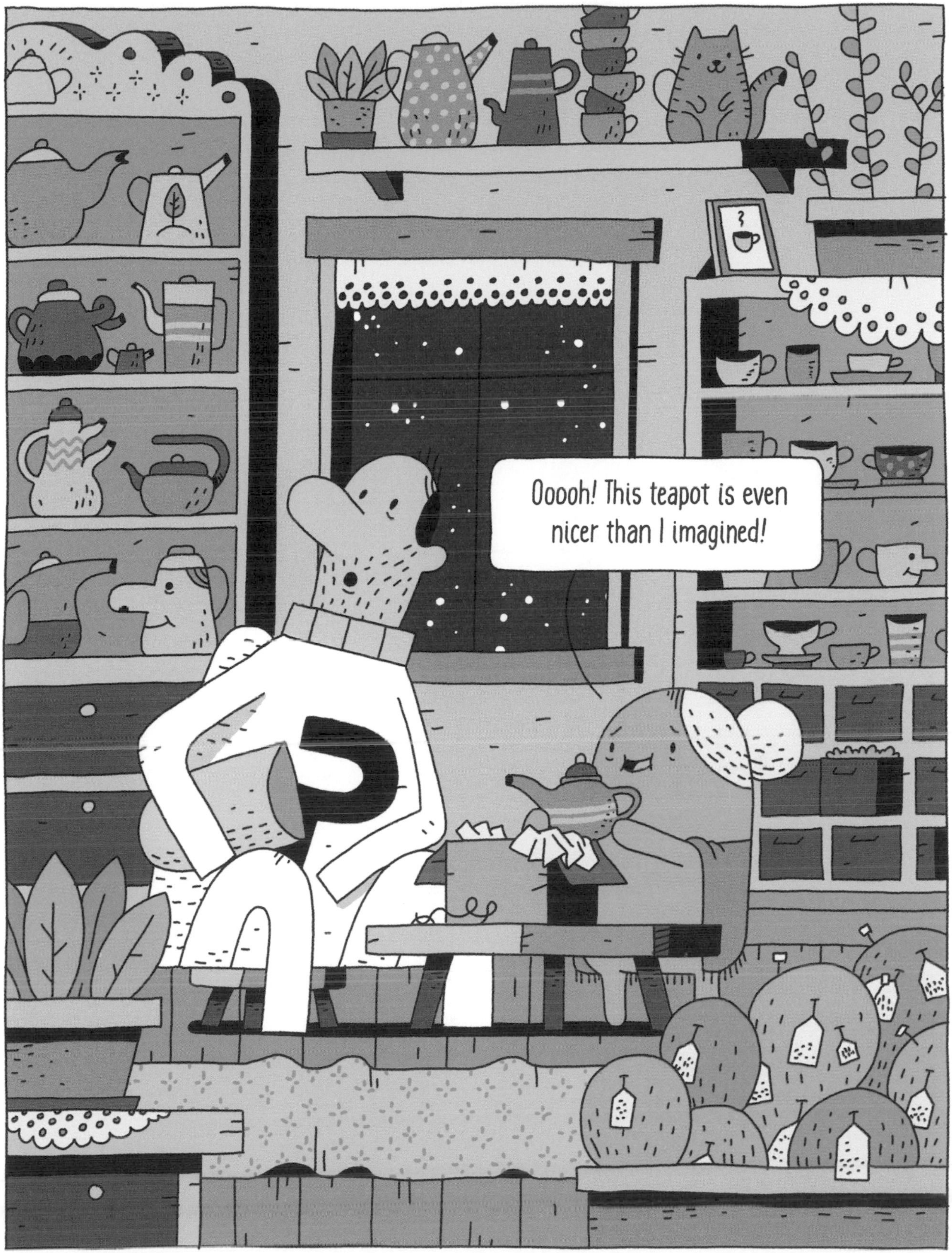
Ooooh! This teapot is even nicer than I imagined!

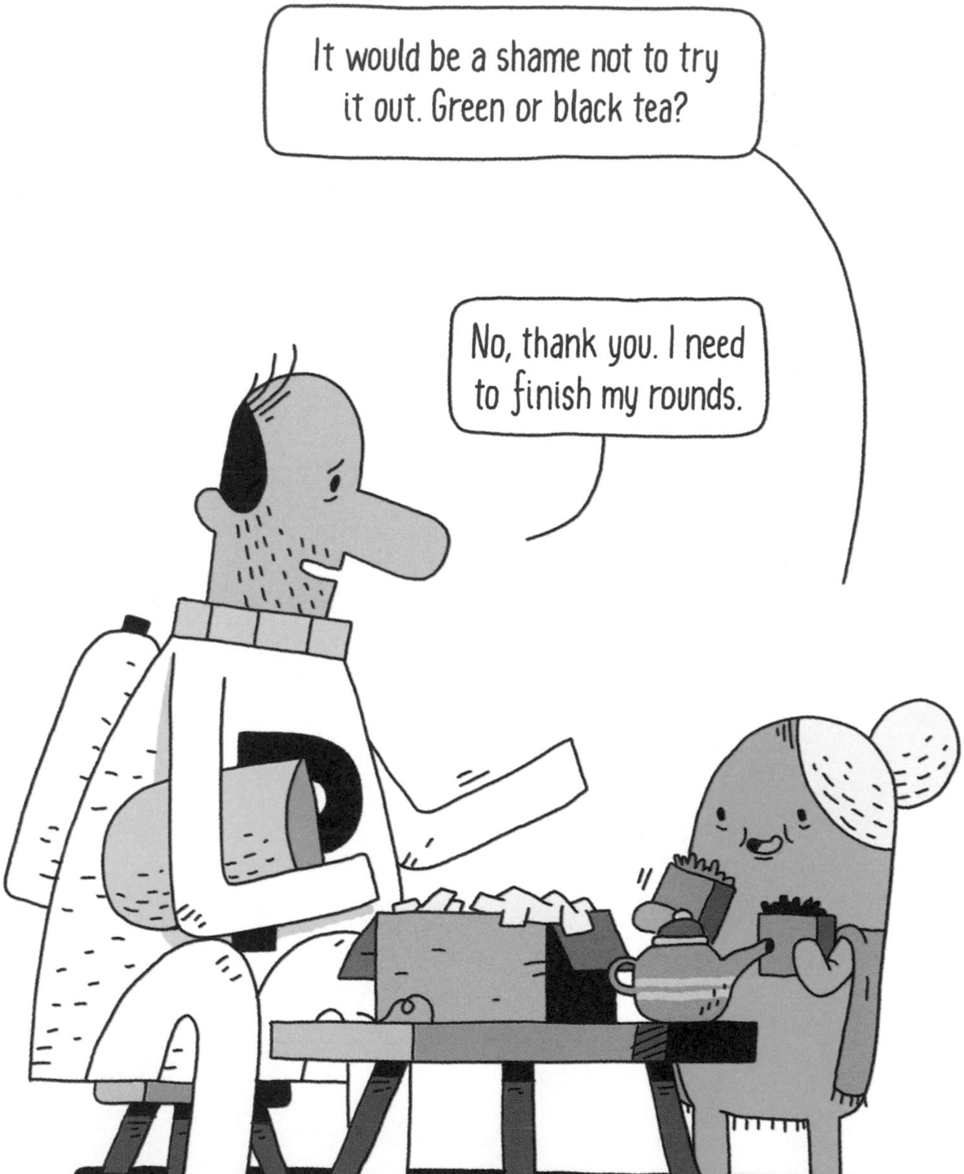
It would be a shame not to try it out. Green or black tea?
No, thank you. I need to finish my rounds.

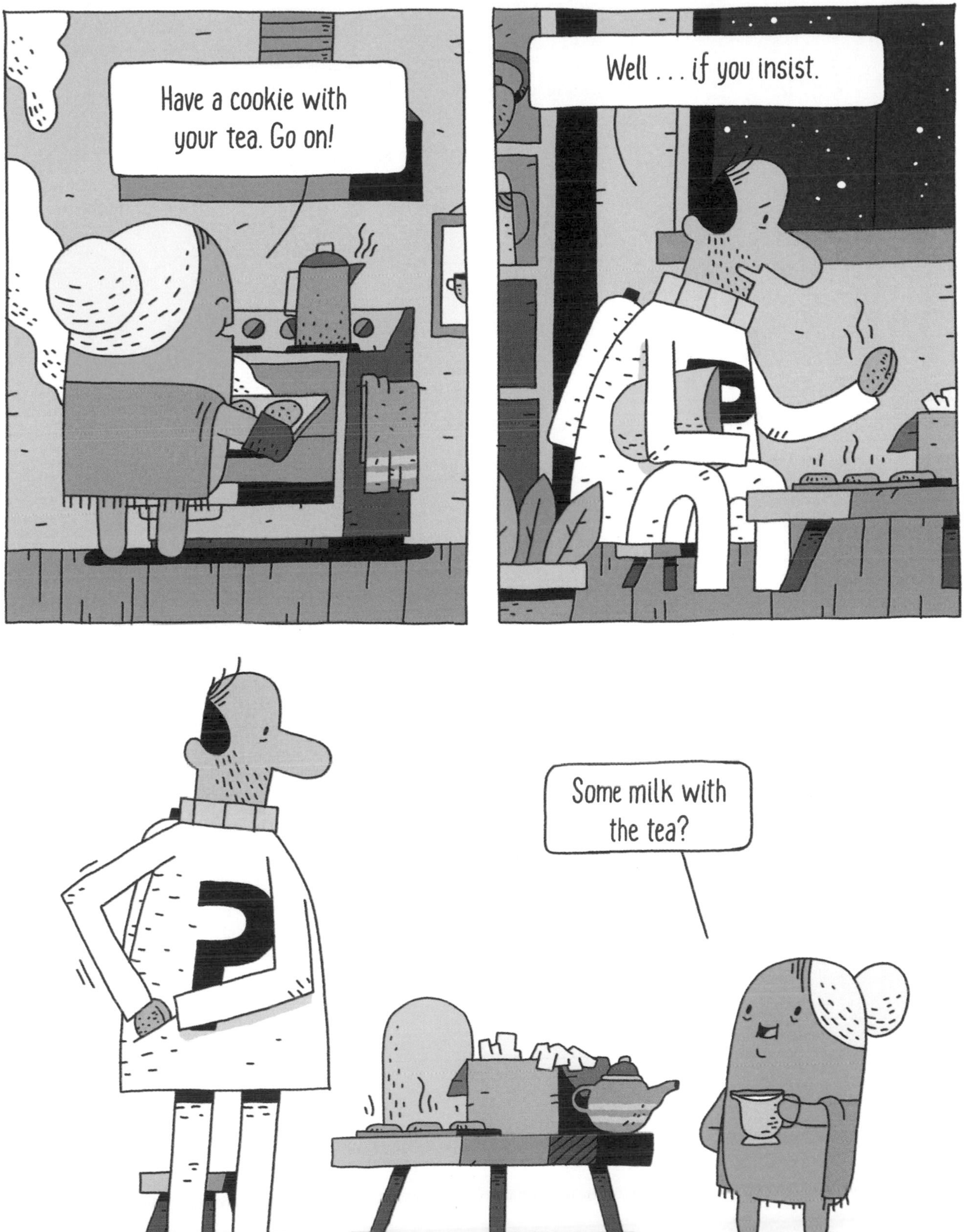
Have a cookie with your tea. Go on!
Well . . . if you insist.
Some milk with the tea?

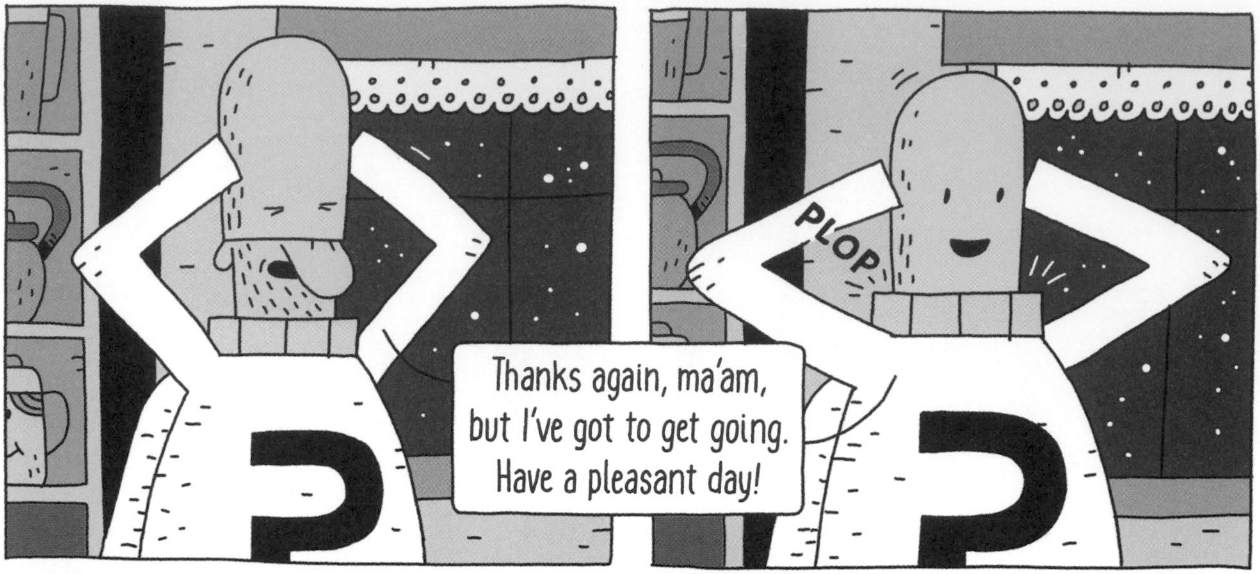
PLOP
Thanks again, ma'am, but I've got to get going. Have a pleasant day!

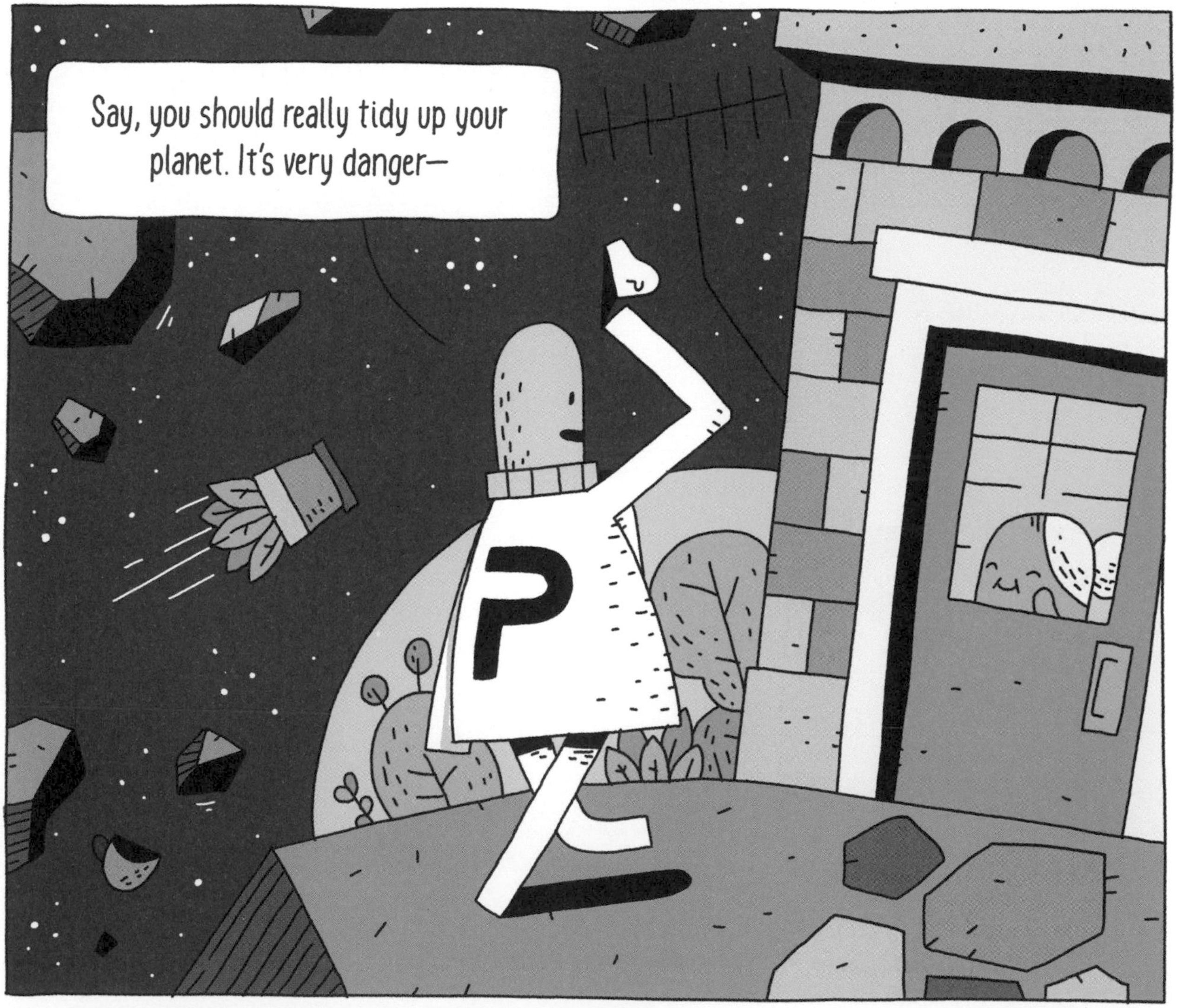
Say, you should really tidy up your planet. It's very danger—

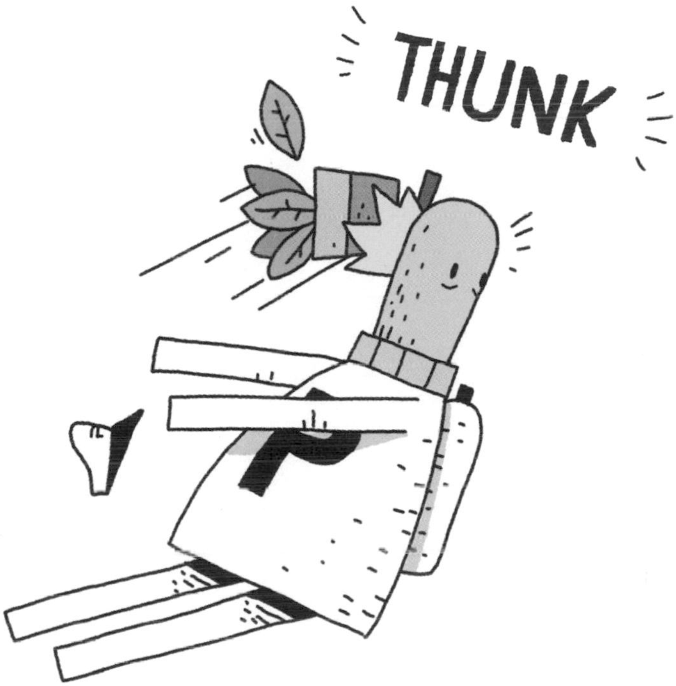
THUNK

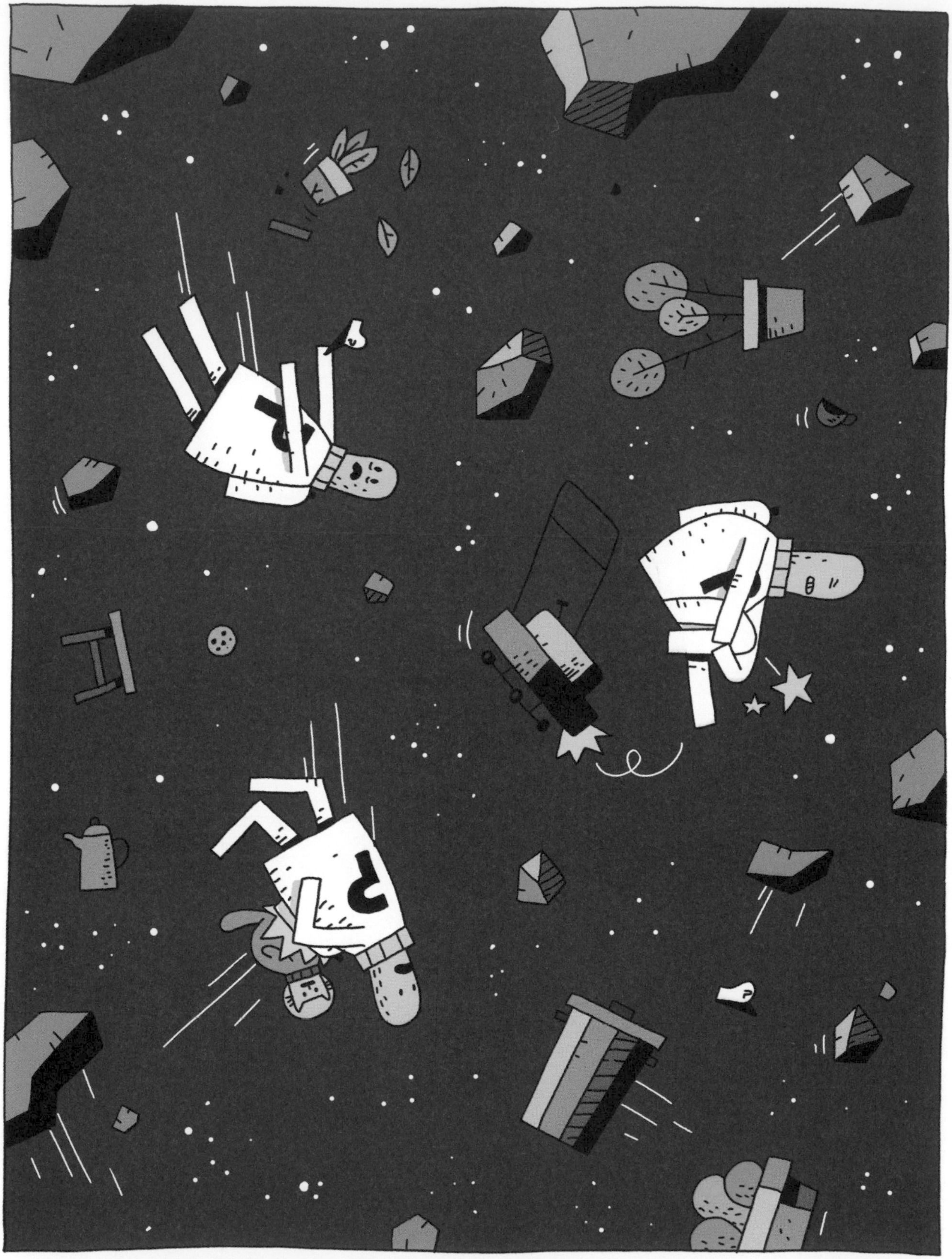

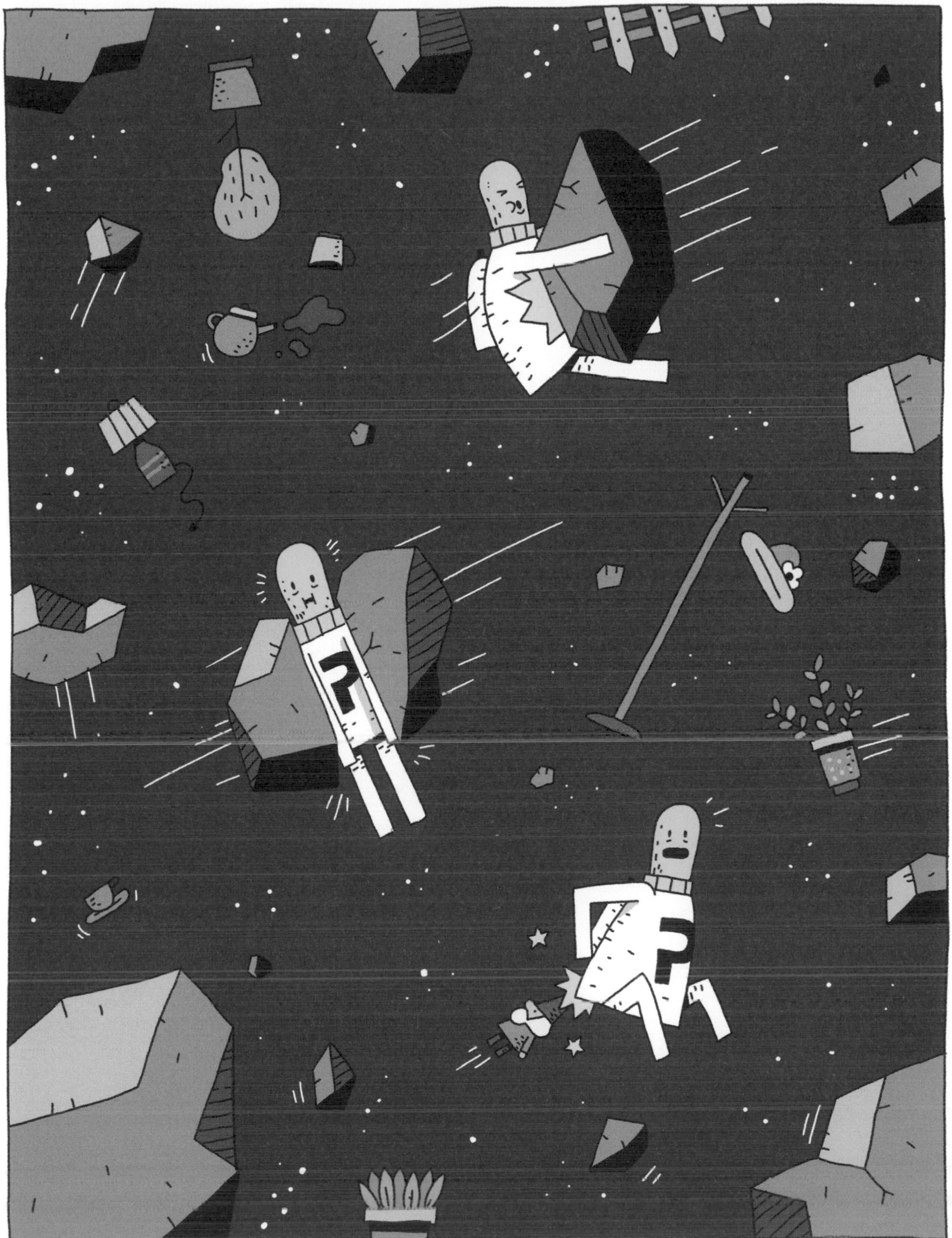

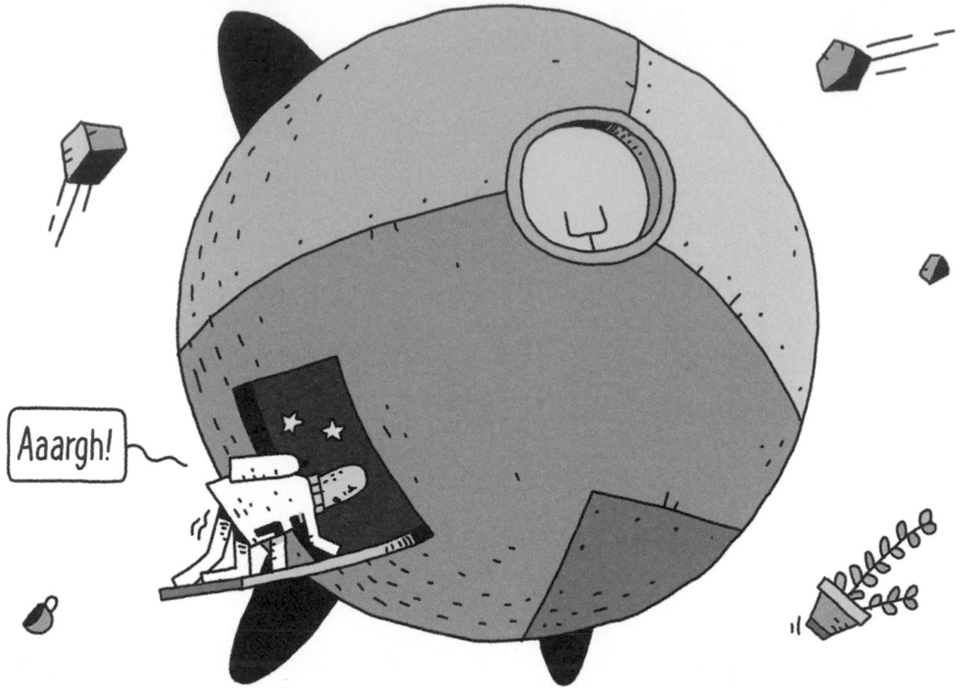
Aaargh!

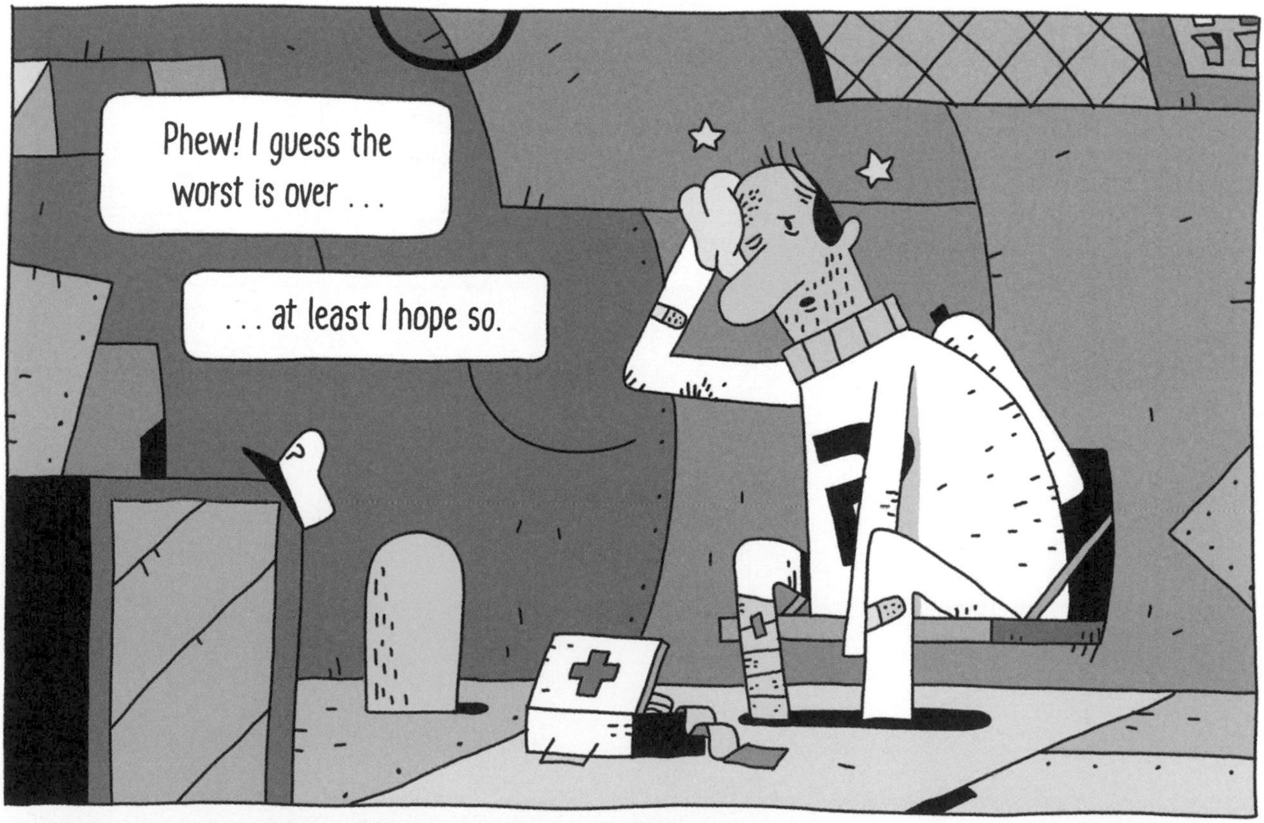
Phew! I guess the worst is over . . .
. . . at least I hope so.

DELIVERY
#3

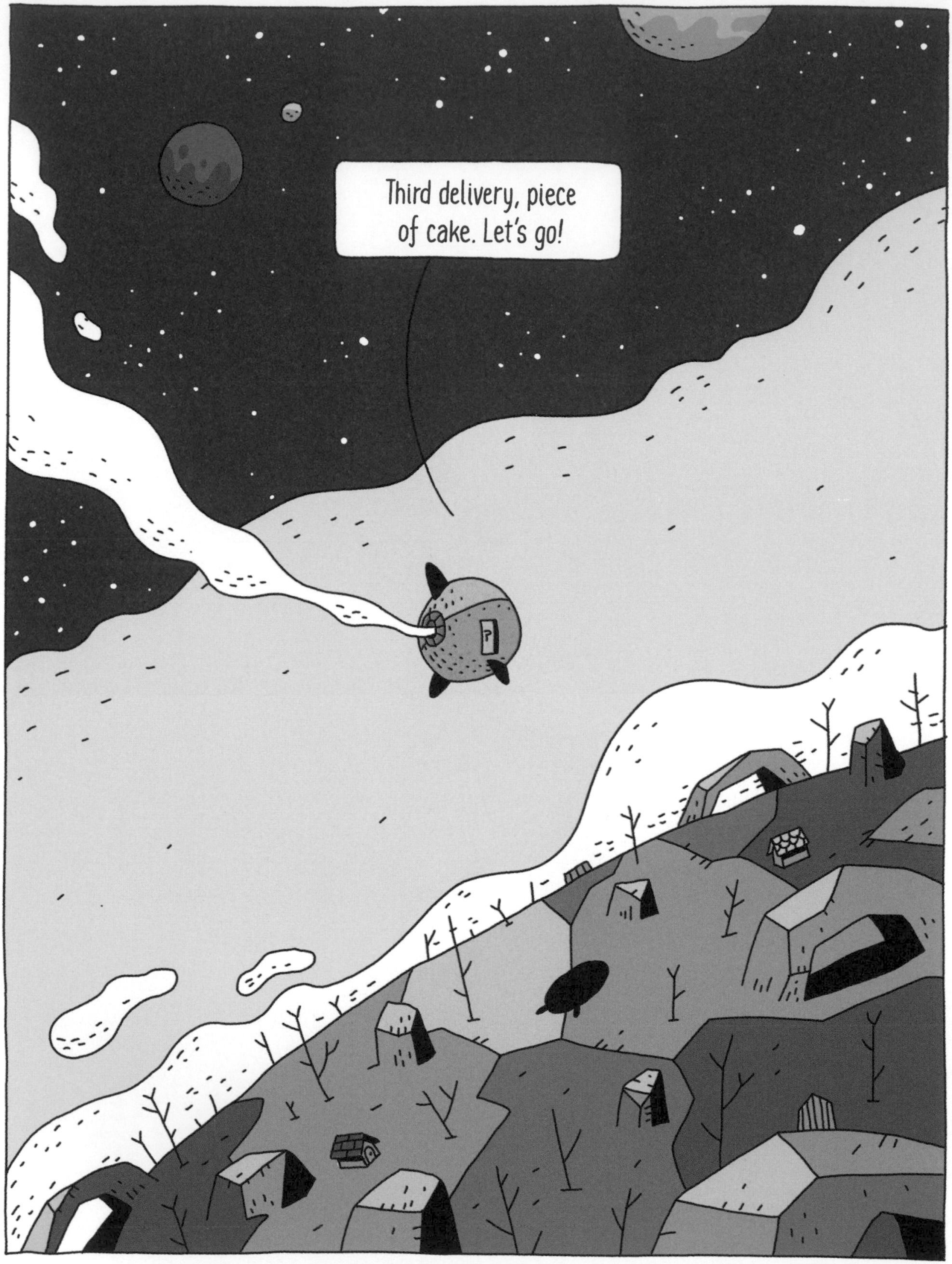
Third delivery, piece of cake. Let's go!

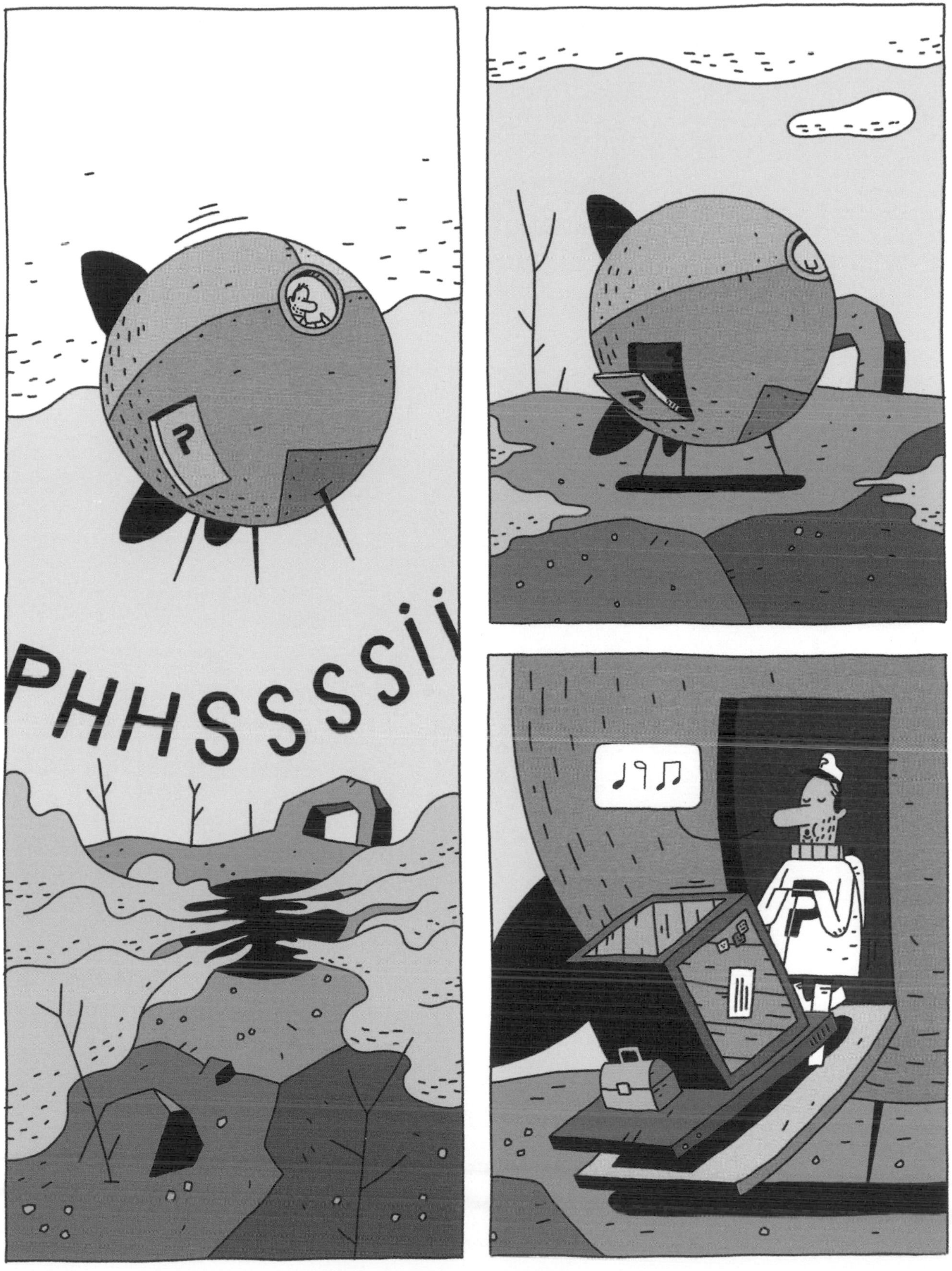
PHHSSSSIIJ

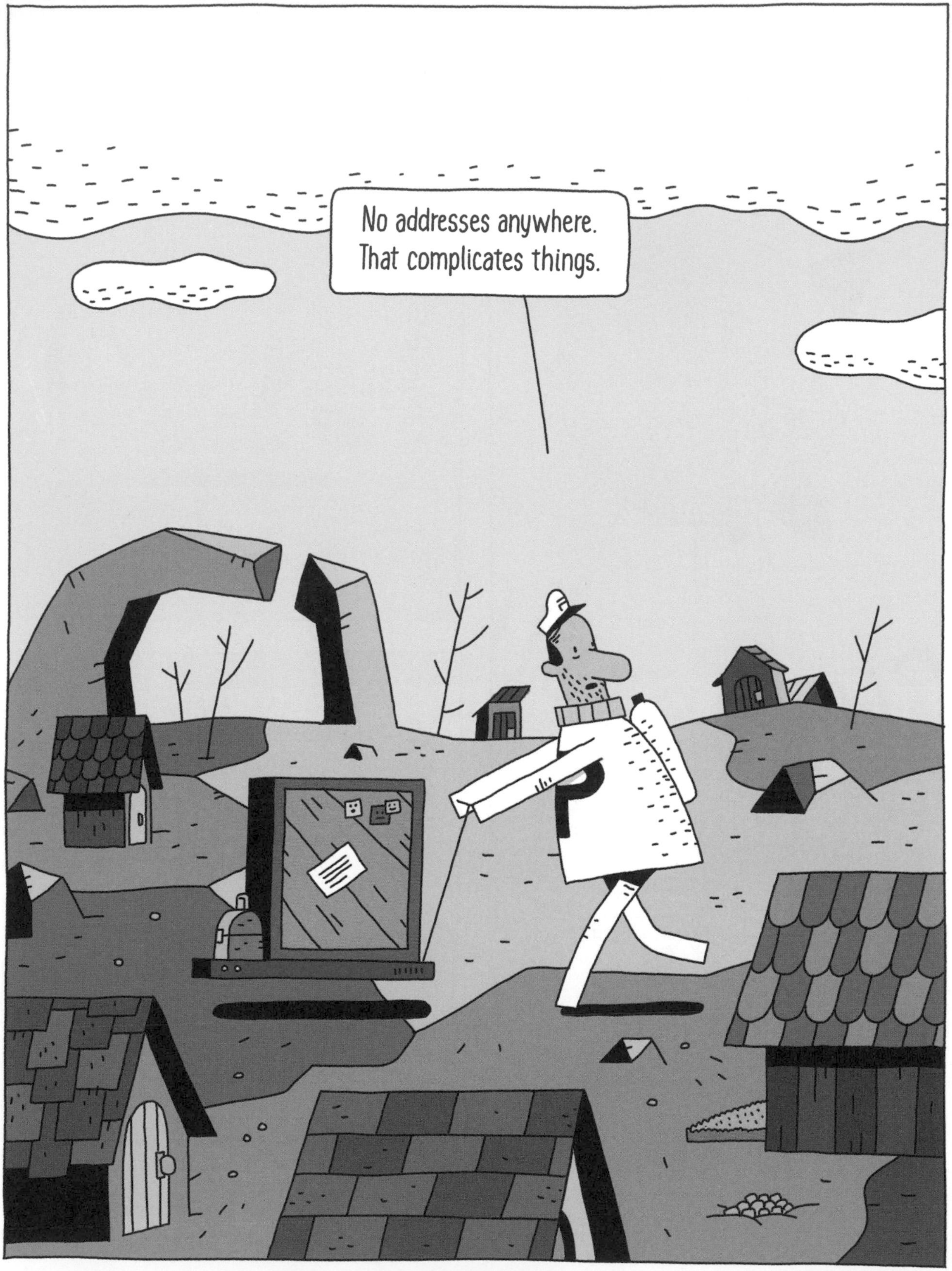
No addresses anywhere.
That complicates things.

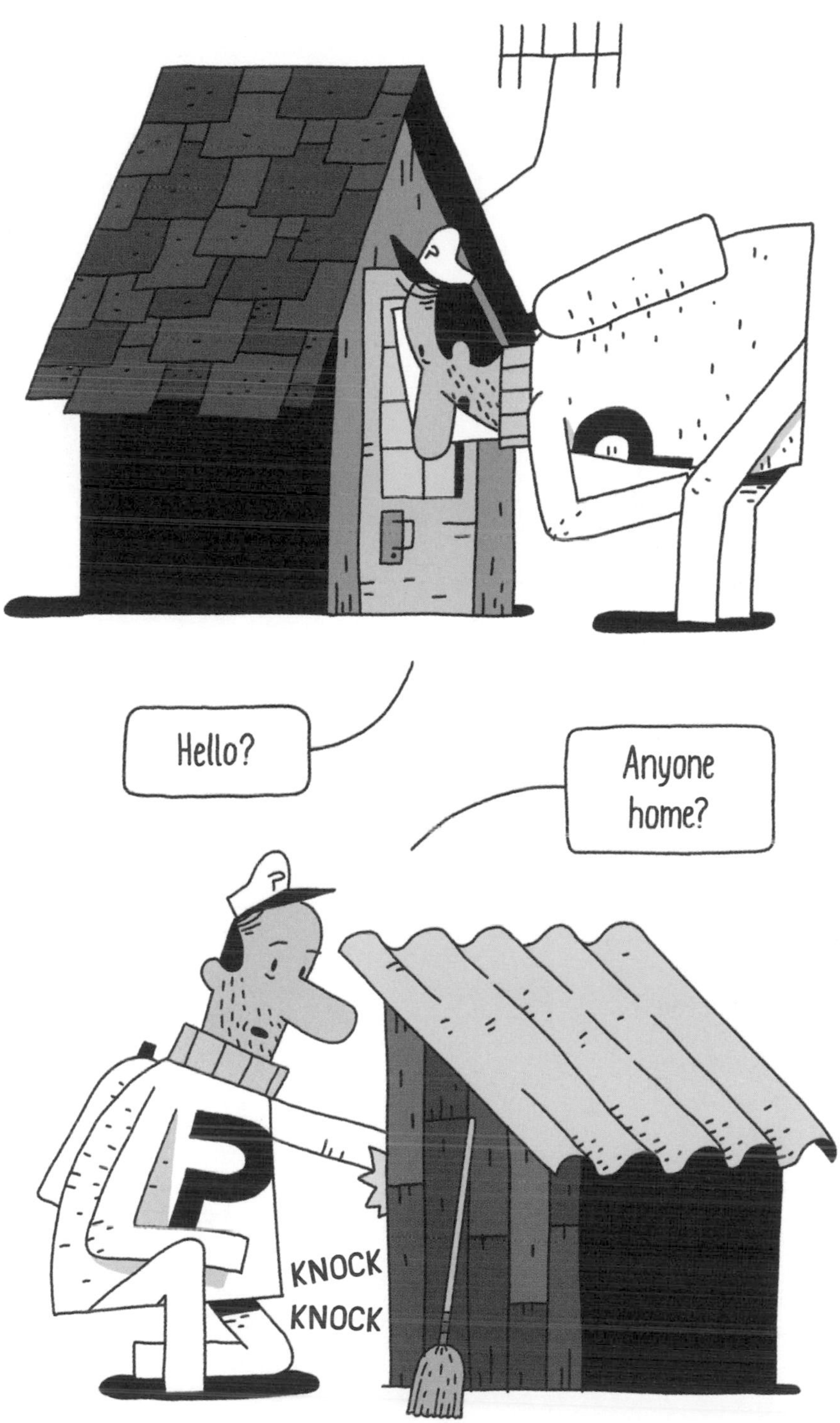
Hello?
Anyone home?
KNOCK
KNOCK

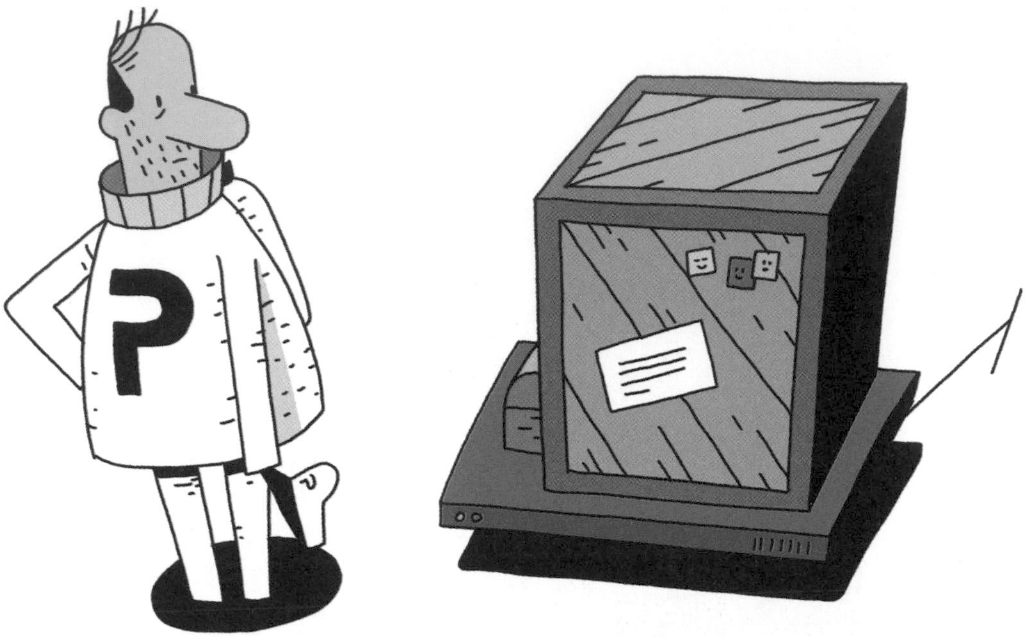

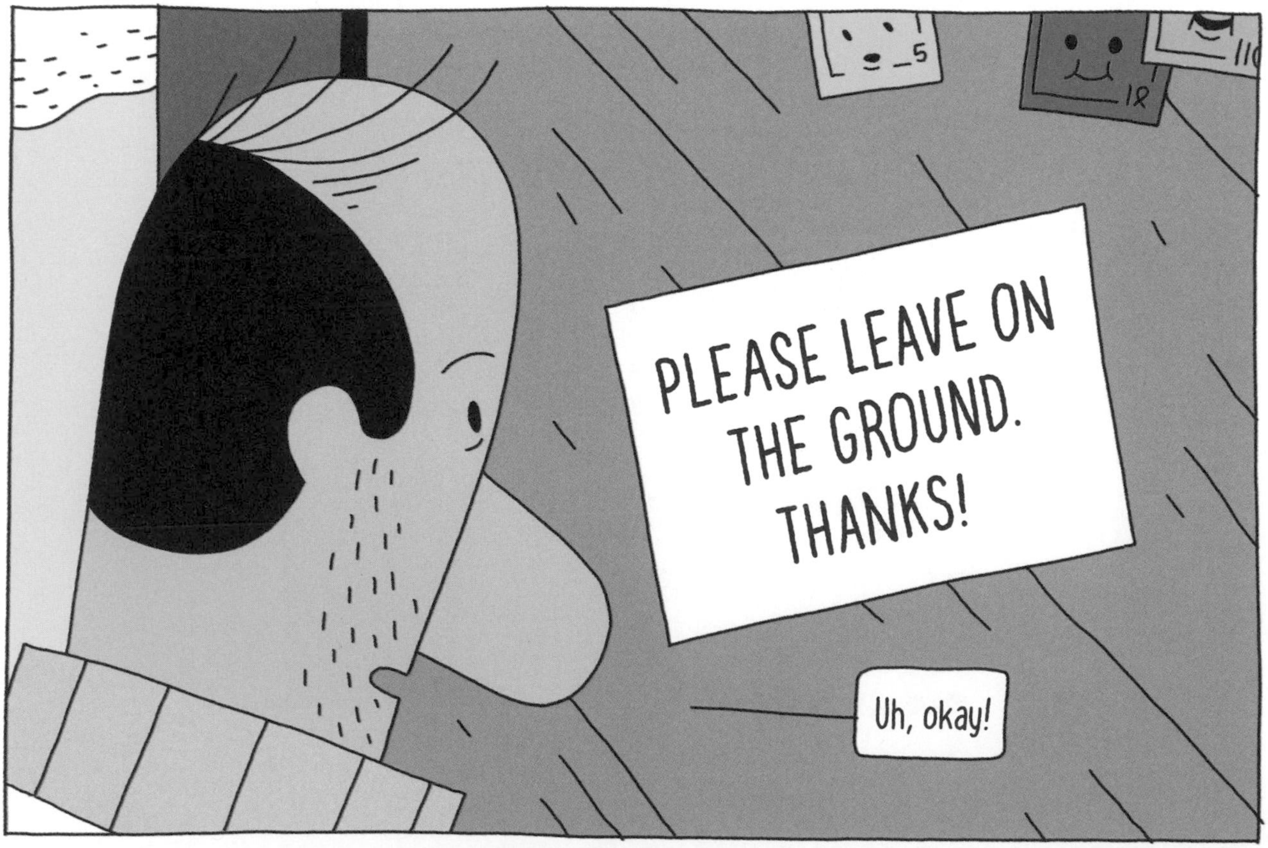
PLEASE LEAVE ON THE GROUND. THANKS!
Uh, okay!

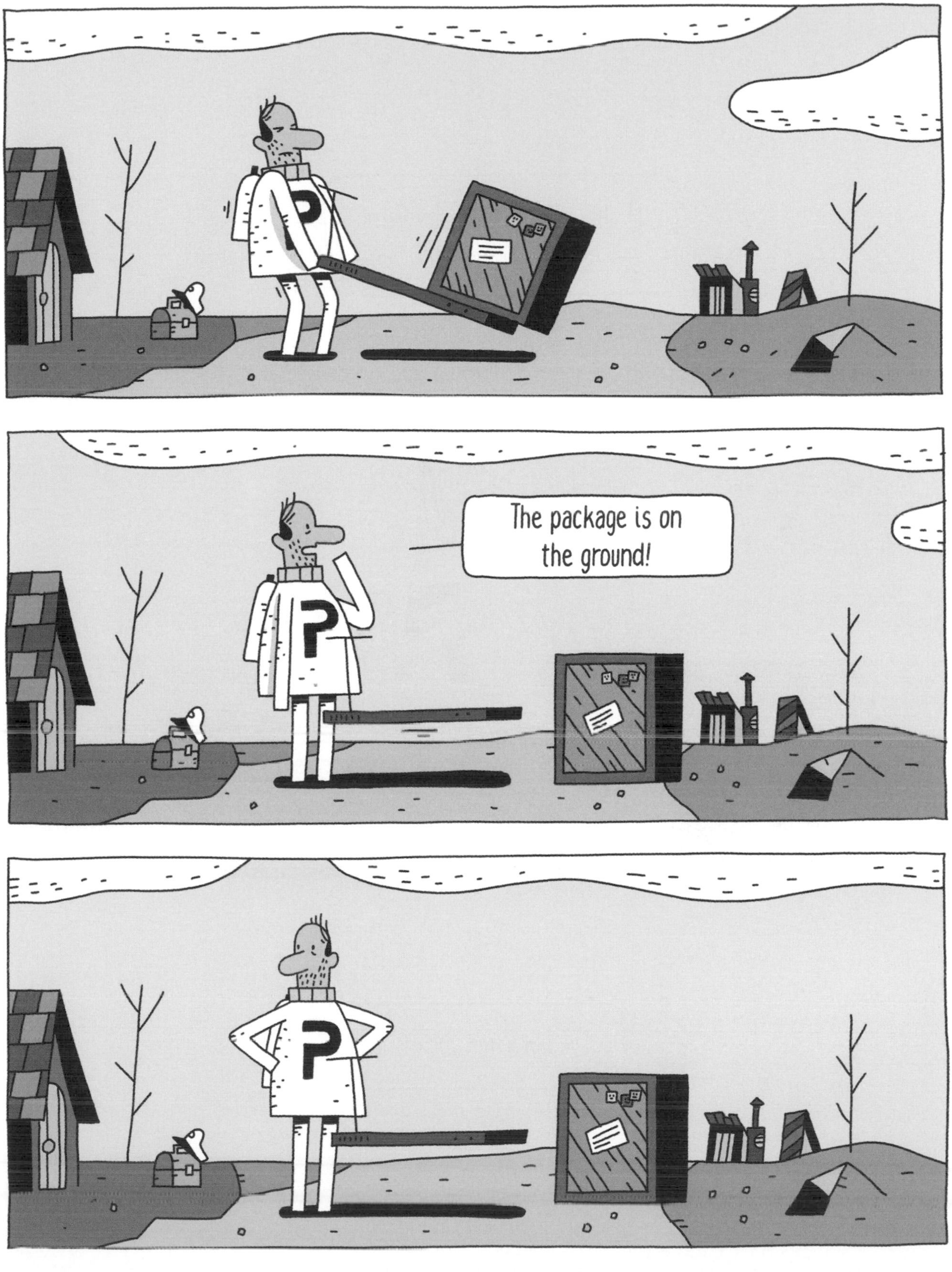
The package is on
the ground!

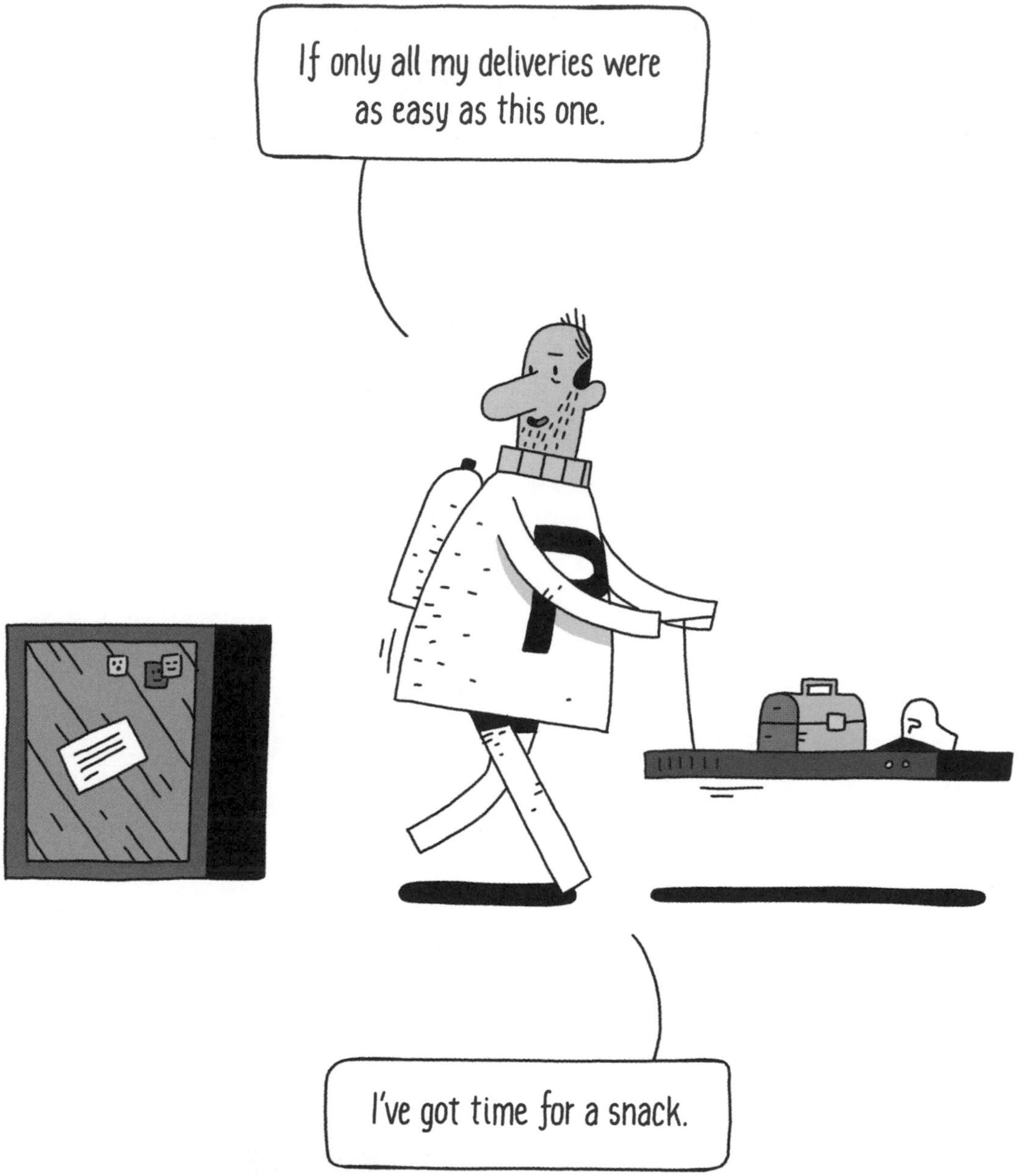
If only all my deliveries were as easy as this one.
I've got time for a snack.

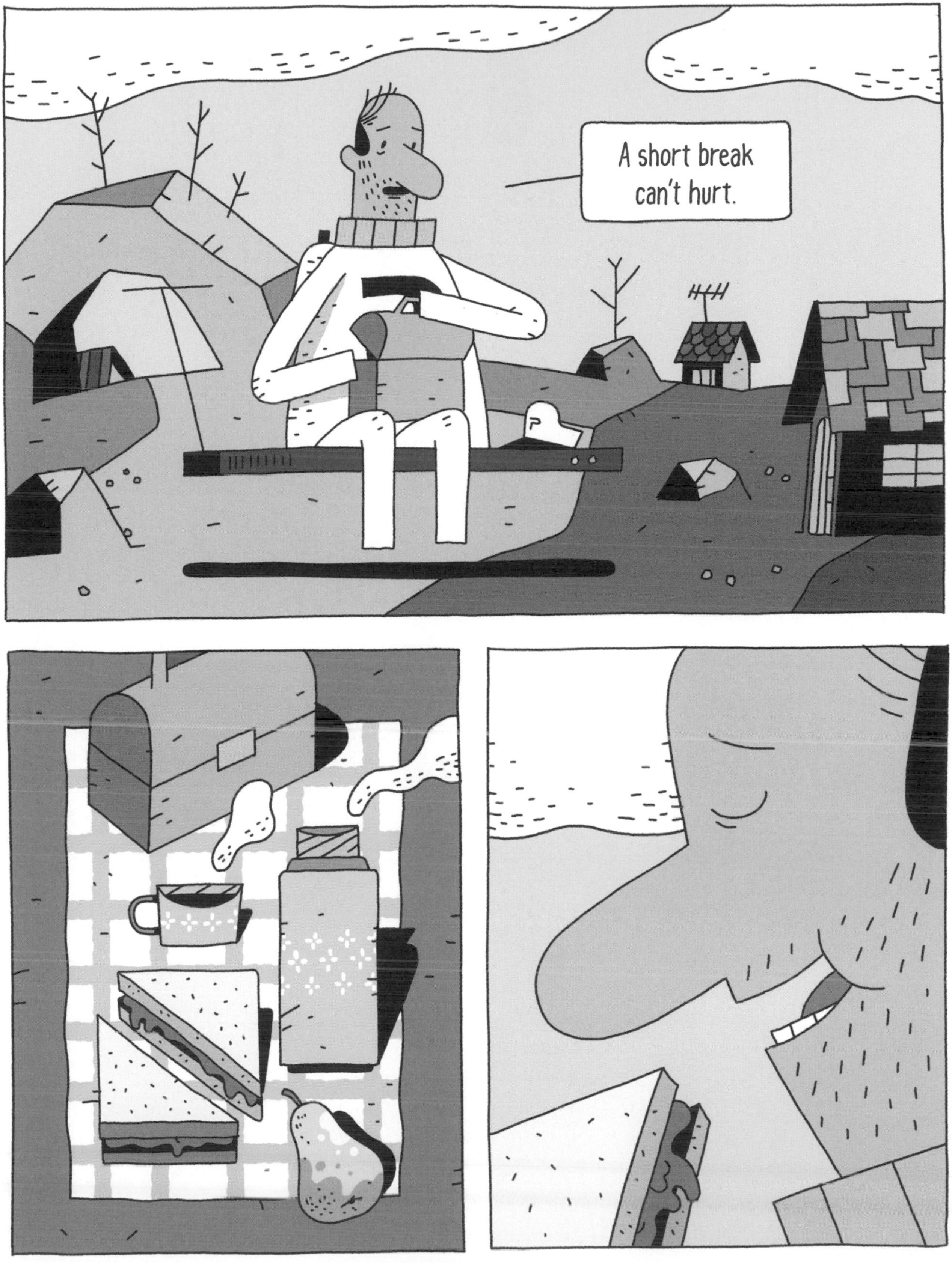
A short break
can't hurt.

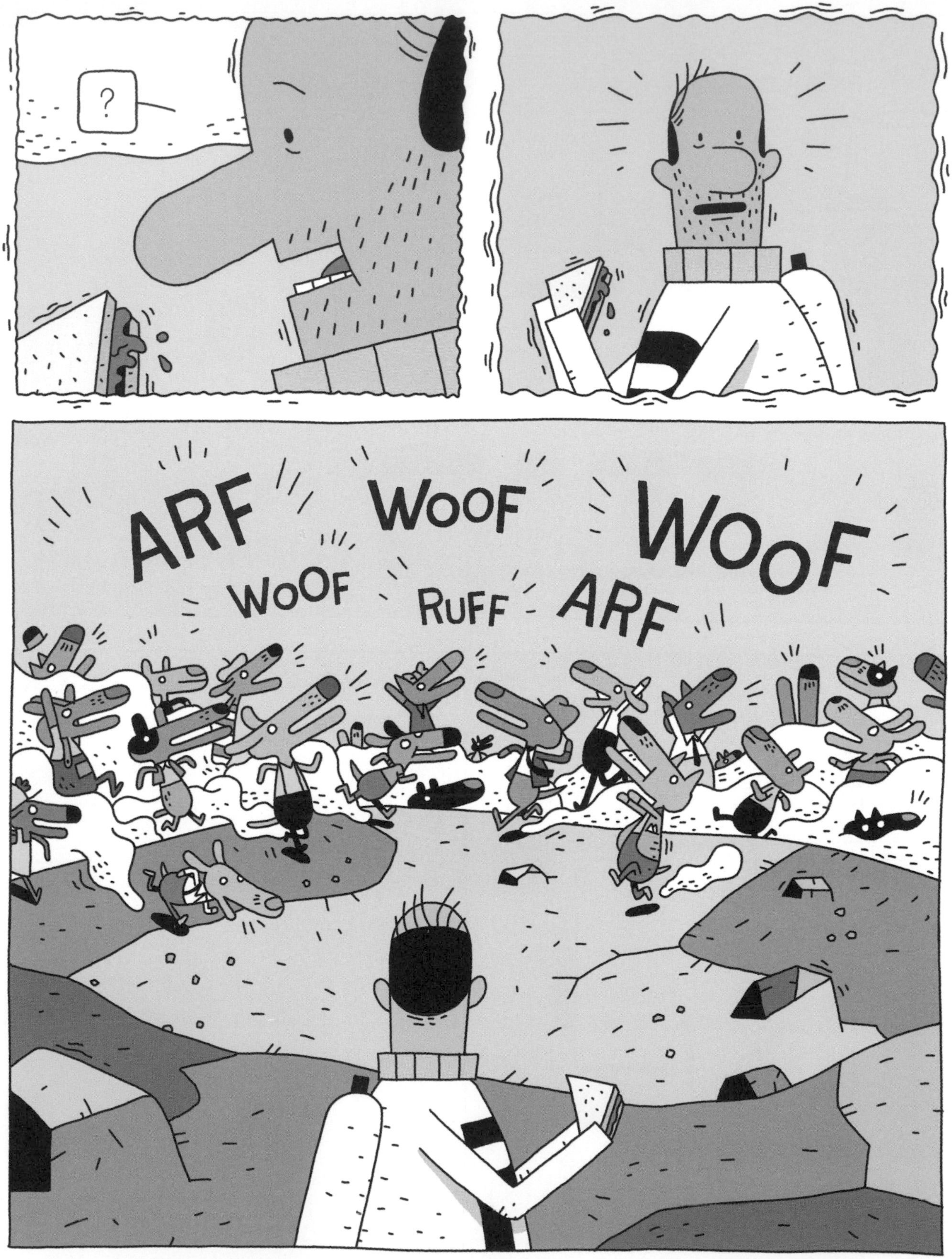
?
ARF
WOOF
WOOF
WOOF
RUFF
ARF

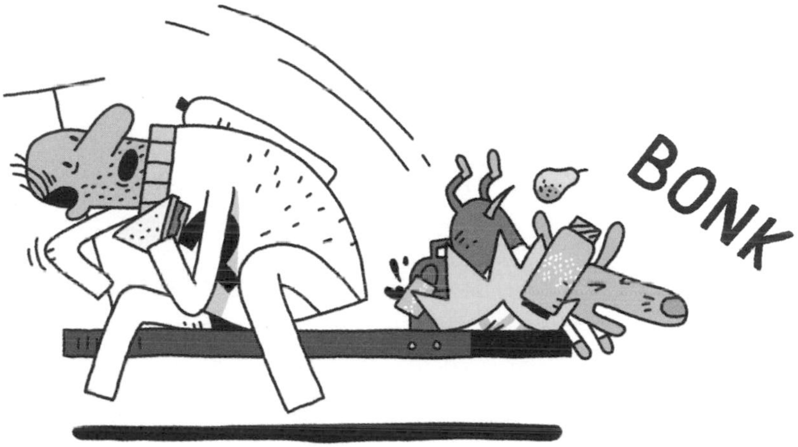
BONK

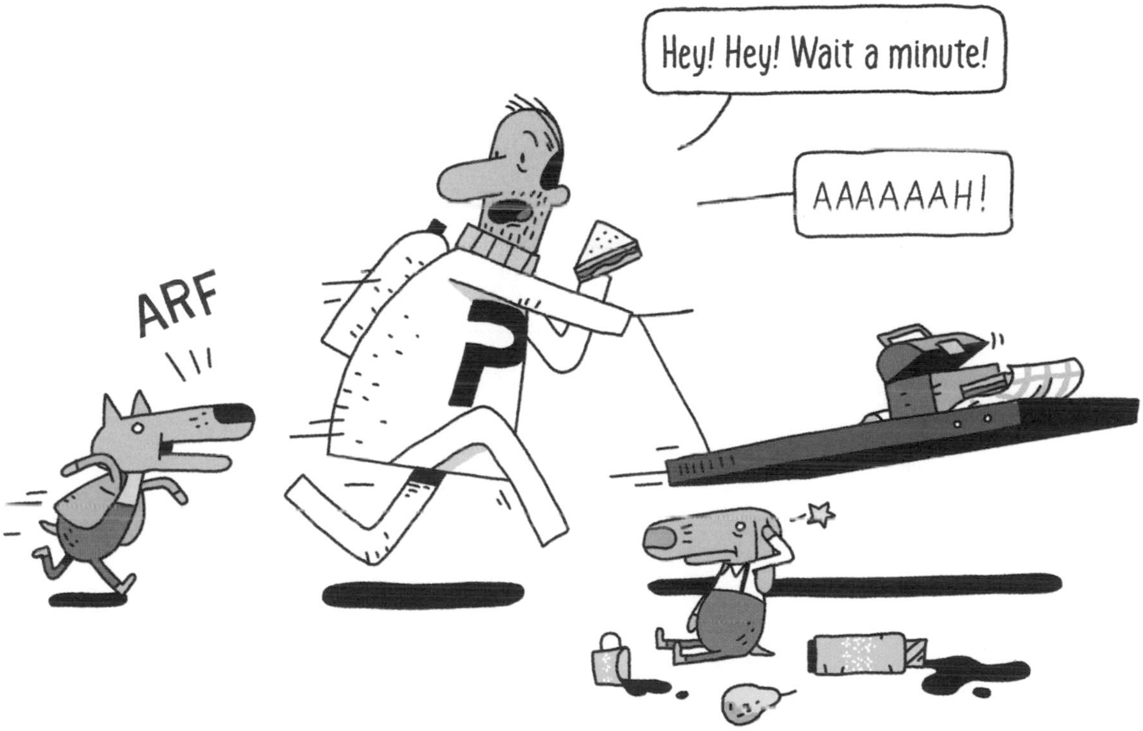
Hey! Hey! Wait a minute!
AAAAAAH!
ARF

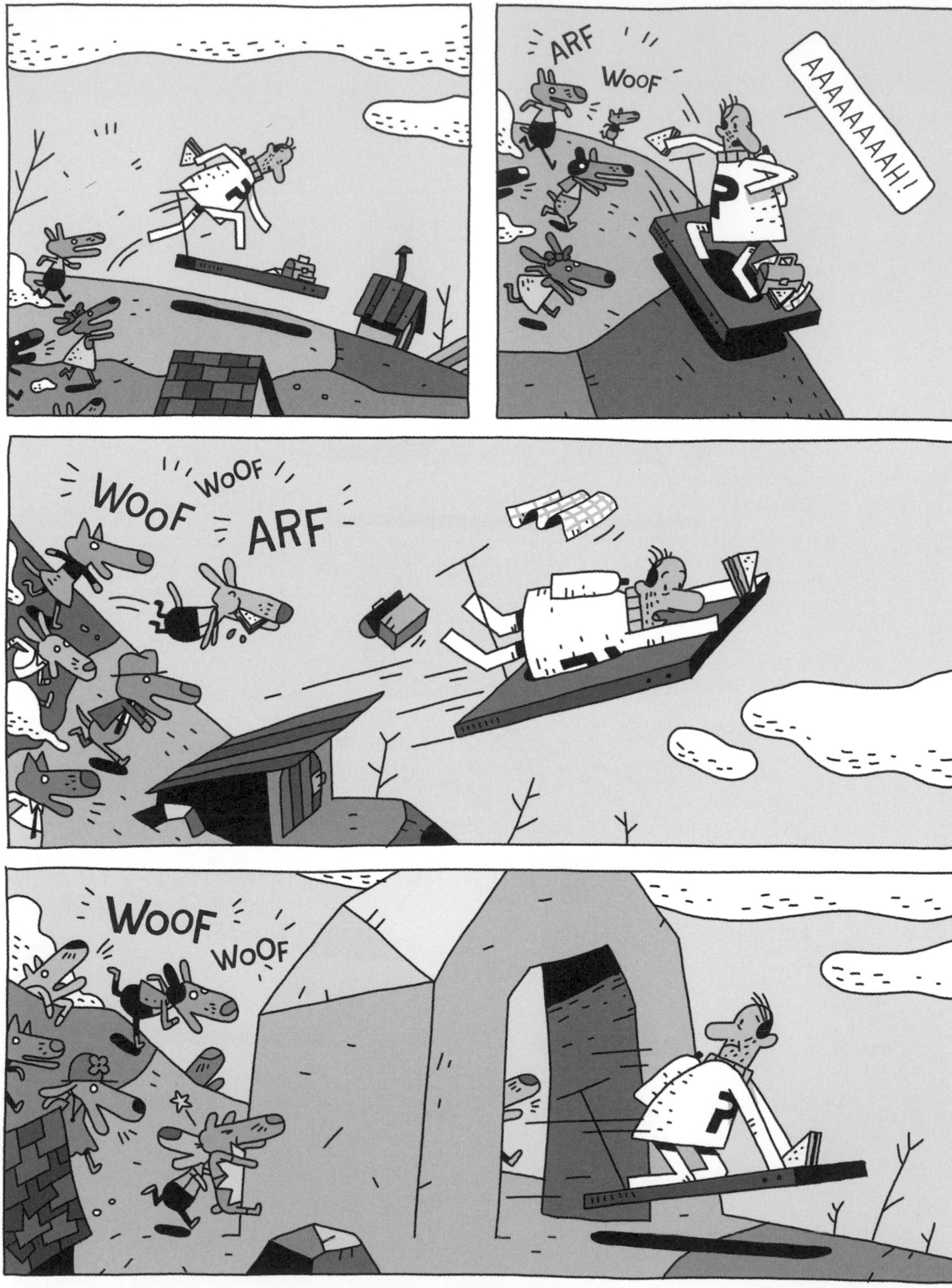
ARF
WOOF
AAAAAAAAH!
WOOF
WOOF
ARF
WOOF
WOOF

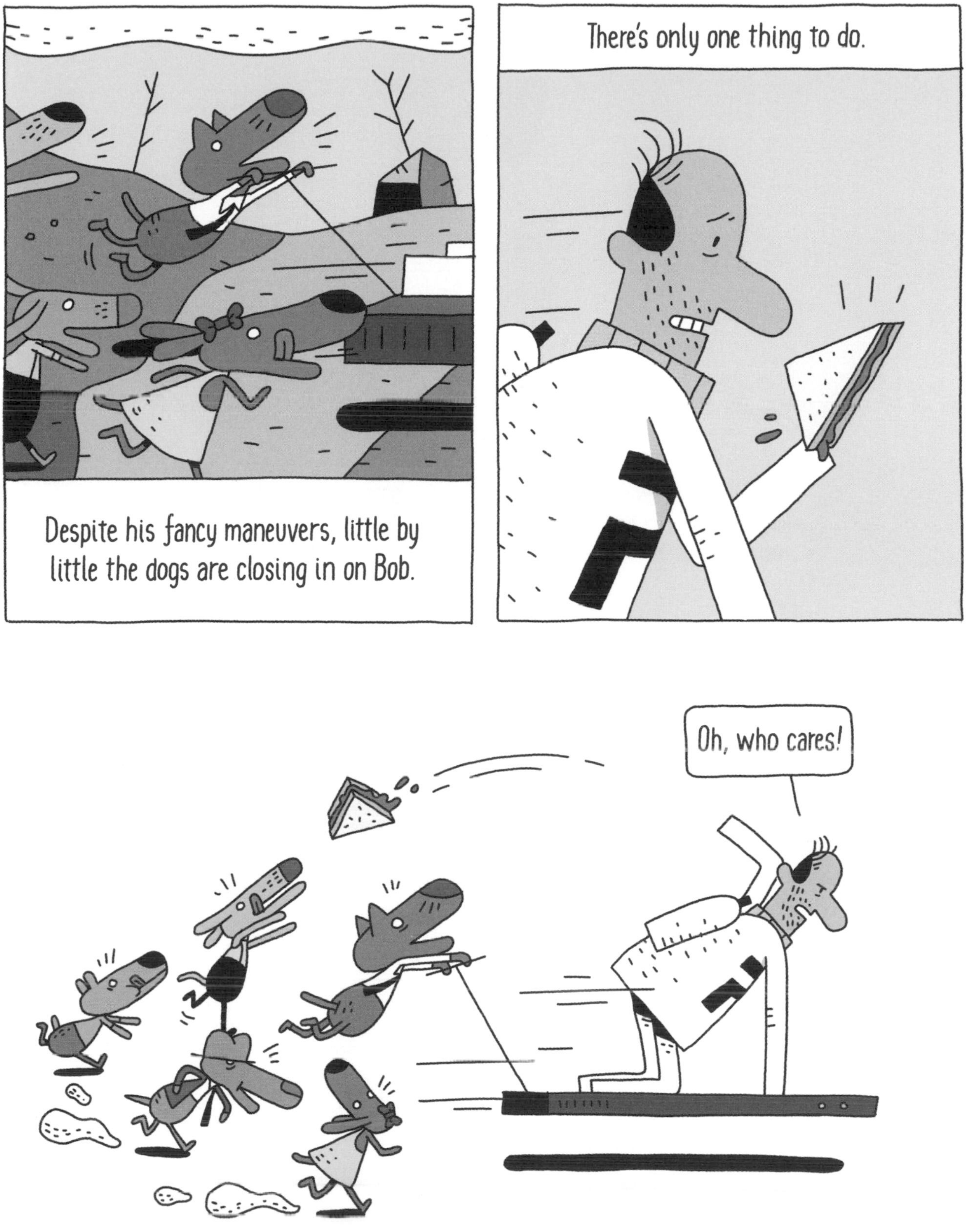
Despite his fancy maneuvers, little by little the dogs are closing in on Bob.
There's only one thing to do.
Oh, who cares!

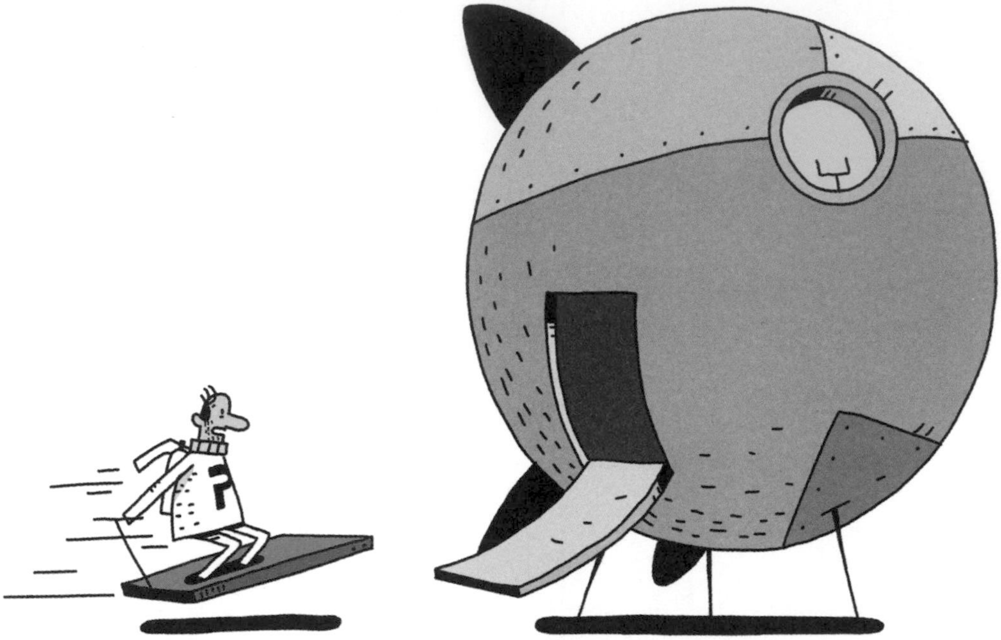

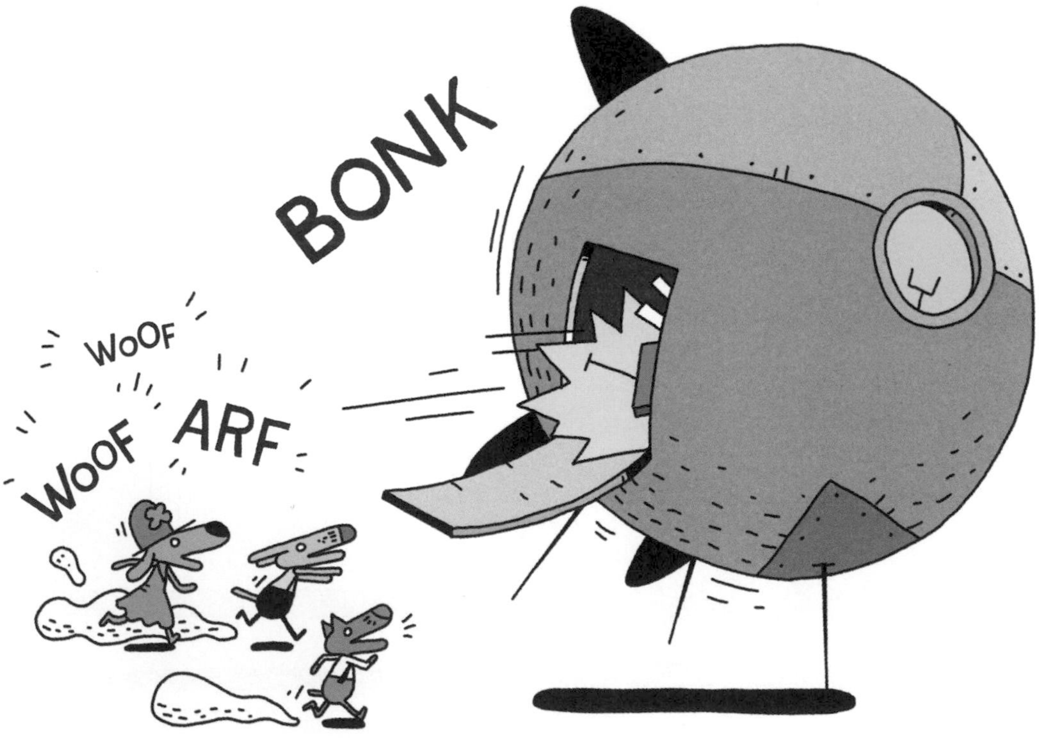
BONK
WOOF
WOOF
ARF

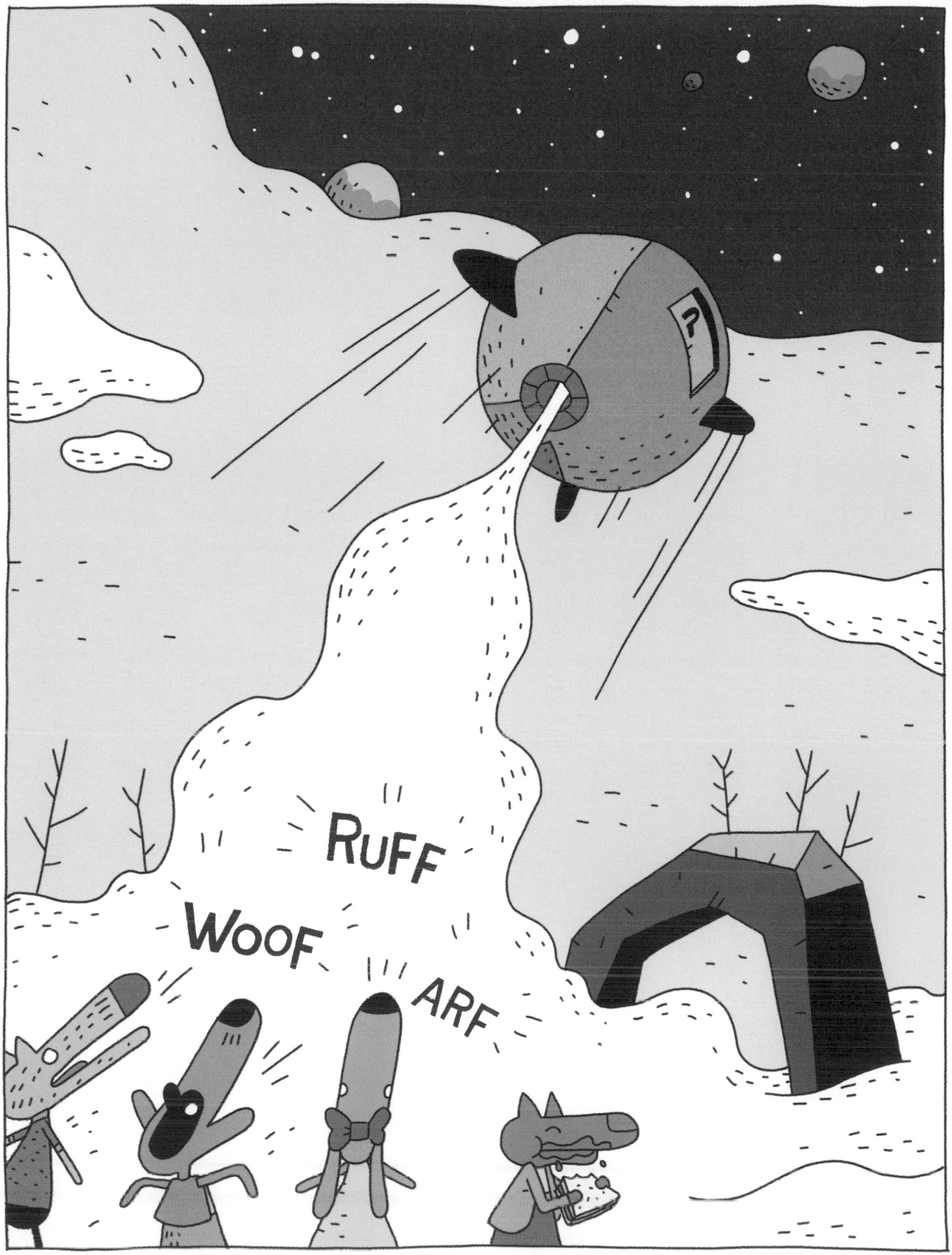
RUFF
WOOF
ARF

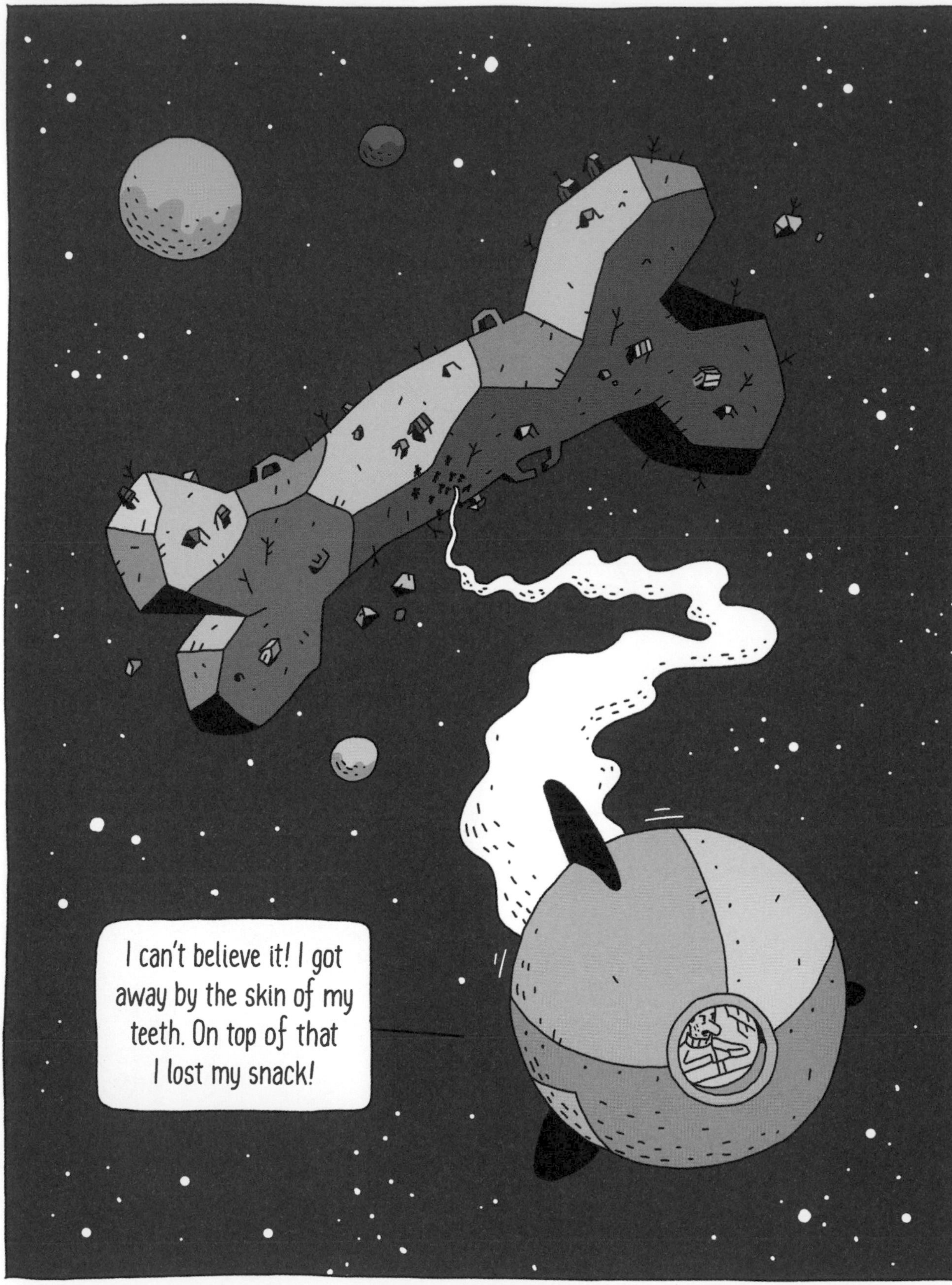
I can't believe it! I got away by the skin of my teeth. On top of that I lost my snack!

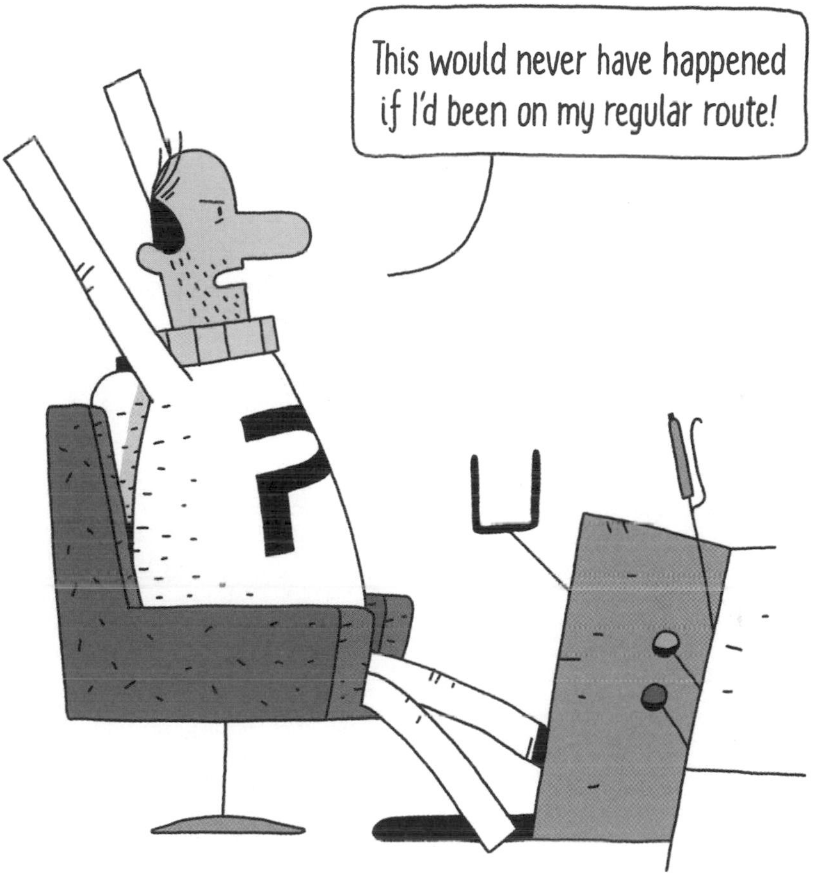
This would never have happened if I'd been on my regular route!

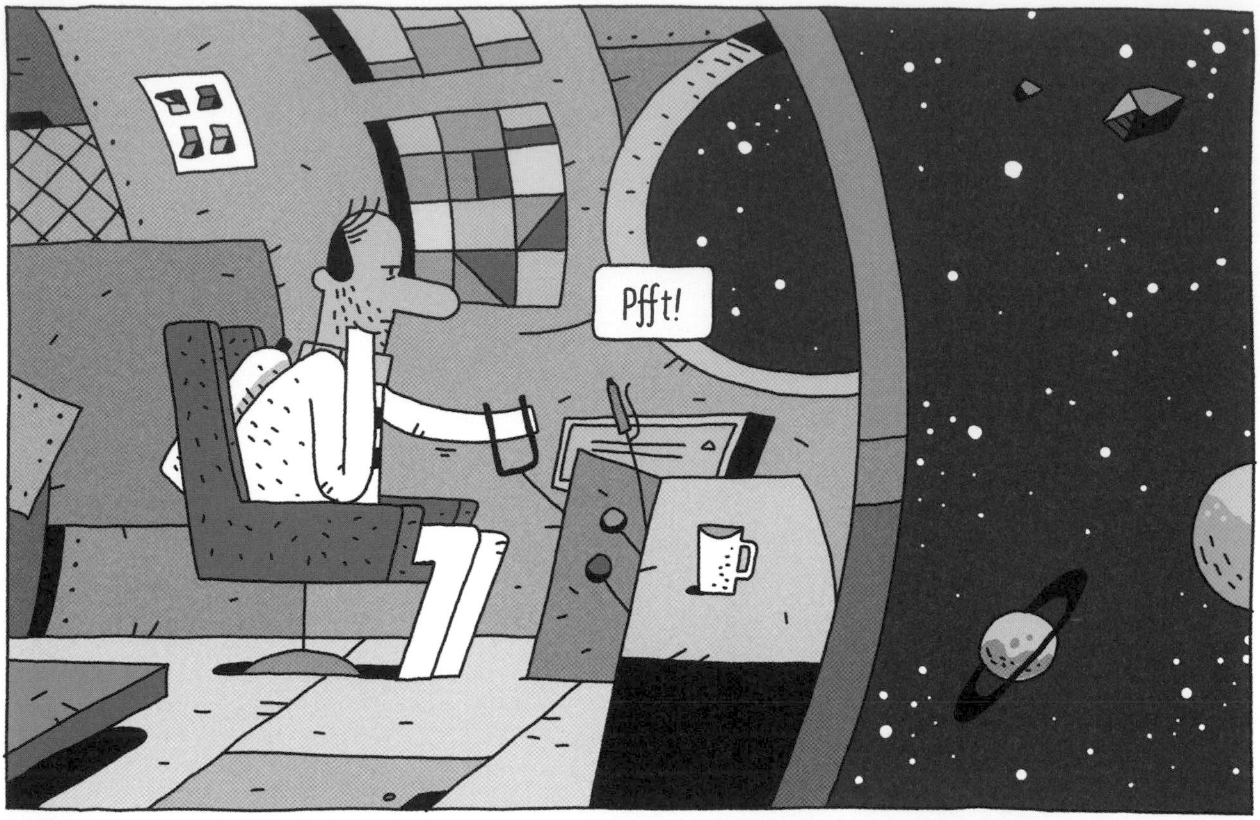
Pfft!

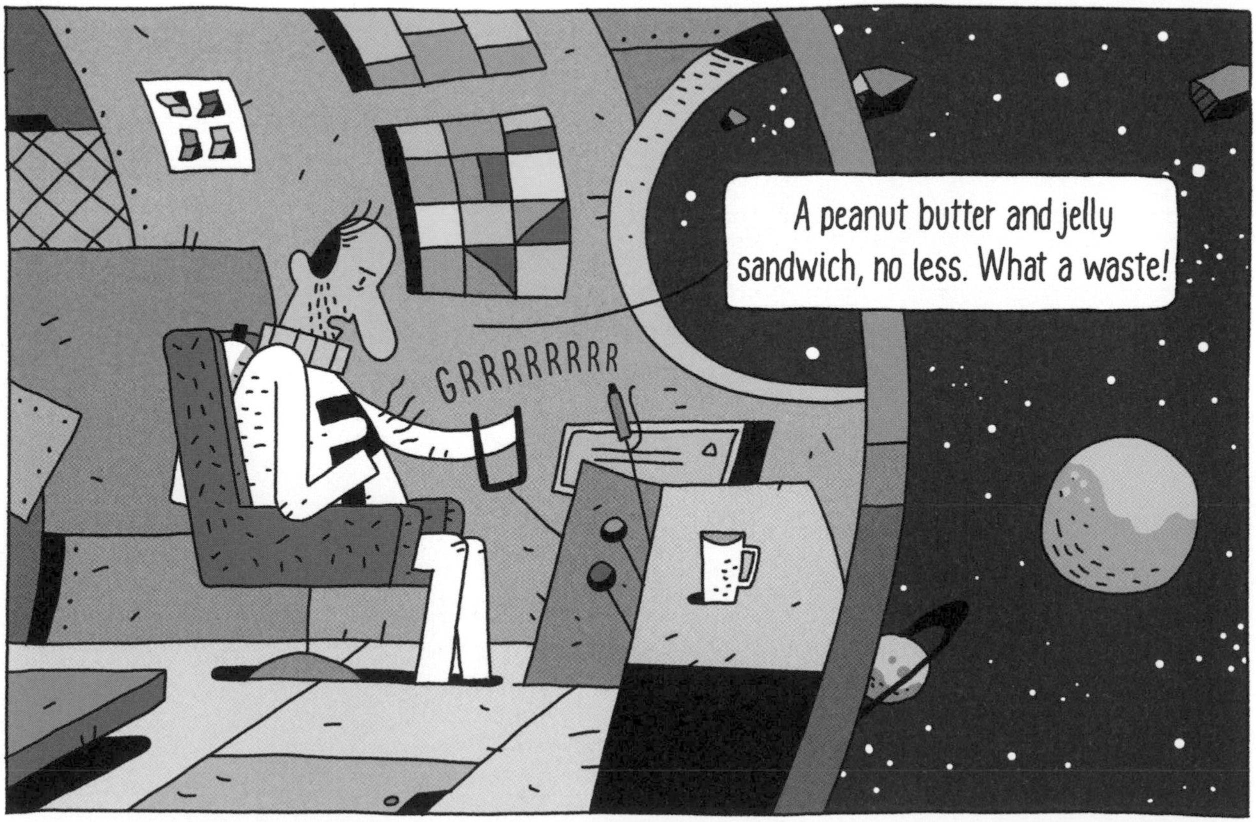
A peanut butter and jelly sandwich, no less. What a waste!
GRRRRRRRR

DELIVERY

#4

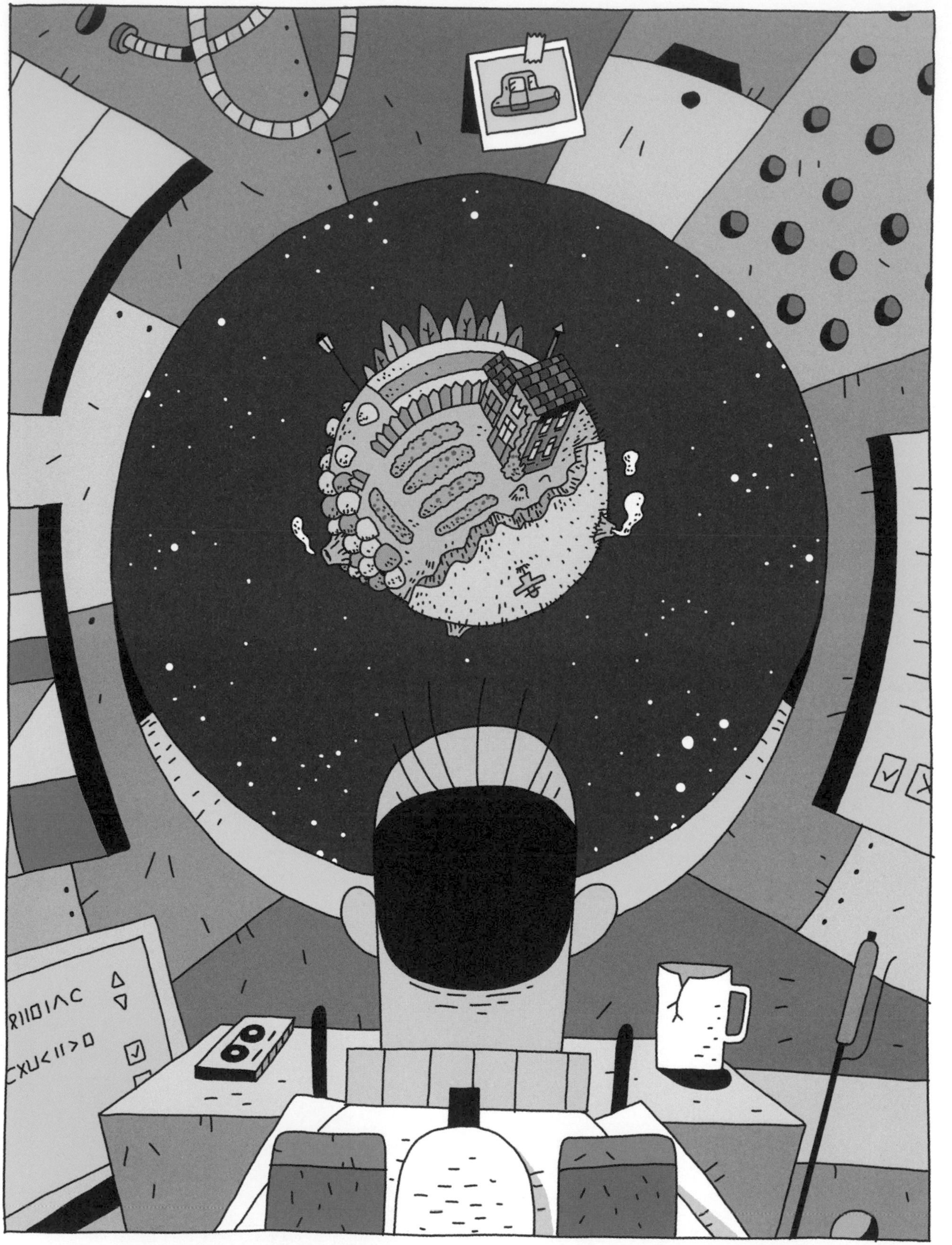

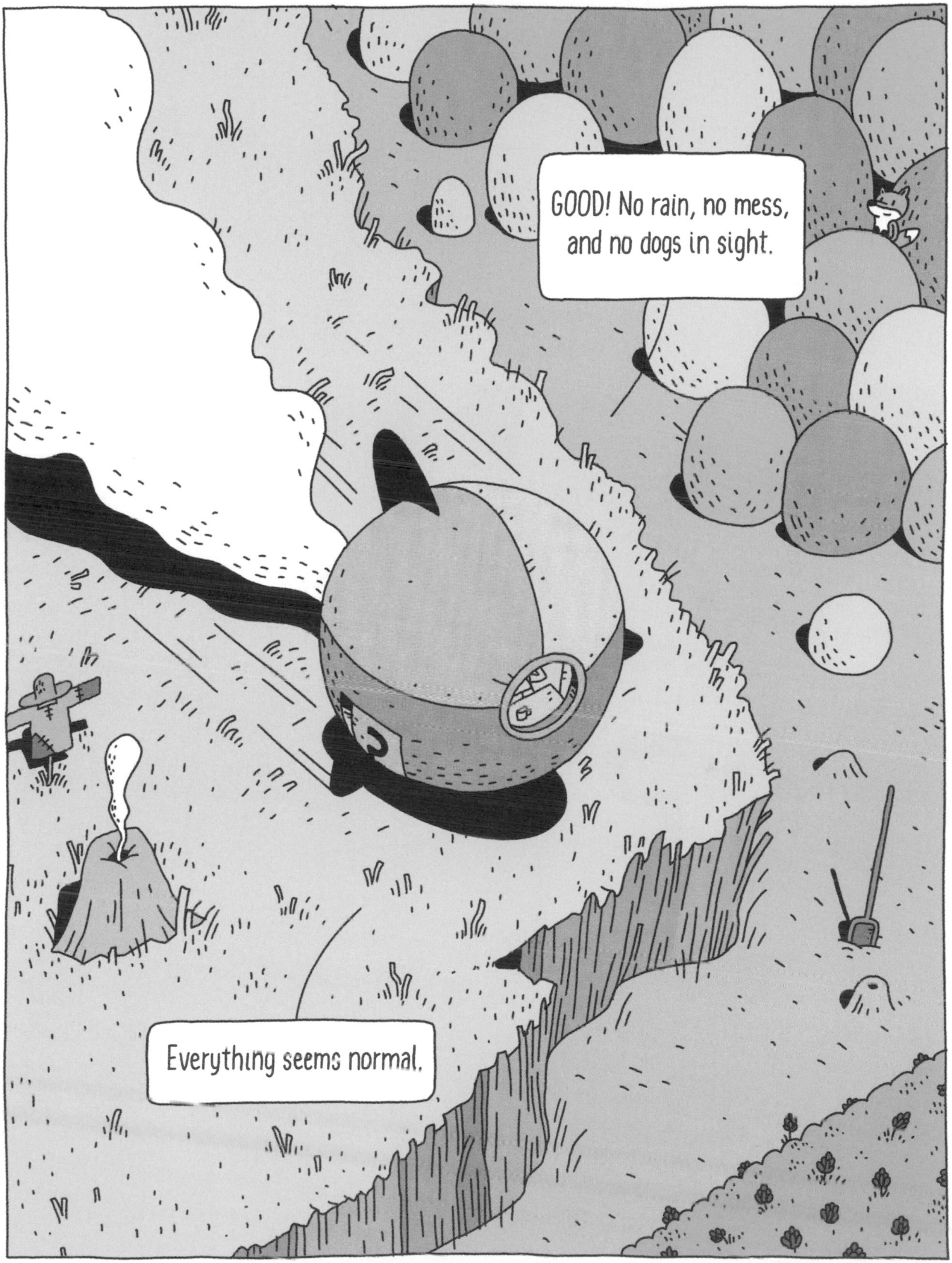
GOOD! No rain, no mess, and no dogs in sight.
Everything seems normal.

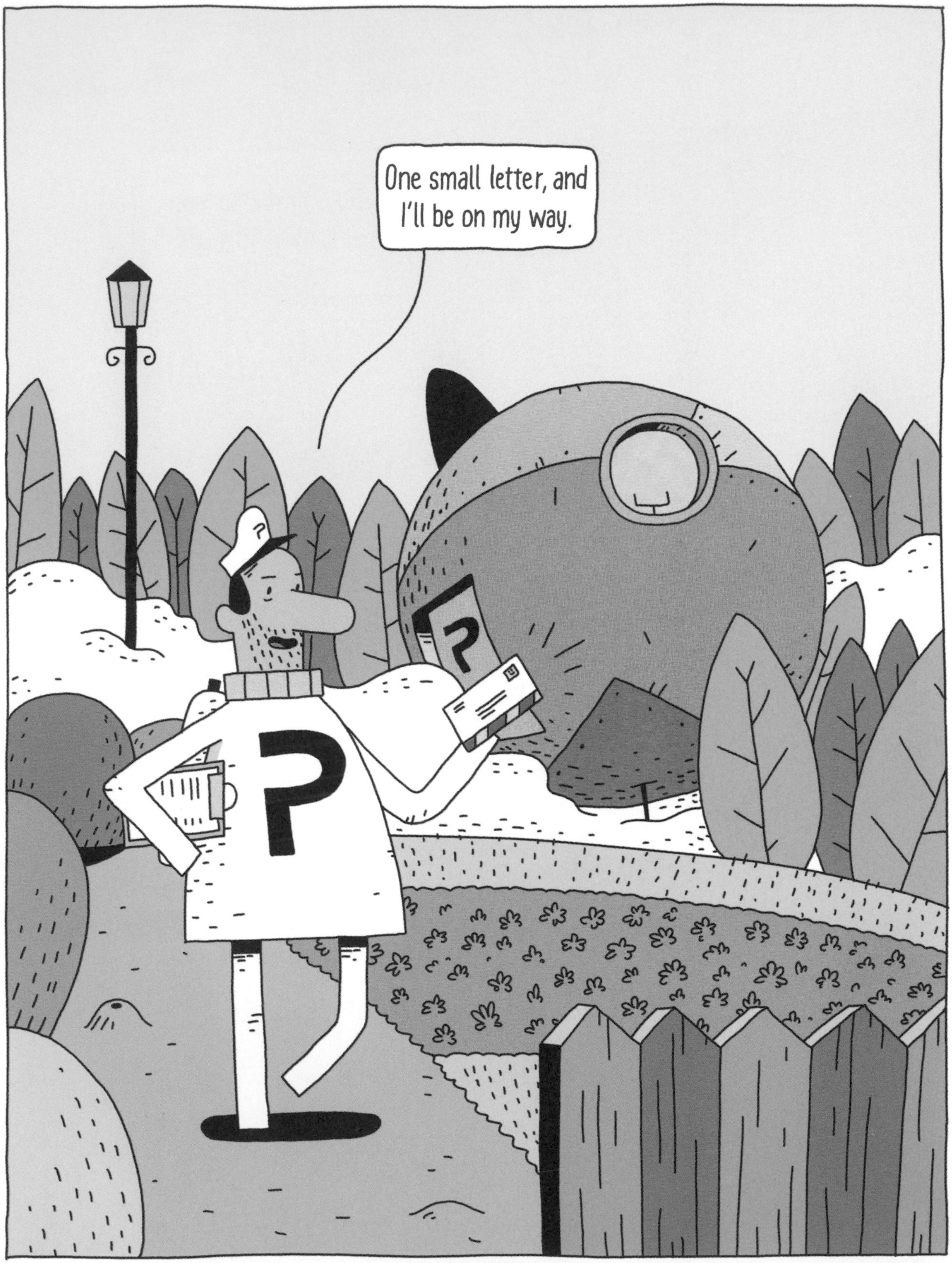
One small letter, and I'll be on my way.

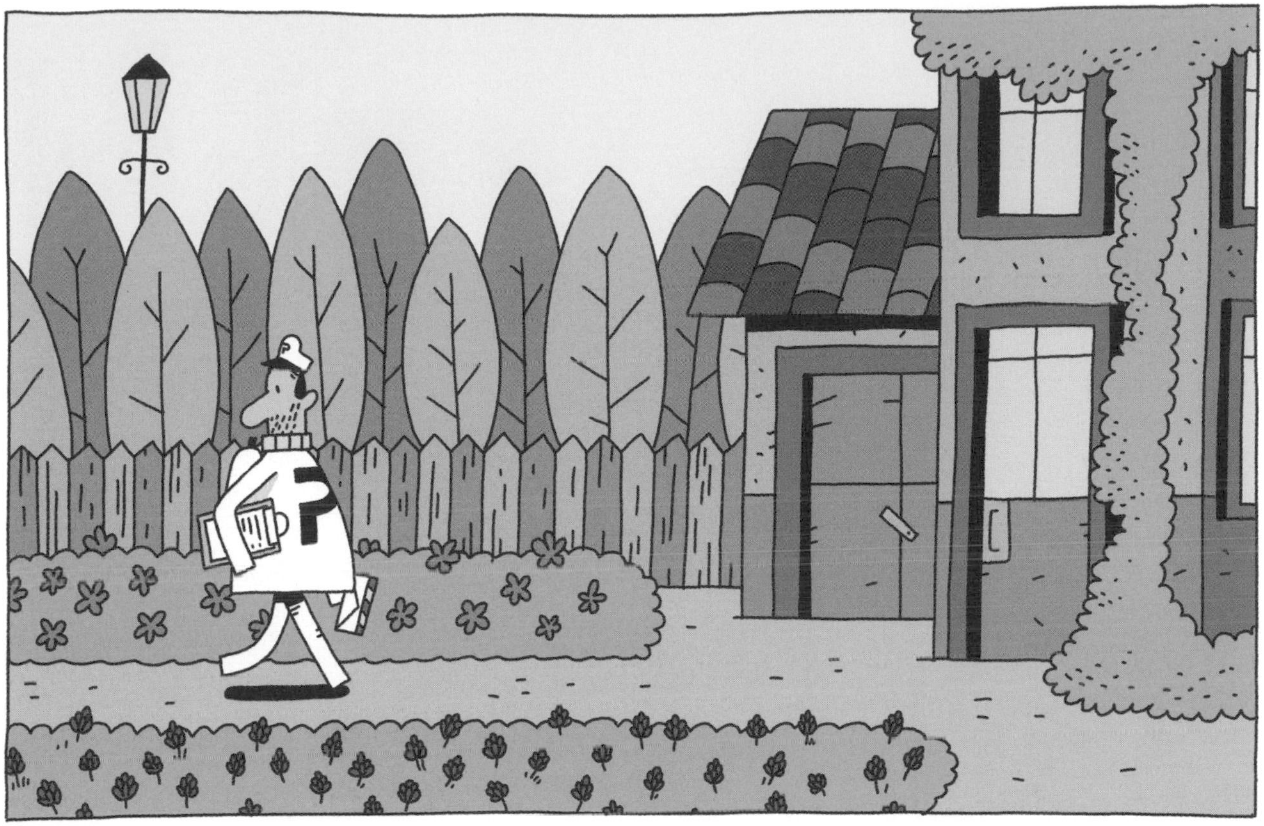

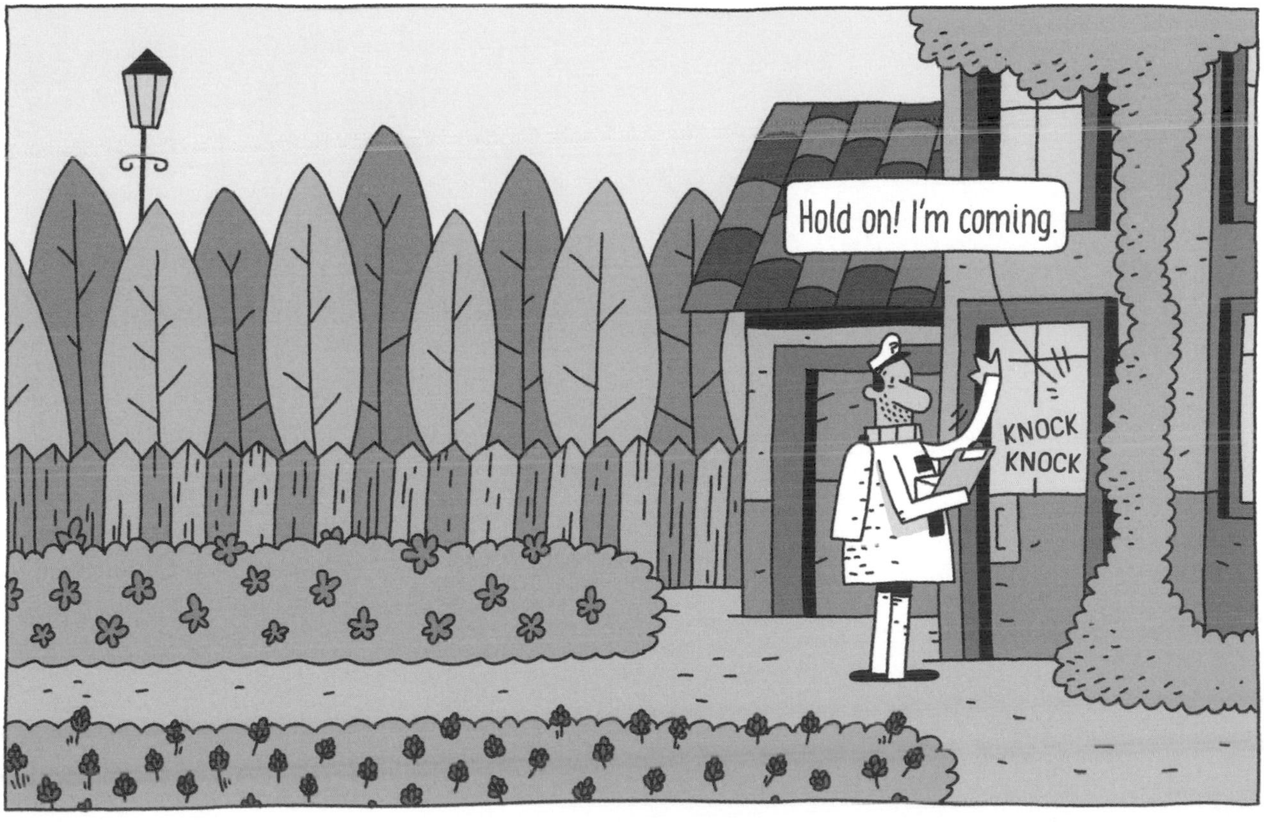
Hold on! I'm coming.
KNOCK KNOCK

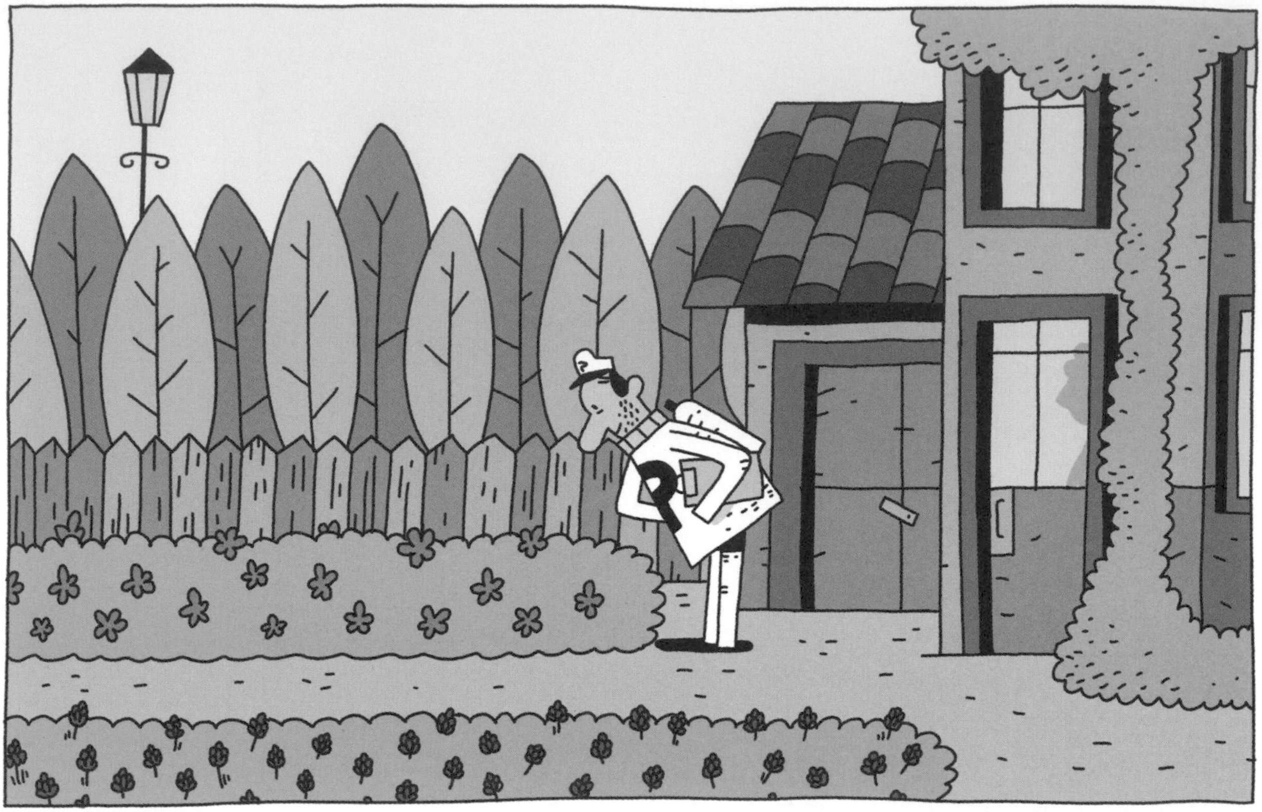

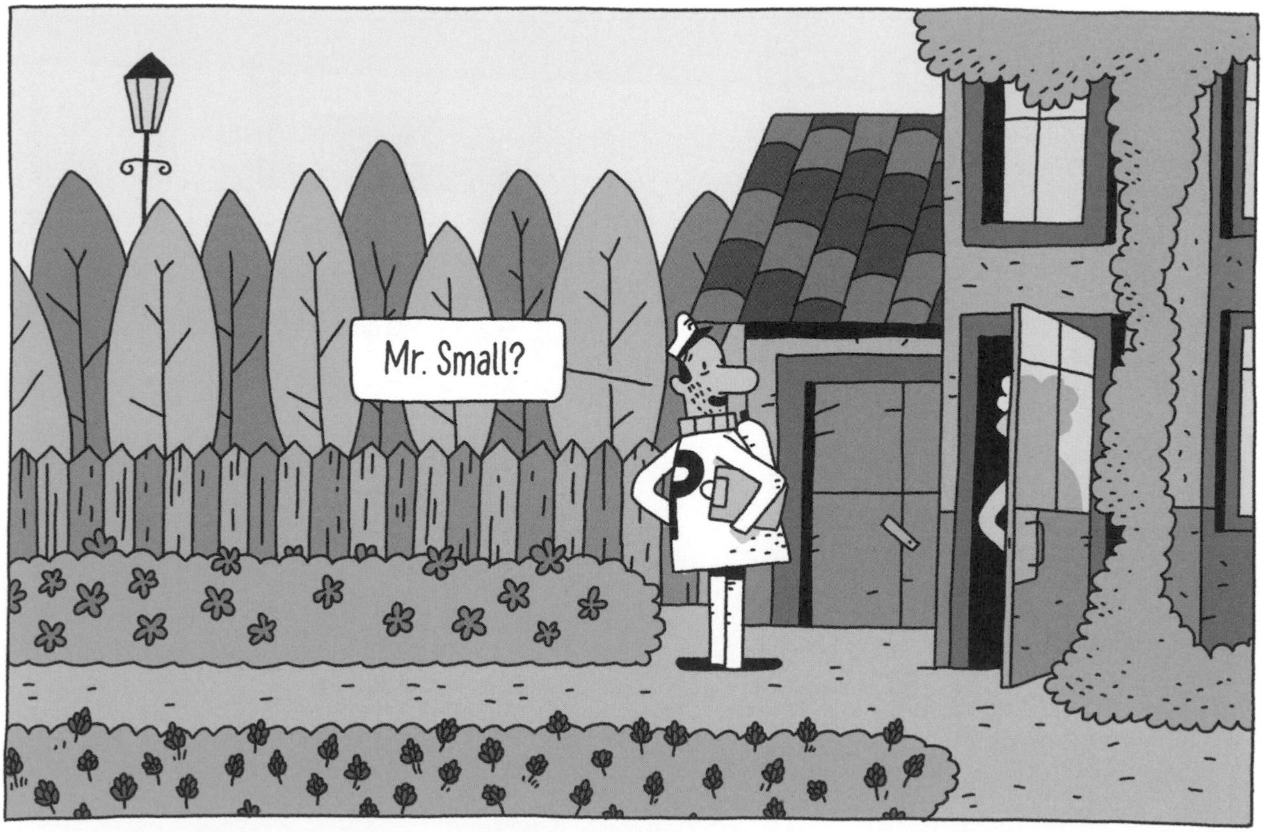
Mr. Small?

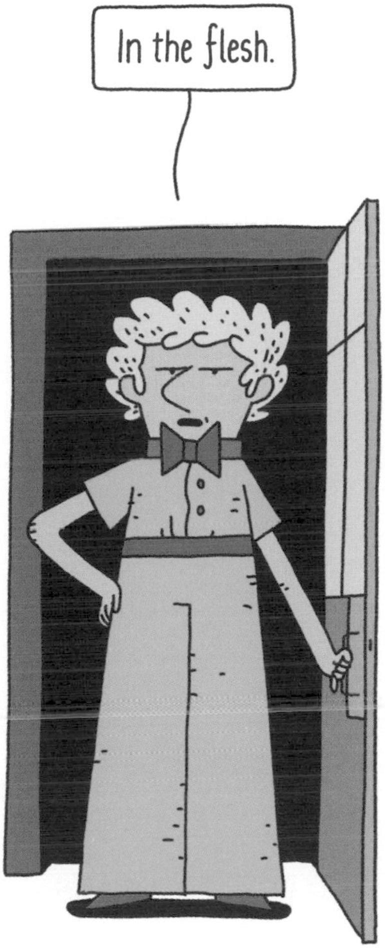
In the flesh.

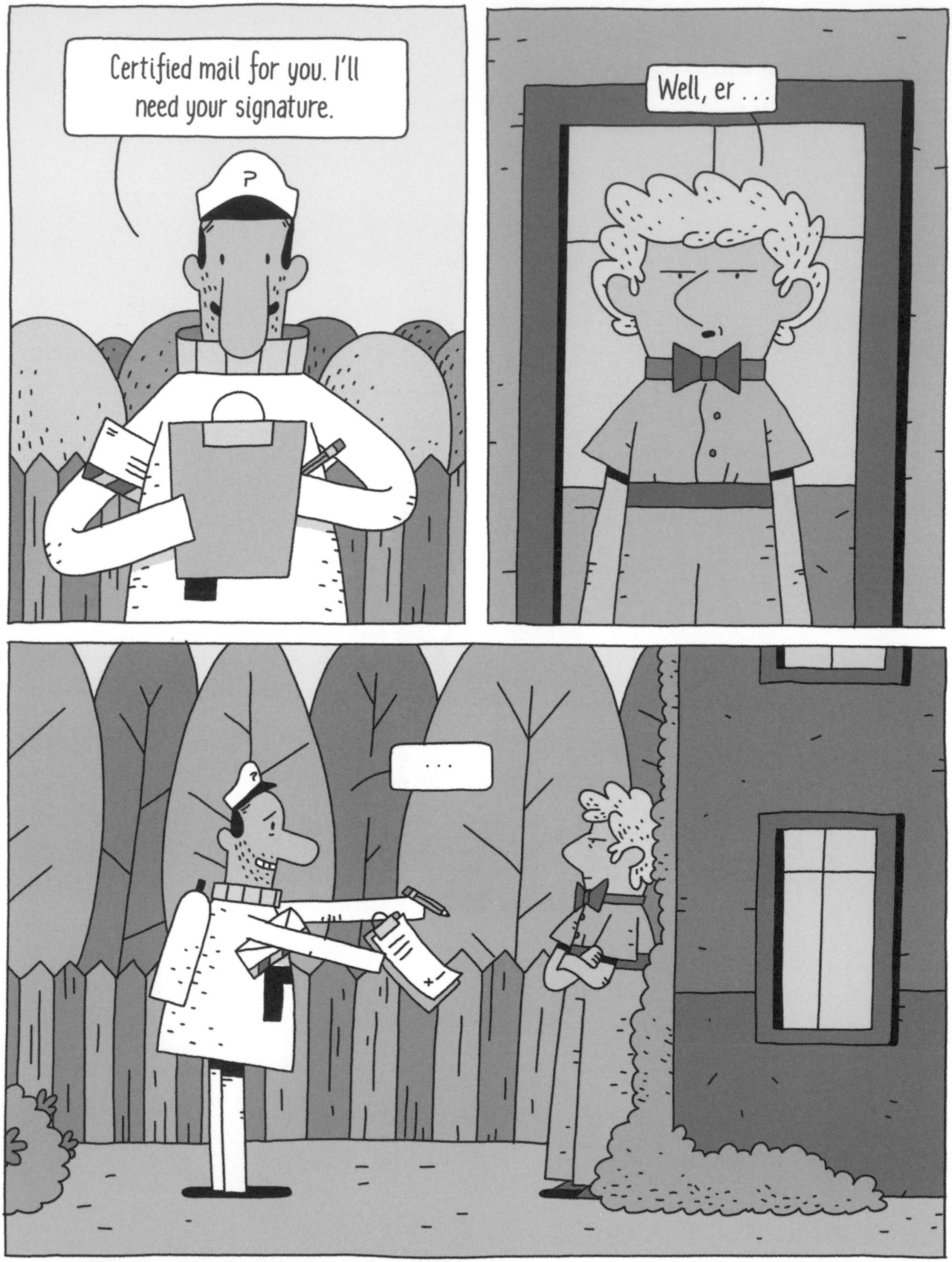
Certified mail for you. I'll need your signature.
Well, er . . .
. . .

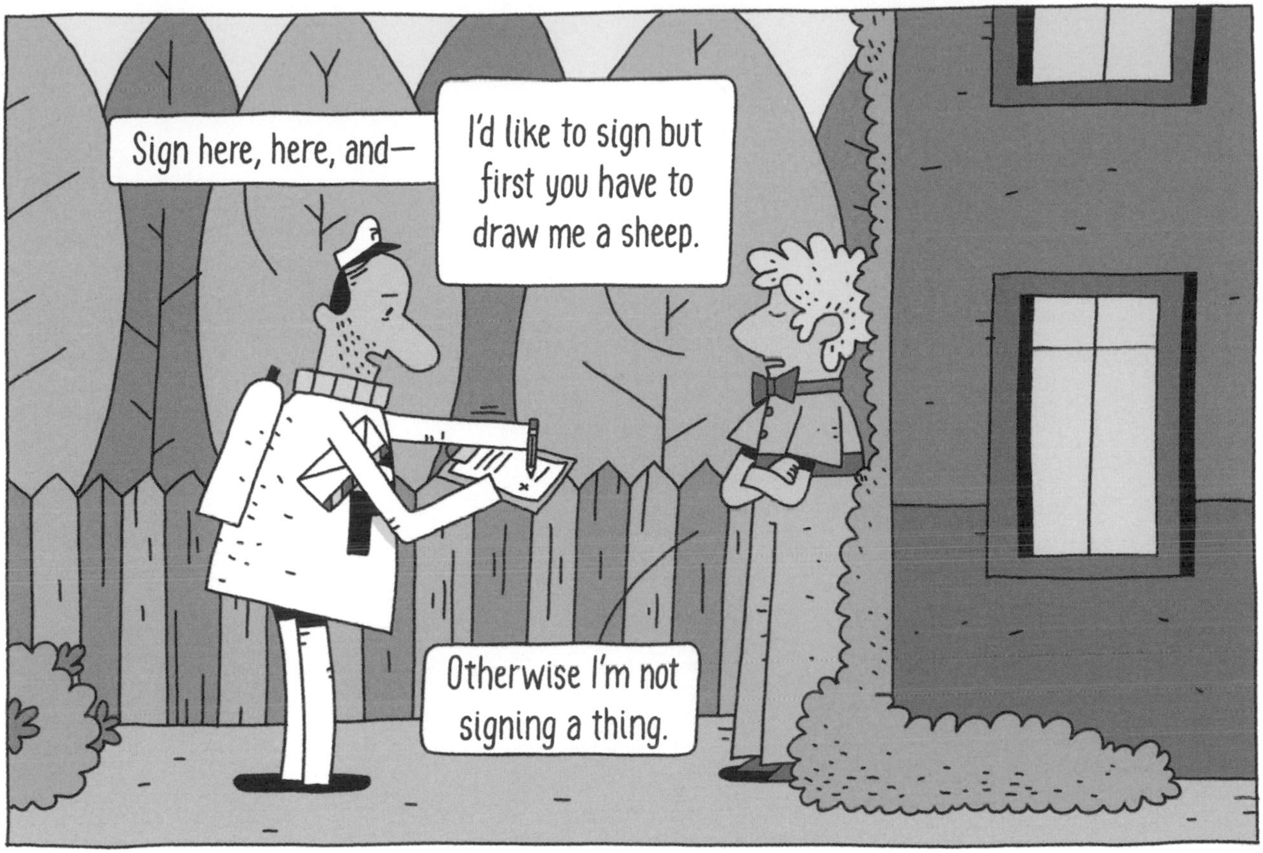
Sign here, here, and—
I'd like to sign but first you have to draw me a sheep.
Otherwise I'm not signing a thing.

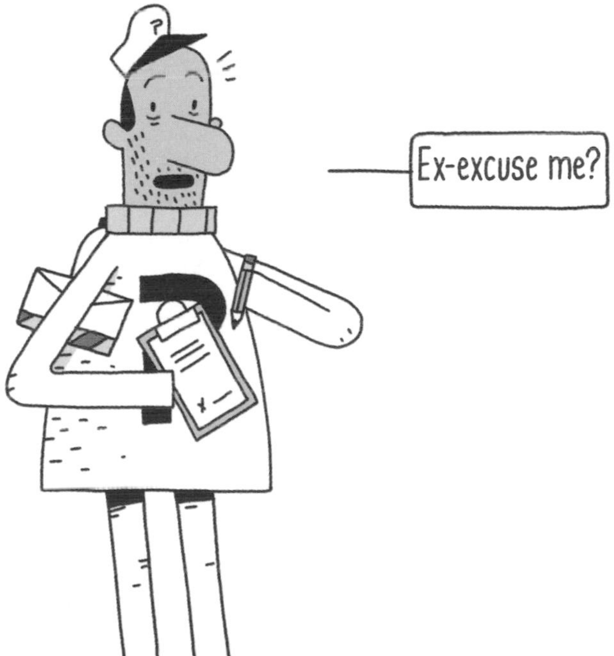
Ex-excuse me?

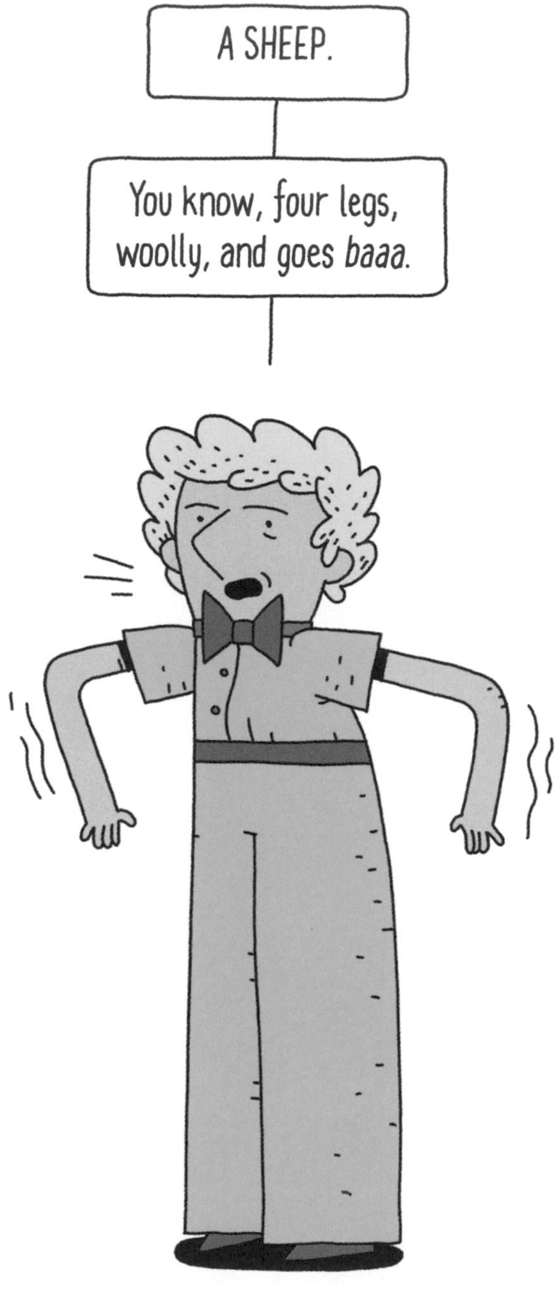
A SHEEP.
You know, four legs, woolly, and goes *baaa*.

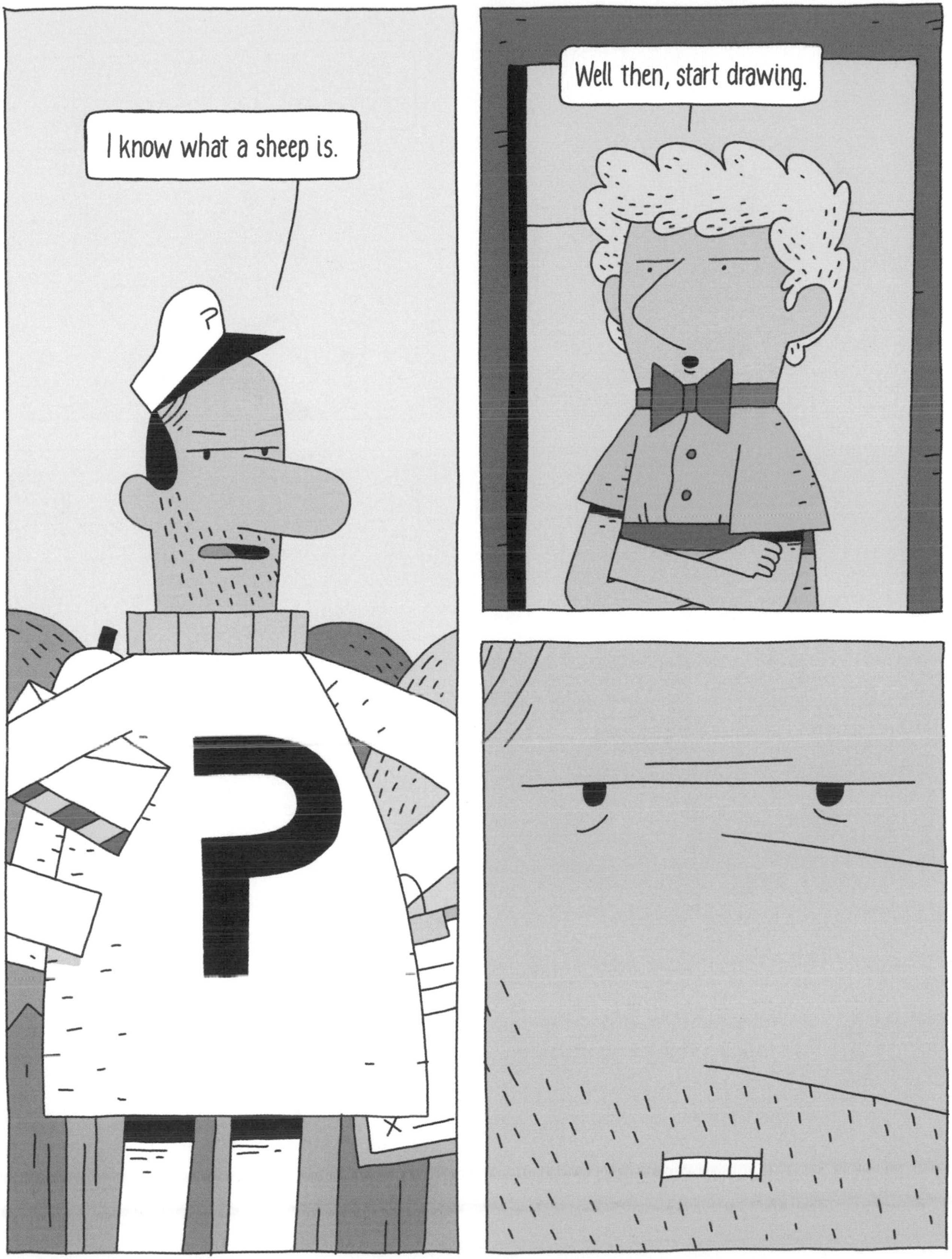
I know what a sheep is.
Well then, start drawing.

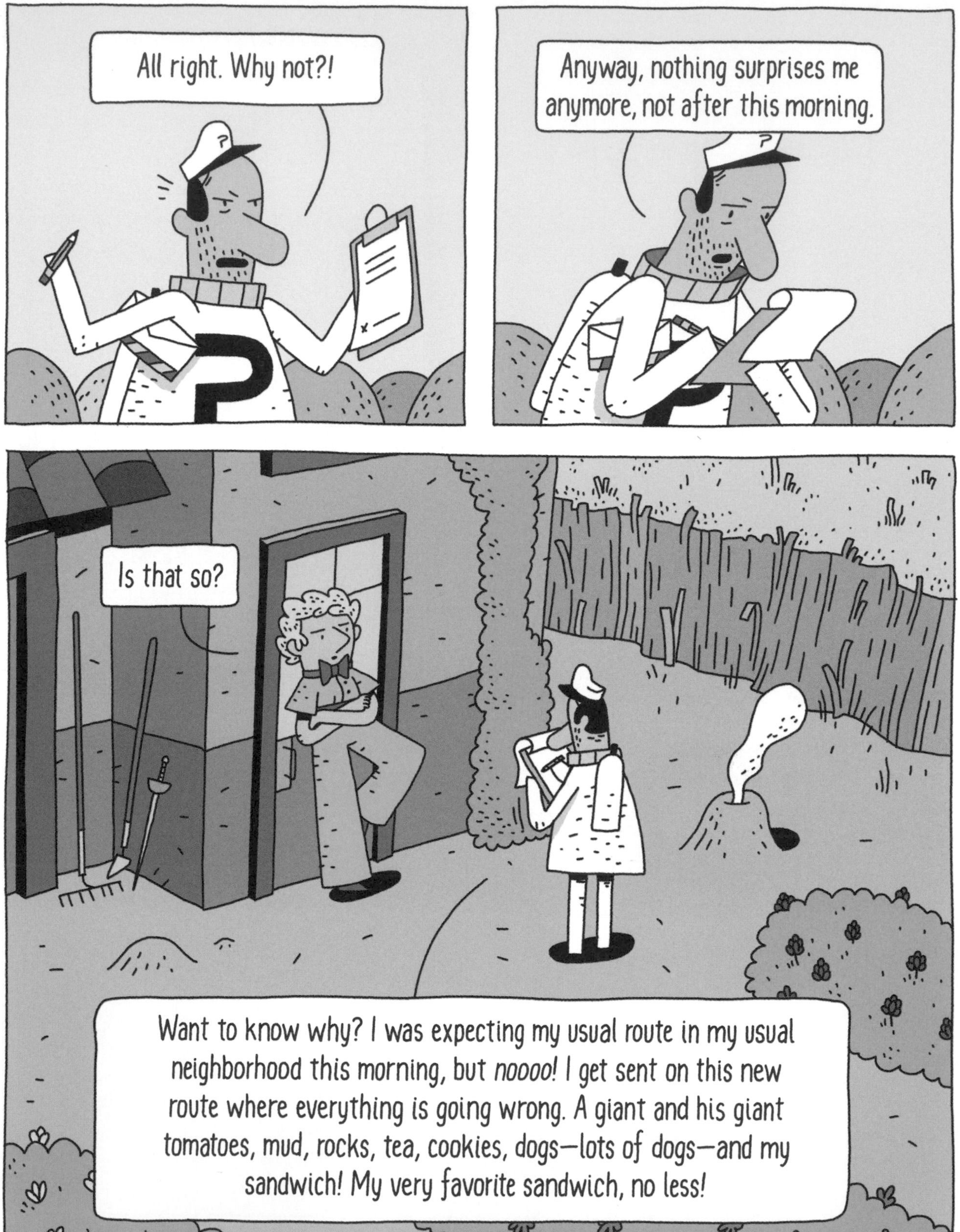
All right. Why not?!
Anyway, nothing surprises me anymore, not after this morning.
Is that so?
Want to know why? I was expecting my usual route in my usual neighborhood this morning, but *noooo*! I get sent on this new route where everything is going wrong. A giant and his giant tomatoes, mud, rocks, tea, cookies, dogs—lots of dogs—and my sandwich! My very favorite sandwich, no less!

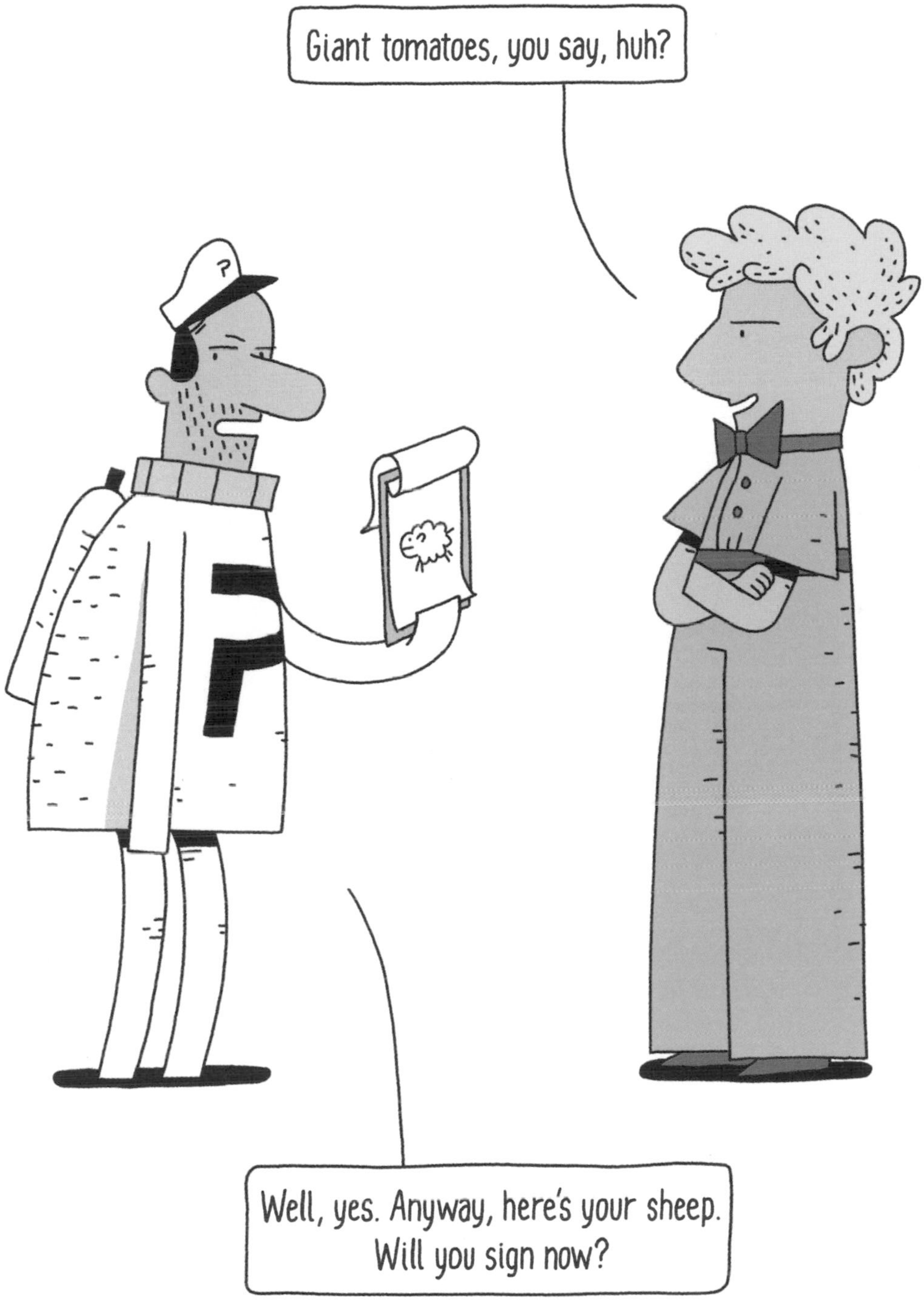
Giant tomatoes, you say, huh?
Well, yes. Anyway, here's your sheep. Will you sign now?

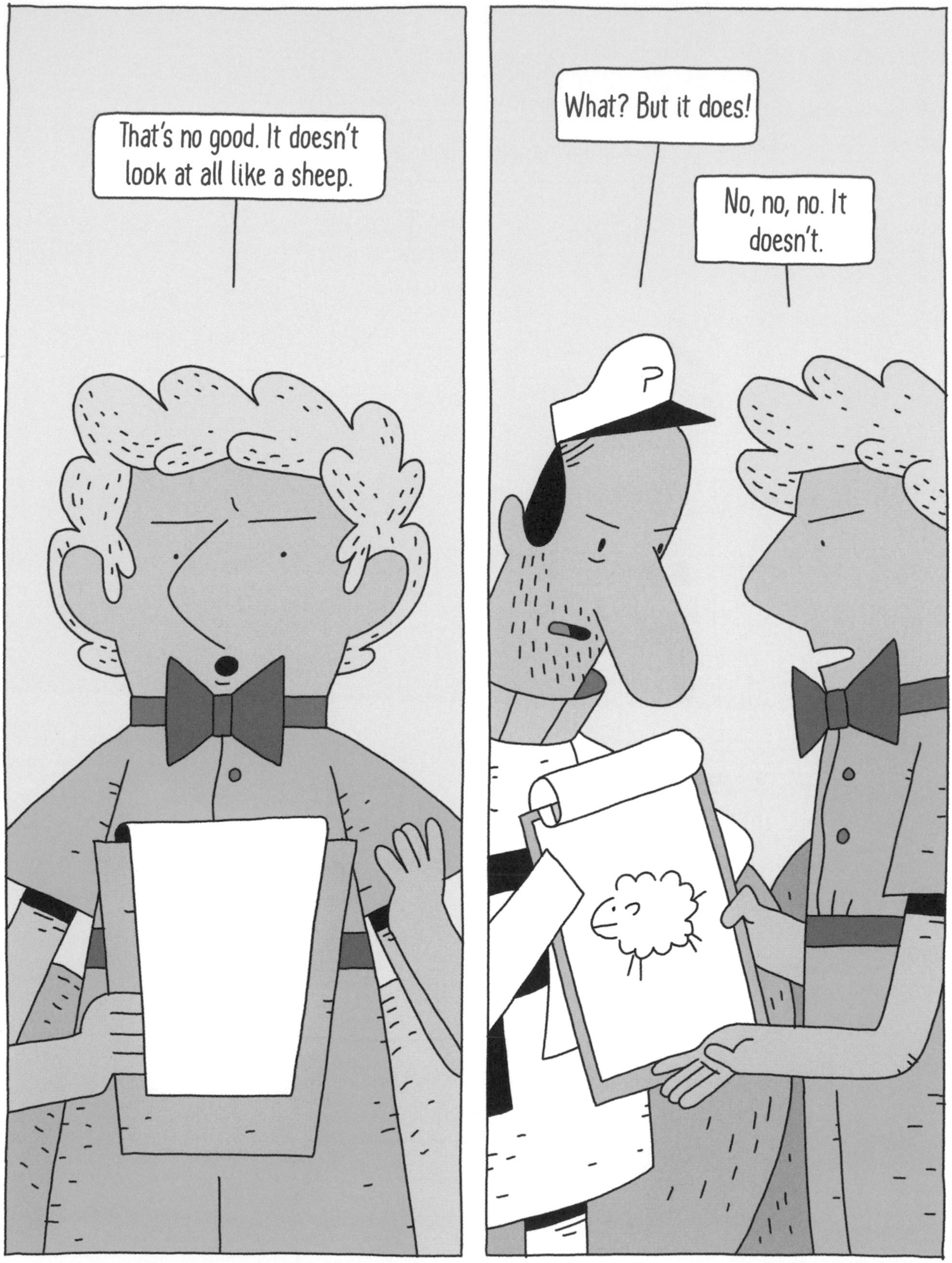
That's no good. It doesn't look at all like a sheep.
What? But it does!
No, no, no. It doesn't.

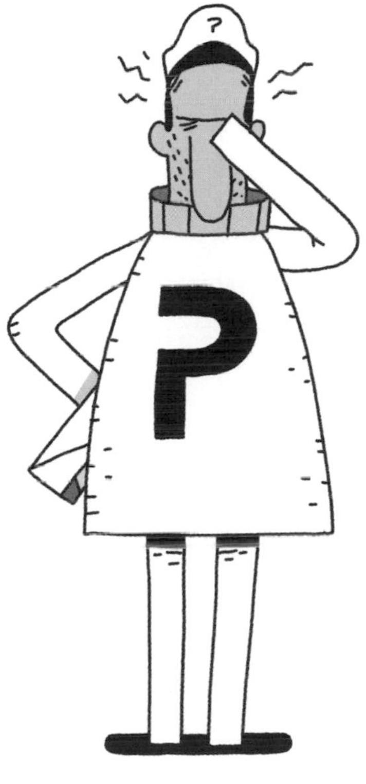
P

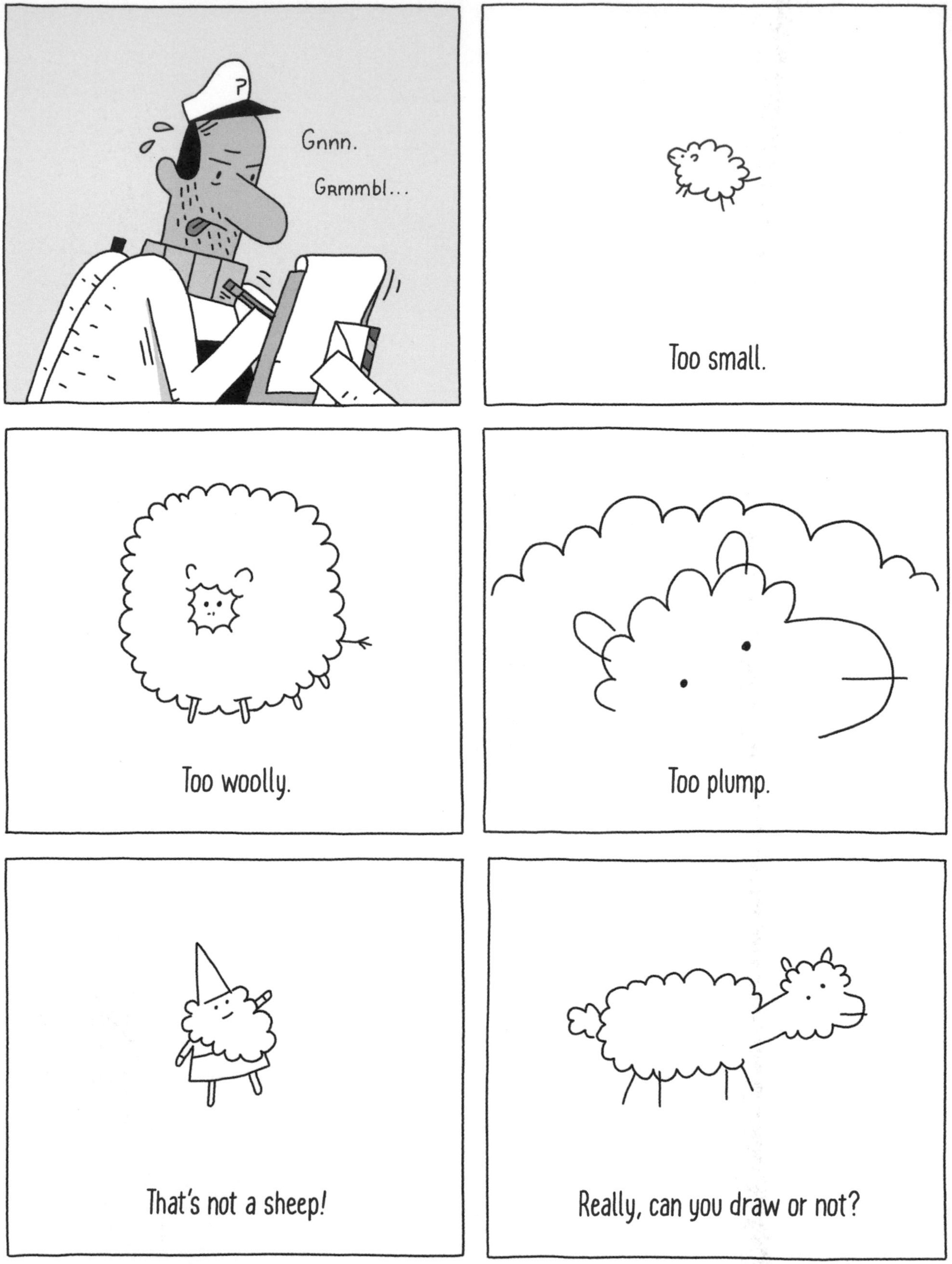
Gnnn.
Grmmbl...
Too small.
Too woolly.
Too plump.
That's not a sheep!
Really, can you draw or not?

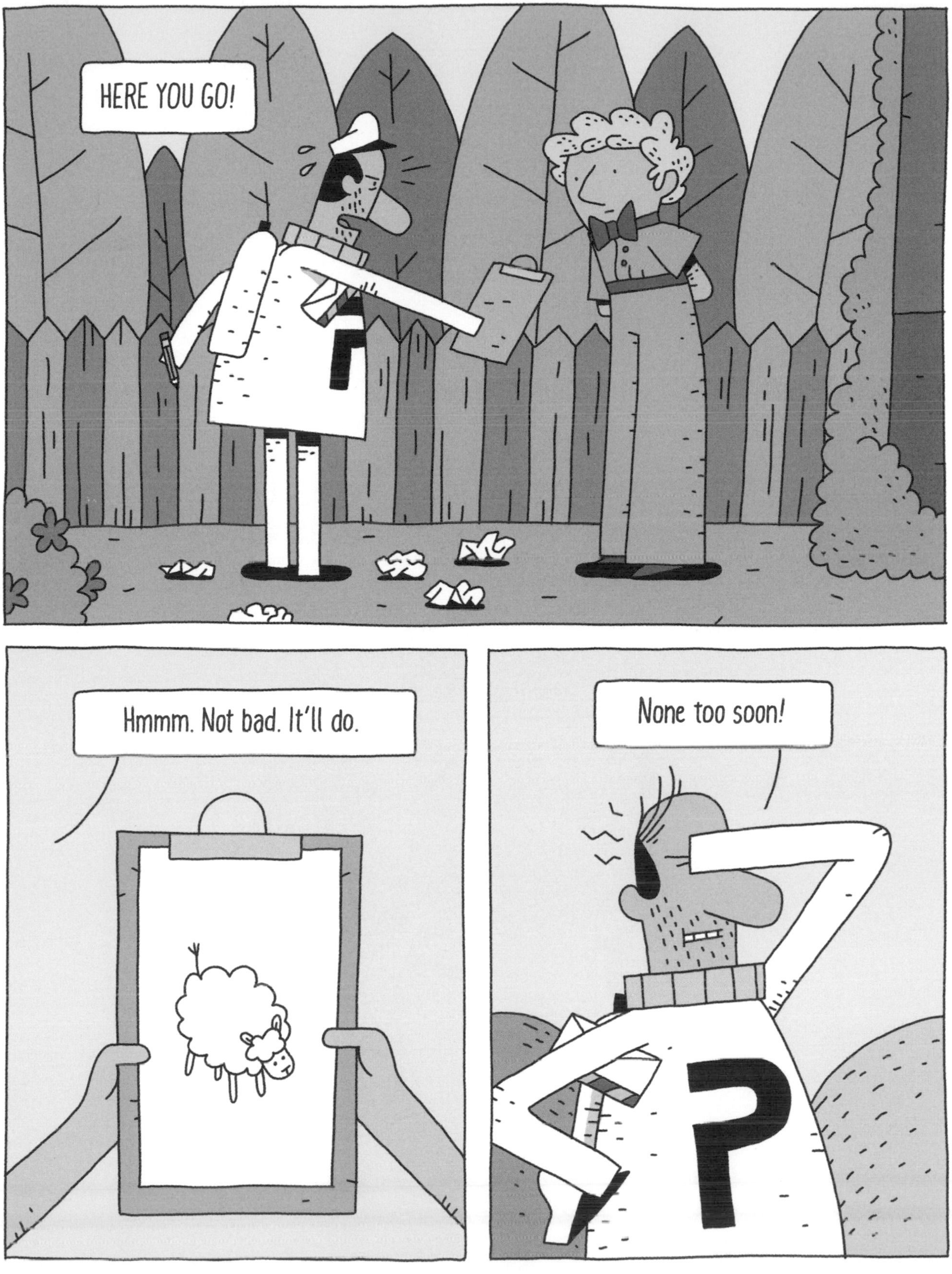
HERE YOU GO!
Hmmm. Not bad. It'll do.
None too soon!

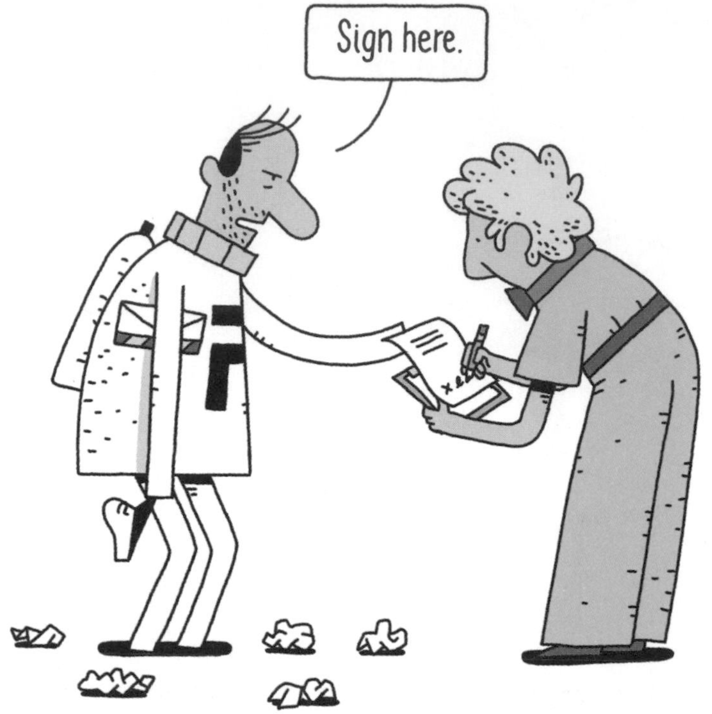
Sign here.

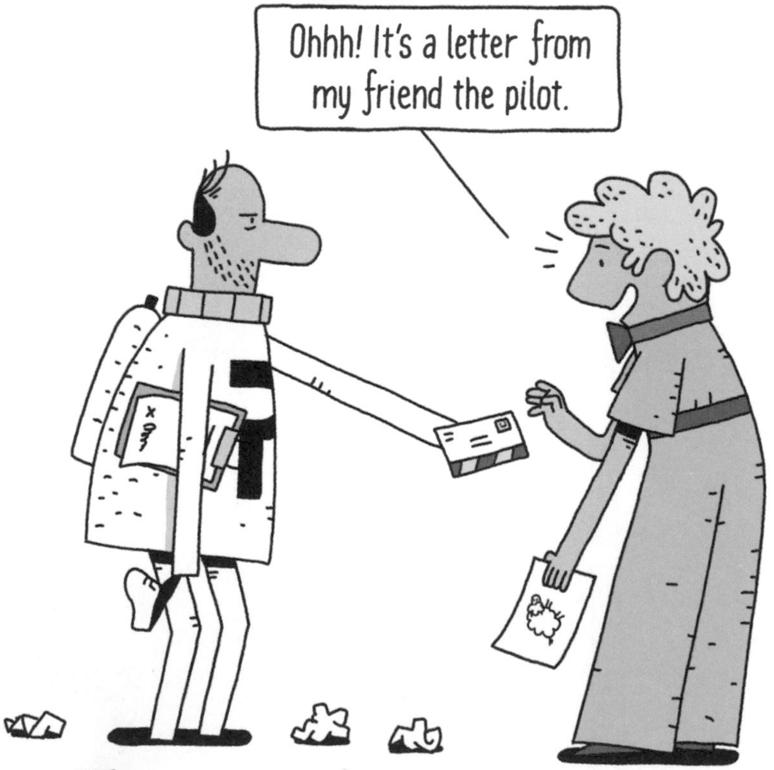
Ohhh! It's a letter from my friend the pilot.

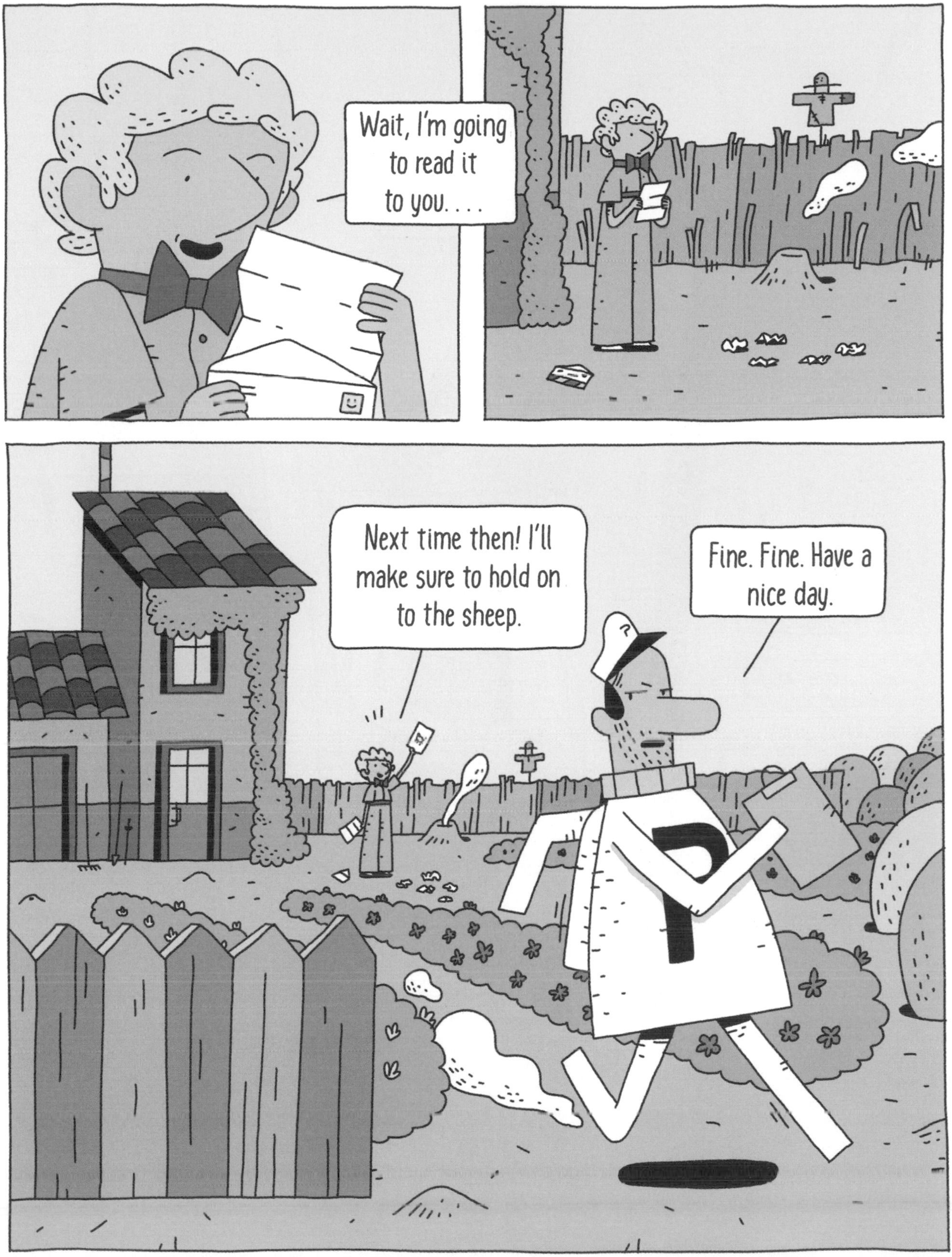
Wait, I'm going to read it to you. . . .
Next time then! I'll make sure to hold on to the sheep.
Fine. Fine. Have a nice day.

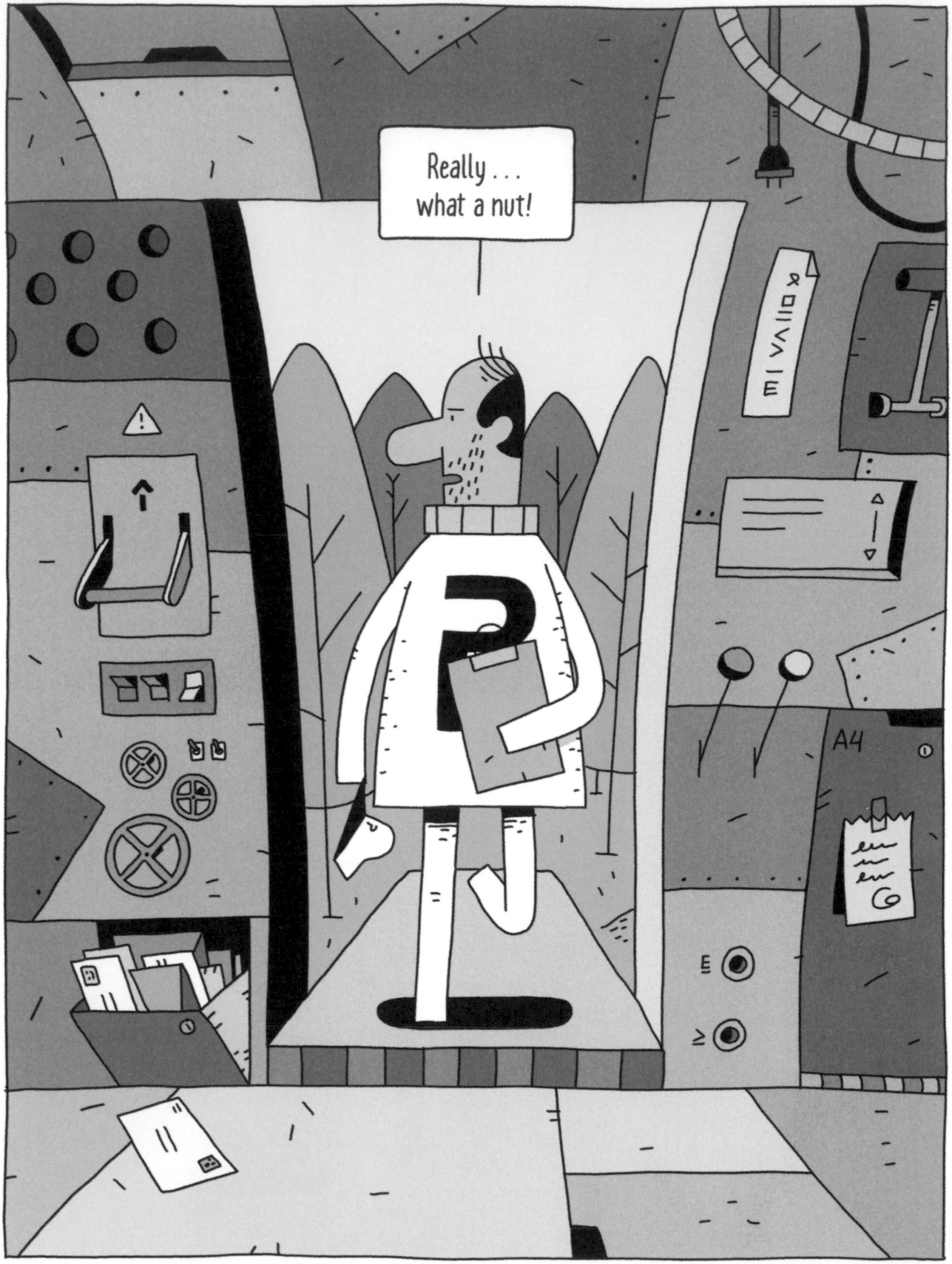
Really . . .
what a nut!
A4

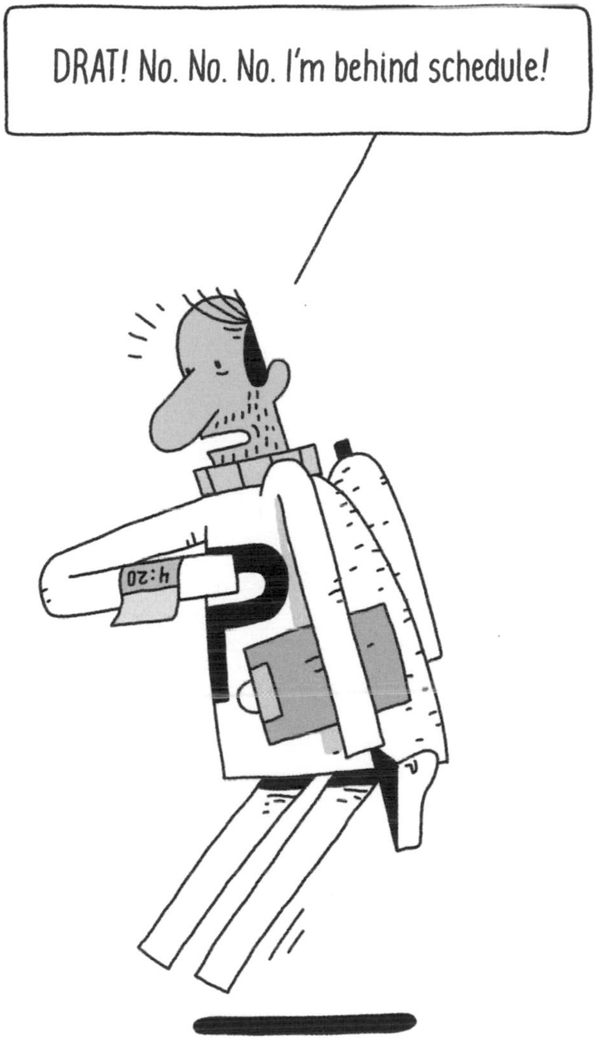
DRAT! No. No. No. I'm behind schedule!
4:20

Let's just say Bob is not having a very good day.

DELIVERY

#5

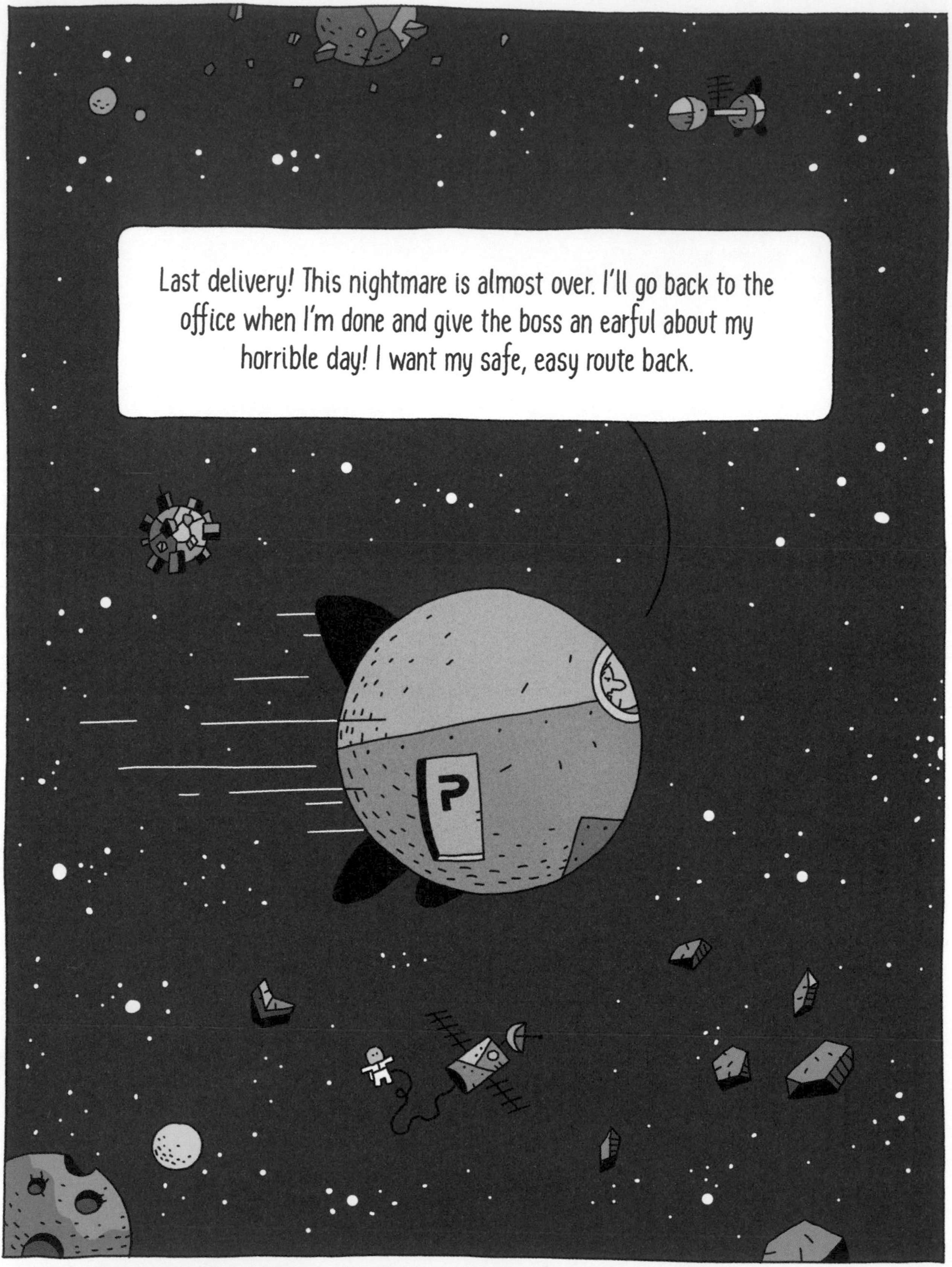
Last delivery! This nightmare is almost over. I'll go back to the office when I'm done and give the boss an earful about my horrible day! I want my safe, easy route back.

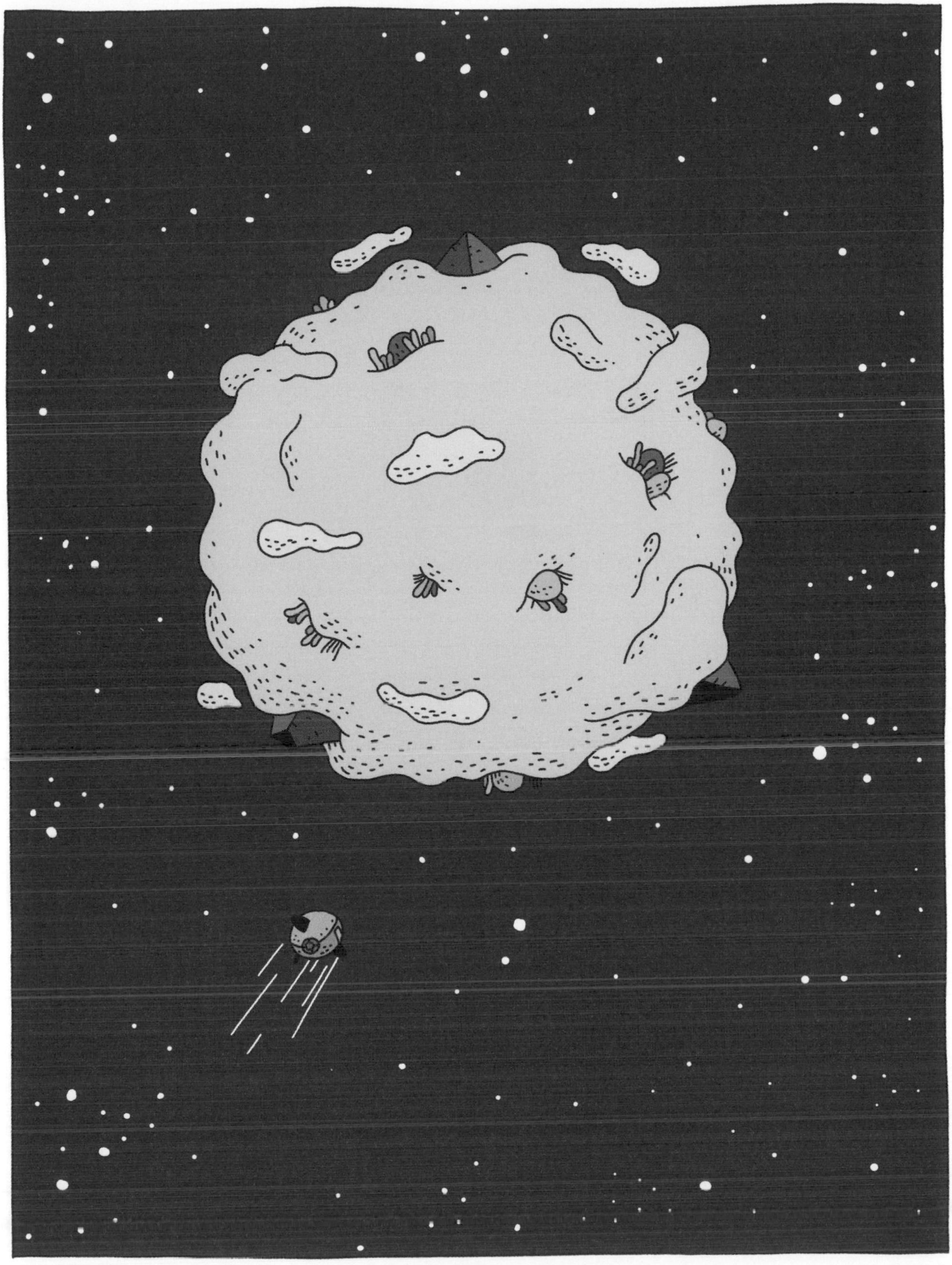

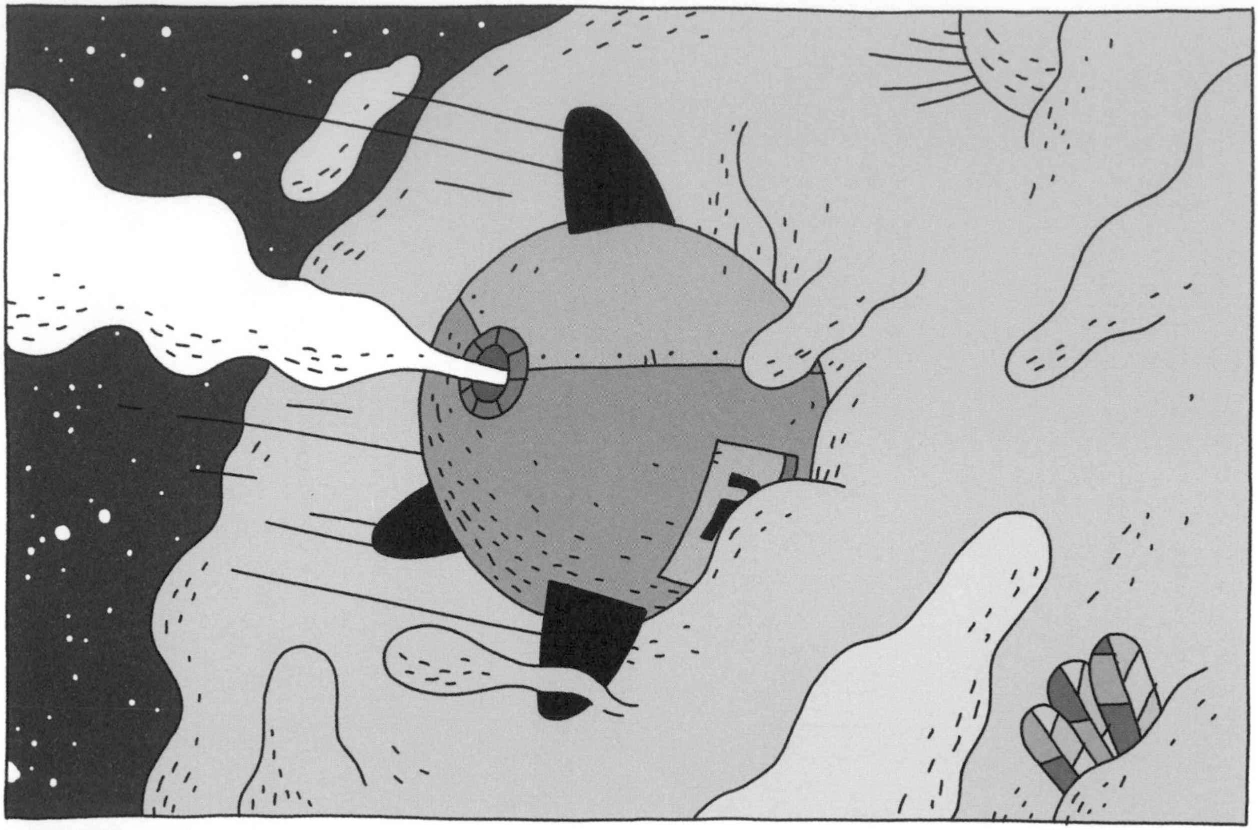

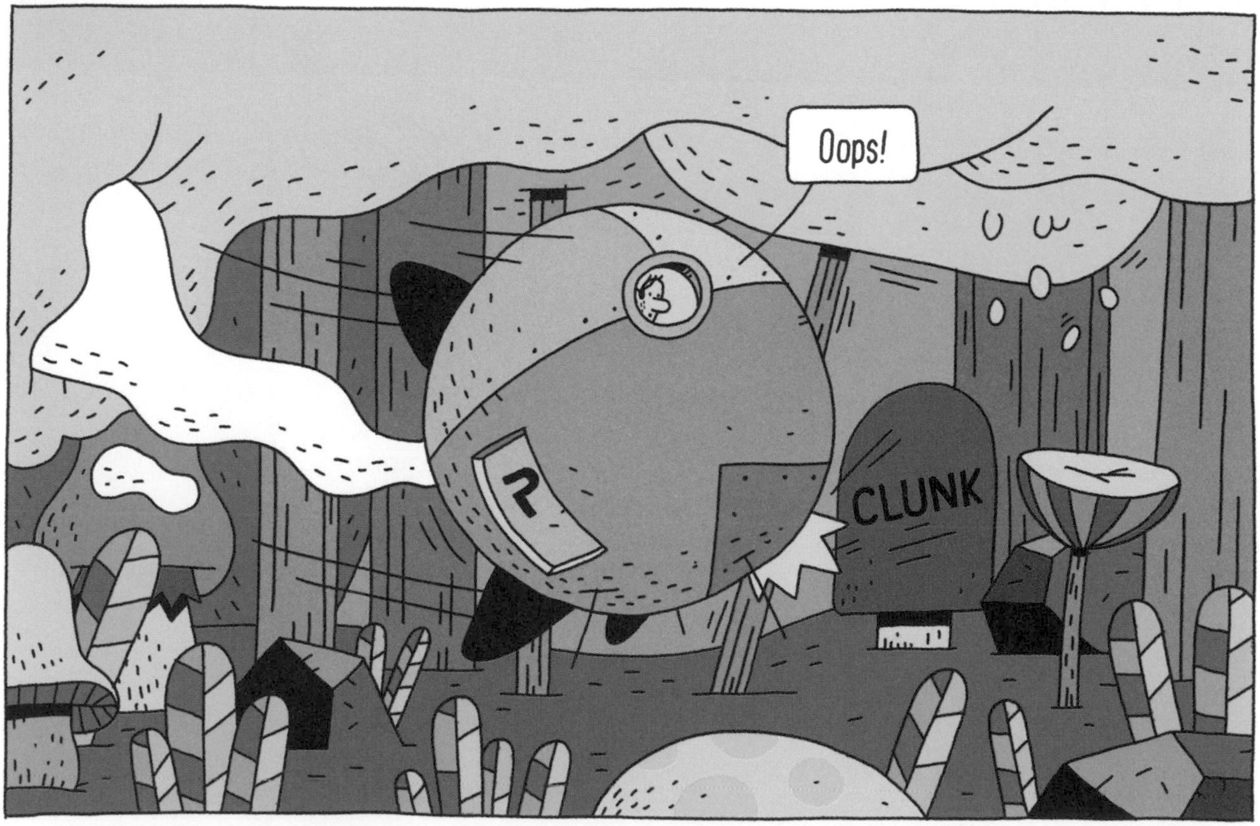
Oops!
CLUNK

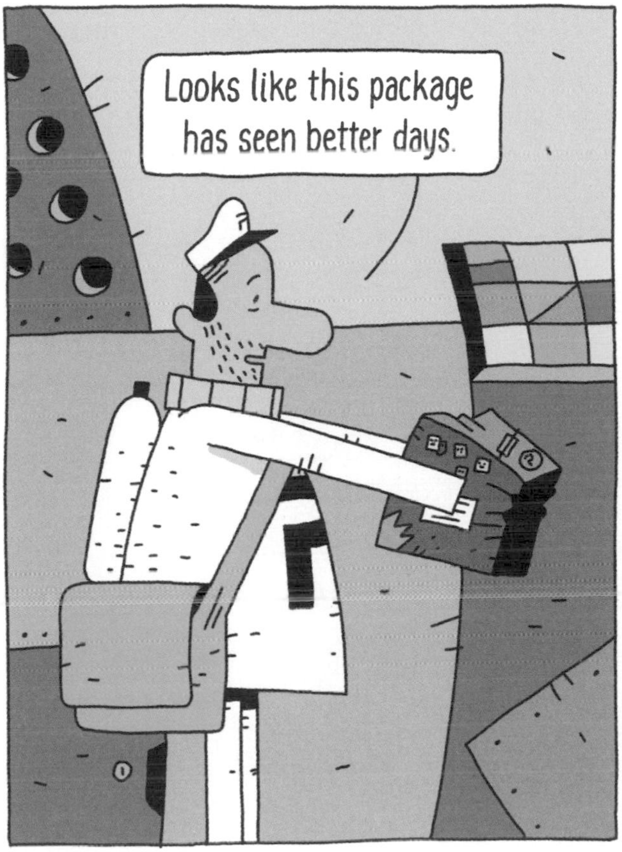
Looks like this package has seen better days.

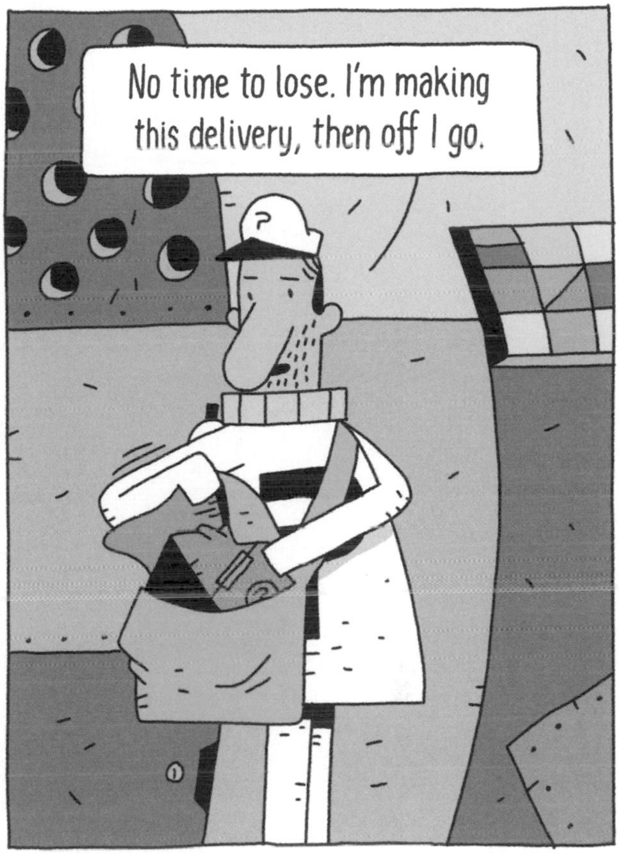
No time to lose. I'm making this delivery, then off I go.

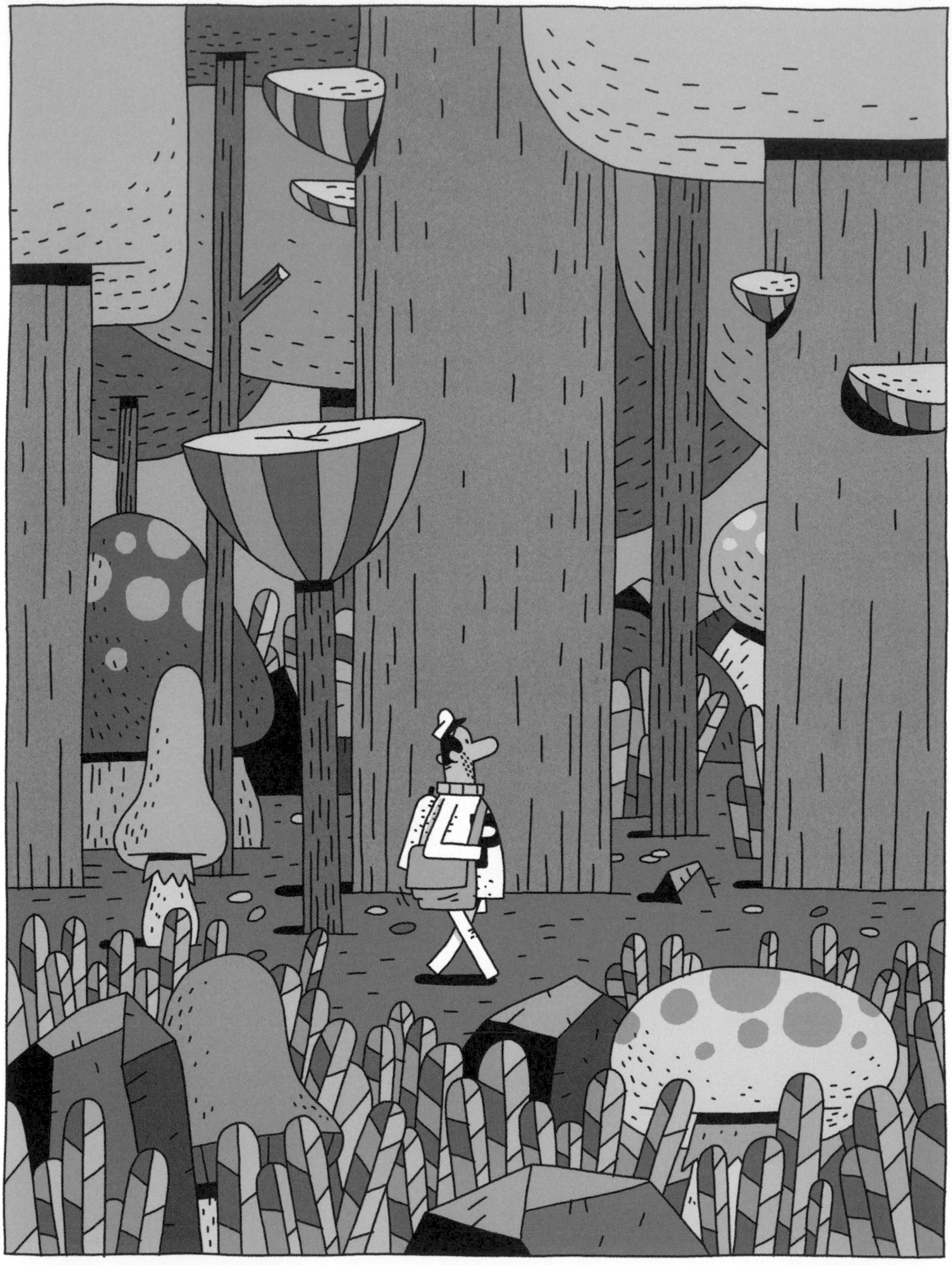

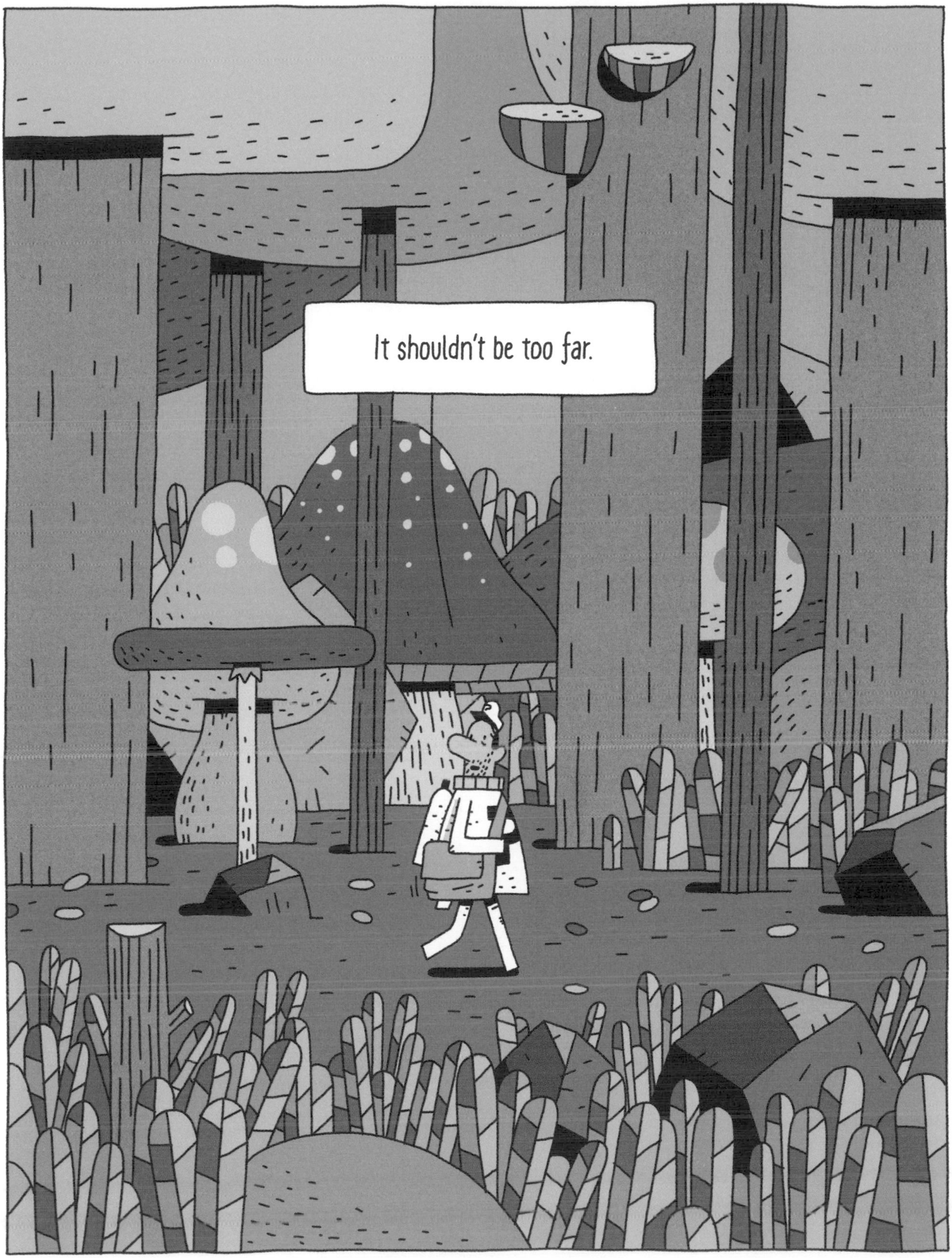
It shouldn't be too far.

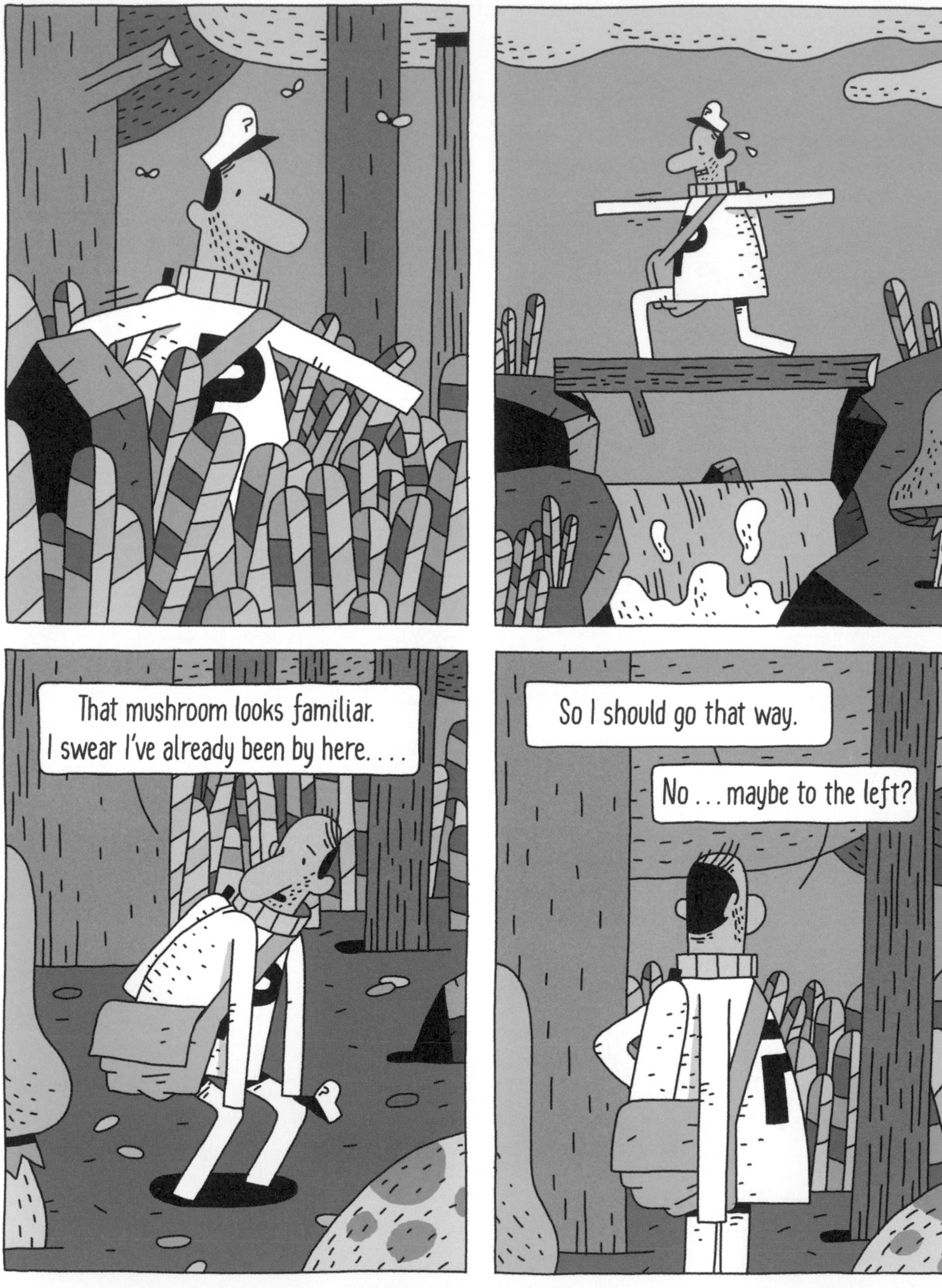
That mushroom looks familiar.
I swear I've already been by here. . . .
So I should go that way.
No . . . maybe to the left?

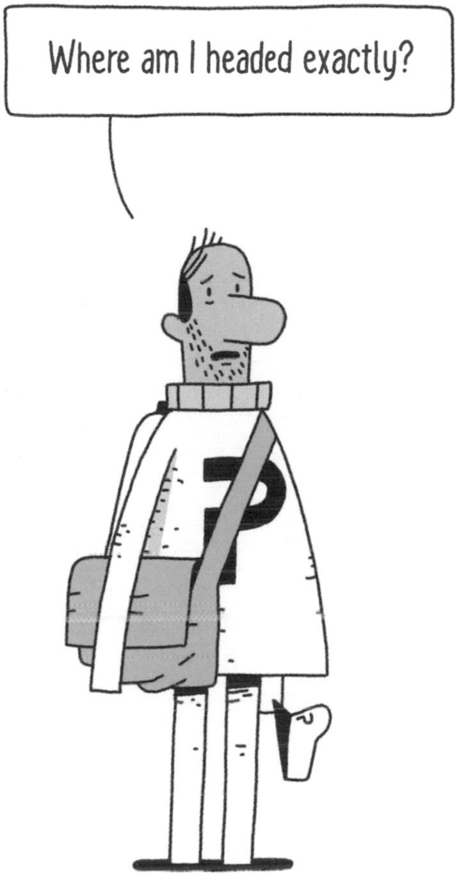
Where am I headed exactly?

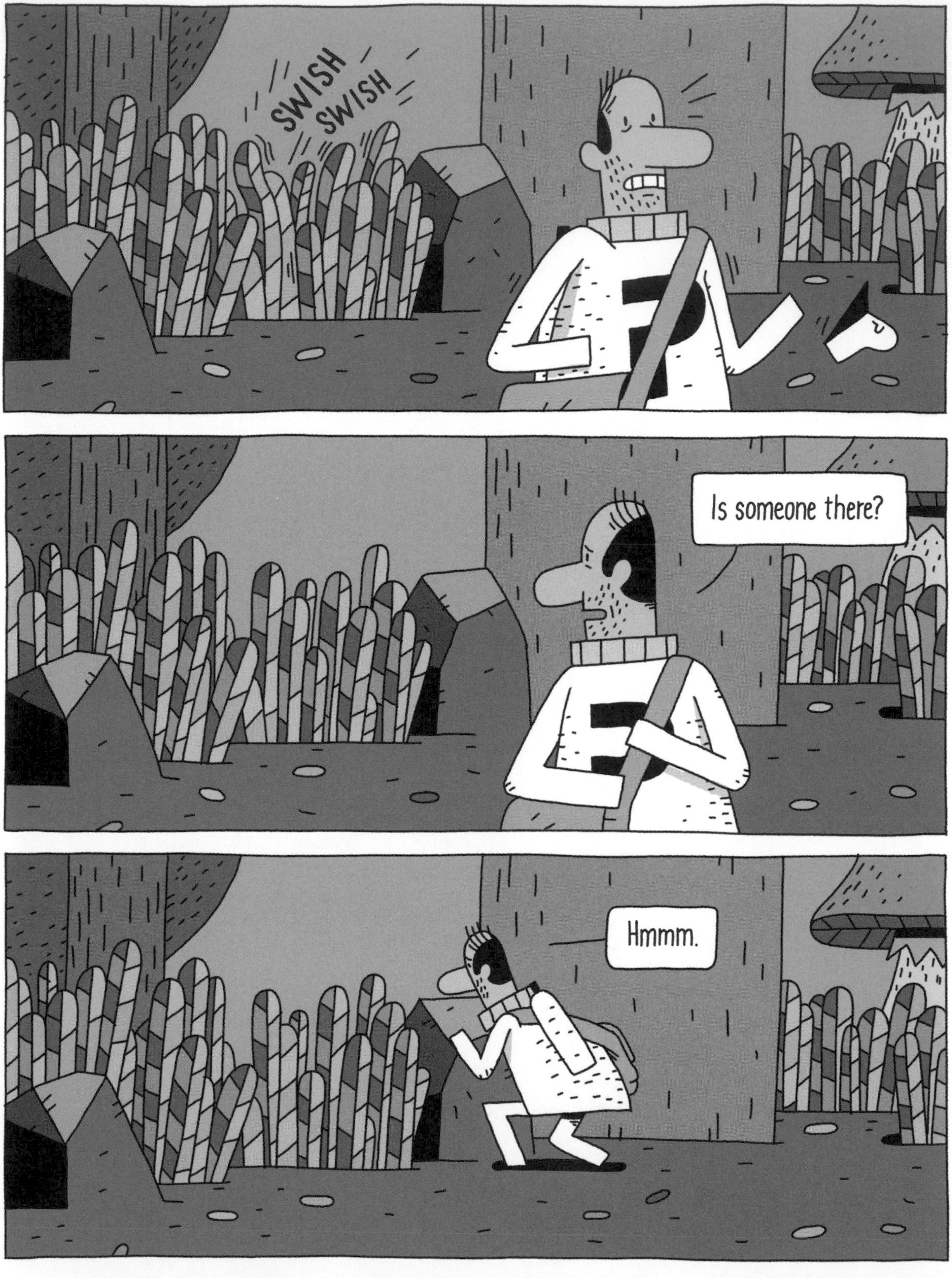
SWISH
SWISH
Is someone there?
Hmmm.

Must be my imagination.

But I'm not sticking around. Let's try going that way.

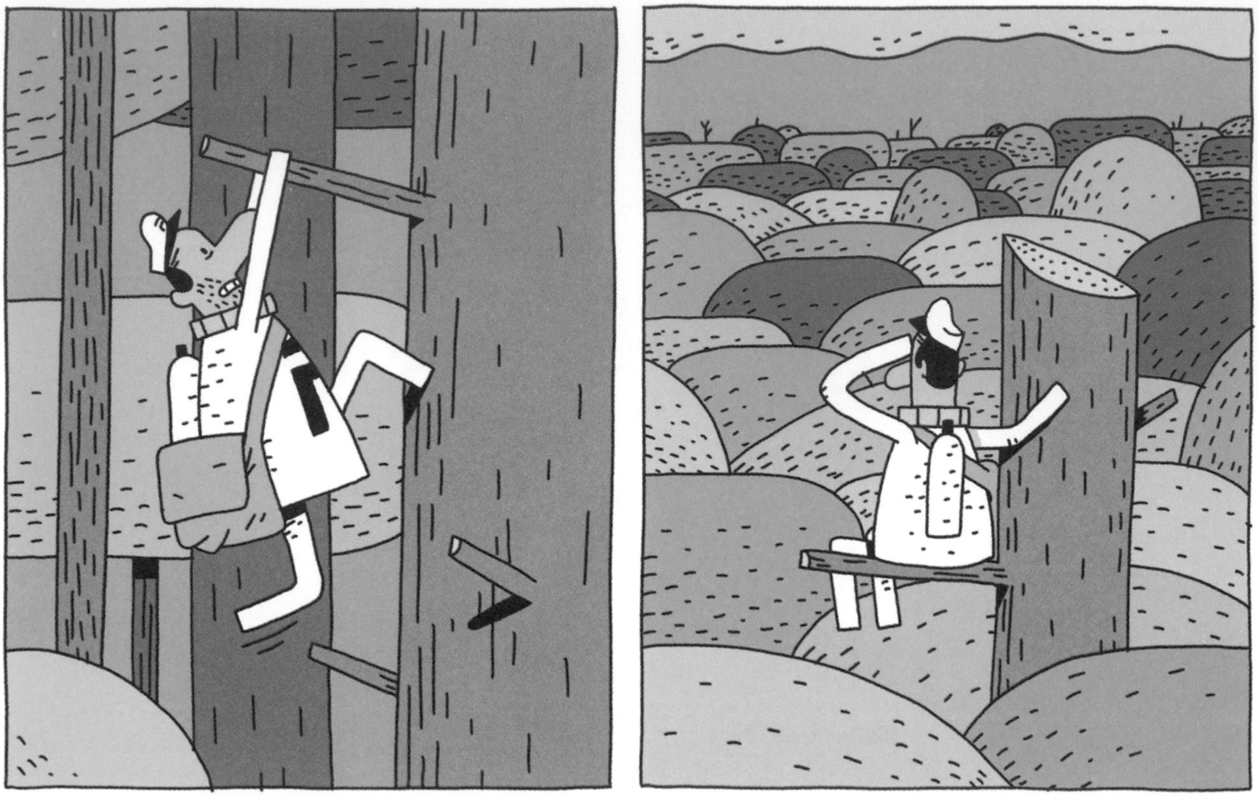

Our friend the postman has no idea where to make the delivery.

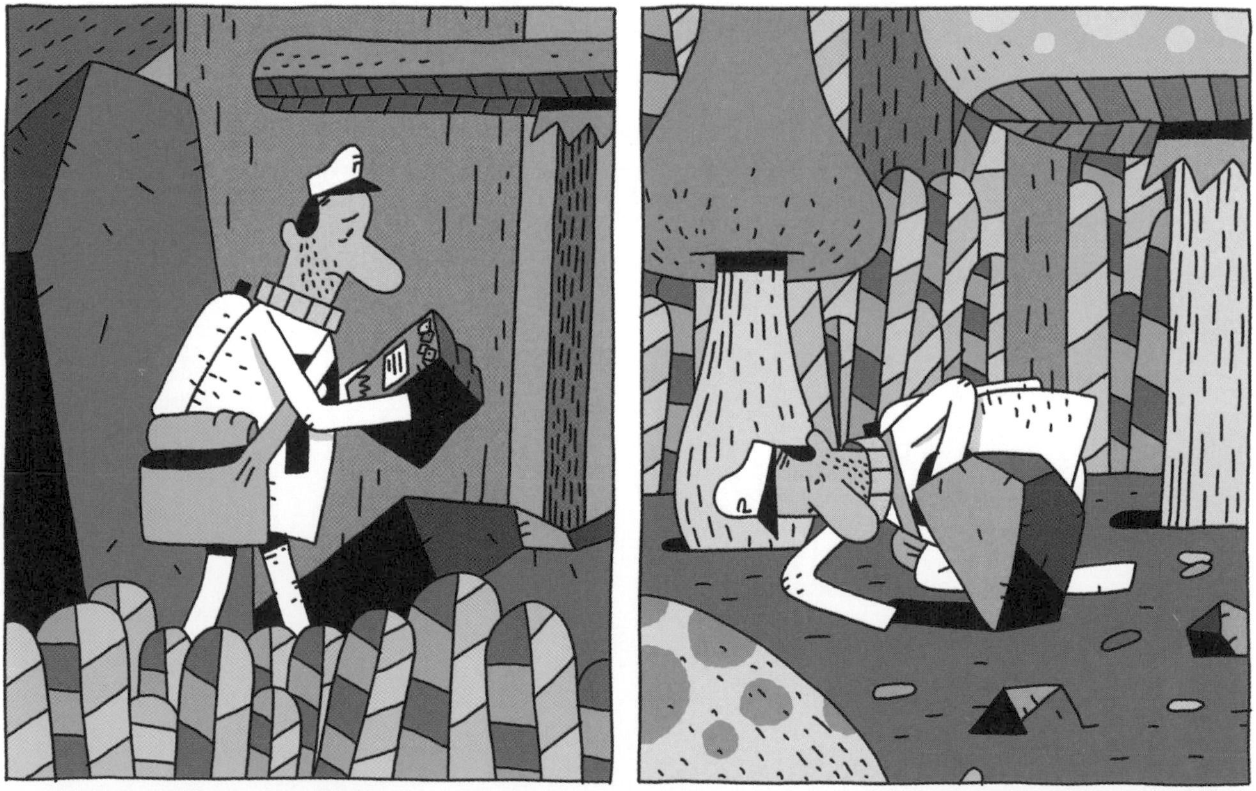

In fact, Bob has no idea where he is.

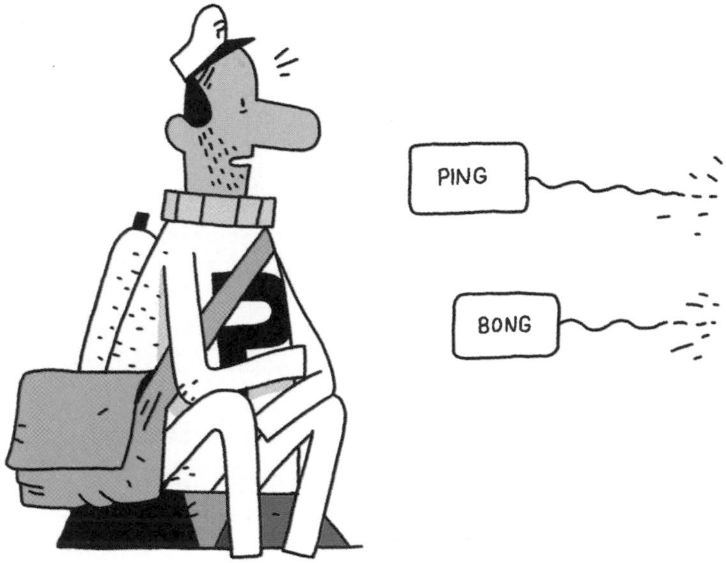
PING
BONG

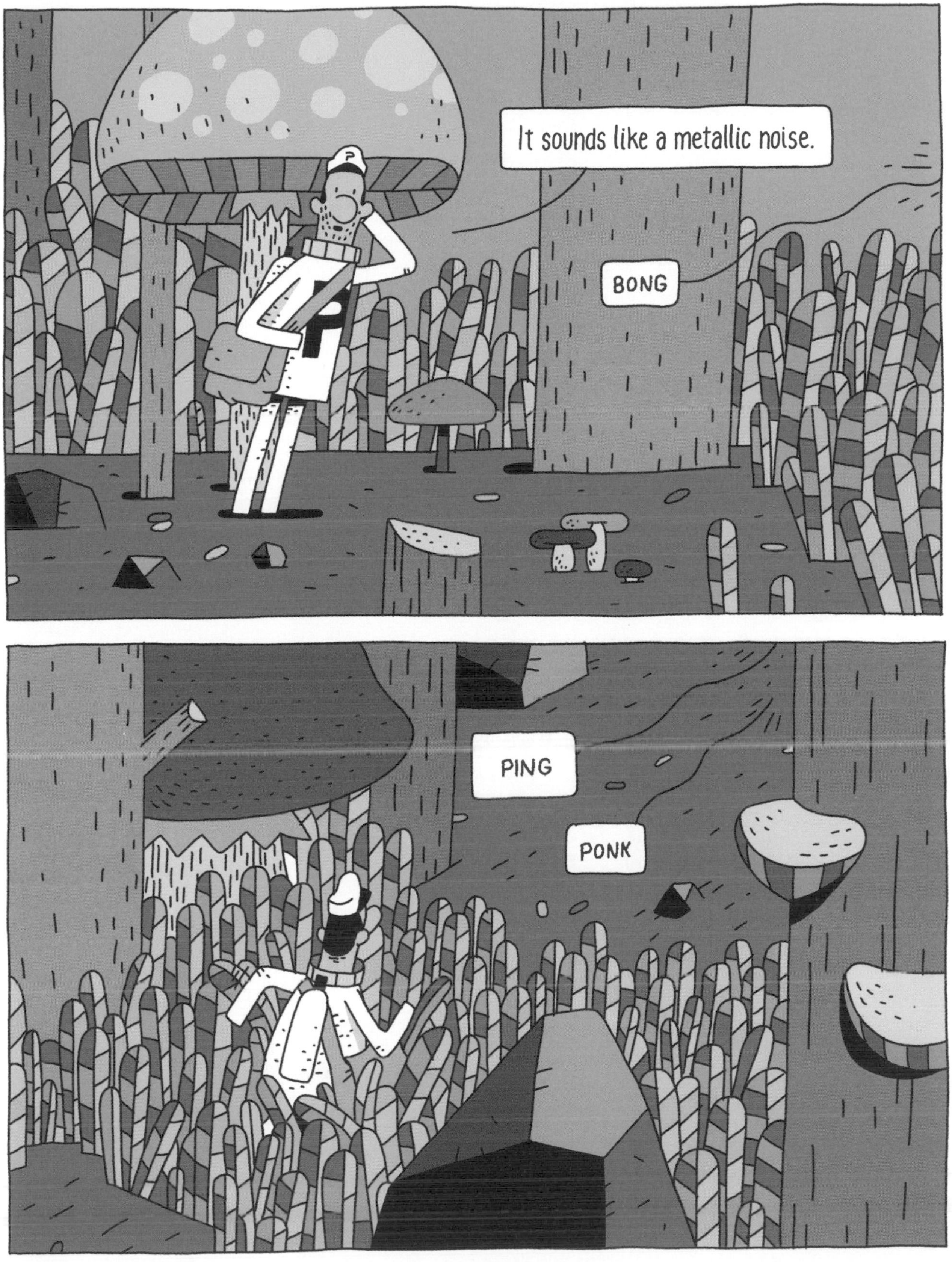
It sounds like a metallic noise.
BONG
PING
PONK

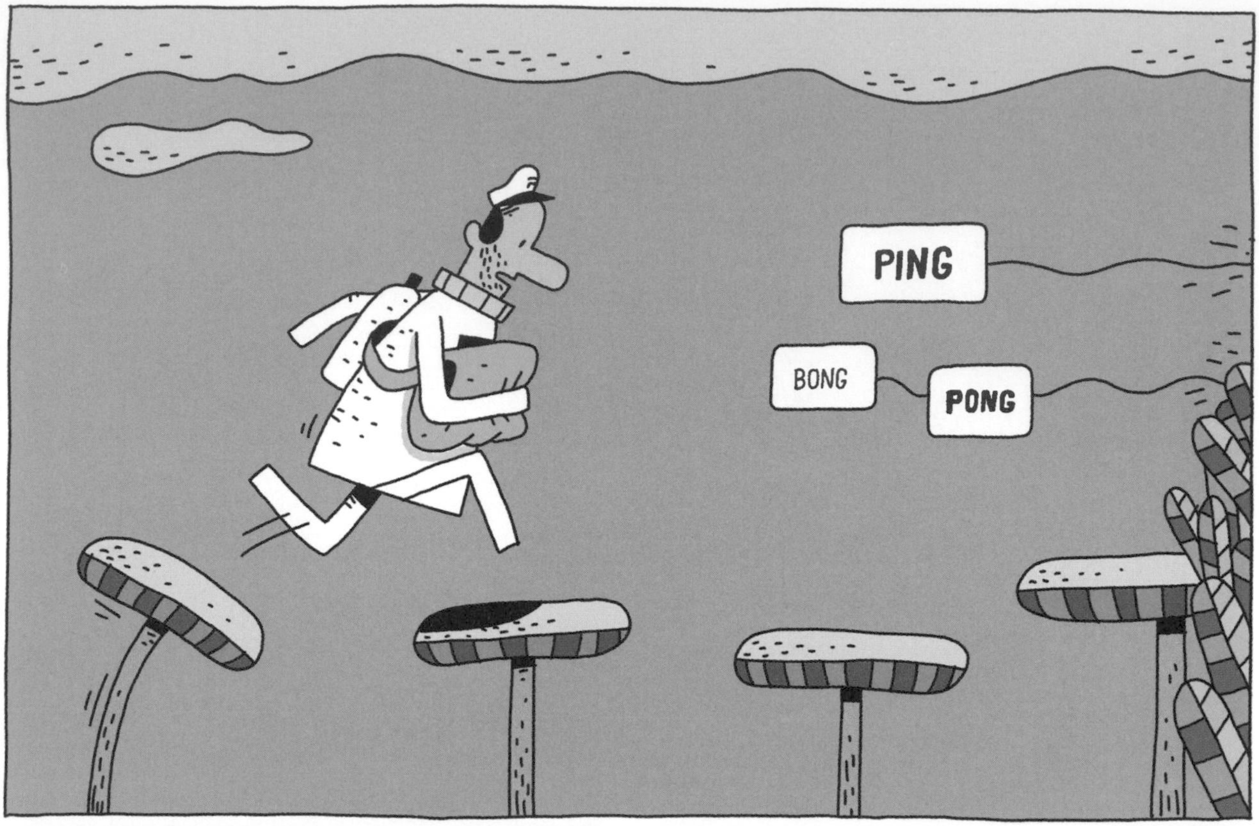

PING
BONG
PONG

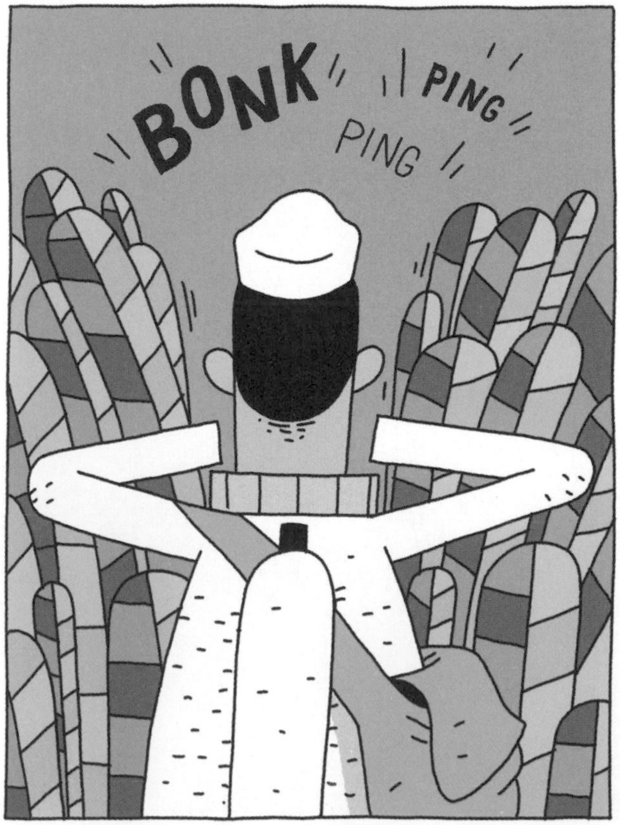

BONK
PING
PING

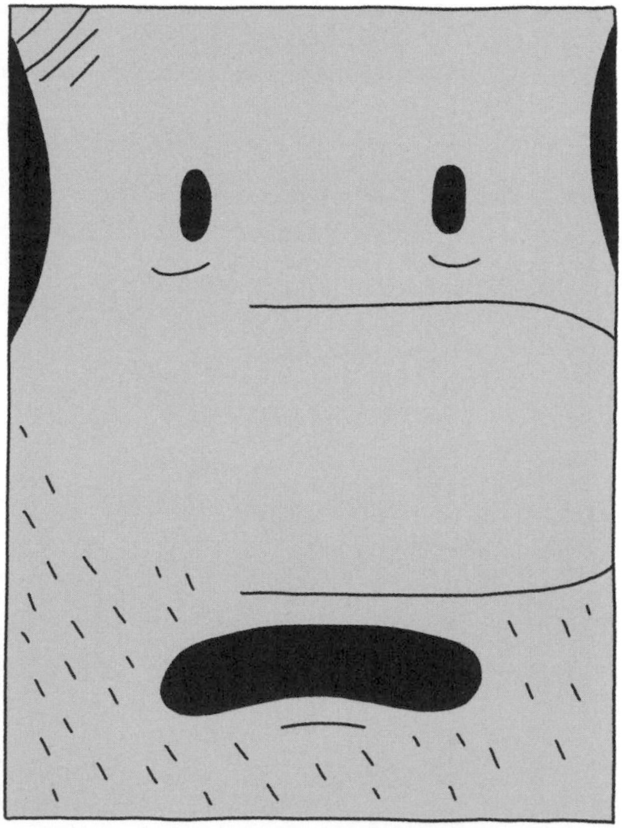

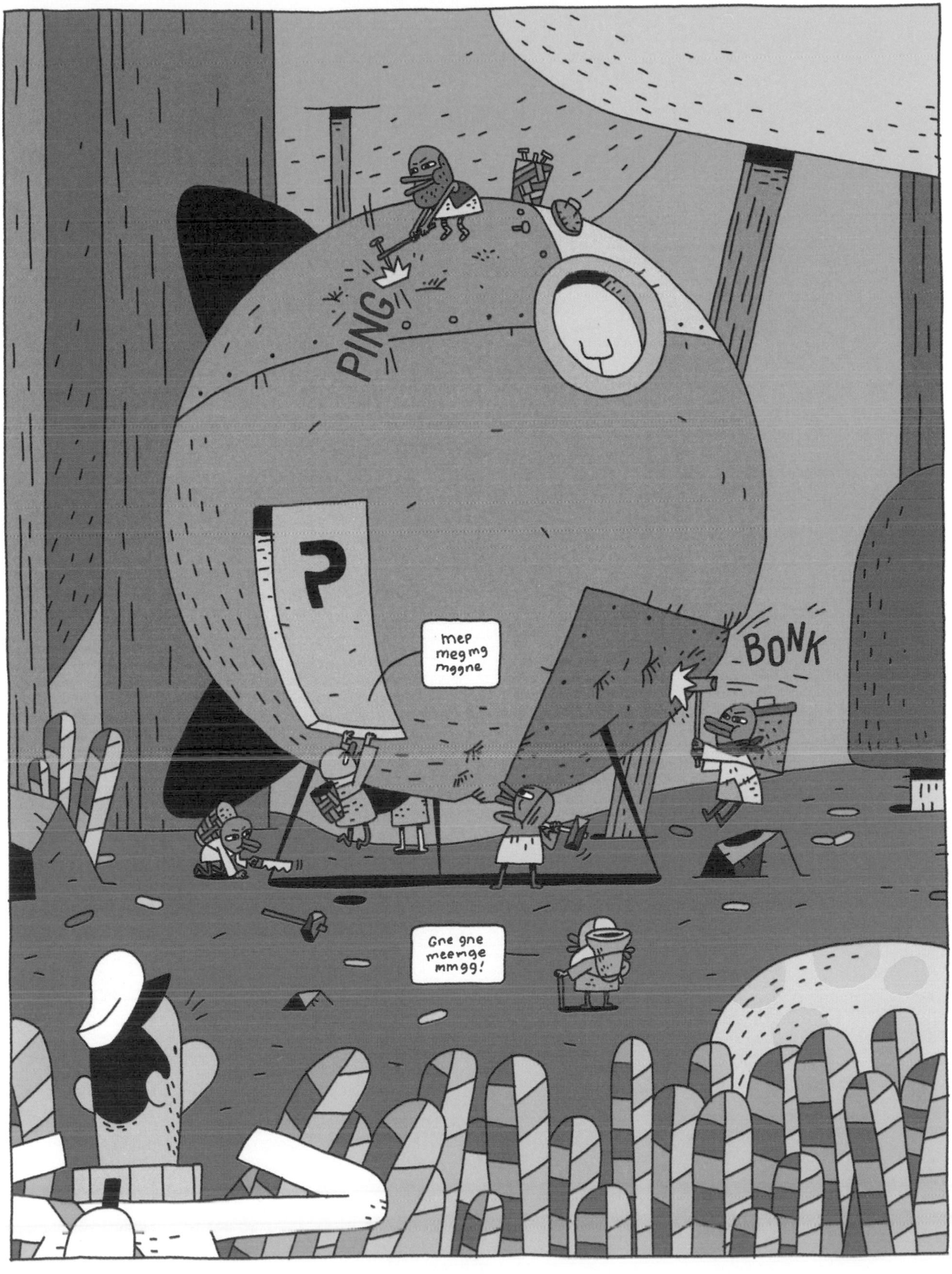
PING
mep megmg mggne
BONK
Gne gne meenge mmgg!

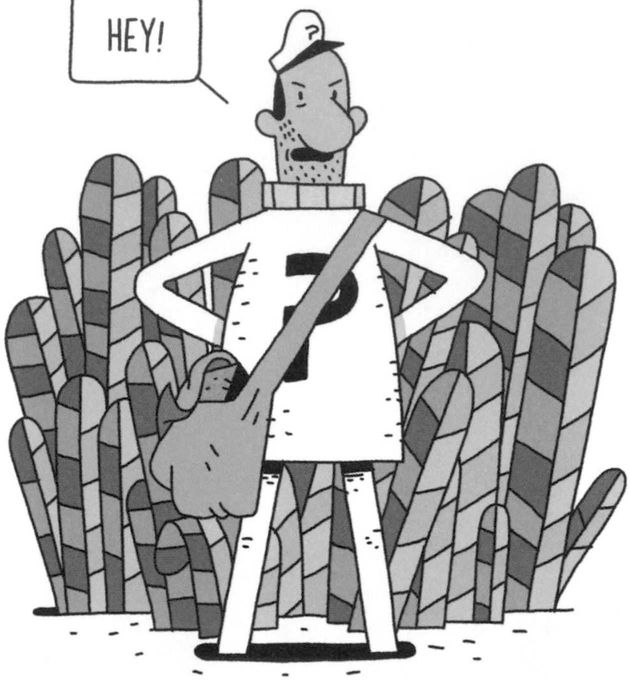
HEY!

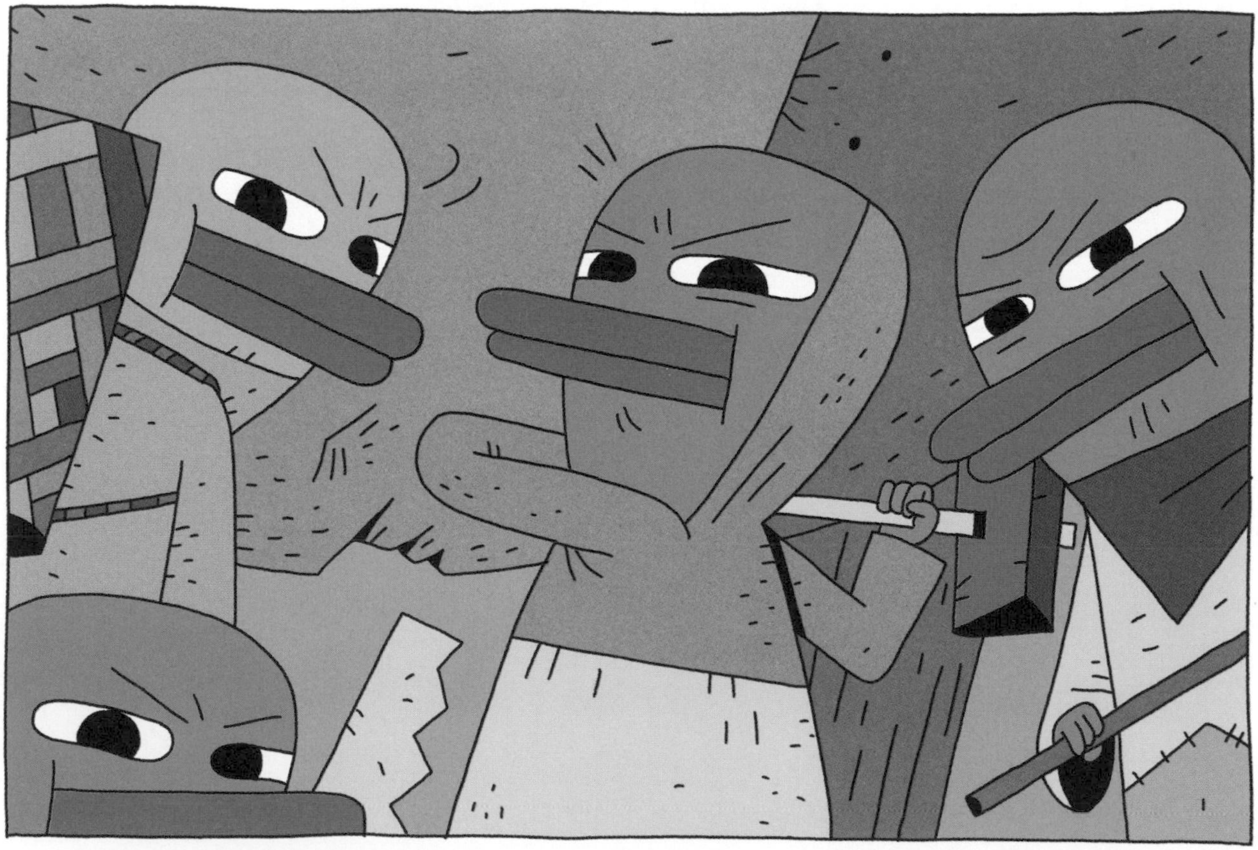

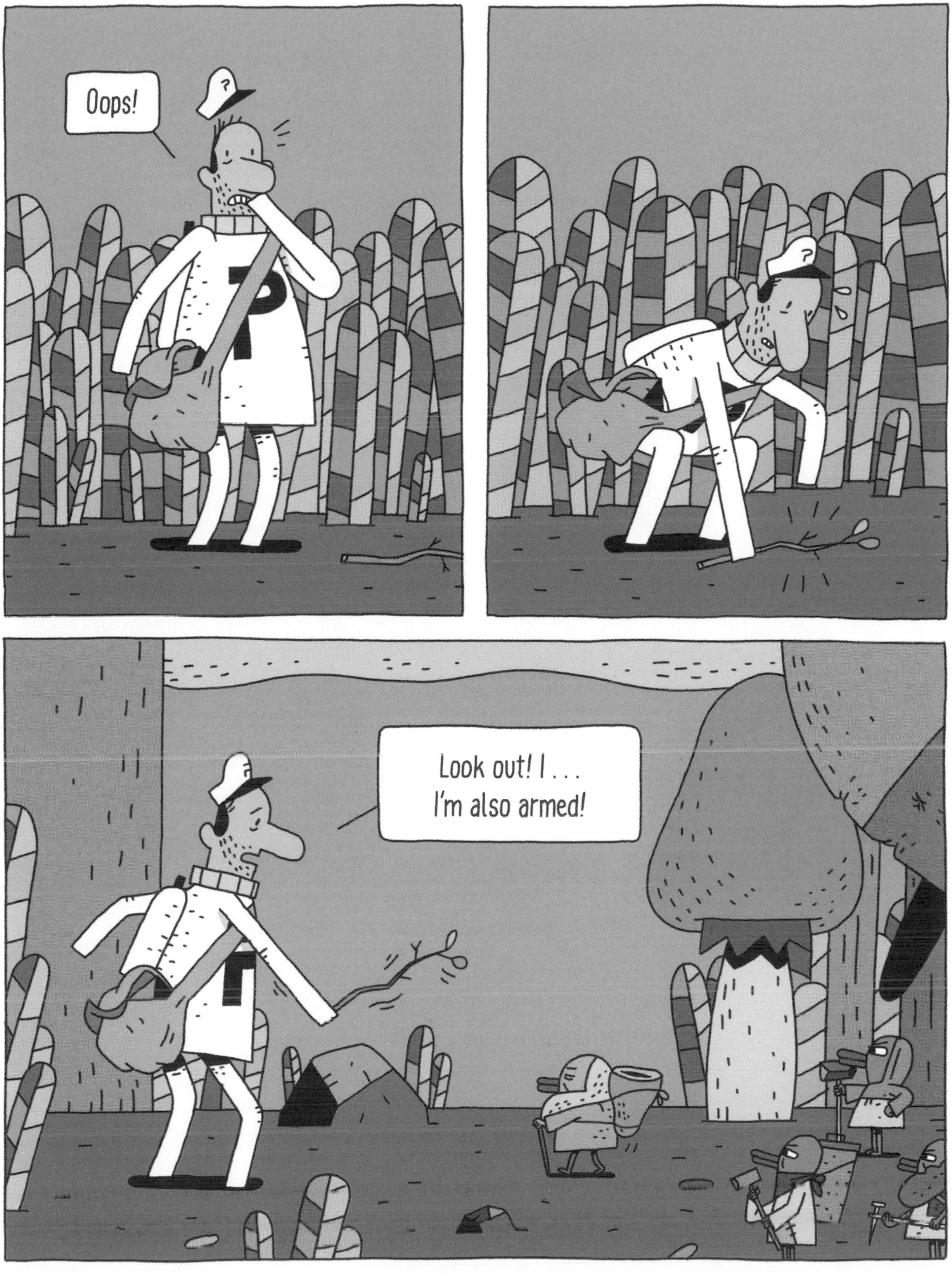
Oops!
Look out! I . . .
I'm also armed!

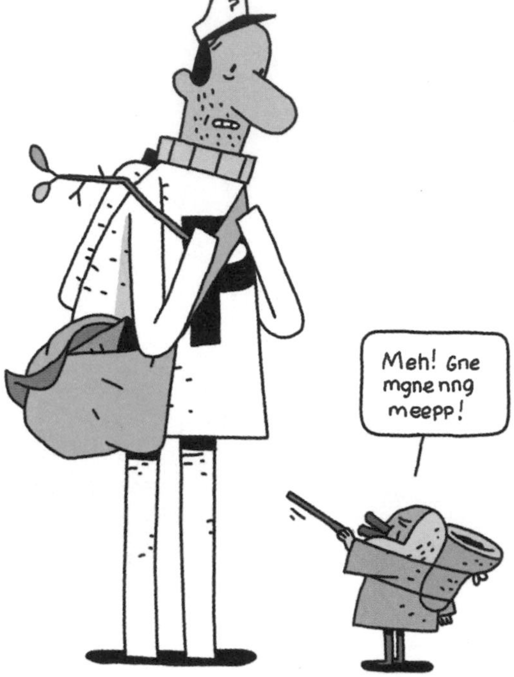
Meh! Gne mgne nng meepp!

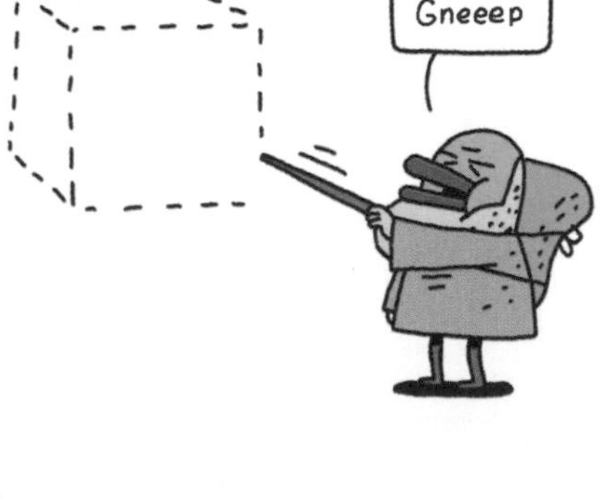
Gneeep

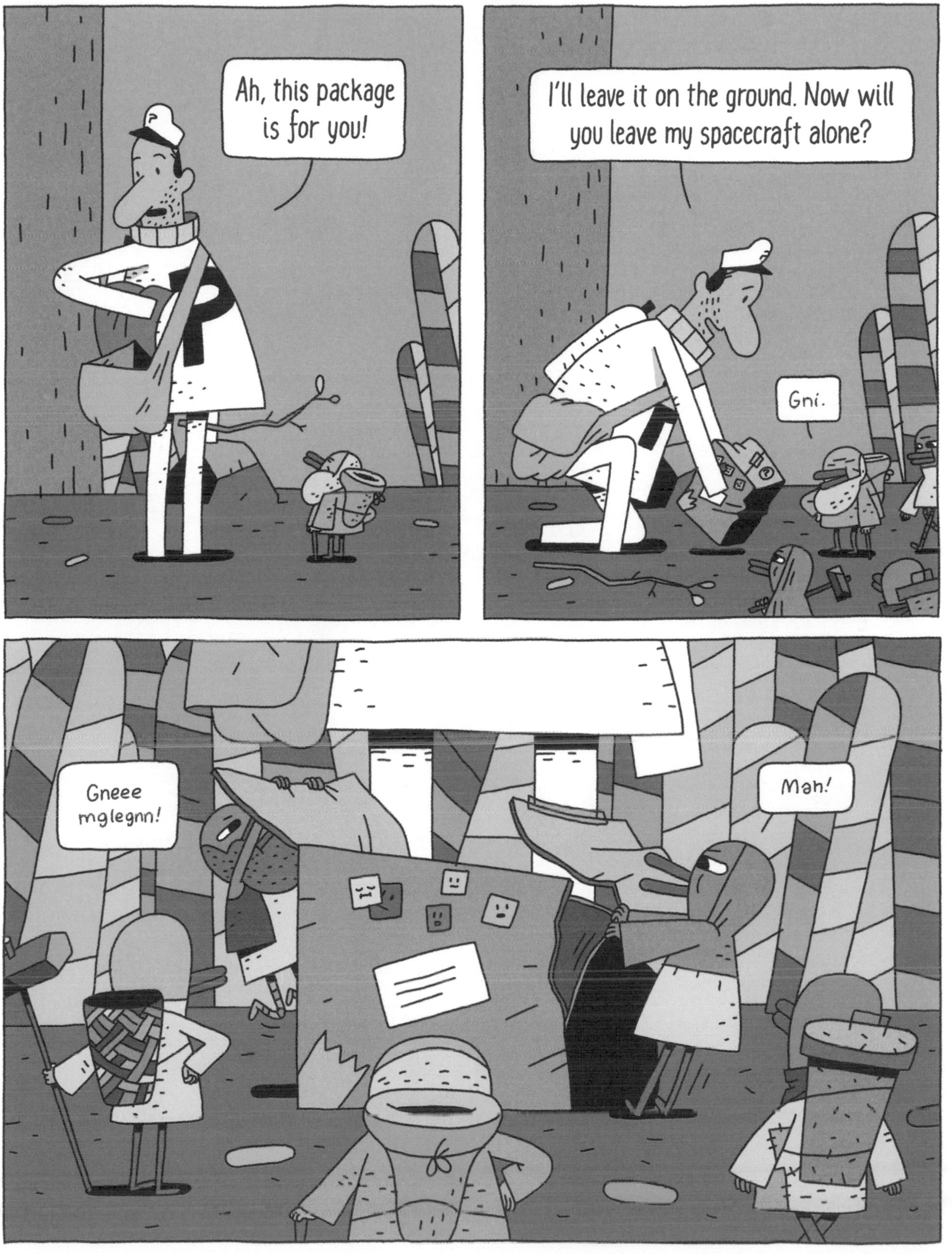
Ah, this package is for you!
I'll leave it on the ground. Now will you leave my spacecraft alone?
Gní.
Gneee mglegnn!
Mah!

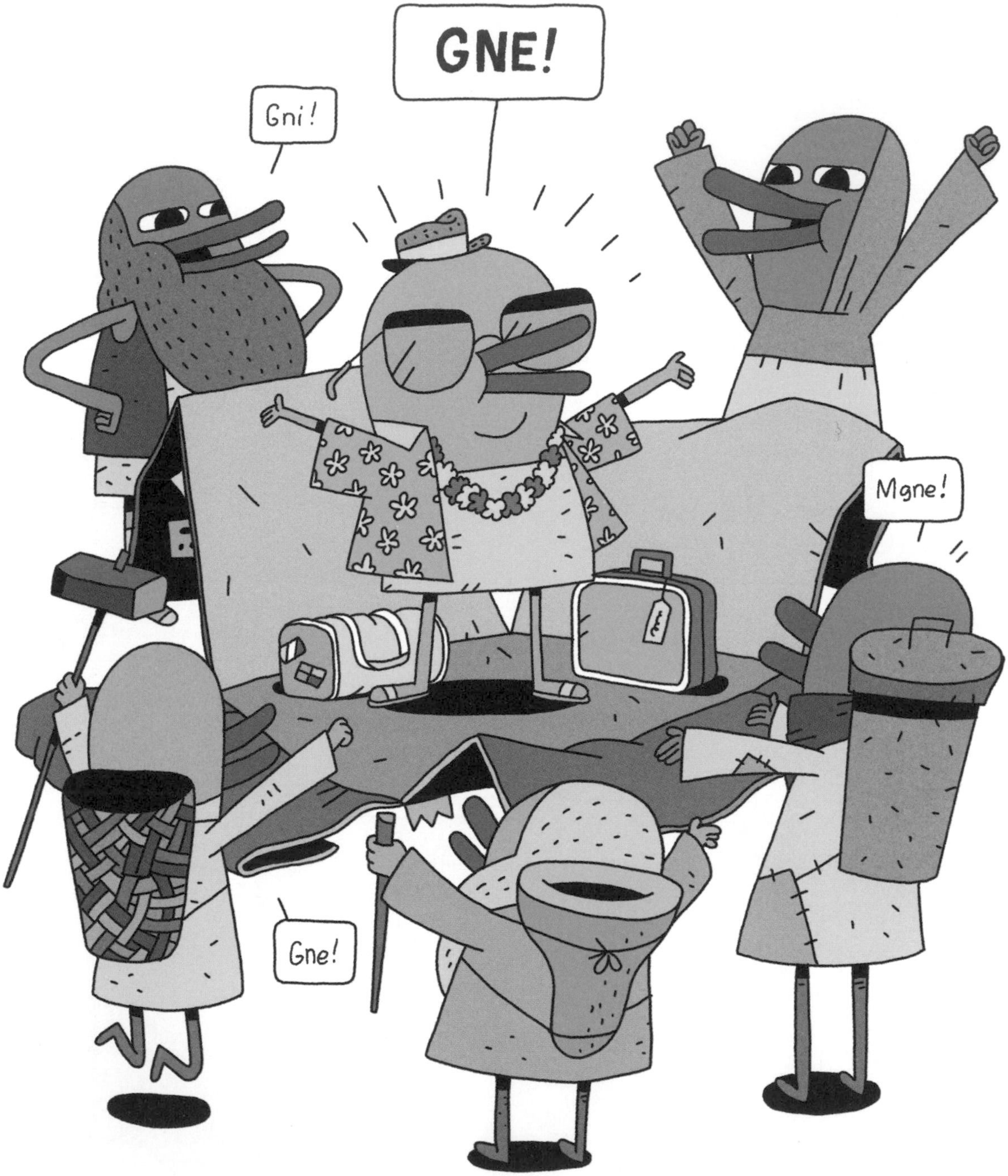
GNE!
Gni!
Mgne!
Gne!

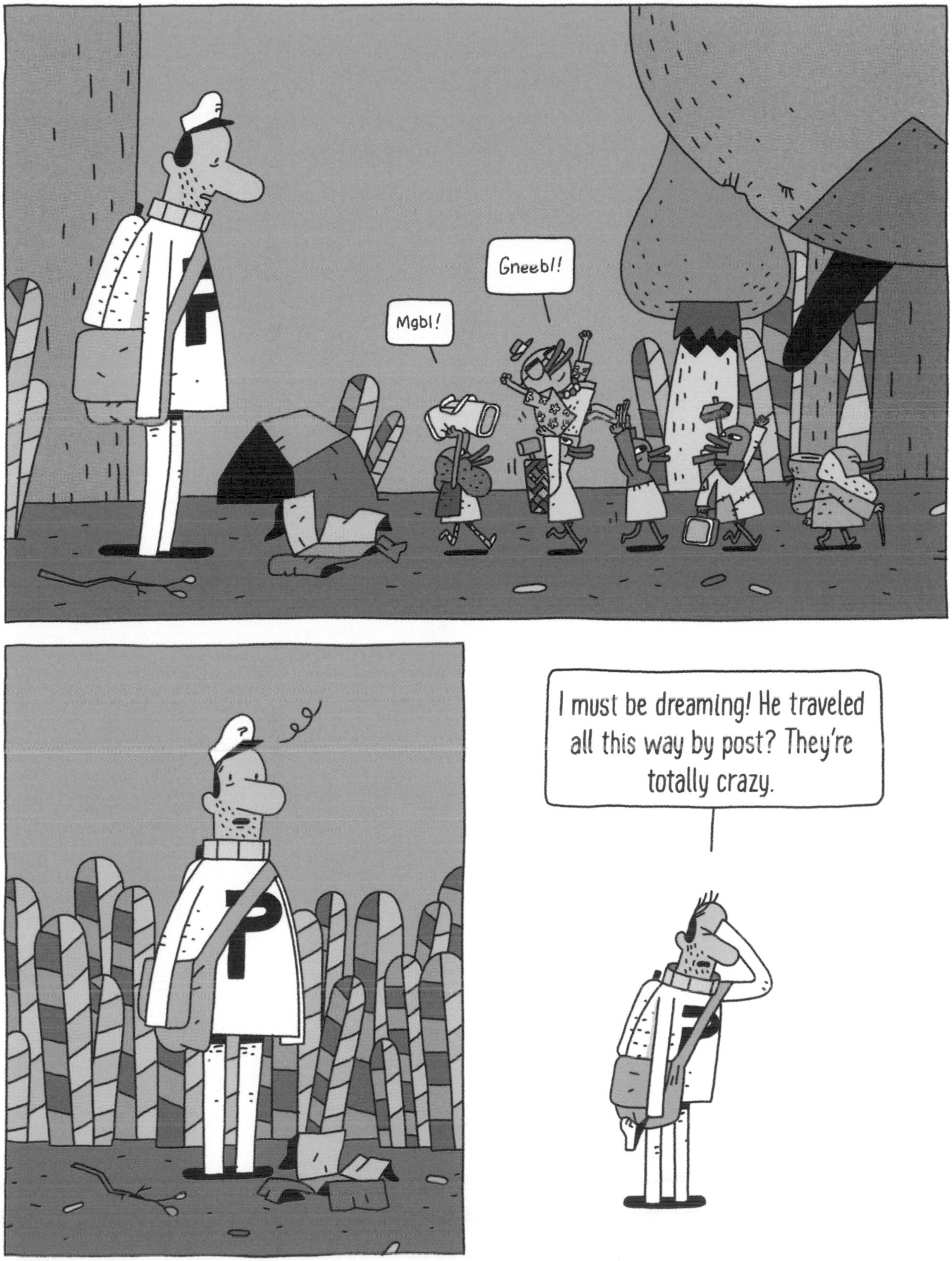
Mgbl!
Gneebl!
I must be dreaming! He traveled all this way by post? They're totally crazy.

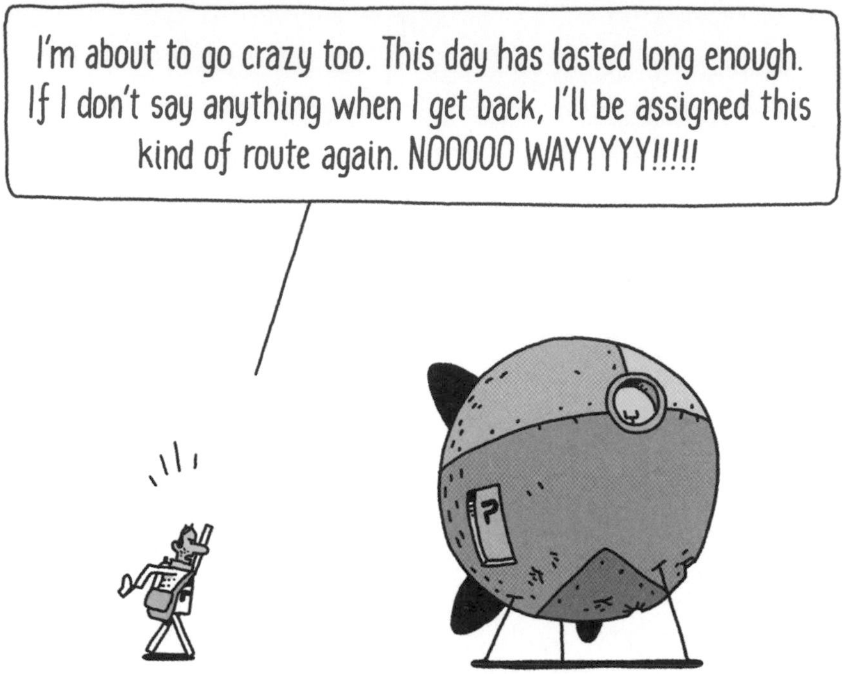
I'm about to go crazy too. This day has lasted long enough. If I don't say anything when I get back, I'll be assigned this kind of route again. NOOOOO WAYYYYY!!!!!

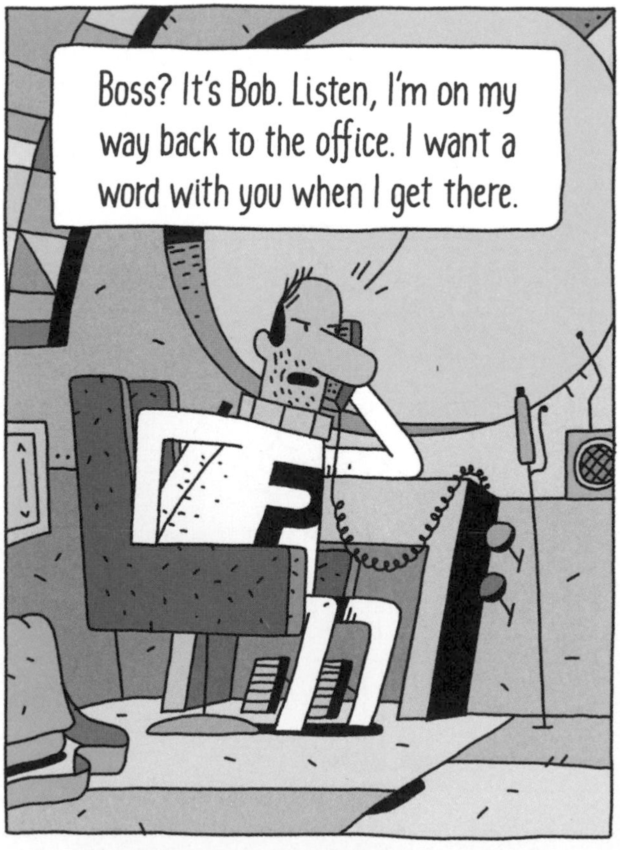
Boss? It's Bob. Listen, I'm on my way back to the office. I want a word with you when I get there.

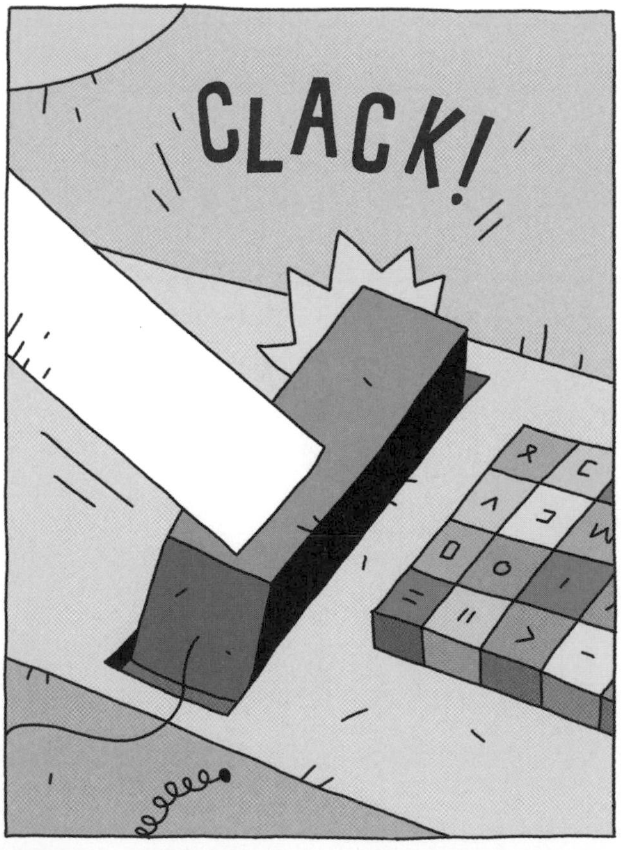
CLACK!

THE RETURN

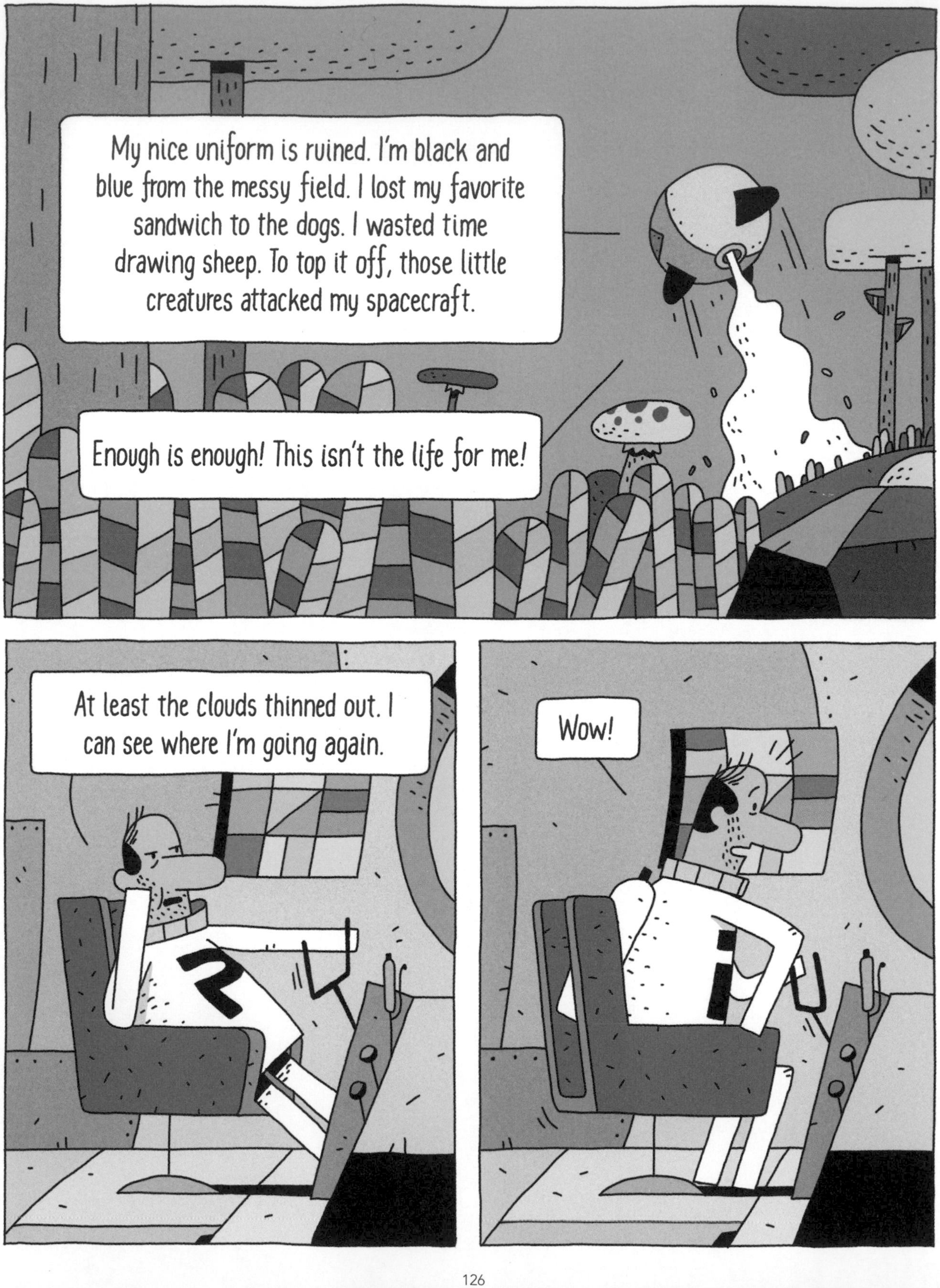
My nice uniform is ruined. I'm black and blue from the messy field. I lost my favorite sandwich to the dogs. I wasted time drawing sheep. To top it off, those little creatures attacked my spacecraft.
Enough is enough! This isn't the life for me!
At least the clouds thinned out. I can see where I'm going again.
Wow!

It's amazing!

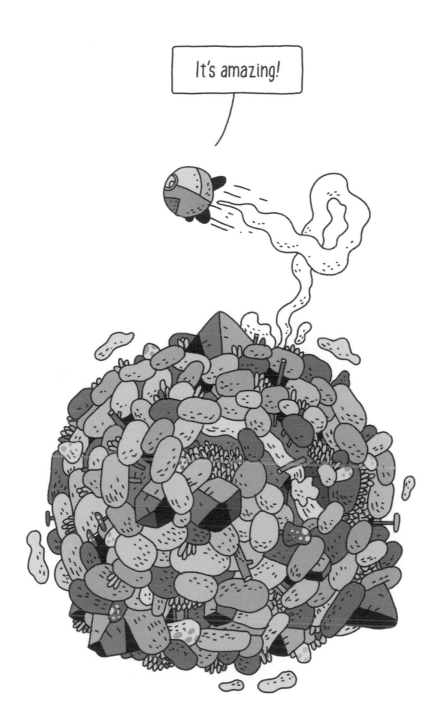

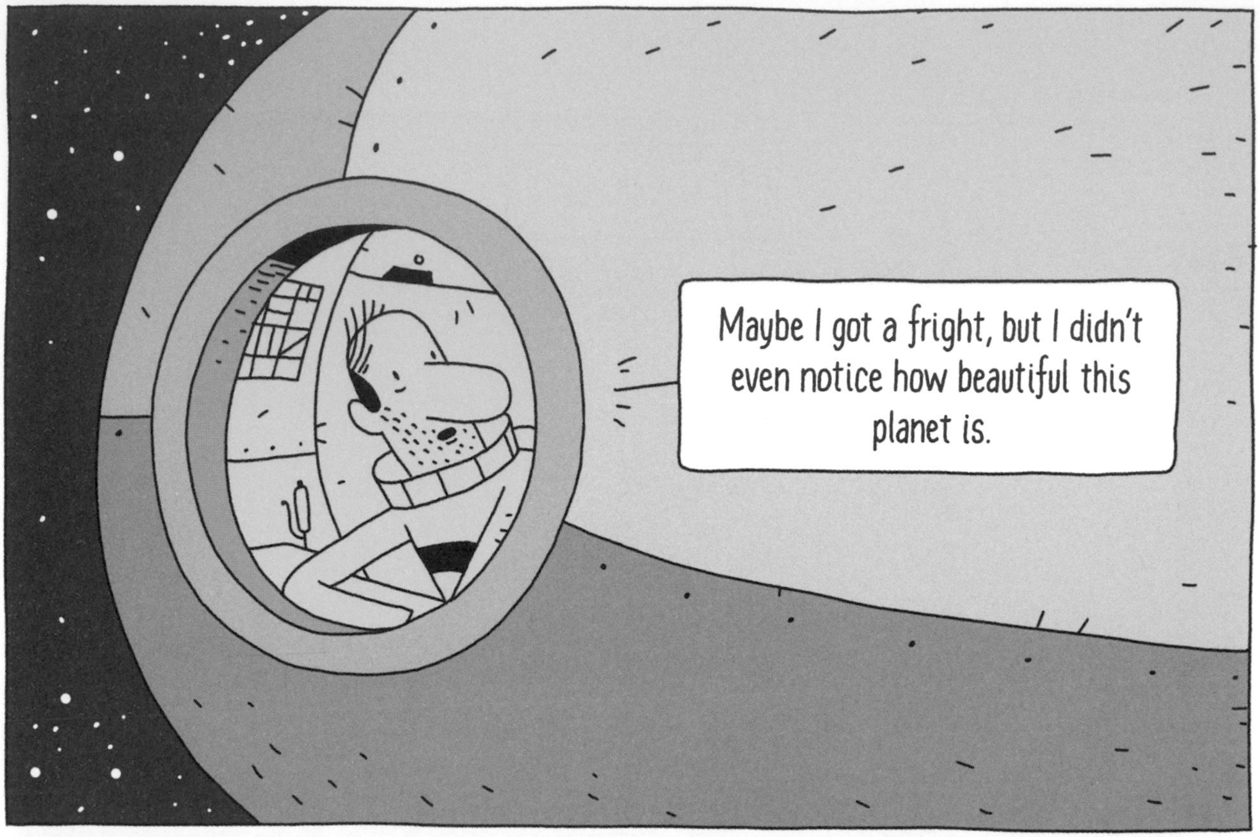
Maybe I got a fright, but I didn't even notice how beautiful this planet is.

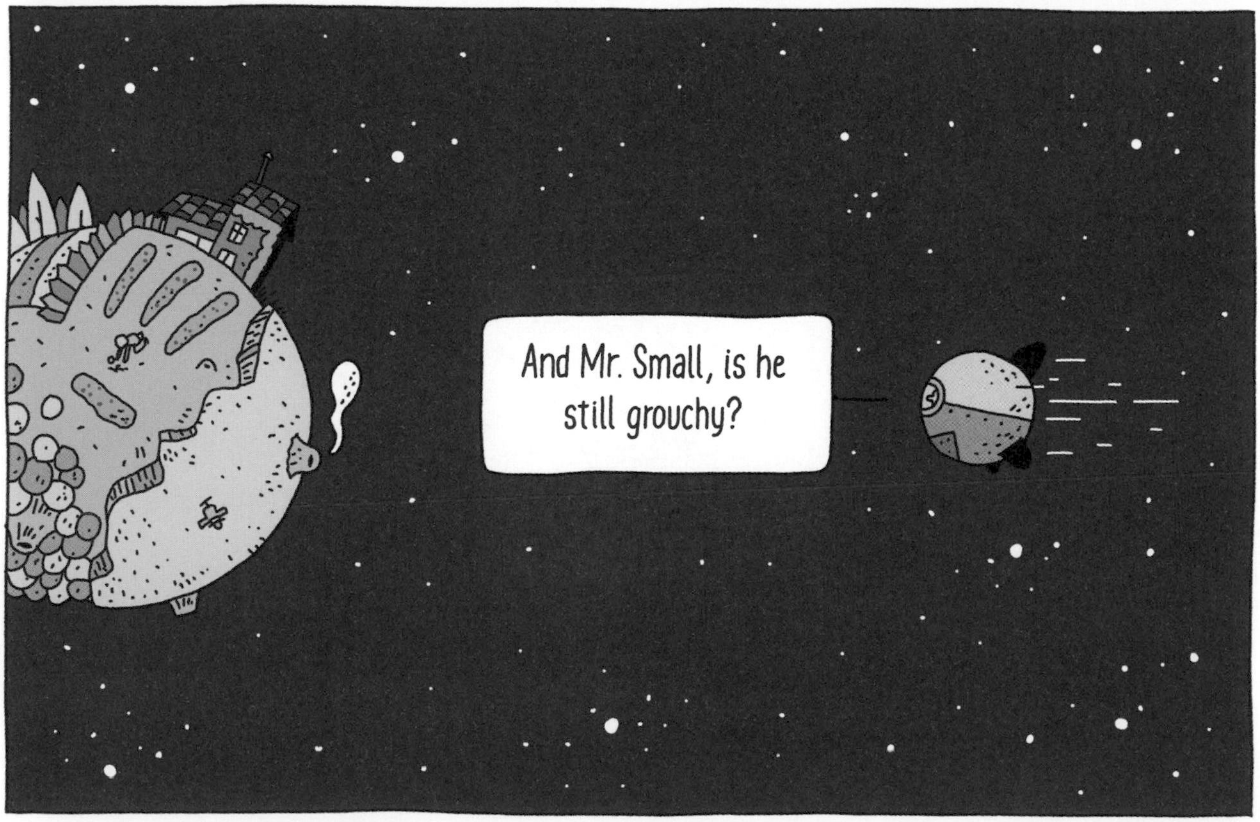
And Mr. Small, is he still grouchy?

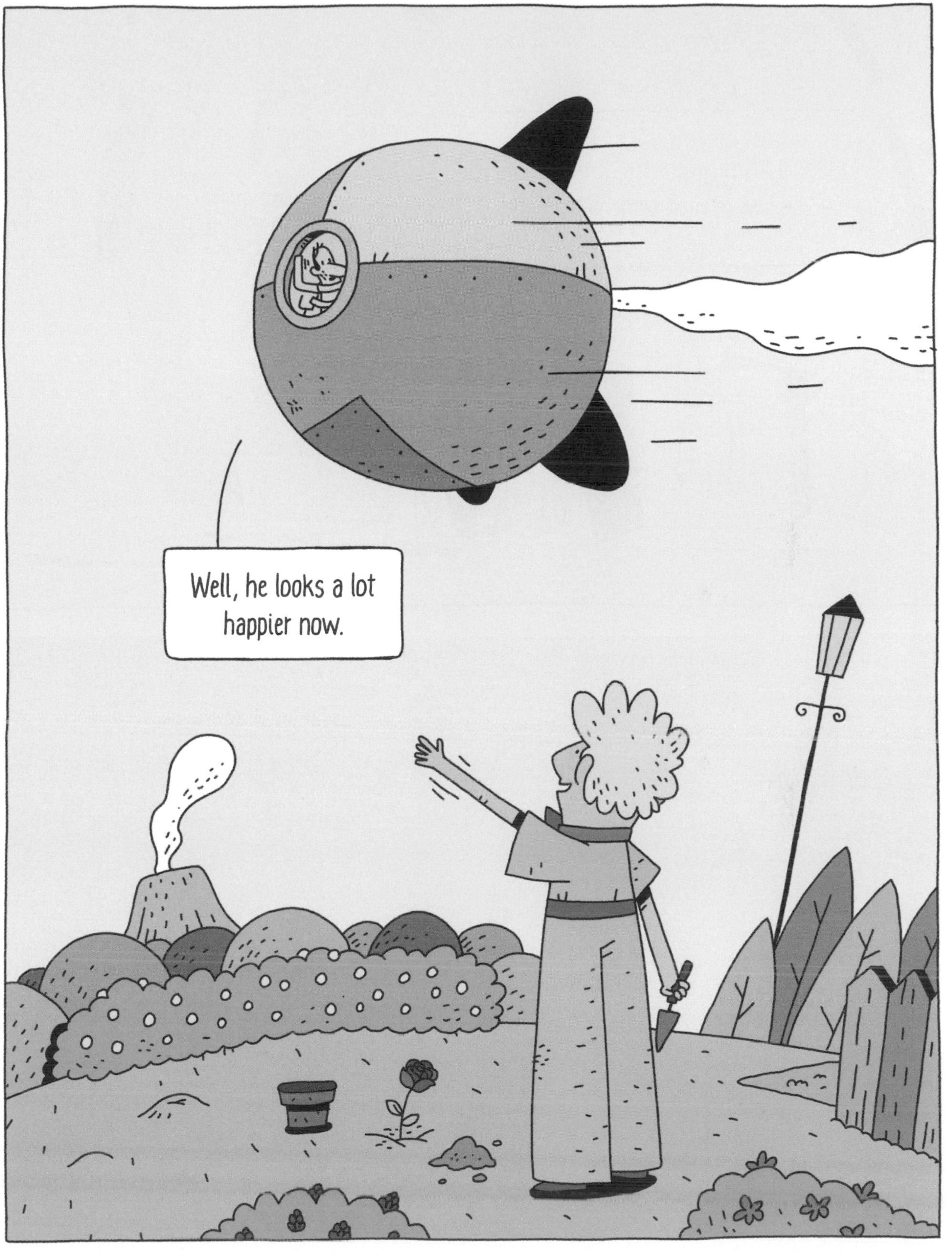
Well, he looks a lot happier now.

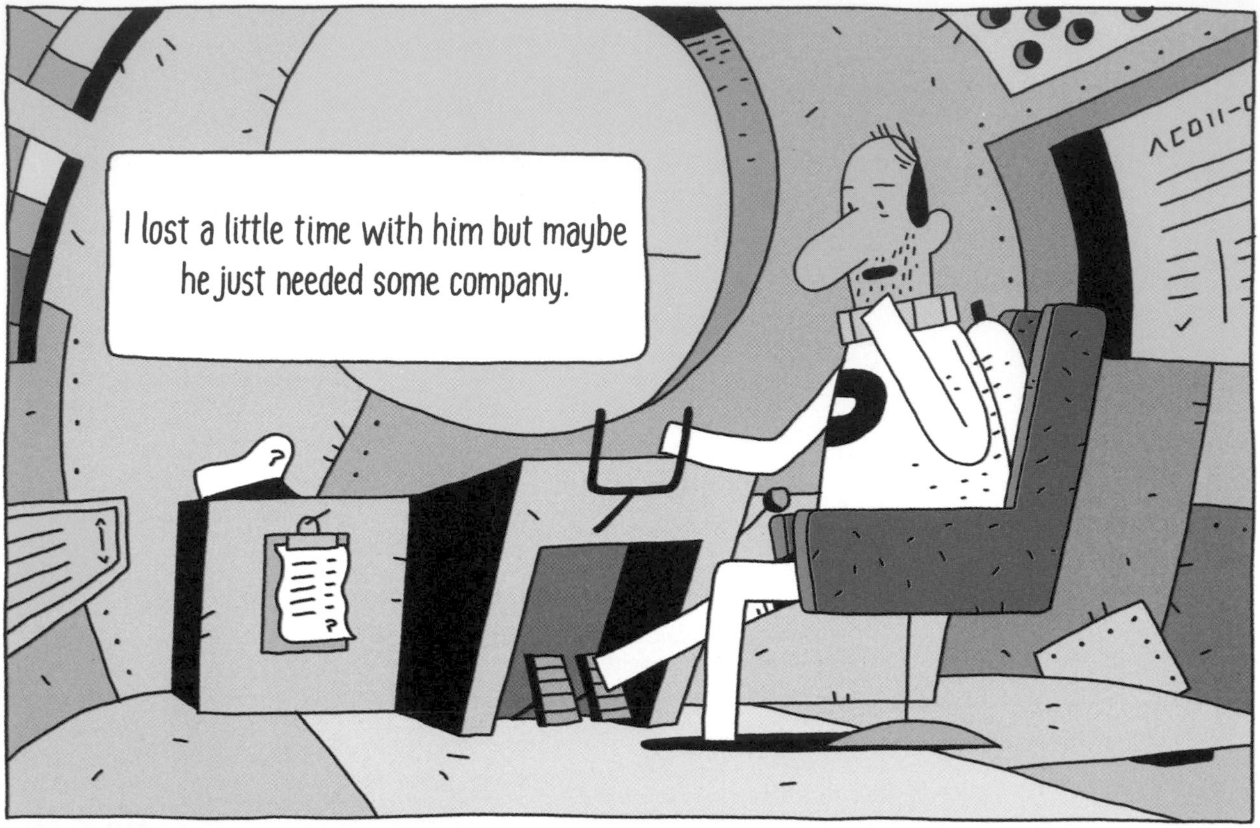
I lost a little time with him but maybe he just needed some company.
ACO11-C

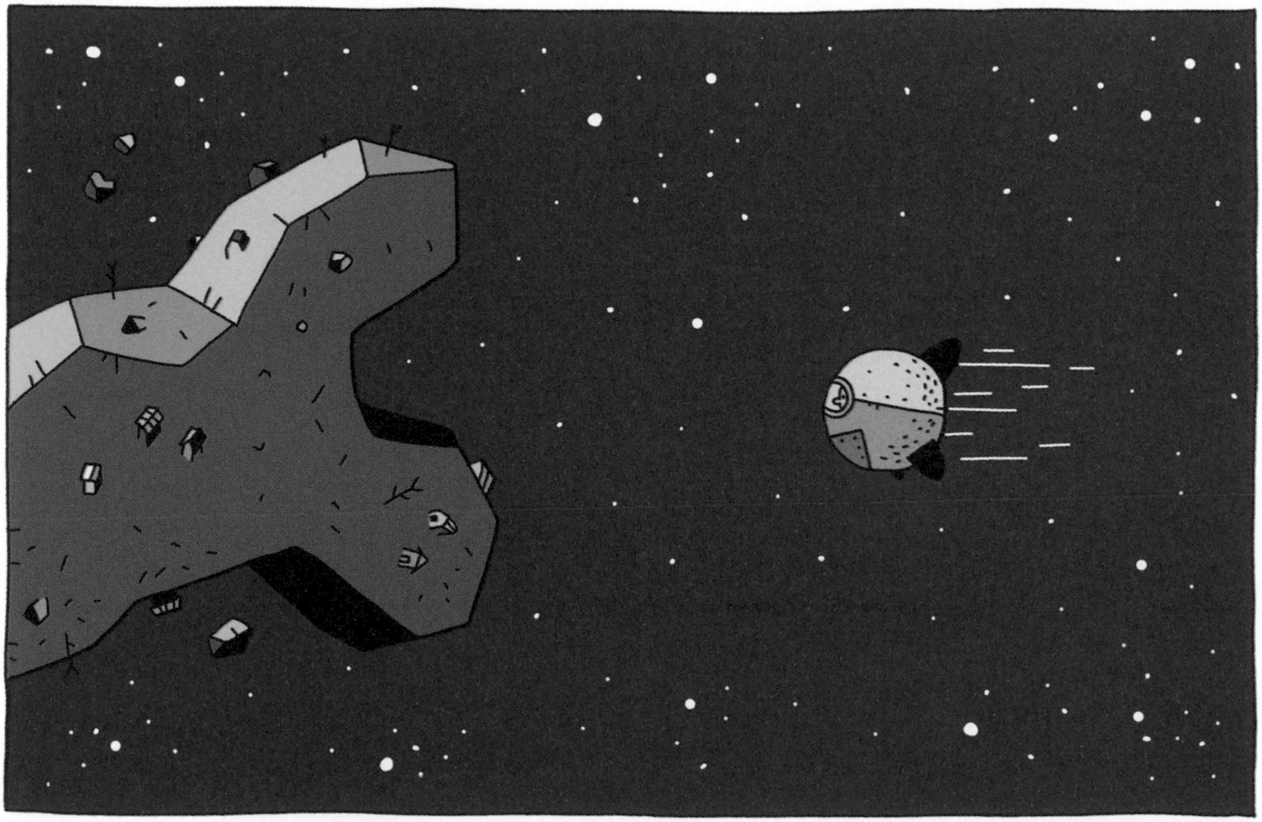

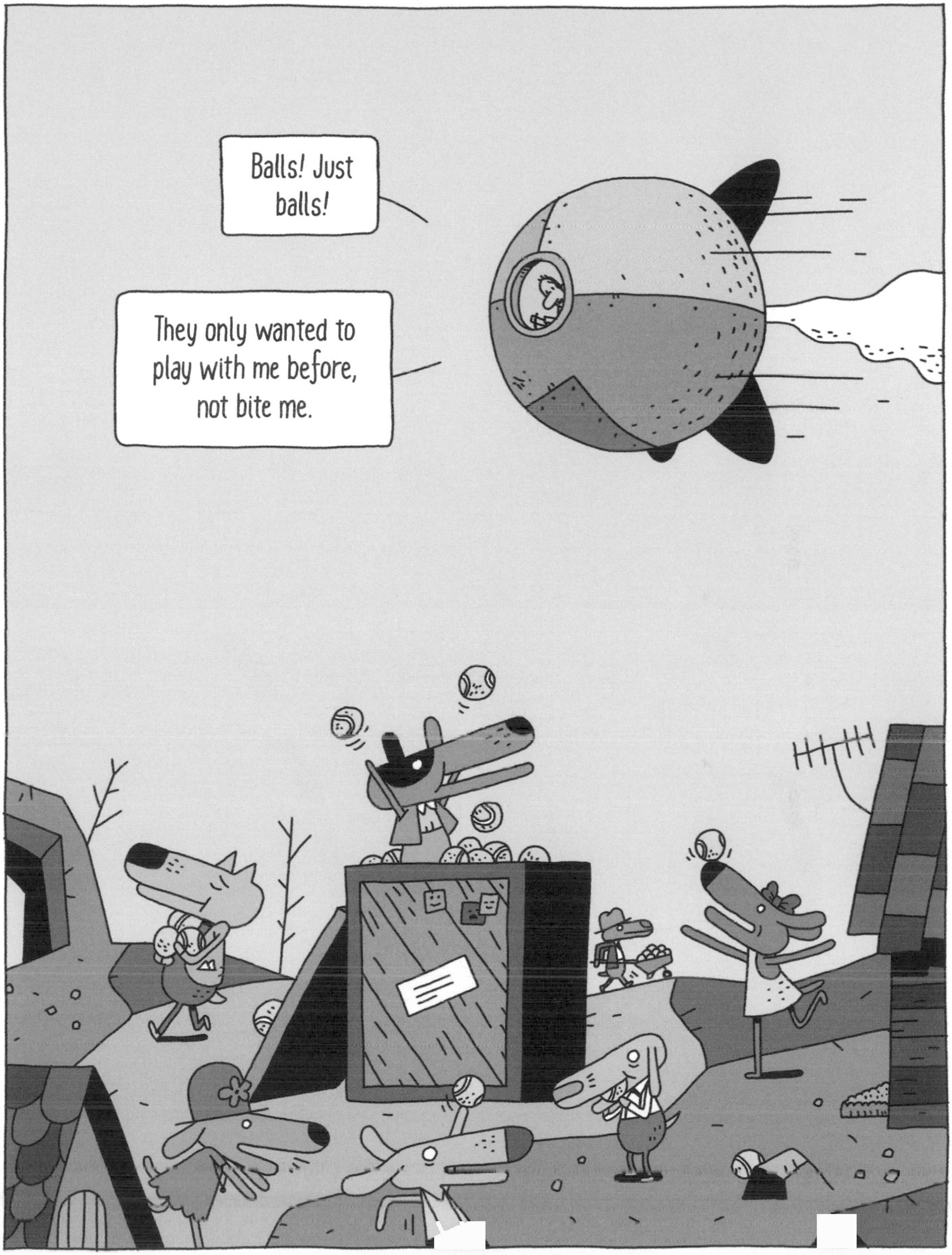
Balls! Just balls!
They only wanted to play with me before, not bite me.

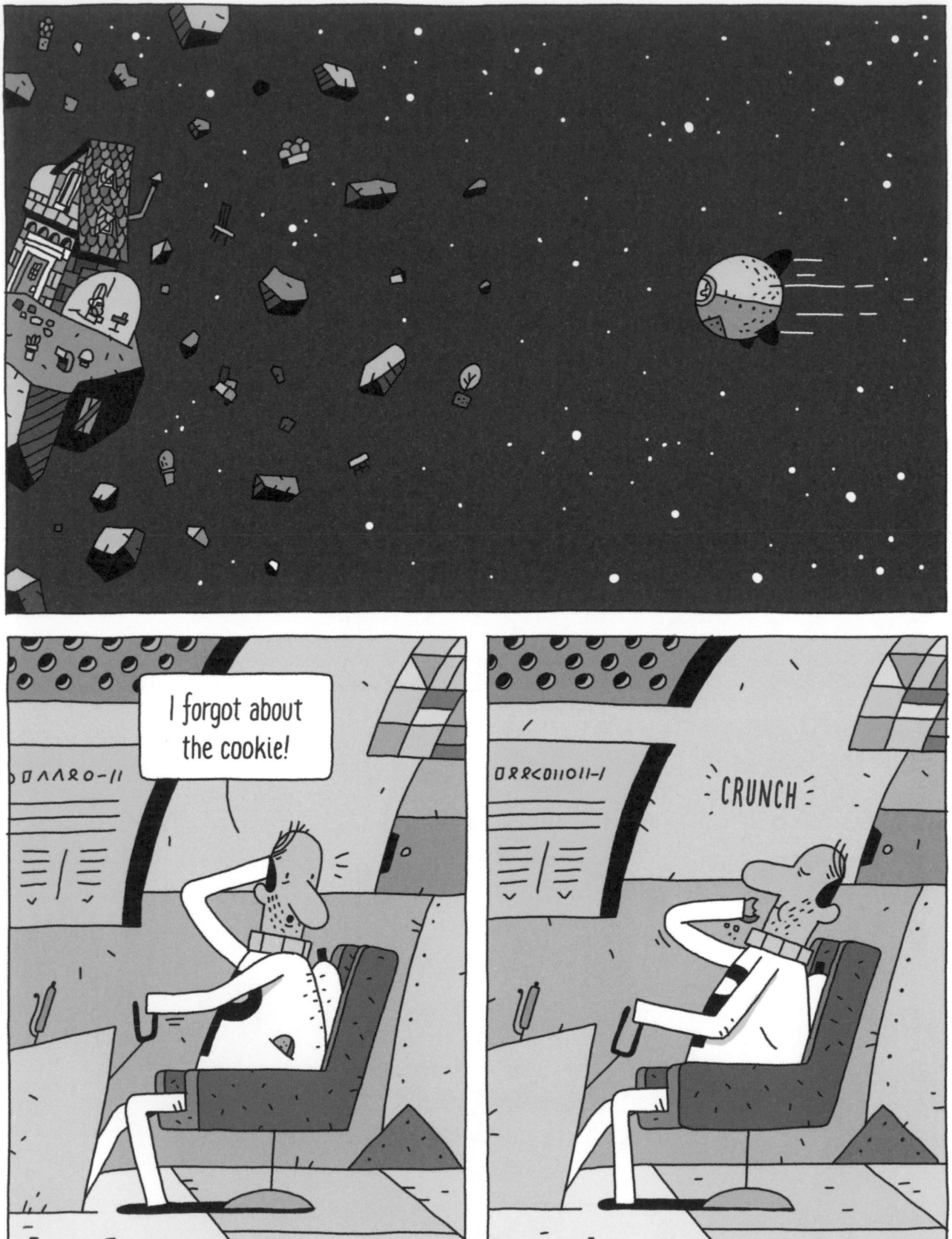
I forgot about the cookie!
CRUNCH

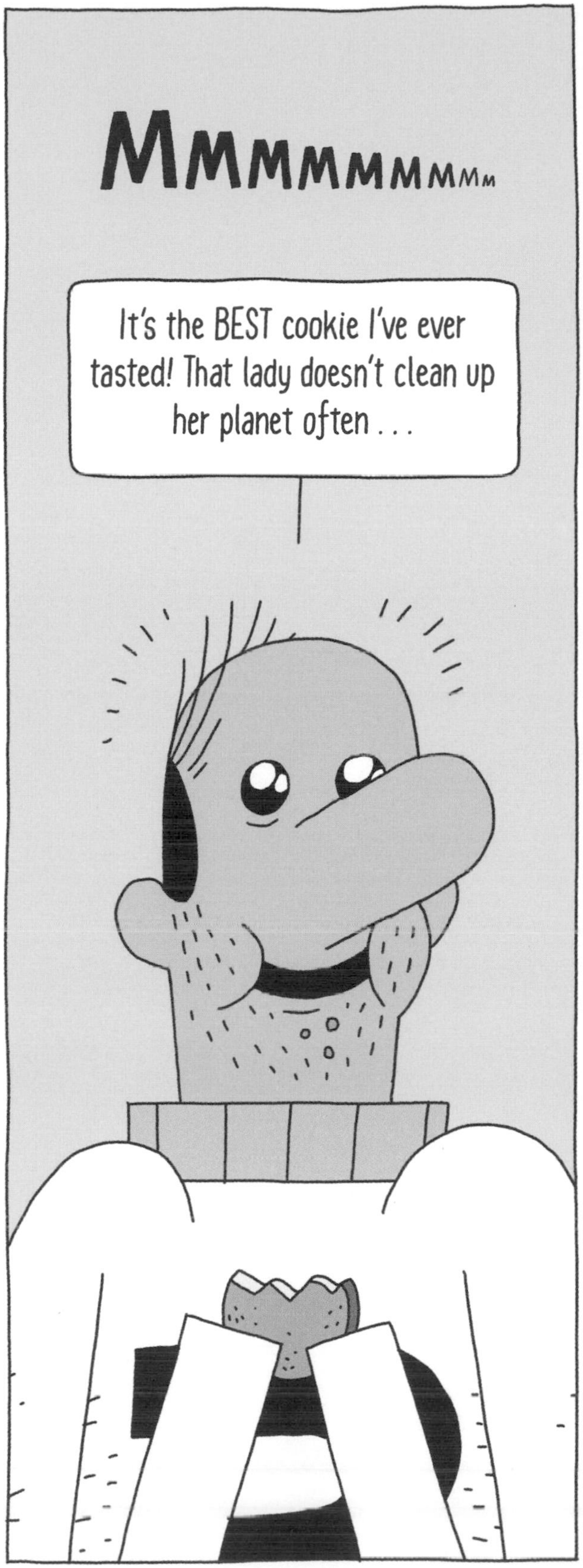
MMMMMMMMM
It's the BEST cookie I've ever tasted! That lady doesn't clean up her planet often . . .

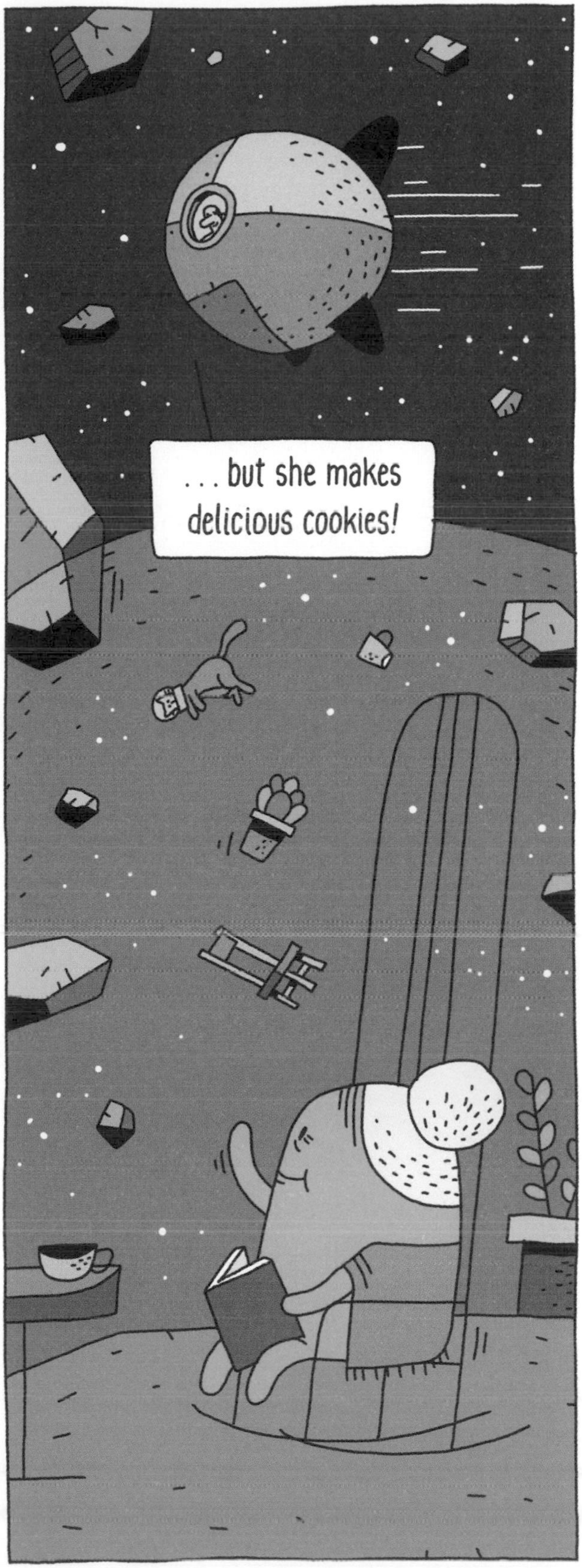
. . . but she makes delicious cookies!

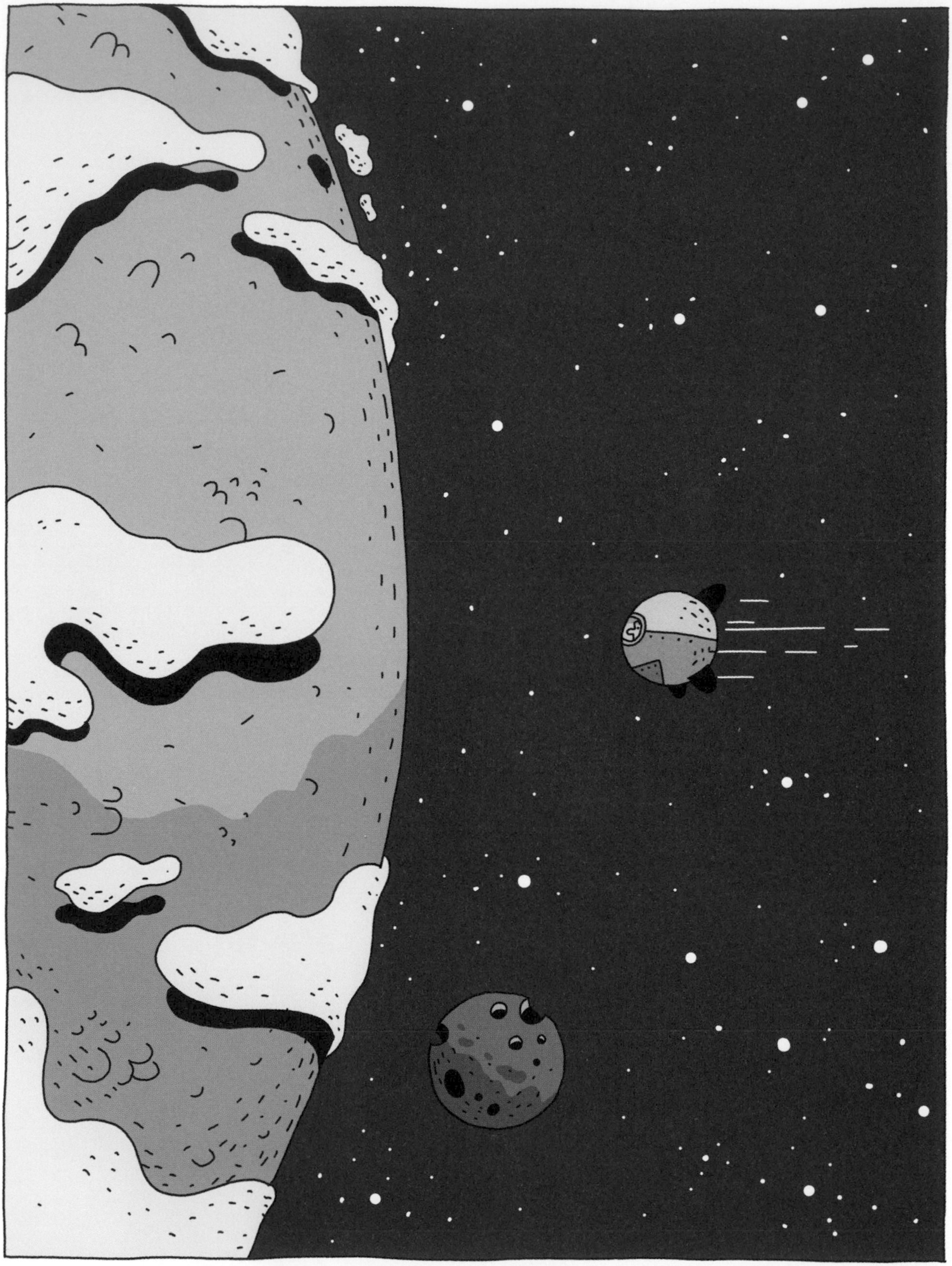

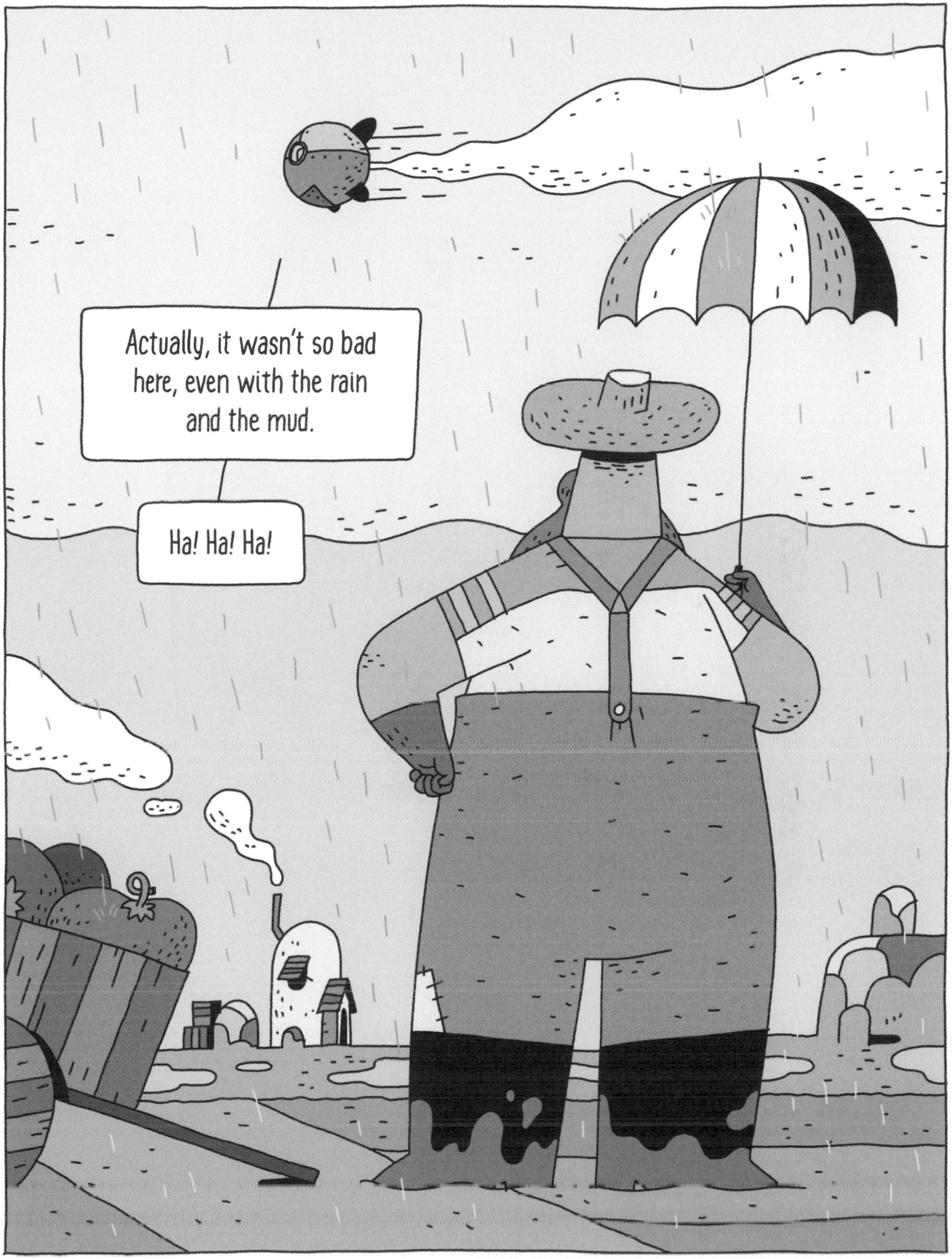
Actually, it wasn't so bad here, even with the rain and the mud.
Ha! Ha! Ha!

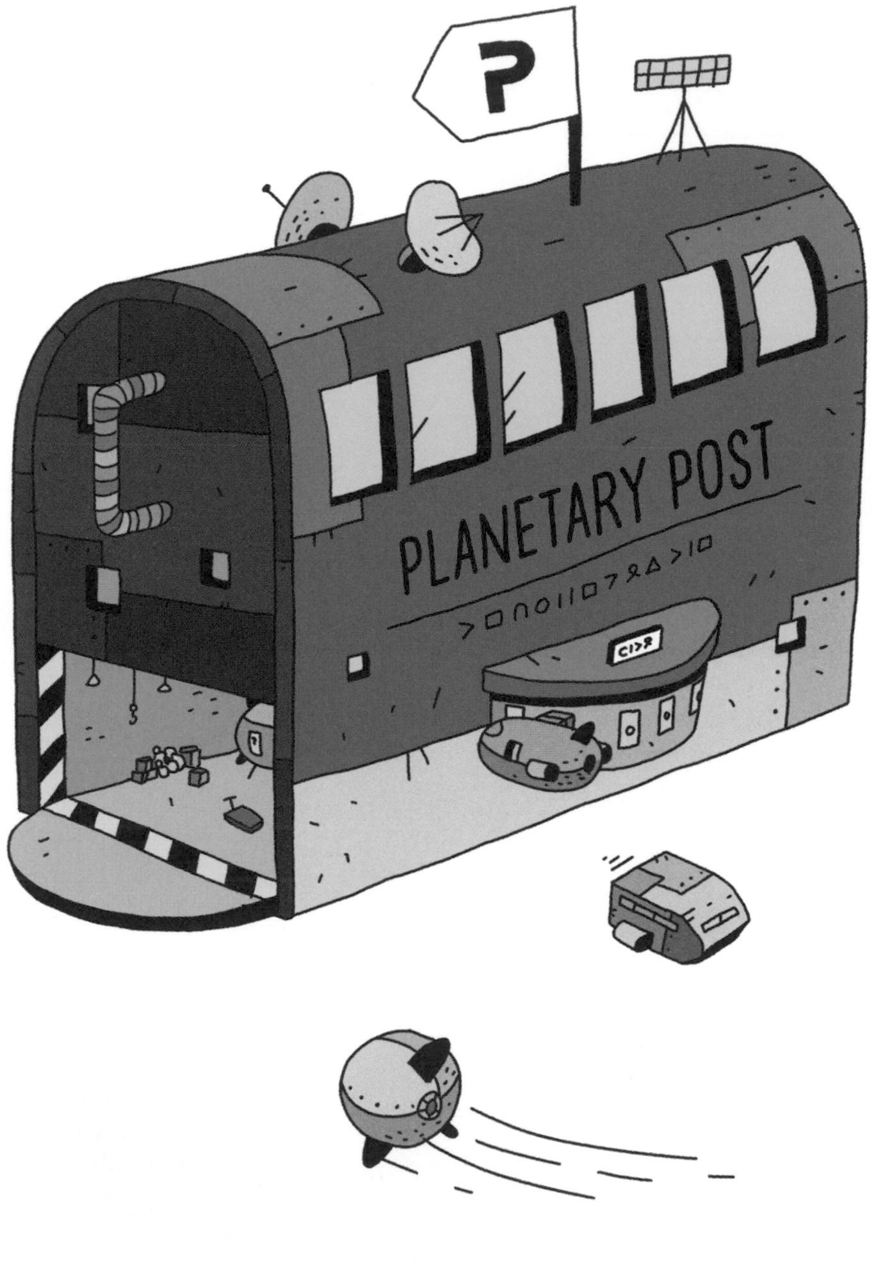
P
PLANETARY POST

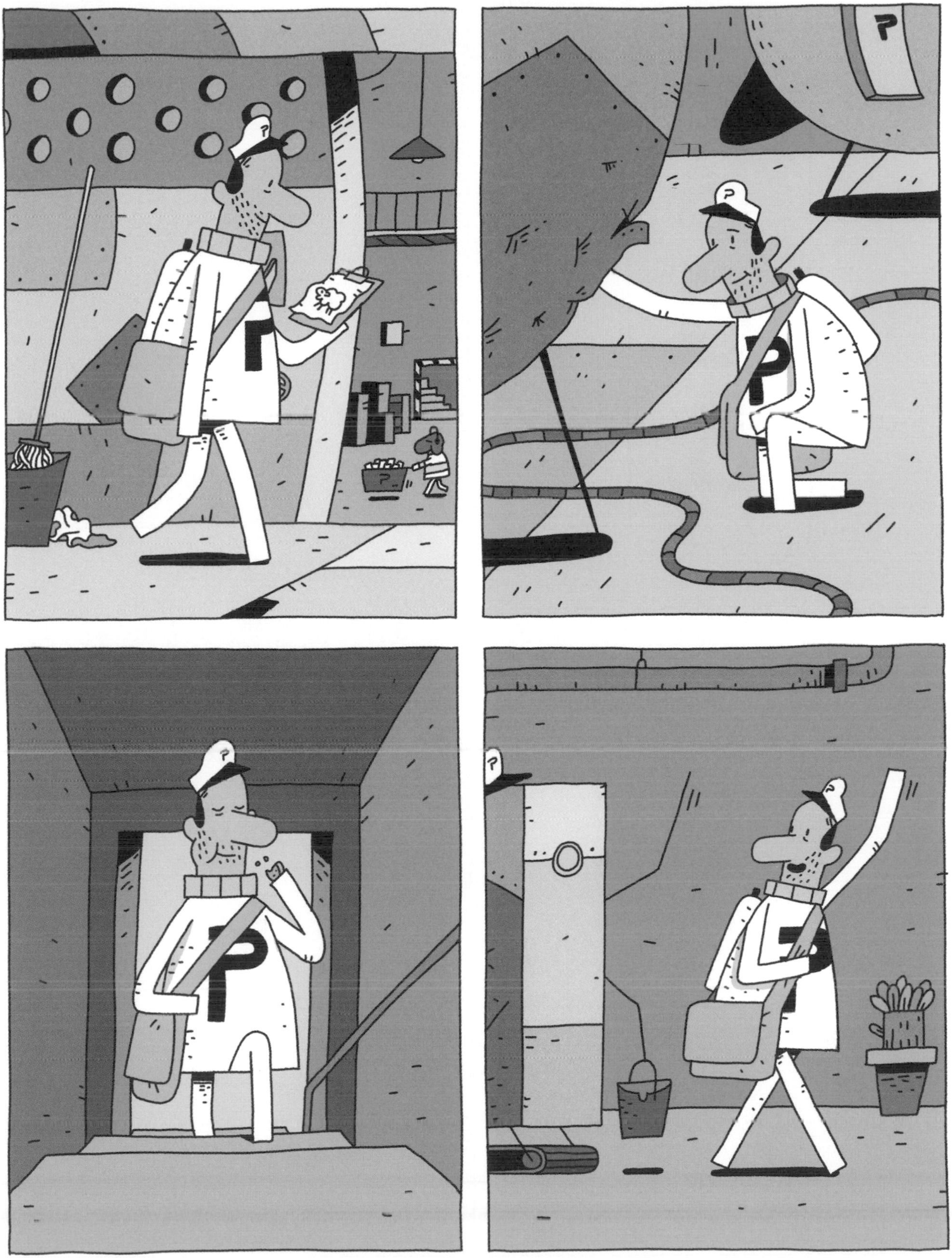

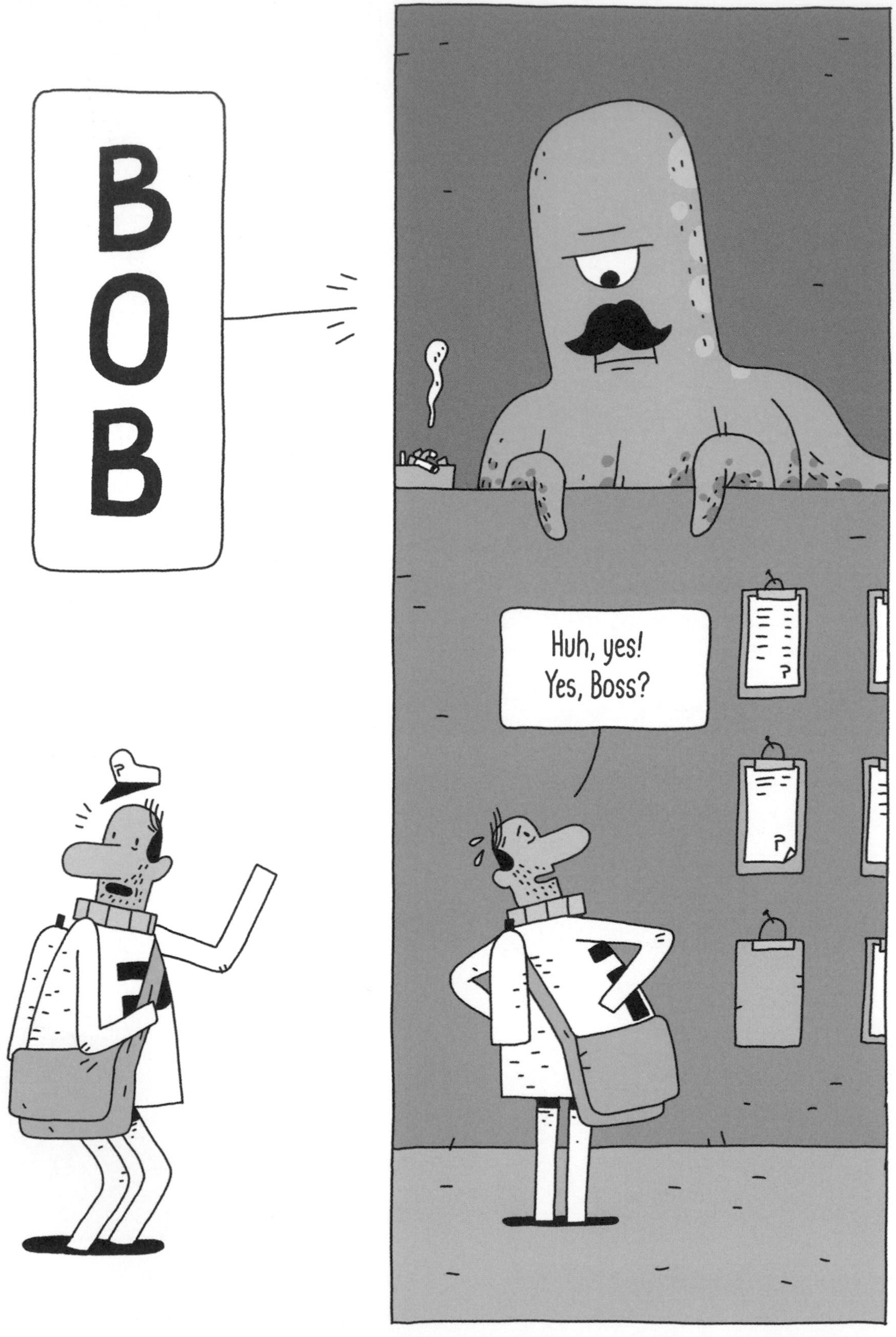
BOB
Huh, yes! Yes, Boss?

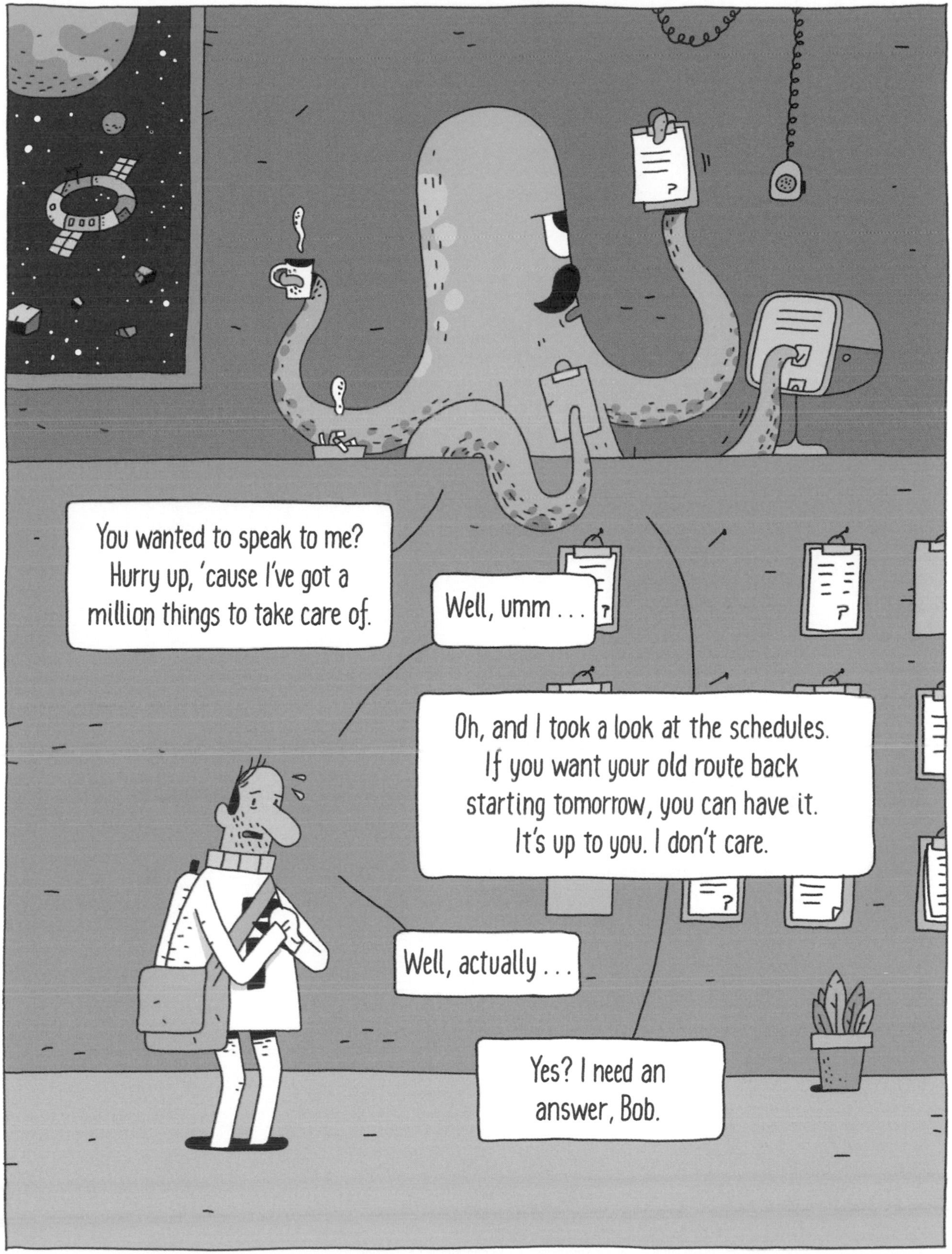
You wanted to speak to me? Hurry up, 'cause I've got a million things to take care of.
Well, umm . . .
Oh, and I took a look at the schedules. If you want your old route back starting tomorrow, you can have it. It's up to you. I don't care.
Well, actually . . .
Yes? I need an answer, Bob.

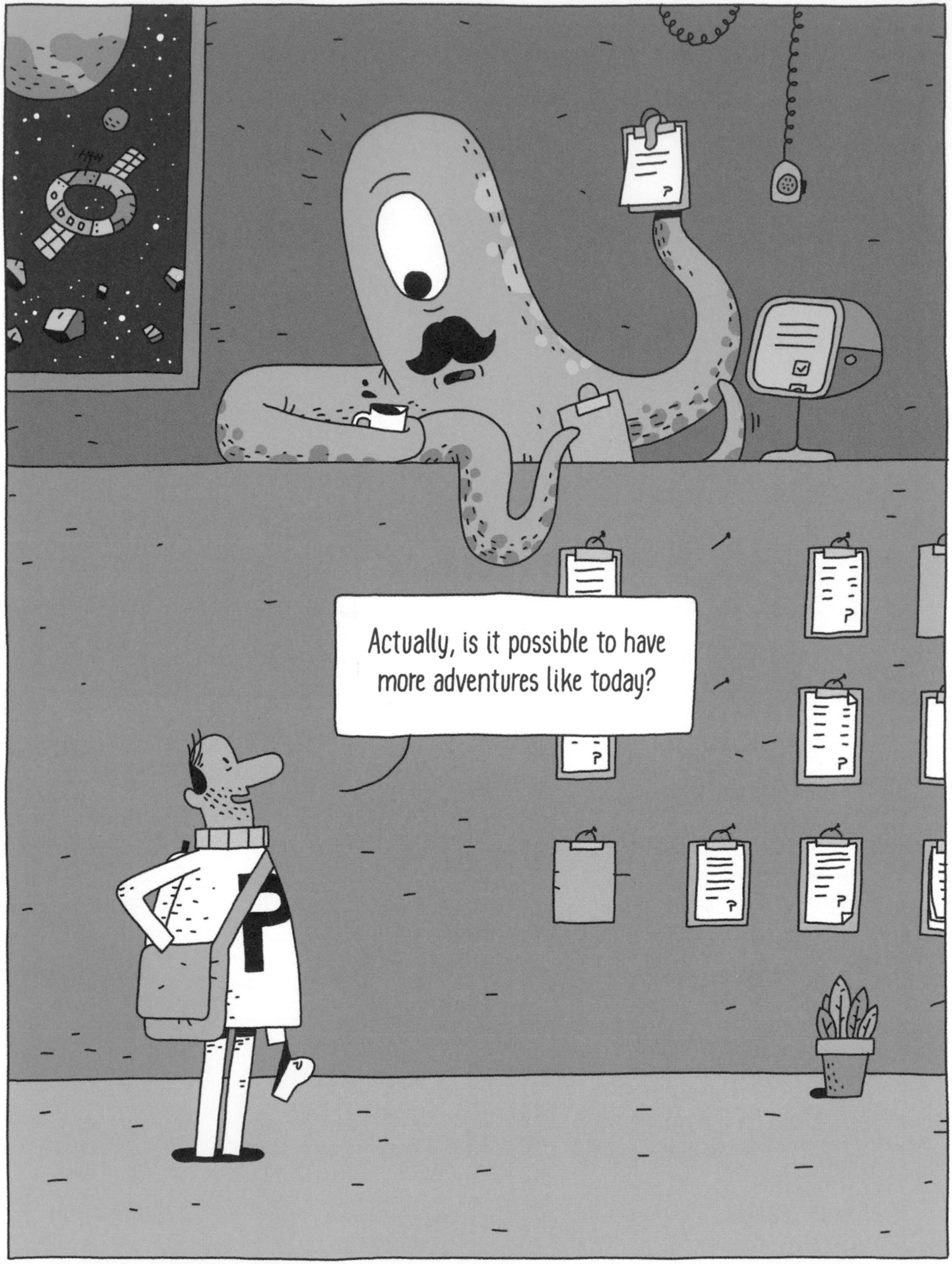
Actually, is it possible to have more adventures like today?

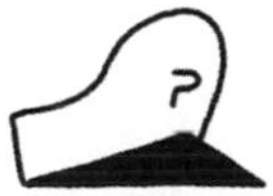

THE END

First published in French by Les Éditions de la Pastèque, Montreal as *Le facteur de l'espace*
Copyright © Guillaume Perreault and La Pastèque 2016
Published in agreement with Koja Agency
English translation by Françoise Bui
English translation copyright © 2020 by Holiday House Publishing, Inc.
All Rights Reserved
HOLIDAY HOUSE is registered in the U.S. Patent and Trademark Office.
Printed and bound in December 2019 at Toppan Leefung, DongGuan City, China.
www.holidayhouse.com
First Edition
1 3 5 7 9 10 8 6 4 2

Library of Congress Cataloging-in-Publication Data
Names: Perreault, Guillaume, 1985– author, illustrator. | Bui, Françoise, translator.
Title: The postman from space / Guillaume Perreault ; English translation by Françoise Bui.
Other titles: Facteur de l'espace. English
Description: First edition. | New York : Holiday House, 2020.
Originally published: Montreal : Éditions de la Pastèque, 2016 under the title, Le facteur de l'espace.
Summary: A letter carrier who delivers mail across the galaxy in his spaceship finds adventure when he is assigned a new route.
Identifiers: LCCN 2019020321 | ISBN 9780823445196 (hardcover)
Subjects: | CYAC: Graphic novels. | Letter carriers—Fiction. | Adventure and adventurers—Fiction. | Humorous stories. | Science fiction.
Classification: LCC PZ7.7.P416 Po 2020 | DDC [E]—dc23 LC record available at https://lccn.loc.gov/2019020321

ISBN: 978-0-8234- 4519-6 (hardcover)
ISBN: 978-0-8234-4584-4 (paperback)